Chapter One

The sound woke Texas Ranger Eli Slater. Something, or *someone*, was on his front porch.

He'd heard footsteps, maybe. Or maybe it was just some animal on a nighttime prowl. Since he lived in the country, something like that was always a possibility.

When he heard another sound, he checked the clock on the nightstand. It was just after midnight. And he cursed because there was no way he would get back to sleep unless he made sure this wasn't a would-be burglar. If that was the case, it'd be a stupid one since the fool was at the house of a Texas Ranger. A heavily armed and grouchy Ranger, since Eli had just finished a long shift only a couple of hours earlier.

He threw back the covers and first glanced at his phone to make sure that he hadn't missed a text from his family. He had three brothers, and since all of them were lawmen, there was a chance that there could be some kind of emergency. But there were no texts or missed calls.

That put a knot in his stomach.

He was glad there was no family crisis, but that could have been a reasonable explanation for why someone was visiting him at this god-awful hour. So, if it wasn't family, then who was it?

He cursed again when he heard the sound for the third time. Definitely footsteps, and not those of an animal. Eli dragged on his jeans, slipped his phone into his pocket and grabbed the SIG Sauer he kept next to his bed. He hoped this would be a quick check that would turn out to be nothing. Maybe a neighbor with car trouble. Then he could deal with it, get right back in bed and hope that he didn't dream about…anything.

Especially *her.*

But hoping hadn't ever helped him much in that department. She made regular appearances in his nightmares. That was his punishment, he supposed. A woman was dead because of him, and Eli figured even a couple of lifetimes wouldn't be enough to help him come to terms with that.

"Who's out there?" Eli shouted when he made it to the living room.

The footsteps on the porch came again, and this time the person was running. Maybe that meant this was possibly some kind of prank from local teenagers.

Since it was July, school was out, and his ranch was just a stone's throw off the road leading into town. It could be that some kids had too much time on their hands. If so, Eli was in an ornery enough mood to arrest their sorry butts for waking him up. Then he'd take them into Longview Ridge to the sheriff's office where his brother, the sheriff, could put them in jail for a few hours.

"Just in case you're too stupid not to know this—I'm Sergeant Eli Slater, Texas Ranger," he added.

SETTLING AN OLD SCORE

DELORES FOSSEN

No more footsteps, but he did hear something else. A strange mewing sound. Maybe a kitten? Oh, man. Had the pranking clowns left a stray cat on his porch?

Eli went to the door, keeping to the side of it while he opened it, and he peered out into the darkness. Nothing. Until he looked down.

What the hell?

It was a car seat, and there was a thin blanket draped over it. At first glimpse Eli thought maybe the cat was inside it, but then the blanket moved, and he saw the foot.

A baby's foot.

That put his heart right in his throat, and he fired glances all around the yard to see who'd done this. No one was in sight.

The baby whimpered, kicking at the blanket, and while Eli still kept watch of the yard, he stooped down for a better look. That look got a whole lot easier for him when the baby's kicking caused the blanket to slide off the car seat.

Yeah, it was a baby all right, and not some automated doll as he'd hoped.

A baby dressed in a pink gown. He wasn't an expert on kids by any means, but he thought that maybe the baby was a couple of months old. And he or she wasn't very happy, with that bottom lip poked out, and staring up at him as if about to start crying at any second.

"If this is a joke, I don't find it funny," Eli called out to the person who'd left the baby.

But a joke didn't feel right. This went well beyond something that bored kids would do. Had someone actually abandoned the baby on his porch? His place wasn't a "safe haven" for leaving unwanted infants; that was usually reserved for fire stations and police departments. But it could have happened.

Still keeping watch in case someone was out there, Eli checked to make sure the little one was okay. There wasn't a scratch on the baby that he could see, and he or she appeared to be clean. That was something, at least. And whoever had left the baby had tucked a bottle into the side of the seat. So someone had been feeding the kid.

"Who did this?" Eli shouted, trying again to get some kind of response from the person responsible for the baby.

But nothing. Well, nothing other than the baby, who started to whimper. Hell. That caused the adrenaline to spike through him, and while he took out his phone, he rocked the car seat a little, hoping it would soothe the child. It didn't. The whimpering turned into a full-fledged cry.

He scrolled through his contacts to his brother Kellan, the sheriff, but before Eli could even press the number, he saw a slash of headlights as a vehicle turned off the main road and started toward his place.

Fast.

The car sped right at him, skidding to a stop in front of his house. His first thought was this was someone who was about to clear up the situation. Maybe someone frantic. A blond-haired woman wearing a gauzy white dress bolted from the car. She was armed, and she aimed the gun that she whipped up right at him.

And he groaned.

Because he knew his visitor—Ashlyn Darrow. As a

lawman, he'd made enemies, had dealt with his share of bad blood, and Ashlyn was at the top of the bad blood list. In her mind she thought he was the bad guy.

He wasn't.

But Eli doubted he would convince her of that—ever. Especially after what'd happened.

Despite him trying to push it away, pieces of the repeating nightmare came. Ashlyn was in that nightmare, but like now she was very much alive. The other woman wasn't.

"Get away from her," Ashlyn ordered.

If Eli had had on his badge, he would have tapped it to give her a reminder that she didn't need. Ashlyn knew full well that he was a Ranger, and she had no badge and no right, legal or otherwise, to pull a gun on him. Still, he had no intention of trading shots with her, not with the baby right at his feet. Just in case Ashlyn pulled the trigger, though, he moved in front of the little girl. He seriously doubted she would do something like that if she knew there was a baby involved.

"Put down your gun," he warned her. "Along with pissing me off, you're endangering a child."

A burst of air left her mouth. It was a humorless laugh. "You've already endangered her. Just like you did Marta."

There it came again. Bits of the nightmares, and it always sickened him that the pieces could be just as potent as the real thing. Two years hadn't toned down the bits, either, and despite the bad blood between Ashlyn and him, Eli thought maybe it was the same for her.

Since talking about Marta Seaver wasn't going to help this situation, Eli went with a question that would hopefully give him the start of the answers he needed. "Put down your gun and tell me what you know about this baby. Were you the one who left her here?"

Even though it was dark, there was enough light coming from the porch that he saw the confusion go through her eyes. Brown eyes, he knew. And he knew them well. Or rather *had known* them.

She shook her head, lowering her gun just a little, but then he saw another emotion. Pure anger. "You know how the baby got here, because you were the one to take her," she insisted.

Now he was the one who was no doubt showing some confusion. "I was in bed asleep." He tipped his head to his lack of shirt and boots. "I heard a noise, came to the porch to check it out, and she was here. A couple of minutes later, you showed up with a gun."

Ashlyn stared at him, repeated the headshake, and she started moving closer. Eli didn't think he was the reason for that, though. The baby started fussing.

"Is she hurt?" Ashlyn asked, her thick breath gusting.

"She seems fine to me, but I didn't pick her up for a closer look. I was about to call Kellan, and then I would have taken her to the hospital just to be sure."

If Ashlyn heard any of that, it didn't register on her face. As the baby's fussing got louder, Ashlyn moved faster. She practically barreled up the steps, and the moment that she reached him, Eli stripped the gun from her hand.

She made a strangled sound of fear and frustration, but she didn't fight to get the weapon back. Instead,

Ashlyn dropped to her knees and picked up the baby, pulling the infant right against her.

"She's okay," Ashlyn said, raw relief in her voice, and she just kept repeating it.

He'd known Ashlyn since they were kids, but it'd been two years since he'd seen her. Not since that night of Marta's death and the shooting that'd nearly ended Ashlyn's life, too. She hadn't actually cried that night, had been more in shock and then too drugged up on the pain meds for her injuries. However, she was crying now, and the tears were streaming down her face.

Eli wasn't immune to those tears, either. Ashlyn's grief already felt like a fist around his heart, and that fist was squeezing hard now.

He tucked both of their guns in the back waist of his jeans and glanced out at her car to make sure no one else was inside. If there was, he didn't see them.

"Whose baby is this? Is she yours?" he demanded, and he made sure his lawman's tone came through loud and clear.

But his tone faltered a bit when he recalled something. Yet more memories of the attack two years ago. Ashlyn had been shot three times, and the bullets had done a lot of damage. Eli was pretty sure he remembered the doctors saying that she'd never be able to have a child.

An injury like that was something that only added to his nightmares. One woman was dead and the other wounded to the point that it had changed her life forever and taken away her chance to become a mother. A biological one, anyway.

"She's mine. Her name is Cora, and I adopted her,"

Ashlyn added as if she'd known he was thinking about the shooting.

Eli hadn't heard about the adoption, but then Ashlyn wasn't exactly a frequent visitor to Longview Ridge. Probably because she hadn't wanted to risk running into him. By avoiding him, she'd also avoided the inevitable gossip that came with living in a small town.

"If you didn't bring Cora here, then who did?" he asked.

Ashlyn still had tears in her eyes when she looked up at him. She opened her mouth, closed it and shook her head for a third time. She glanced away from him as if trying to figure out how to answer, and with the baby gripped in her arms, she quickly stood.

"Oh God," she blurted out. "They could be watching us. They could still hurt her."

That got his attention, and even though Eli still didn't have all the answers he wanted, he hurried Ashlyn inside his house and shut the door. Eli immediately started to pat Ashlyn down, working his hands around the baby.

Ashlyn made a sound of outrage. One that Eli ignored.

"You showed up here out of the blue and pulled a gun on me," he grumbled. "Just in case you're carrying our bad blood to the next level, I don't want you trying to kill me."

She didn't exactly jump to defend herself or claim that killing him had never been on her agenda. That didn't ease the tight muscles in his chest.

"I would have done anything to get her back." Ashlyn's voice trembled as she kissed the baby again. But then she froze for a moment before she looked up at him. "And they knew that. Oh God. They knew that."

"They?" Eli challenged. Once he was certain she wasn't armed, he engaged the security system and looked out the side window of the front door.

"The men who took Cora." Her breath shuddered, and she started to sob again.

Eli didn't have a stone heart, so that got to him. So did the fact that an innocent little baby was somehow involved in this. Whatever *this* was.

"Keep talking," he insisted while he continued to keep watch. Ashlyn had left on her car headlights so that helped him see the road that led to his house. "Tell me what happened." And then he would almost certainly need to call Kellan. First, though, Eli wanted to hear the specifics so he'd know what to relay to his brother.

"I was in bed at my house. Cora was asleep in the nursery." Ashlyn's voice got shakier with each word. So did she. Whatever had happened had spooked her, and he was positive that she wasn't faking it. "Two men broke down the door. Cops," she spat out, aiming a glare at him. A glare that quickly softened as if she'd heard what she'd said and realized it didn't ring true.

"Two cops broke into your house?" He didn't bother to take out the skepticism. "Did they have a warrant? Did they ID themselves?"

Ashlyn shook her head. "They were wearing uniforms, badges and all the gear that cops have. They used a stun gun on me." She rubbed her fingers along the side of her arm, and the trembling got worse. "They took Cora, but I heard them say they were working for you."

Eli's groan was even louder than she one she made.

"And you believed them." The look he gave her was as flat as his tone. He didn't spell out to her that she'd been gullible, but he was certain Ashlyn had already picked up on that.

She squeezed her eyes shut a moment. "I panicked. Wasn't thinking straight. As soon as I could move, I jumped in my car and drove straight here."

The drive wouldn't have taken that long since Ashlyn's house was only about ten miles away. She lived on a small ranch on the other side of Longview Ridge that she'd inherited from her grandparents, and she made a living training and boarding horses.

"Did the kidnappers make a ransom demand?" he pressed. "Or did they take anything else from your place?"

"No. They only took Cora. Who brought her here?" Ashlyn asked, her head whipping up. "Was it those cops?"

"*Fake* cops," Eli automatically corrected. "I didn't see who left her on my porch, but they weren't exactly quiet about it. She was probably out here no more than a minute or two before I went to the door and found her."

He paused, worked through the pieces that she'd just given him, and it didn't take him long to come to a conclusion. A bad one. These fake cops hadn't hurt the child, hadn't asked for money or taken anything, but they had let Ashlyn believe they worked for him. There had to be a good reason for that. Well, "good" in their minds, anyway.

"This was some kind of sick game?" she asked.

It was looking that way. A game designed to send her after him.

"They wanted me to kill you?" Ashlyn added a moment later.

Before Eli answered that, he wanted to talk to his brother and get backup so he could take Ashlyn and the baby into Longview Ridge. First to the hospital to confirm they were okay and then to the sheriff's office so he could get an official statement from Ashlyn.

"You really had no part in this?" she pressed.

Eli huffed, not bothering to answer that. He took out his phone to make that call to Kellan, but he stopped when he saw the blur of motion on the other side of Ashlyn's car. He lifted his hand to silence her when Ashlyn started to speak, and he kept looking.

Waiting.

Then, he finally saw it. Or rather he saw *them*. Two men wearing uniforms, and they had guns aimed right at the house.

Chapter Two

Ashlyn immediately noticed the change in Eli's body language, and she heard the single word of profanity that he said under his breath. And she knew something else was horribly wrong.

"Did those cops come back? Those *men*?" she corrected.

Not cops. Now that she had her baby safe in her arms and was seeing things a little clearer, she knew that. Well, unless they were dirty lawmen, but she doubted they would have shown up in uniform and full gear if they had been.

"Someone's out there," Eli confirmed, and while volleying his attention between the window and his phone, he fired off a text to someone. Kellan, no doubt. "Get down and stay down," he added as he finished the text.

Ashlyn held Cora close to her while she hurried to the sofa and dropped down on the side of it. "How good is your security system?" she asked, trying to tamp down the fear that was racing through her.

"Good," Eli verified. "But yours would have been, too, and yet they still managed to get in."

That only caused her heart to pound even harder. Because he was right. After she'd nearly been killed two years ago, after Marta had died, Ashlyn had added a security system with motion detectors, but no alarms had gone off when the men had broken in.

She groaned. "They jammed it." Eli didn't verify that, didn't need to. It was the only thing that made sense. Actually, it was one of the few things that actually made sense. They'd jammed it so they could get to her before she could grab a weapon or try to defend herself. But why had they set her up to go after Eli?

If that's what had actually happened.

"The men aren't coming closer," Eli told her. "They're behind the trees across the road from your car. As soon as Kellan gets here, I'll go out there and confront them."

She was shaking her head before he even finished. "If you go out there, they could gun you down."

"Maybe. But they would have had a chance to do that when I stepped on the porch and found the baby. And they could have killed you when they broke into your house or even after you arrived here."

That robbed Ashlyn of what little breath she'd managed to gather. Mercy, he was right. They could have shot her instead of using the stun gun. Once they'd overpowered her, they could have done whatever they'd wanted.

"What's going on?" she mumbled.

"The hell if I know, but trust me when I say this, I will find out."

Eli glanced back at her again, and even though the lights in the room were off, she could see his intense expression. Of course, plenty of things were intense about

Eli. He was the tough Slater brother, the hard-nosed Texas Ranger who could intimidate with a single look.

Like now.

Of course, the intimidation was lessened some by the fact he was bare to the waist and his jeans weren't even zipped. For just a split second, before she could push it away, Ashlyn saw the hot cowboy that she'd once crushed on way back in high school.

"You'd better not be lying to me about any of this," he snarled.

And just like that, he caused the "crush" thoughts to vanish in a flash. "Everything that I've told you is the truth."

It was. But with their history, she couldn't blame him for asking. However, she could perhaps blame him for what'd gone on.

"If these men wanted me to kill you, then maybe it's because of a case you're working on. Maybe it's because of Marta," she added.

Ashlyn waited for the glare that she was certain he would send her way, but there wasn't one. Maybe because he got an interruption when his phone rang. He put the call on speaker while he continued to keep watch, and it didn't take long before she heard the familiar voice.

Sheriff Kellan Slater.

"I'm just up the road, and I have the two men in sight," Kellan explained. "You're right. They're armed. From what I can see both have handguns, and one has a rifle with a scope."

Eli's scowl deepened, and she thought she knew why. The handguns might not be much of a threat to them if the men stayed across the road because of the range of the bullets, but they could use the rifle to fire into the house. If that's what they planned, that is. But as Eli had pointed out, they hadn't shot at either him or her when they'd had a chance.

"Gunnar's on the way," Kellan added a moment later. "I'd like to hold off doing anything until he gets here, and he can block the road from the other end."

Gunnar was Deputy Gunnar Pullam, whom Ashlyn had known most of her life. Like Kellan, he didn't live too far away, which hopefully meant he'd be there soon. That way, if they could pen in the men, they might be able to catch and then question them.

"You have IDs on these two?" Kellan asked Eli.

"No. But I believe they might have brought Ashlyn's adopted baby to my house and left her on my doorstep."

"What?" Kellan sounded just as stunned as Eli had been when she'd first shown up.

"Yeah," was all Eli said. "I need to grab my boots from my bedroom," he added to Kellan. "If we have to chase these guys, I don't want to be barefoot. Ashlyn is on the floor, and she'll stay down."

"I'll keep watch," Kellan assured him. "Hurry."

The urgency in Kellan's voice came through loud and clear, and it gave Ashlyn another jolt of adrenaline that she didn't need. At least Cora had stopped fussing and had fallen back asleep. That hopefully meant the baby wasn't picking up on the terror that Ashlyn was feeling.

Eli ran back to his bedroom, and within seconds he returned with his boots, holster and shirt. He laid his phone on the small table next to the door while he put them on and continued to volley glances out the window.

It didn't take Eli long to dress, and when he put on the shirt, she saw his badge was already attached, and just like that the memories washed over her like a tidal wave. He'd been wearing the badge the night of the shooting. She could feel and smell the air in the parking lot of the seedy bar where Marta had asked Ashlyn to meet her. It'd been thick, humid. Smothering.

Ashlyn could also feel the bullets slam into her.

She felt the cold shock that followed. Then, the pain. Especially the pain. It hadn't been just physical, either, after she'd seen Marta, her best friend, lying in a pool of her own blood.

Dead.

So was the person who'd fired those shots, Drake Zeller, a drug dealer scumbag whom Eli had managed to take out. But not before Zeller had put three bullets into Ashlyn and a fatal one into Marta. The only person who was still standing, still unharmed, after the gunfight was Eli—and he was the reason Zeller had been after Marta. Ashlyn had simply been collateral damage.

"Gunnar will have the road blocked in about five minutes," she heard Kellan relay to Eli, but then the sheriff cursed. "Wait. The men are on the move."

That pushed away the thoughts of that horrible night, and Ashlyn automatically tightened her grip on the baby. She considered asking Eli if she could have her gun back, but she didn't want it that close to Cora.

"Hell," Eli spat out as he ran out of the foyer and into the living room, very close to the sofa where Ashlyn was. He took up position at the window, which would give him a different angle to the front yard and the road.

"Are they getting away?" she asked.

"Can't tell yet. They're no longer in sight, but they could have just dropped back."

And with that rifle, they'd still be a threat. Maybe, though, Gunnar would have had time to finish that roadblock.

Eli's phone dinged, and his forehead bunched up when he looked down at the screen. "I've got another call with a blocked number." He paused. "It could be these thugs. I'll put you on hold while I find out."

While volleying glances at the window, Eli switched over the call, but he didn't say anything. He just waited, and several seconds later, she heard the man who came onto the line.

"Still alive, Sergeant Slater?" the caller asked.

Ashlyn gasped because she recognized that voice, too. Unlike Kellan's, though, this one gave her no reassurance. "That's one of the men who kidnapped Cora," she told Eli. Eli immediately hit a button his phone, maybe to record the conversation or even try to have it traced.

"That's right," the man said, his voice dripping with sarcasm. "You didn't do what you were supposed to do, so this is about to get very messy."

The muscles in Eli's face went even tighter. "Who are you, and what the hell do you want?"

"Best not to answer either of those on the grounds it might incriminate me." He laughed. "Ready to play, Sergeant Slater?"

"I'd rather know the rules of the game first," Eli fired back.

"Here's the only rule you need to know. Your current houseguest, Ashlyn Darrow, is responsible for this."

She shook her head and was about to insist that she'd done nothing to warrant her child's kidnapping, but then everything inside Ashlyn went still. Eli saw her reaction, too, and he grumbled out more profanity.

"What did Ashlyn do?" Eli demanded.

"That's a question you should ask her," the man said, and with that, he ended the call.

Eli immediately switched back to his brother, and he also aimed her a hard look. "According to Ashlyn, the man who just called me is one of the guys who kidnapped her baby. Can you see the men now?"

"No. But I'm moving in closer. Gunnar's doing the same from the other side. We'll try to pen them in. I'll call you when I can."

The moment Eli ended the call, he gave her another of those looks. "Start explaining."

She shook her head again. "I asked the San Antonio cops for the reports of the night of Marta's murder. And I went to the prison to visit Leon Taggart."

There was no need for her to explain more about that. Leon and Marta were both Eli's criminal informants. Both Marta and Leon had prior drug arrests, but Marta had been small potatoes compared to Leon. And Leon had ultimately been blamed for setting up the ambush attack that'd resulted in the bloodbath the night Marta had been killed.

"Why the hell would you go visit Leon?" Eli asked. She was surprised he could speak with his jaw clenched so tight.

He wasn't going to like her answer.

"I wanted to hear Leon's take on what happened." She paused, because she had to drag in enough breath to continue. "He worked out a plea deal to get the death penalty off the table so there was no trial, no testimony, and I wanted to see if—"

"If I'd been the one to set up what went on that night. You think I purposely had Marta go into that alley so a drug-crazed snake could gun her down."

That thought had kept crossing her mind until she'd become obsessed with it. "I just had to know the truth."

"And you thought you'd get that truth from a criminal with a long record. One who confessed to putting Marta on the scene because he didn't like the competition. She was giving the Rangers and cops more reliable info and therefore getting paid more than he was, and he wanted to put her out of commission."

Ashlyn hadn't expected Eli to see it any other way. But then, he hadn't nearly been killed that night. "I had to be sure." Her gaze flew to his. "And this proves I'm right. There is something off, or why would these men have taken Cora?"

That felt like a punch to the stomach. Oh God. In her quest to find the truth, she'd put her precious baby in danger.

"Why go and visit Leon now?" Eli pressed, not answering her question. "It's been nearly two years."

Ashlyn wasn't sure he would understand. Heck, she wasn't sure she did, either, but enough time had passed that she'd finally felt able to start confronting some of her demons. Cora was responsible for that. Ashlyn hadn't wanted her daughter to be burdened with her mom's emotional baggage, and she'd thought the way to start dealing with that was to visit Leon.

Before Ashlyn could even attempt to answer Eli, she

saw him shift his body a little, changing the angle of the view he had outside the window. He had his attention focused on something, or maybe someone, and he was suddenly so still. Holding his breath and waiting.

"Get all the way down to the floor," Eli suddenly shouted. He scrambled toward her.

His loud voice woke Cora, and the baby started to cry again, but Eli's shout wasn't nearly as deafening as the next sound.

A gunshot.

It blasted through the window where he'd just been standing. A second and third one quickly followed. And the shots set off the security system. The alarms immediately began to blare through the house.

Eli practically threw himself over Cora and her. Good thing, too, because the bullets sent glass flying through the room, and it clattered and pinged to the floor next to her. It no doubt hit Eli, too. She hoped those hits had only come from the glass and not the shots.

As the bullets continued to slam into the house, he turned, pivoting so that his back was to her, and he took aim at the door. It didn't take her long to figure out why he'd done that. The latest shots were hitting the door. It was as if the gunman was trying to tear right through the wood.

And there was something else…

"Is the shooter getting closer?" she asked, her voice trembling. Plus, the alarm was so loud that she wasn't sure how he'd managed to hear her.

"Yeah," he verified.

Oh, mercy. Closer meant he could maybe get into the house and gun them down. Cora could be hurt.

Eli used his phone to turn off the blaring alarms. Probably so he could hear the gunman if he made it onto the porch.

"Move behind the sofa," he instructed. "If things get bad, crawl down the hall and go into my bathroom. Get in the tub."

She nodded and moved as he'd said, but things were already bad. The shots were coming nonstop.

"Where're Kellan and Gunnar?" she asked.

"I'm not sure, but some of those shots are theirs," he explained.

Ashlyn listened. That was hard to do with her pulse crashing in her ears, but she thought she could hear the different firearms. It meant Kellan and the deputy were in a gunfight with these men, but they weren't stopping the one shooting through the door. The one who no doubt had the rifle.

Eli scrambled away from her again, heading back to the window. Putting himself in the line of fire, but a moment later she heard him deliver his own shot. It was even louder than the others had been, and it caused Cora to cry harder. Ashlyn tried to soothe the baby by rocking her, but the noise had obviously frightened her.

When Eli's phone rang, he put the call on speaker, and she braced herself in case it was from the kidnapper. But it was Kellan.

"Hold your fire," Kellan immediately said. "The shooter with the rifle is on the run, and Gunnar and I are moving in. But keep watch. We lost sight of the other one."

"Where'd you last see him?" Eli asked.

Kellan didn't even pause. "He was headed toward your house."

Chapter Three

Eli had figured the danger wasn't over, but he sure as hell hadn't expected one of the thugs to come toward the house when he had two cops in pursuit and another lawman waiting for him inside. The smart thing to do would have been to try to escape, but this guy wasn't doing that. That made him either an idiot, cocky or desperate.

None of those was a good option. All three would be the perfect bad storm, especially considering the guy was armed and ready to commit murder.

Eli fired glances all around the yard. No sign of the man, but Eli knew he was out there somewhere, and if his brother and Gunnar were in pursuit of the other gunman, then that meant Eli needed to make sure this clown didn't get anywhere near Ashlyn and the baby.

He made a quick look over his shoulder at them, to make sure they were still behind the sofa. They were. But now that the security alarms weren't blaring through the house and no one was shooting at them, he could hear Ashlyn's ragged breaths and the baby's whimpers.

Hell.

Ashlyn had to be terrified, perhaps even getting some flashbacks of the night she'd been shot. And that wasn't even the worst of it, because this was a parent's worst nightmare, to have a child in the middle of an attack.

No baby should be put through this, and once he had the situation under control, he needed to make sure it never happened again. That's why he wanted to take the gunman alive. Maybe Kellan and Gunnar could do the same so they could pit the two against each other and get to the truth. Maybe, too, this wouldn't be connected to Marta's murder, but it wasn't looking that way.

Your current houseguest, Ashlyn Darrow, is responsible for this, the kidnapper had said.

Eli didn't intend to just accept the word of a guy trying to kill him, but it left him with an even more unsettled feeling. Had Ashlyn really triggered this by digging into the old case file or visiting Leon? And if so, why would it have caused someone to respond with violence like this?

Leon was in prison. Locked up in a maximum security facility where he was serving a life sentence. It was exactly where he belonged since he'd been the one who'd lured Marta, and therefore Ashlyn and Eli, into that alley with the drug dealer. No way could Leon dispute that, either, because there'd been multiple witnesses.

But Leon had always claimed that he'd been set up.

There'd never been an ounce of proof to that claim and plenty of evidence to indicate Leon had simply wanted Marta dead because he resented her and also because she was about to rat him out for his new criminal association with the drug dealer who'd been killed. Still, it chewed away at Eli that there could be something else about the violence that'd gone on that night. Something he'd missed.

Something that had led to the situation they were in now.

Eli was so focused on watching for the gunman that the sound of the bullet was an unexpected jolt. It caused Ashlyn to gasp.

"The shot wasn't fired near the house," he told her.

It had come from the east side of his land, probably where his brother and Gunnar were. Eli prayed that one of them hadn't been shot. He figured Ashlyn was doing plenty of praying, too, because he heard her mumbling. Also heard her whispering reassurances to the baby.

There was another shot. Also in the distance. But it had no sooner rung out when Eli finally saw something. Not Kellan or Gunnar. This was a man wearing camo who was doing a low military-style crawl on the ground by a line of trees on the side of the house. He was close.

Too close.

Eli shifted and took aim out what had once been a window. It was now just a gaping hole from the other rounds of gunfire. And he waited for a clean shot, maybe to the guy's shoulder. Something to slow him down enough so that Eli could get out there and disarm him.

His phone beeped with a text message, and since Eli didn't want to take his attention off the crawler, he slid his phone across the floor to Ashlyn.

"It's from Kellan," she relayed a moment later. Her breath gusted even more. "He had to kill the shooter."

Eli groaned, but he'd known that could be the likely outcome. That's why it was even more important to keep thug number two alive.

"Kellan and Gunnar are on the way back here," Ashlyn added.

"Text him back and tell him that I've got the gunman in my sight, and he's on the west side of the house in the cluster of pecan trees."

He immediately heard her do that, and Eli knew it would send Kellan and Gunnar that direction. Maybe if the thug knew he had three lawmen bearing down on him, he'd surrender.

Or not.

No sooner had that thought popped into Eli's head, the gunman moved out of the crawling position to crouch behind one of the trees. No doubt getting into position to continue the attack. Continuing it didn't take long, either. It was only a couple of seconds before the guy leaned out and took aim at the house.

Eli couldn't risk another bullet being fired this close to the house, because it could go through the walls and hit the baby. That's why Eli fired first. His shot slammed into the guy's shoulder, just as he'd planned, but the gunman didn't go down. Instead, he lifted his gun again, ready to take the shot that Eli couldn't let him take. Eli tapped his trigger again, sending another bullet into the man's chest.

That put him on the ground.

Cursing, Eli took out Ashlyn's gun, and as he'd done with the phone, he slid it across the floor to her. "Stay put," he warned her, and hoped that she would listen.

She probably would only because she wouldn't want to risk taking the baby outside.

"Be careful," she said, but that didn't sound like her first choice of things to tell him. Right now, she likely just wanted him to stay alive so there'd be someone to help her protect the baby.

When she peered out from the sofa to get the gun, he saw the uncertainty in her eyes. Probably because she knew that his going out there was a risk. One he had to take so that he could get to the shooter before the guy bled out. A dead man wouldn't be able to give him any answers.

"Kellan's almost certainly already done it, but go ahead and call for an ambulance," Eli instructed.

Eli heard her do that, too, while he did a quick mental check of the security of the house. The place was all locked up except for the front window with the shattered glass. It wasn't a big enough hole for someone to climb through, but he'd need to keep watch just in case there was a third thug, lying in wait.

That definitely didn't help loosen the knot in his stomach.

Eli unlocked the front door, glanced around. And he listened. There was nothing other than the groans of pain coming from the injured gunman. Those moans let Eli know that the guy was still alive. Probably still armed, too, and that's why Eli couldn't just go charging toward him.

He gave the living room one last glance to make sure Ashlyn was still behind cover. She was and was no longer peering out from the sofa. And with that safeguard ticked off his mental to-do list, he walked out on the porch. His foot brushed against the side of the baby carrier, a reminder that it needed to be processed for trace and fiber evidence, and he took the steps one at a time while still keeping watch.

The gunman groaned again, and as Eli got closer, he saw the guy was lying on his back and clutching his chest. And yeah, he still had a gun in his hand. A gun now soaked in blood. Eli had hoped he'd been wearing a Kevlar vest and had only had the breath knocked out of him. But this was much more serious than that.

The man was dying.

Eli didn't feel any sympathy for the man, this clown who'd come to his house with guns blazing, but he wanted him to hang on.

By the time Eli reached the man, he heard the hurried footsteps behind him. Eli automatically pivoted, his heart jumping to his throat with a fresh slam of adrenaline, but it was just Kellan and Gunnar.

"The ambulance is on the way," Kellan relayed, but then he cursed when he saw the man. And the blood. The guy would be dead before the ambulance could get there.

"Wait on the porch," Eli told Gunnar. "Ashlyn is inside with her baby."

Gunnar nodded and ran to the door to stand guard in what Eli hoped would be an unnecessary precaution. Eli and Kellan continued to the man, and the first thing Eli did was take the gun from his hand because a dying man could still be dangerous and pull a trigger.

Kellan had a small flashlight that he aimed at the shooter's face. Brown hair, nondescript features except for a scar that cut through his right eyebrow. Eli was certain that he'd never seen him before.

"Who are you?" Eli demanded.

The guy managed a sneer. "I got a family," he said. "And you won't get an ID off me from my prints. No record."

Even though it wasn't an answer to his question, that response told Eli plenty. This was a hired gun, and his family would get a payout whether he lived or died. Or at least that's what this clown believed.

"Once you're dead, your face will be plastered on every news station in the state," Eli warned him. "Someone will recognize you, and once I have an ID, I can and will go after your family as accessories to kidnapping and attempted murder of a Texas Ranger. How do you think that'll play out for you, for them, huh?"

No sneer this time, but the guy did cough, and there was a rattling sound in his chest while his hands stayed pressed to his wound. "My family had nothing to do with this. You were just the job."

"Funny, but it felt very personal to me." Eli knelt down, got right in his face and made sure he looked like the badass Ranger that he was. "You endangered an innocent baby. I won't forget that, and I'll go after your family until I put every last one of them in a cage. Now tell me who the hell you are and why you did this."

The man shook his head, dragged in a ragged breath, but Eli saw the realization in his dying eyes. The realization that Eli wasn't bluffing. "I'm Abe Franklin," he finally said, his voice barely audible now. "And if I tell you who hired me, you have to promise to protect my family. Promise me," he repeated.

Eli would have lied to get the name of the guy's boss, but in this case, no lie was necessary. If his family was indeed innocent, then they'd be protected. "I promise," Eli assured him.

Even though the man clearly only had a few seconds left, he still took his time answering. "The woman with the kid, Ashlyn Darrow, was supposed to shoot and kill you once she thought you'd taken the baby. And then the woman would be arrested for your murder."

Eli had already come up with that theory, but it didn't give him the info he needed. "Who set that up? Who hired you?"

"She said you and Ashlyn wouldn't see it coming, that you wouldn't suspect her at all."

"She?" Eli demanded.

"The woman who hired me. She said you wouldn't suspect her because you thought she was dead." The next breath was much thinner. The cough, more of a death rattle. "Her name is Marta Seaver."

Chapter Four

Ashlyn eased Cora into the infant seat that Eli had arranged to have in the back seat of the cruiser. The baby remained asleep, thank goodness, and Ashlyn hoped she stayed that way for the next couple of hours. Cora had already had enough interruptions to her routine and sleep.

Even though it would only be a short drive from the hospital where they'd just been examined to the sheriff's office, Eli had insisted on them riding in the bullet-resistant cruiser. He'd told Ashlyn that he didn't want to take any chances. Since her baby's life could be at risk, neither did she.

But Ashlyn wanted to know why there was that dangerous risk in the first place.

And who was really behind it.

She hated that the hired thug claimed that Marta was his boss. Hated even more the man had died before giving them the truth. Of course, to him maybe that was the truth. The person who hired him could have told him that. It was just as possible, though, that he'd used his dying breath to lie.

Judging from the phone calls Eli was making, he

was considering that it was at least a possibility that Marta was alive.

On the drive to the hospital and during Cora's exam in the ER, Eli hadn't left their sides. He'd stood guard, continuing to keep watch. That gave Ashlyn the chance to hear him contact the admin office at the San Antonio hospital where Marta had been pronounced dead. When he hadn't been able to reach someone who had answers, he'd left messages both there and then at the funeral home that had handled Marta's remains.

She listened to those calls and others he made. Some to the two CSI teams who were at her house and his to remind them to relay to him anything that they found. He'd done the same to the medical examiner and his brother Kellan. Ashlyn had no doubts that he would get that info.

However, what concerned her was that it wouldn't keep her daughter out of further danger.

When her mouth began to tremble and the tears threatened, again, Ashlyn clamped her teeth over her bottom lip and forced herself to stay steady. It wouldn't help anything if she fell apart, and it would likely only rile Eli even more. He was obviously upset, not just at the attack but probably at her, too. She'd been a fool to believe those thugs when they'd told her Eli had kidnapped Cora.

And it could have gotten Eli killed.

Ashlyn hated to think that she would have pulled the trigger, but she'd been out of her mind with fear and worry when she'd driven to his house. If Eli and she had gotten into a scuffle… But she stopped herself from going there. It hadn't happened, period, and she didn't need to play "what if."

"Marta's dead," Ashlyn repeated once Eli had finished his latest call to the crime lab.

Eli made a sound of agreement. It was the same reaction he'd had the first time she pointed out that obvious fact shortly after he had told her what the gunman said. Eli definitely hadn't argued with her then, or now.

"But you called the funeral home and the San Antonio hospital," she pointed out. "So you must think her being alive is at least a possibility."

He made another of those annoying noncommittal sounds but then glanced at her. Well, actually his glance went to Cora first, then her. "Just covering all the bases." He paused and didn't say anything else until his attention was back at keeping watch out the window. "I checked Marta's pulse that night and didn't feel one."

Ashlyn had known he'd done that. Once backup had arrived, Eli had stooped down and touched his fingers to Marta's neck. He hadn't said anything, but Ashlyn had seen it in his eyes. The dread. The grief.

The guilt.

Or maybe she'd seen the guilt only because she had blamed him for what had happened to Marta. Ashlyn still did blame him. Though it was hard to hang on to every drop of that blame after what Eli had done tonight. He'd put his life on the line for Cora and her.

"Thank you for protecting Cora," she said.

The next sound he made seemed to be one of dismissal. It had an "I was just doing my job" ring to it, and maybe that's all it was, but at the core of it was something very personal. A different kind of personal than the old attractions that had once been between them.

She and Eli had been in that alley when Marta was shot. When she'd been shot, too. And whether either of them wanted it, it had created this connection between them. One that came with bad memories and a shared nightmare that was still haunting them. Maybe it always would.

While Gunnar drove down Main Street, Eli continued to keep watch, and he checked his phone whenever it dinged with a text message. Since Cora's car seat was between them, Ashlyn couldn't see what was on his phone screen, but she could certainly see Eli. The muscles flexing in his jaw. The tightness of his mouth. The formidable expression.

She'd always thought he had the face of a warrior, and that was especially true now. Like all his brothers, he had the cocoa-brown hair and stormy gray eyes, but there was an edge to Eli. Something unsettled. He was dangerous-looking. As if the only thing he was searching for was the next fight. A fight he was certain he would win.

Maybe it was the adrenaline and fatigue, but Ashlyn remembered when he'd kissed her. So many years ago. They'd been practically kids, and it was something that the bad memories of Marta should have washed away.

But it hadn't.

He'd kissed like a warrior, too.

"Are you okay?" Gunnar asked.

It took Ashlyn a couple of seconds to realize he was talking to her and that he was volleying glances at her in the rearview mirror. Heaven knew what her expression must have been for him to ask that now, but she hoped she hadn't shown any signs of remembering that warrior kiss from Eli.

"I'm just tired," she settled for saying.

Gunnar nodded. "Once Kellan gets your statement, maybe we can find a place for you to take a nap."

She doubted she'd be able to sleep, but Gunnar's comment told her that she probably wouldn't be leaving the sheriff's office before morning. Not that she especially wanted to leave. Ashlyn definitely didn't want to go back to her house until they'd figured out why this attack had happened.

Or if there'd be another one.

"Remy will be coming in for questioning," Eli told her after he read another text on his phone.

Ashlyn immediately shook her head and tried to process that. Eli didn't have to explain who Remy was. She knew. Remy Sager was Marta's boyfriend, and he'd been crushed when she died. And in a rage from the pain of losing the woman he loved.

"You actually think Remy had something to do with the attack?" Ashlyn asked.

"Just covering all the bases," Eli repeated.

She supposed he had to start the investigation somewhere, and with both gunmen dead, Eli would need to find the reason for the attack. But Remy seemed as much of a long shot as contacting the funeral home and the San Antonio hospital.

"Has Remy threatened you recently?" she asked.

Eli shook his head. "But it's hard to know what's in a person's mind. Some people don't just jump right into revenge. They stew on it for a while and then come at you when you're not expecting it."

Maybe, but it didn't make sense in this case. "Remy didn't hold a grudge against me, and he never threatened me. Whoever did this wanted me to kill you. You would have been dead, and I would have gone to jail. The grudge or whatever this is seems to be against both of us."

A grudge that was a sick kind of poetic justice to have her end up killing the man that she had blamed for Marta's death. Well, in part she had blamed him, anyway, but Remy had put the full blame on Eli. Ashlyn hadn't witnessed firsthand the exchanges between Eli and him because she'd been in the hospital recovering, but some of the nurses had told her about Remy's accusations and threats against Eli. Then the cops from San Antonio PD had brought it up, too, when they'd interviewed her.

"Remy could have let his grief fester to the point that he wants someone else to pay for Marta's death," Eli pointed out. His voice was calm enough, but she figured that was a facade. Someone had just tried to kill them, and that had to eat away at him. Plus, he would want to get the bottom of it, and that meant taking a hard look at Remy. Doing so would dredge up the past and put the nightmarish memories right in front of them again.

Gunnar pulled to a stop in front of the sheriff's office, and as Eli had done at his house and at the hospital, he positioned himself in front of her when she scooped the baby into her arms. He kept right by Cora and her when they hurried inside, where she immediately spotted Kellan in the doorway of his office.

The bullpen was empty, which likely meant everyone other than Gunnar and Kellan was out working the investigation. No sign of Eli's other brother, Owen, who was a deputy, and she hoped he was home with his toddler daughter. Since Owen lived just a short distance from Eli, Ashlyn wanted him to stay close to home in case something else went wrong. Whoever was carrying out this grudge—or whatever it was—might use Owen to get to them.

Kellan didn't waste any time, and he quickly ushered them into his office. Away from the front door and the windows. A reminder that another gunman could be out there. That didn't help calm any of her still-raw nerves.

"The doctor said Ashlyn and the baby weren't hurt," Eli relayed to his brother the moment Kellan shut his office door behind him.

Kellan nodded and motioned for Ashlyn to take the chair across from his desk. Because her legs felt as if they might give way, she did. "I'll need diapers and a bottle for her soon," she let them know.

Kellan gave another nod. "What kind of formula and diapers?"

After Ashlyn told him, he fired off a message to someone, most likely arranging for those items, and then he turned to Eli. "Remy won't be in until nine in the morning," Kellan explained. "And he's bringing his lawyer with him."

That didn't surprise her. Word of the attack had almost certainly gotten out, and Remy would know that he would be a suspect.

"If Remy did this, he'll have an alibi," Ashlyn said,

and judging from the quick looks of approval, Eli and Kellan had already considered that.

"We'll get his financials," Eli assured her. "If Remy paid for those thugs, we'll find it."

She didn't have any idea how much it cost to hire would-be killers, but Ashlyn suspected it would be enough of a withdrawal to get their attention. That meant Remy would have covered those tracks, too. Except there was a problem with the whole theory that Remy was responsible for this.

"Remy isn't rich," she reminded them, her gaze holding on Eli. "From what I've heard, he drained his savings trying to bring a civil lawsuit against you." A lawsuit for Marta's wrongful death that a judge had dismissed before it could even go to trial.

If Eli had a reaction to the reminder of the legal attempt against him, he didn't show it. He kept the same stony expression he'd had in the cruiser. "He could have borrowed the money or sold something to get it," Eli pointed out just as quickly. He turned to his brother. "SAPD is interviewing Abe Franklin's family. They might know who actually hired him."

Ashlyn latched onto that hope even though she knew it was a long shot. "What about the second gunman?"

Kellan glanced at his computer screen, his eyes scanning over the info he saw there. "Charles Cardona. He's got a record as long as Abe Franklin's. No family other than an ex-wife. The Austin PD will interview her."

So, the investigation was already in full swing. No surprise there, since someone had targeted a Texas Ranger. Law enforcement all over the state would hopefully see this attack on one of their own, and that would spur them to get to the bottom of it ASAP.

Eli and Kellan exchanged a glance, and it seemed as if something passed between them. A cue, maybe, because Eli turned to her. "Tell us about the baby," Eli insisted.

Ashlyn felt herself go stiff, and she tightened her grip around Cora. His comment definitely didn't sound friendly, more like a lawman's order. "I adopted her six weeks ago. She's three months old."

They both stared at her, definitely waiting for more, and the uneasy feeling in her stomach turned to a hard knot. Because she suddenly knew why they had those lawmen eyes on her.

"Dominick McComb," she muttered. Just saying his name tightened her stomach even more, but Ashlyn shook her head. "He's Cora's biological grandfather, and he wasn't happy about the adoption. But he wouldn't have done this. He wouldn't have done anything to put Cora at risk."

Eli lifted his shoulder as if maybe not buying that. "Why wasn't he happy about the adoption?"

Obviously, they weren't going to accept that Dominick was innocent. And maybe Ashlyn didn't, either, but it chilled her breath to bone to even consider that Dominick might be behind this. Unlike Remy, Dominick had money along with a cool facade that didn't make cops take a second look at him. That made him even more dangerous than Remy, but she didn't think that danger would apply to anything he did with Cora.

Ashlyn took a moment to steady herself before she answered. "Cora's biological parents were Olive Landry and Dominick's son, Danny. Danny died of a drug overdose when Olive was pregnant, so Olive decided she'd put the baby up for adoption. Olive and I met, and she liked me. She's a college student, only nineteen," Ashlyn added.

"Olive didn't want Dominick to raise the child?" Eli pressed.

"No, and neither did Danny," Ashlyn said without hesitation. "Dominick has a police record, and Olive thought he, well, bullied Danny. Dominick tried to stop the adoption, but that didn't go anywhere."

"A judge denied him custody," Eli spelled out. "But he does have supervised visitations." Obviously, he'd gotten that information during one of those many calls he'd made.

Ashlyn nodded. "He sees Cora every two weeks. But not alone. When he visits, I'm there, and so is a social worker. And then there's the nanny he hired."

"A nanny?" Eli questioned. Obviously, that wasn't something Eli had known, and he was probably wondering why a man with very limited, supervised visits would need the services of a nanny.

"His visits weren't long, only an hour each time, but Dominick was hoping that Cora would eventually have overnight stays at his house. He thought it was a good idea to have a nanny in place, one who already knew Cora." She paused. "He's never been hostile toward me. And he's very loving with Cora. That's why I don't believe Dominick would have hired those men."

"Maybe the gunmen didn't have orders to fire into the house or endanger the baby." Eli's argument came so fast that she realized he'd already given this some thought. "Unlike Remy, Dominick has the funds to hire thugs."

Yes, he did, and she couldn't completely dismiss the notion that the thugs hadn't followed orders. Maybe they panicked when things hadn't gone as planned. Still…

"Why would Dominick have sent gunmen after you?" she asked Eli. "He doesn't even know you."

"Dominick doesn't have to know me, but I'm sure he's heard of me," Eli assured her.

He let that hang in the air, and Ashlyn tried to figure out his train of thought. It didn't take her long to do that. It'd been all over the news about Marta's death, and Dominick could have easily found out the details with some simple internet searches. If Ashlyn had indeed murdered Eli, she would be in jail. Maybe even dead. The gunmen could have been instructed to kill her and make it look like a suicide because she was so distraught over killing Eli.

And then she would have no longer been in the way of a custody challenge from Dominick.

His police record and Olive's wishes might be dismissed with the adoptive mother out of the way. Dominick could even possibly use this as a way of discrediting Olive and accusing her of handing over Cora to someone mentally unstable enough to commit murder.

"Oh God," Ashlyn said under her breath.

"Yeah," Eli agreed. Obviously, he'd had no trouble figuring out what was going through her head. "He'll be brought in for questioning, too. And since Dominick does have the money to hire more guns, Cora and you will need to be in protective custody. For the time being, that'll be with me."

Her head snapped up, and she fired a glance first at Eli, then Kellan. "Eli insisted," Kellan explained.

"I'm seeing this through to the end," Eli added when her attention shifted back to him. "No one puts a baby in danger and then tries to kill me. Whoever's behind this won't get away with it."

She wasn't sure if that was a threat or a promise. Maybe it was both. But before Ashlyn could point out the problems of the two of them being under the same roof, there was a knock on the door. The sound caused her to gasp, a reminder of just how on edge she still was. Her body tensed, bracing for a fight, but it wasn't a threat. It was Gunnar.

"Here are the baby supplies," Gunnar said, holding up several large bags. "Want me to put them in the cruiser?"

Eli nodded. "You'll be driving us to Jack's?"

"Jack?" Ashlyn repeated. She knew who he was, of course. Marshal Jack Slater, another of Eli's brothers, and he lived on the grounds of their family ranch.

"We're going to his place," Eli verified. "He's out of town on a case, and he said we could use it. We can't go back to our houses because the CSIs are still there."

She didn't want to go to their houses, but she was still shaking her head about Jack's. "What if hired guns follow us there?"

"We'll take precautions." Eli's gaze held for several moments on Cora. "Lots of them. Trust me, keeping your daughter safe is my top priority."

Ashlyn heard the unspoken part of that. He wanted

her to put aside their pasts and declare a truce. For Cora. That was probably the only thing that could have caused her to nod.

"Thank you," she managed to tell Eli.

Obviously, he wasn't comfortable with that because his mouth tightened again. "Are you okay with Ashlyn giving her statement tomorrow?" Eli asked Kellan, and he checked the time. "It's late, and I'm sure we could all use some rest."

"Tomorrow's fine," Kellan agreed, and he looked up at Gunnar. "Stay there with them tonight at Jack's. I'll get someone out there to relieve you first thing in the morning."

Ashlyn stood to get ready to leave, but she stopped when Eli's phone dinged with a text message. He frowned, then scowled when he read it and then immediately made a call. She hadn't been able to see what was on his phone screen, but Ashlyn held her breath, praying this wasn't the start of another attack.

"What the hell do you mean by a glitch?" Eli snapped to the person that he'd called.

The next part of the conversation was all one-sided so Ashlyn looked at Kellan to see if he knew what was going on. He shook his head, lifted his shoulder.

"Find them now," Eli growled a couple of seconds later, and he stabbed the End Call button as if he'd declared war on it. There was an angry fire in stormy eyes.

"What's wrong?" Kellan and she asked in unison.

A tight muscle flickered in Eli's jaw. "Marta's funeral home and hospital records are missing. Both the hard copies and the digital files. It looks as if someone stole them."

Chapter Five

Eli's fun meter was already at zero, and hearing about Marta's missing files sure as hell didn't give his mood a boost. He wanted answers, damn it, and this certainly wasn't helping.

Neither were his sleeping arrangements for the night.

Of course, Eli seriously doubted that he'd be getting much sleep, but he was going to need at least a nap if he wanted his brain to continue to function. And that nap would need to happen at his brother's house. With Ashlyn and her baby daughter under the same roof.

Ashlyn didn't look any more pleased than he did about the sleeping arrangements when Eli ushered her into the wood-and-stone house, and Eli knew her disapproval wasn't because of the place itself. She was no doubt troubled by that "being under the same roof" part, too.

He stepped in, glanced around, trying to see it from a lawman's eyes rather than a visitor's. It definitely wasn't sprawling like the main house where Kellan lived and helped run the family ranch. This one only had a combined living and kitchen area, two bedrooms, an office, two baths and was, well, laid-back. Which was a fairly apt description of his brother Jack. This was a place where you could flop on the sofa, drink a beer and watch the game on the big-screen TV mounted on the wall above the fireplace.

Now it was going to be a place where Eli would keep Ashlyn and Cora safe. He started that by arming the security system, which he knew was top-notch. It was a precaution that Eli and all his brothers had taken after their father was murdered.

"I'll put these in the guest room," Gunnar said, holding up the bags of baby supplies. "I'll also close the curtains and make sure all the doors and windows are locked," the deputy added, and he went into the hall.

"You really believe Marta's missing records are a glitch?" Ashlyn came and asked Eli. It was just a rephrasing of what she'd already pressed him on, and during one of his responses, Eli had indeed used the word *glitch*.

His word choice, though, was because the alternative just pissed him off. There was no good reason for someone to steal the files. That's why he'd demanded a full investigation on it. However, there was a bad reason for a person to do this.

"I don't believe Marta's alive," he said. "But someone could have stolen and wiped the files to muddy the waters." If he had to run down leads on who'd do something like that, then he wasn't focusing on the actual person who'd sent those armed idiots after them.

She nodded, swallowed hard and then glanced around as if to give herself a distraction. "The place looks like Jack."

It didn't surprise him that she would realize that

since she knew his brothers as well as she did him. Almost as well, he mentally corrected, since she hadn't been around them much lately. However, Ashlyn had been Eli's girlfriend in high school.

Now he mentally cursed.

Because he had to add an asterisk to that girlfriend label. She'd lost her virginity to him when she was seventeen, a memory that was certainly etched in his brain. His body wasn't going to let him forget it, either.

Once, they'd been as close as a couple could be, and while Eli hadn't exactly been planning their future when he'd been in high school, it had stung when they'd drifted apart after Ashlyn had gone off to college. Then there'd been other relationships, both his and hers, and the timing hadn't worked for them to get together for even a round of ex-sex.

Then Marta had died, and everything had gone to hell in a handbasket.

He'd never been thankful for the bad blood between them, but it would stop the old heat from rising now. He hoped. Because that wasn't a distraction he needed when he already had enough of them.

"Will we really be okay here?" she asked, and even though he'd purposely kept the light dim, he had no trouble seeing the fear that was still in her eyes. "I want the truth. Don't tell me something just to ease my mind."

He thought about that a moment, then nodded. "No mind-easing then. The security system will alert us if anyone tries to break in. Both Gunnar and I will be here, and we'll both have our guns ready."

Their gazes met. Held. "Will that be enough?" she

asked. Ashlyn pulled the baby even closer to her. "Because nothing bad can happen to Cora. I can't lose her."

The fear was in her voice, too. And the love. Eli recognized it because his brother Owen had a daughter as well, and he got an up close and personal look at that parental love whenever he visited them.

"It'll be enough," Eli assured her. It wasn't a lie. He hoped. And because he didn't want her to see any doubts in him, he tipped his head to the hall. "As soon as Gunnar's done checking the place, I'll show you to the guest room. You'll feel better once you've gotten some rest."

She nodded, almost absently, and with the baby cuddled in her arms, she went to the bookshelves on the sides of the fireplace. Her gaze combed over the framed pictures, some of Eli and his brothers. Others were of the champion horses that Jack had raised and trained.

Her attention lingered on the one that was on the center shelf. It was a shot of Kellan and his now fiancée, Gemma, and they were standing next to Jack and his then-lover, Caroline Moser. It had obviously been taken during happier times, because they were all smiling.

"Caroline Moser," Ashlyn said. She looked at him. "How is Jack?"

Eli knew that was a Texas-sized question with a couple of layers. Their father had been murdered a little over a year ago, and his killer still hadn't been caught. Ironic, since Eli and all his brothers were lawmen.

"Jack's okay," Eli answered, but he had no idea if that was even true. That's because the one person who could tell them their father's killer was Caroline, and a head injury prevented her from remembering.

Ashlyn's glance was more of a flat look to let him

know that she didn't buy the part about Jack being okay. Or any of them, for that matter. They'd lost their father and couldn't bring his killer to justice. That ate away at all of them. Eli liked to think that he had less in the eating away department because he was still feeling lower than dirt about Marta's murder. Both deaths, though, had left plenty of holes in him.

"It's all clear," Gunnar announced when he came back into the living room. He tipped his head to the sofa. "I'll crash in here for a while. That way, I can hear if anyone drives up."

Eli had been about to make the same offer, but since Gunnar got to it first, he'd crash on the floor outside where Ashlyn would be. Jack wouldn't mind if Eli slept in his bed, but the master was at the end of the hall with the office in between it and the guest room. Until Eli was certain there was no longer a threat, he didn't want to be that far away from Ashlyn and Cora.

He led Ashlyn into the guest room and immediately saw a problem. "Sorry, no crib. I can try to get one—"

"No. It's okay. We won't be here that long."

It sounded as if she had some other plan in mind. Or maybe it was just wishful thinking. Either way, he didn't press it.

"I can put Cora on a quilt on the floor," Ashlyn added, and she brushed a kiss on the baby's head. "I don't want her on the bed because she's started to roll over, and she might fall off."

Since she had her hands full, Eli helped with the bedding issue. There was an extra cover folded on top of the dresser, and he spread it out on the floor. He was pretty sure he'd find some more bedding in the hall closet for Gunnar and him.

"The bathroom's attached," Eli explained, tipping his head to one of the doors. "Don't know if it's got what you need, but if not, let me know and I'll have one of the ranch hands bring it over."

Ashlyn nodded again and muttered a thanks. "What happens next?" she asked just as Eli had turned to leave. "About the investigation," she clarified when he stared at her.

Hell. For just a split second, he'd let the old heat creep into his body, and it was a reminder of how easy it would be to lose focus.

"I'll see if Kellan has any updates. Then I need to make some calls to the hospital and funeral home. I want to talk personally to the folks who dealt with Marta's records." And he didn't give a rat that it was the wee hours of the morning. He wanted answers right away.

"You'll let me know if you find anything?" she pressed.

He nodded and got out of there. The best way to regain focus was to put some distance between Ashlyn and him. Of course, there was no chance his body was going to let him forget that she was just a door away.

Eli went back into the living area where Gunnar was already stretched out on the sofa. Not asleep yet, but from the looks of it, he soon would be, so Eli went into the laundry room just off the kitchen to make his calls. He tried the contact number at the hospital first.

No answer. Which didn't please him.

That displeasure went up a significant notch when the answering service for the funeral home transferred his call, only to have it unanswered as well. It went to voice mail, and Eli left a scathing message for the person in charge to call him immediately. If he hadn't heard from them in a few hours, he would have SAPD go to the place with a search warrant. A warrant he was certain that he could get since he could tie it to the attack tonight.

Eli was about to try Kellan next, but before he could do that, his phone buzzed, and he saw his brother's name on the screen. Good. Well, maybe. He hoped Kellan wasn't calling with more bad news.

"It looks like we got a break," Kellan said the moment that Eli answered. "I'm sending you something that I'm sure you'll want to see."

WHEN CORA GRINNED at her and flailed her arms and legs in excitement, Ashlyn couldn't help but smile back. She was still shaken from the attack the night before, still trying to get past the fatigue of too little sleep, but it was impossible to stay gloomy when looking at her little girl.

Ashlyn finished dressing the baby, picking her up from the quilt on the floor and giving her kisses on her cheeks and neck. The sound that Cora made wasn't quite a laugh, more of a breathy babble. Like the grin, it also lifted Ashlyn's spirits. Yes, there was a lot of danger and uncertainty right now, but she didn't have a single doubt about the love she felt for her baby.

A child she'd thought she would never have.

It didn't matter that she hadn't been the one to give birth to Cora. The little girl was hers in every way that counted, and she would make sure she was not only safe but happy.

"It's me," Eli said a split second before there was a knock on the door.

"Come in," Ashlyn answered.

He did, almost hesitantly, and he seemed relieved that she was up and dressed. Ashlyn had made sure of that. She'd gotten up before Cora so she could grab a quick shower so that she would be ready to go if something went wrong. And so that Eli wouldn't walk in on her when she was wearing only a T-shirt that she'd slept in.

With his hands crammed in the pockets of his jeans, Eli walked in. Not too close, though. He stood there eyeing Cora while the baby eyed him. Ashlyn studied him as well and wished that she hadn't.

Mercy, no one should look that good after the horrible night they'd had. Yet he managed it in his jeans that were snug and loose in all the right places. The gray shirt also had a too-good fit, and it was nearly the same color as his eyes. The top three buttons were undone, but in her mind it was as if it were fully open so she could see his chest—which she knew was as incredible as the rest of him.

He followed her gaze, nearly causing her to curse because he'd caught her gawking at him, but then Eli only shrugged. "I raided Jack's closet for some clean clothes."

Oh, so maybe he hadn't realized the gawking after all. Good. There was enough heat still stirring between them without her adding that to the mix.

Cora made another of those cooing babbles and reached out a hand to Eli. Apparently, Cora had the knack for making Eli smile, too, because the corner of his mouth hitched, and he went to them, sinking down onto the floor. He stunned Ashlyn when he pulled Cora into his arms.

"She's a cute kid," Eli muttered. "And she smells good."

It took Ashlyn a few seconds to get her mouth working. "Baby soap. There was some in the supplies that Gunnar brought in. I bathed Cora in the bathroom sink." She paused. "You seem pretty comfortable holding a baby."

He shrugged again. "I've had some practice with Owen's daughter, Addie. She's a year and a half old now, and we've all taken our turns babysitting."

A surprise that Eli would involve himself in that, but then Owen's wife had died in childbirth so he'd likely needed the help.

"Don't puke on me," Eli playfully told Cora as he lifted her into the air.

Cora didn't puke, but she did act as if Eli was the greatest thing since baby formula. The playfulness didn't seem right, not with everything else going on. Not with the old wounds that were still between Eli and her.

Not with the heat.

All the memories began to swirl together, and that's when Ashlyn knew she had to get this back on track. "Any updates on the investigation?" she asked.

"A few. One big one," he added a moment later. He looked at her. "Remy recently came into a lot of money, nearly a hundred grand. It's an inheritance from his grandmother."

She took a moment to process it. That was certainly plenty enough to hire those two gunmen. "When did Remy get this money?"

"A week ago, but he's known it would be coming for several months now."

So he'd had plenty of planning time. Even though she wasn't a cop, Ashlyn had no trouble figuring out that Remy had means, motive and even the opportunity for the kidnapping and attack. Since Marta had been a criminal informant, Remy could have even used Marta's old contacts to find the gunmen.

But Ashlyn immediately rethought that last part.

"Marta didn't associate with violent people," Ashlyn pointed out. "Yes, she'd had an arrest for drug possession when she was eighteen, but she'd turned her life around. She helped the cops. She helped *you*."

"She did," Eli readily admitted, but then he didn't say anything else for several seconds. "But drugs and violence overlap. She knew Leon, who in turn knew Drake Zeller."

Eli didn't spell out for her that Drake had certainly been violent, since he'd been the one who'd shot both Marta and her. Even though Leon hadn't fired any shots, he'd been convicted of setting up the ambush.

"Of course, Leon claims he didn't personally know Drake," Ashlyn reminded him under her breath.

Eli went silent again, and he handed Cora back to her before he stood. Ashlyn expected him to just walk out and put up that wall between them again. But he didn't leave. He put his hands on his hips and glanced up at the ceiling before his attention came back to her.

"I've gone over every detail a thousand times of that night Marta was killed," he said. "I'm sure you have, too."

She had, and Ashlyn confirmed it with a nod.

"I didn't set up the ambush," Eli went on. "Neither did you or Marta. That leaves Leon, since Drake couldn't have put it together on his own. The anonymous tip I got about the drug bust came through official channels, through a number that only the criminal informants used."

A number that Eli knew—that's what she was about to point out. It was the old argument that Ashlyn had used because she hadn't believed Leon was gutsy enough to do something like that. It was too dangerous, and from everything she'd learned and heard about Leon, he was basically a coward.

But Marta hadn't been.

And now for the first time Ashlyn had to consider this from a different angle. She had to consider the unthinkable. What if Marta had set up the ambush in the alley? And maybe Marta had done that to kill Eli. Of course, Ashlyn couldn't think of a good reason why Marta would want Eli dead, but it was something she needed to at least admit was possible. Along with admitting something else.

What if Marta was still alive?

"Did you find out anything about Marta's missing records?" she asked.

Eli stared at her as if he wasn't pleased with the shift in conversation. Maybe because he'd wanted or hoped for an air-clearing between them. Of course, he probably already knew that the "air" wasn't as murky between them as it had been before the attack. He'd saved her and Cora's lives, and that changed things. So did this old attraction rearing its head. Someday, soon, they'd talk that all out, but for now the investigation had to come first.

He dragged in a long breath before he finally answered. "Terrell Wilburn, the mortician who handled Marta's remains, is on vacation, but I'm in the process of tracking him down so I can question him. The owner doesn't understand why the file is missing, but he said Wilburn might have copies of it. They're looking into it. So am I."

That wasn't a surprise. Eli would dig until he found answers. "And the hospital?" Ashlyn pressed.

"They're sticking with the glitch theory. They're converting from hard copy to digital and think it got lost in the shuffle. I don't believe it."

"You think Marta's alive and there was a cover-up?" she pressed.

"No. But someone might want me to think that. I'm having SAPD show Remy's photo to the employees at both places. Something might pop."

Yes, but it was just as likely that Remy would have hired someone to steal those files. If he was the person behind the attack, that is.

"The cops questioned the families of the two dead gunmen," Eli went on a moment later. "If they know anything about who hired the men, they're hiding it well. If there is something to hide, the Rangers will be monitoring their bank accounts to make sure there aren't any unusual deposits."

Good. Because then a deposit like that could be traced back to the source. Hopefully, anyway.

Eli continued to stare at her as if there was something

else he wanted to say. "There's coffee in the kitchen if you want a cup."

She doubted that was what was actually on his mind, but before Ashlyn could press it, his phone dinged with a text message. Whatever he saw on the screen caused his forehead to bunch up.

"Dominick just came into the sheriff's office," Eli relayed. "He's demanding to see you and the baby."

Chapter Six

Eli was absolutely certain he wouldn't like anything about this visit to the sheriff's office. For starters, it put Ashlyn and the baby out of the house and on the road—since she had insisted on making the trip with him.

It was too big a risk.

Of course, so was staying put, as Ashlyn had argued. Getting answers was what they needed if they were to figure out what was going on, but Eli wasn't convinced it was necessary for Ashlyn to go with him to get those answers. Hell, he wasn't sure they'd be getting any useful information from Dominick.

The only thing that was certain so far was that Eli despised the man for demanding to see Ashlyn and the baby. Even more, he hated the new round of worry and fear that this had put in Ashlyn's eyes.

Eli cursed himself when that thought sank in. Now he was thinking about worry, fear and her eyes. None of that would help this investigation.

At least Ashlyn had agreed with him about Dominick not seeing the baby. Actually, she'd been as adamant about that as Eli had been. Until they were certain that

Dominick had had no part in hiring those thugs, then he wouldn't have access to his granddaughter.

Eli was betting that wouldn't go over well with Dominick.

And that was the reason he'd taken precautions before they'd left Jack's house. First, he'd called a sitter, Gloria Coyle. The woman hadn't actually watched Cora yet, but Gloria was someone they had both known most of their lives. Ashlyn had contacted her shortly before the adoption to ask her if she'd be able to watch the child if ever there was some kind of emergency. This definitely fell into that "emergency" category, so Gloria had agreed to meet them at the sheriff's office. She could wait with Cora in the break room while Ashlyn chatted with Dominick.

That wouldn't be a fun conversation, either.

After Dominick said whatever it was he had to say to Ashlyn, then Eli wanted a crack at questioning the man. As a Texas Ranger, he didn't have a set jurisdiction, so it would be perfectly legal for him to do that as long as Kellan agreed. Which he would. His brother was as eager to get to the bottom of this as he was.

This time when they arrived at the sheriff's office, Eli had Gunnar park the cruiser at the back of the building. One of the other security measures Eli had taken was to ask Kellan to unlock the back door so he could get Ashlyn and Cora in fast. Kellan had also posted a deputy there to make sure a hired gun hadn't thought it was a good place to lie in wait for an ambush.

When Gunnar pulled to a stop, Eli glanced around for any signs of a threat. None. But he saw his other brother Owen waiting in the doorway. So this was the deputy that Kellan had assigned to the protection detail. Owen immediately stepped out, helping Ashlyn get the baby into the break room. The transfer was fast, exactly what Eli wanted.

Gloria was already there, waiting, and she went to Ashlyn to give her a hug as soon as Owen had shut and locked the door. Ashlyn thanked the woman, and while they talked about the baby's bottle and such, Eli turned to Owen.

"Dominick's in the interview room," Owen said. "He's got a bad attitude and two lawyers." He glanced at the baby. "Please tell me he won't get near that little girl."

"Trust me, he won't," Eli assured him.

There must have been something in his tone that got Owen's attention, because he lifted an eyebrow. "That sounded…personal."

Eli scowled. "Don't read anything into it."

Owen's eyebrow stayed up. "Hey, this is your brother, remember? I used to have to cover for you when you sneaked off with Ashlyn for some…private time."

"That was high school," Eli snapped.

And if they'd been in high school now, that remark from Owen would have earned him a butt-whipping. Not because it wasn't true. It was. But Eli didn't like that smug look on Owen's face. Still, he supposed it was better than the angry gloom and doom that all of them had been sporting since this whole ordeal had begun.

Ashlyn handed off the baby to Gloria, but Eli didn't have to be a mind reader to know that was hard for Ashlyn to do. With the memories still fresh from the attack, she probably didn't want the baby out of her sight.

Something he considered using to try to talk her out of coming here to see Dominick, but her expression was easy to read, too, when she looked at him.

She was ready to do this.

"I'll wait back here with Gloria and the baby," Owen assured Ashlyn. "We'll keep the door locked and the security alarm on."

Ashlyn thanked him, and as if it were the most natural thing in the world, she brushed a kiss on Owen's cheek. A reminder that once Ashlyn and his brother had been friends. Heck, maybe they still were. Ashlyn had shut Eli out of her life, but it was possible she hadn't done the same to the rest of his family.

She gave the baby one last kiss and then one last glance before she followed Eli out of the break room. He shut that door, too, so that Dominick wouldn't be able to hear the baby if she cried or fussed.

"Is the adoption ironclad?" Eli asked her as they walked up the hall.

"Yes." She didn't hesitate, but she did give him a long look. "Why do you ask?"

"I just don't want Dominick to spring any surprises on you. I don't want him trying to get temporary custody because he could convince a judge that you can't keep Cora safe."

He expected for that to put some alarm in those already emotion-heavy eyes. It didn't. Ashlyn shook her head. "He has no legal claim."

"What if you were out of the picture?" he added.

Now there was some alarm. "You mean if I were dead." The breath that she blew out was part huff. "It still wouldn't happen." But she didn't sound exactly convinced of that.

Eli wasn't convinced of it, either, and even though Dominick might not have a legal claim to the child, the truth was, the birth mother also wouldn't have a claim, because she'd signed the papers and was the only surviving birth parent. Custody would be up in the air since Ashlyn didn't have any close family heirs. That could create the right amount of custody chaos for Dominick to make his move.

He didn't spell that out for Ashlyn. Planting that seed was enough to make her even more aware—and skeptical—of anything Dominick said.

When they made it to the interview room, Kellan was already there waiting for them. "Dominick wants to talk to you first," he told Ashlyn, "and then you'll have to leave for the actual interview. You can watch from the observation room though if you like."

She nodded, murmured a thanks, and she walked in behind Kellan when he opened the door. Eli had no trouble spotting Dominick because he recognized him from his driver's license photo that Eli had pulled up during his background search on the man. Dominick was tall with a well-toned build. Despite the thread of gray in his dark brown hair, he looked ten years younger than he actually was.

There were two guys wearing suits on either side of Dominick, and one of them stood when Dominick did. The lawyers gave Eli the once-over with some stink eye thrown in, but Dominick nailed his gaze to Ashlyn.

"Where's Cora?" Dominick immediately asked. "Is she all right?" He went to Ashlyn and reached out for her. The man likely would have grabbed her by the shoulders if Eli hadn't stepped in front of him.

Dominick spared him a glance, one laced with annoyance, before he glared at Ashlyn. "Where is she?" Dominick repeated.

"Cora's fine," Ashlyn answered.

Eli wasn't sure how she managed it, but her voice stayed cool. As did the stare she gave Dominick. She was likely sizing him up, trying to figure out if there was a trace of guilt.

"I want to see her." Dominick made that demand through clenched teeth.

"She's in protective custody," Eli volunteered. "No visitors allowed."

This time Dominick gave him more than just a glance, and the annoyance went up a huge notch. "I'm Cora's grandfather."

"Not legally, and if this is why you wanted to talk to Ashlyn, then you've wasted her time and yours." Eli took hold of her hand, turning as if to leave, and it got the exact reaction he wanted.

"You can't just go," Dominick snapped. "You must know I'm worried sick about my granddaughter being put in danger like that. Gunmen," he spat out like profanity. "It's obvious someone's after Ashlyn, and Cora could get hurt. She'll need more protection than what some local badge can give her."

Eli tapped his badge. "I'm a Texas Ranger, and since both Ashlyn and Cora are unharmed and safe, I think I did an okay job. Plus, I don't have any ulterior motives of trying to get custody of Cora. Unlike you."

Dominick pulled back his shoulders. There was the

heat from temper in his expression, but it only lasted a few seconds before the ice came. Oh, yeah. He was capable of hiring thugs to come after Ashlyn.

"Are you suggesting that my client was responsible for the attack?" one of the lawyers snarled.

Eli lifted his shoulder. "If the overly priced shoe fits..."

That brought the other lawyer lurching out of his chair, but with his cold stare still on Eli, Dominick waved the man down after only sparing him a glance. Obviously, Dominick was accustomed to having even his unspoken orders followed.

"I have an alibi for last night," Dominick said, tossing some of that chilly shade on Ashlyn. "Of course, you could say that doesn't matter, that I could have hired those men. But I didn't."

"Can you prove that?" Ashlyn asked, taking the question right out of Eli's mouth. He tried not to beam with pride, but that was some backbone Ashlyn was showing under very difficult circumstances.

Eli hadn't thought the frost in Dominick's eyes could go up any, but he was wrong. It did. "Give the *Texas Ranger* access to my bank account," Dominick snapped, speaking to the lawyers, though this time there wasn't even a glance involved. "That'll prove I didn't hire anyone."

"Thanks for that," Eli said. "But actually it only proves that you didn't use money from the one account that you'll let us examine. It's my guess that a man who wears a suit like yours probably has more than one account."

Eli added a grin that he knew was prime fuel for a

hissy fit, which he hoped Dominick would have. Heck, maybe the man would even take a swing at him, and Eli could use the assault to get a warrant to dig even deeper into financials. Goading a possible suspect was a cheap trick, but Eli wasn't above using it to get this man behind bars.

With the pulse throbbing on his throat and his eyes narrowed to slits, Dominick certainly looked as if he wanted to throw a punch, but he finally took a step back. His attention slashed from Eli to Ashlyn.

"You know I wouldn't do anything to harm Cora," Dominick insisted. "I love her."

The love part certainly sounded sincere, but Eli had seen people do all sorts of stupid things in the name of love.

"Do I need to go through a judge to get an order to force you to allow me to see my granddaughter?" Dominick added when Ashlyn didn't say anything.

Ashlyn stared at him for a long moment. "If you truly love her, you won't insist on visiting her when hired guns could follow you to her location. You could put her in danger, and I think any judge will agree with me about that."

"I'd be careful," Dominick blurted out, but then he waved that off. He turned away from them, and Eli didn't think it was his imagination that the man was grappling with that temper of his that was simmering just beneath the surface.

When Dominick turned back around, he fastened his gaze to Eli. "I don't know if you're good at your job or not, but I am aware that you have a history with Ashlyn."

It didn't surprise Eli that this man had had him investigated, and it only proved what Eli had said to Ashlyn earlier. Dominick could have used their past to put together an attack, one that would be harder to trace back to him.

"I don't think you've looked at all the possible angles about the attack at your house," Dominick added.

"Are you about to tell me that I should be investigating Remy Sager?" Eli came out and asked.

Dominick's glare turned to a frown. Apparently, he wasn't happy that Eli had spoiled his big reveal.

"That's a good start," Dominick grumbled. Now there was some sarcasm in his voice, proving to Eli that the check Dominick had done on Ashlyn and him had gone deep. Of course, Eli hadn't expected anything less. "But you need to look at others, because I believe what happened to Ashlyn and Cora is connected to Marta Seaver's murder."

"Oh?" Eli was pretty sure his sarcasm was better than Dominick's. A small victory, but he didn't like this jerk's attitude.

"Oh," Dominick repeated like profanity. "I know that Leon Taggart is in jail for his part in setting up her murder, but he might have a reach beyond prison bars. You might want to look at Leon's old friend Oscar Cronin."

The name was familiar to Eli. *Very* familiar. Oscar owned a pawnshop, and he had an extremely shady past. That past and his friendship with Leon were the reasons Eli had kept tabs on the man. However, Eli hadn't considered that Oscar would play into this.

"You believe Oscar hired those gunmen on Leon's behalf?" Eli asked.

Dominick shrugged. "I believe that's something you should find out since Oscar's paying regular visits to Leon at the prison."

"I will find out," Eli assured him. "And maybe while I'm checking, I'll ask myself why you just handed me Oscar Cronin on a silver platter. I have a suspicious nature about things like that." He turned to Ashlyn. "Are you ready to go?"

"She can't just leave," Dominick howled. "Not until she's told me where Cora is."

Ashlyn proved the man wrong when she walked out the door with Eli. Dominick might have followed them, but Kellan stepped inside the room, blocking Dominick's way. He then closed the door behind him when he went in to start the official interview.

Eli was about to congratulate Ashlyn for how well she'd held up through that barrage Dominick had doled out to her, but when he felt her shaking, he cursed. Obviously, talking with the idiot had gotten to her after all, because she was pale, too.

"I can't lose Cora," she muttered. "I just can't." And he got the feeling she wasn't just talking about the danger from an attack but also the threat that Dominick could pose.

She went in the direction of the break room but then stopped and ducked into the observation room instead. "I just need a minute to steady myself," she said, her voice suddenly as unsteady as the rest of her.

Eli went in with her. "Don't let him get to you like that."

It was lousy advice, like telling someone not to blink if they heard a loud noise. Ashlyn's fears and concerns were natural, and there wasn't anything he could say to her to soothe that. But apparently his stupid body thought there was something he could *do* in the soothing department, because Eli put his arms around her and eased her to him.

Eli expected her to push him away. She didn't. He expected himself to put a quick end to the hug and curse himself for doing it.

He didn't.

There was some cursing himself involved, but his arms stayed firmly planted around her. From the corner of his eye, he saw Kellan start the interview with Dominick, and Eli considered turning on the audio so he could hear. However, he nixed that idea since he figured it would only add to Ashlyn's shakiness. He'd listen to the recording of the interview once he had Ashlyn and the baby back at the ranch. That way, it would give his own temper a chance to cool down.

"I'm not usually this shaky." Her voice was a whisper. A breathy one. It hit against his neck.

"I'm betting you don't usually have someone kidnap your baby and then try to kill you."

Now he cursed again. And winced. Because obviously someone had tried to kill her in that alley the night Marta had died. Eli braced himself for her to verbally blast him for that, but when she pulled back just enough to meet his gaze, there was no blasting involved.

Hell.

There was plenty of heat, though. It was masked a little behind her worried and somewhat confused expression, but it was there. And for one bad moment, he got a flashback. Not the kind that came from being a lawman. This one was of her nearly naked and cuddled up with him on the seat of his truck.

"Thanks," she said, her voice still a whisper. Yeah, the breath was there, too, but this time it landed against his mouth. She noticed it, too, because she pulled back even farther. "Sorry. Sometimes I forget why that's a bad idea. Then I get an old picture of us in my head, and I remember."

"In a memory contest, I bet I would win."

Of course, the moment the words came out, he wanted to hit himself, but he decided just to own the stupid remark. Eli gave her as much of a smile as he could manage. It wasn't a good one, but it seemed to be enough to stop her from trembling. It even gave her a little bit of color in her cheeks.

"Thanks," she repeated, but this time her tone had something they both wanted. Awkwardness. It was a hell of a lot better than his remembering how she looked naked.

Or wanting to kiss her.

Ashlyn dragged in a deep breath, pulled back her shoulders. "So, was Dominick trying to muddy things by bringing up Leon and Oscar?"

It was a good question, the right one to diffuse this restless energy between them, and it helped Eli get his thoughts back where they belonged. "Maybe. I'll talk to the warden at the prison and see what I can find out. Unless Leon's come into some money lately like Remy, then he hasn't got the funds to hire two guns. I don't know anything about Oscar—yet."

And speaking of Remy, that was Eli's cue to see if the man had arrived yet. That would also put some distance between Ashlyn and him. "I need to talk to Owen. After that, Gunnar and I can drive Cora and you back to the ranch."

She glanced at Dominick, who appeared to be in the same riled mood he was when Ashlyn was in the room with him, and she shook her head. "I'll listen to Dominick, and then we can go."

Eli didn't think the listening part was a good idea, because it would likely upset her, but he couldn't blame her. If he were in her shoes, he'd want to know every possible aspect of the investigation. He flicked on the switch for the audio and went in search of Owen. He wouldn't dawdle, though, because the memory of Ashlyn trembling was still way too fresh in his mind.

When Eli made it to the bullpen, he glanced around and soon spotted Owen. "Any sign of Remy?"

"Not yet. He called to say he was delayed because he's waiting on his lawyer. He'll be here in about an hour."

An hour was going to feel like an eternity with Cora in the break room and Dominick just up the hall. Eli knew it was stupid for him to feel as if he had such high emotional stakes when it came to the baby. But he did.

"I'll call Remy and tell him to get his butt in here ASAP," Eli grumbled. And if not, he'd see about getting a warrant for his arrest. Remy ticked all the boxes when it came to suspects, and Eli didn't want the man dodging them while he came up with an alibi or a way to escape justice.

"Hold off on that call," Owen said, his attention on the screen of his desk computer. "I just got a report from SAPD." Owen looked up at him. "They sent an officer out to talk to the mortician who works at the funeral home that handled Marta's remains."

"Terrell Wilburn," Eli supplied. He didn't like that suddenly tight look on his brother's face. "And what did he have to say?"

"He's dead." Owen's tense look only got worse. "Someone murdered him yesterday afternoon. A gunshot wound to the head."

Eli felt the shock of that ram straight into him. He doubted it was a coincidence that the mortician had died just hours before the kidnapping and the attack.

"Who killed him?" Eli asked.

"SAPD doesn't know yet. There's more," Owen quickly added. "The killer apparently stole Wilburn's laptop, but Wilburn had some hard copy files in his office. There was a folder with Marta's name on it."

"And?" Eli prompted when Owen paused.

"It was empty," Owen said. "It looks as if the killer took whatever was in it."

Chapter Seven

Ashlyn listened to every word of Dominick's interview. Of course, he claimed he was innocent of hiring the gunmen. And maybe he was. But she had no intention of letting him see Cora until they had the person responsible for the attack behind bars.

Whenever that would be.

It sickened her to think that the search could go on for days, weeks or even longer, but she had to hold on to the hope that maybe there wouldn't be another attack. That whoever was behind this was done. But she had to be sure. For the sake of her baby, she needed to be certain that no one else would come after them.

After Dominick and his lawyers were gone, Ashlyn went into the break room to check on Cora. She was asleep in Gloria's arms, and Owen was still standing guard. Seeing both steadied her nerves a little so she went in search of Eli so she could find out when they'd be going back to Jack's place. Not that Ashlyn especially wanted to go there, but she didn't like the alternative of staying in the sheriff's office where Dominick could return.

She coiled her way around the hall and spotted Eli in

Kellan's office. The two were huddled over a computer, and judging from their stern expressions, something hadn't gone the way they wanted. When she stepped in, both men looked at her, but then Kellan gave Eli a nod. Obviously, that was a cue for Eli to fill her in. The fact that he had to take a deep breath first told her that she wasn't going to like this much, either.

"Someone murdered the mortician who handled Marta's remains. They stole his file on her and his computer." Eli said it quickly and continued before she could do anything more than gasp. "We're starting the paperwork to have Marta's remains exhumed."

Ashlyn still didn't manage more than a gasp, but she did make her way to the chair to sit. Her legs suddenly didn't feel very steady. Someone was dead. Someone connected to all of this.

"There's no concrete proof that Marta didn't die the night of her attack," Kellan added, "but we need to be sure."

Yes, they did. And a few minutes ago, Ashlyn would have insisted that she needed no such proof as seeing her friend's body. But now with the mortician's murder, it was something that had to be investigated.

The memories of Marta's murder came, of course, and like always they were smeared together with the pain of her own shooting. With the anger and betrayal she felt about Eli. But that had changed, too, she realized.

Everything had changed.

"Why would Marta have faked her death?" Ashlyn asked when some of the numbing shock finally wore off.

"Maybe she wasn't the one who did it," Eli said, but

his attention wasn't on her. It was on the front door, and she followed his gaze to the man who'd just stepped in.

Remy.

She wanted to ask why Remy, or anyone else for that matter, would do something like that, but Remy spotted them, too, and he made a beeline toward them.

Ashlyn stood, steeling herself up for what would no doubt be an onslaught of anger fueled by grief. Until today, she'd understood that, but now she looked at Remy as someone who might have tried to murder Eli and her.

Had he actually done that?

She studied him as he stormed closer. Tall with black hair and dark brown eyes. Attractive in a bad-boy sort of way. A way that had certainly appealed to Marta. Even after Marta had turned her life around and gone straight, she'd kept that thing she had for bad boys.

"I don't appreciate getting a threat about being arrested." Remy aimed that snarl at Eli. "My lawyer still hasn't shown up."

"Then get him here right now because you've had more than enough time," Eli fired back, and his snarl was harder than Remy's. "We've got questions, and you're going to give us those answers."

Remy flickered an annoyed glance at Ashlyn. This time, she saw the blame he sent her way. Blame for what Remy saw as her part in not preventing Marta's death. Or at least that's what she thought it was, but maybe it was all an act. Because maybe Marta wasn't actually dead.

"Yeah, yeah," Remy grumbled to Eli once his gaze

was back on him. “Somebody tried to off you, and you’re looking to pin it on me.”

“I’m looking for the truth,” Eli assured him. “I heard you inherited some money, and once your lawyer’s here, I’ll want to ask you some questions about how you might have used those funds. After all, hired guns cost big bucks.”

Remy gave him an arctic stare. “I didn’t do that, and you’ve got no proof that I did.”

Eli lifted his shoulder. “I’ll be pressing you more about that—again when your lawyer gets here. And after you’ve cleared up that matter, I’ll want to know if you helped Marta fake her death.”

Remy had already turned to leave, but that stopped him in his tracks. “What did you say?”

“You lawyered up,” Eli reminded him, and yes, there was some cocky smugness in his tone and expression. “I can’t talk to you about that until he or she gets here.”

Remy’s glare vanished, replaced by some confusion. He frantically shook his head. “Marta faked her death?” That certainly didn’t seem like old news to him. His eyes were wide now, and his mouth was slightly open.

“You lawyered up,” Eli repeated.

“To hell with the lawyer.” Remy practically knocked into her when he rushed toward the desk where Eli was standing. “Is Marta alive?” He volleyed glances at all three of them while he repeated the question.

“Are you waiving your right to counsel?” Kellan clarified.

“Yes!” Remy snapped. “Now tell me about Marta.”

Kellan read the man his rights first, and with each

word of the Miranda warning, Remy's impatience skyrocketed. "Is she alive?" Remy shouted.

"We don't know. That's the truth," Eli added when Remy looked ready to yell again. "Someone stole her records and murdered the mortician who handled her remains. Tell me what you know about that."

Remy dropped back a step, and he pressed his hand to his chest. "Nothing. I don't know anything about it." He dragged in some rough breaths, and his gaze slashed to Ashlyn. "You saw her dead. You told me you saw her dead."

"I did." Of course, now Ashlyn had to wonder if what she'd seen was true.

"I felt for a pulse," Eli went on, "and she didn't have one. Marta was dead at the scene. I'd bet my badge on that."

Remy shook his head. "But what about the missing records? What about the dead mortician? Does that mean someone wanted to cover up that she's actually alive?"

"No," Eli quickly answered. "They could be just smoke screens." He paused a heartbeat. "Tell me about the disagreement you had with Marta's family about where she was to be buried."

Remy blinked, obviously not expecting that to come up. "Uh, her dad, Gus, wanted to bury her in Oklahoma. I wanted her buried in San Antonio so I could visit her grave. Marta would have wanted that, too," Remy quickly clarified, "but Gus wouldn't bend. He put her in the ground in a place she didn't want to be."

Some of the shock was gone now, and in its place was some venom and bitterness.

"Did that rile you enough to play mind games?" Eli pressed. "Mind games that include getting back at Ashlyn and me?"

Remy's eyes were narrowed when they came back to Eli. "No. I told you I didn't try to kill you. Even though you both deserve it," he added in a grumble. "You let Marta die in that alley, and now you're on a witch hunt to add more misery to my life."

"No witch hunt," Eli tried to assure him, but Remy interrupted him.

"Was it one of you who broke in to my house?" Remy demanded.

Ashlyn sighed. "No," she insisted, but Eli only tapped his badge to remind Remy that he was the law, not the criminal.

Remy didn't look as if he believed them. "Well, somebody broke in night before last and stole my laptop and cell phone. I got a new phone with the same number, but I didn't have all my computer files backed up online."

That got her attention. Eli had said the mortician's computer and files had been stolen, too. She didn't know the timing of that, but she had to wonder if it was connected to the break-in at Remy's. Of course, Remy could be lying about that.

"Now you demand I come in for questioning and tell me stuff about Marta," Remy went on. "What the hell am I supposed to think?" But he waved that off. "I've changed my mind. I'll wait for my lawyer. I won't say anything else until he gets here."

"Suit yourself." Kellan tipped his head toward the hall. "Come with me. You can wait in the interview room."

Ashlyn watched them leave and waited until they were out of sight before she turned to Eli. "You believe him?" she asked.

Eli rubbed his hand over his forehead. "I'm not sure. He hates both of us, and I don't know how far he'd take that hate."

Neither did she. But maybe they could find out. "I can call some of Marta's old friends and find out if they've noticed anything off about Remy. I'll need my cell phone for that, though, because it has the contact numbers. It's still at my house. I didn't bring it with me when I went looking for Cora."

He nodded. "Calling her friends is a good idea, but don't mention the fake death theory to any of them just yet. I want to talk to Marta's dad first."

Just hearing that caused her stomach to twist. Unlike Remy, Marta's father hadn't held the anger and hatred for them, but he had been torn up by his daughter's murder. She doubted that grief had gone away even after all these months.

"The CSIs are done processing our houses," Eli told her. "I got word about that right after I left the observation room." His gaze came to hers. Lingering. And reminding her of what had happened between them there.

A hug.

She might be able to convince herself it had only been that. Might. But she couldn't do much convincing with Eli giving her that smoldering look.

Ashlyn cleared her throat, glanced away. "I'll need to drop by my house and check on my horses and the ones I board. I could get my cell phone and some of my things while I'm there." She paused, gave that some thought. Actually, a lot of thought. "I don't feel comfortable taking Cora back there just yet."

"Because you're smart, that's why. It's not safe. If there are more hired guns, your house and mine would be the first places they'd go. I'll take you to your house later today. *With backup*," he emphasized. "It'll have to be a quick in and out, and we won't be taking Cora with us. She can stay at Jack's with Gloria and a couple of the deputies."

Good. She hated the idea of leaving her baby, but she would hate it even more if Cora was with them during another attack. And Eli was right. If there were other gunmen, her house would be a prime target.

"I'll call Gus now," Eli said, taking out his phone.

With her breath held, she watched as Eli located Gus Seaver's number, and after he put his phone on speaker, he tried the call. No answer. When it went to voice mail, Eli left a message for the man to contact him. Eli had barely finished it when Gunnar stepped through the door.

"Remy's lawyer is here," Gunnar said, "and so is a guy named Oscar Cronin. He wants to see you. He says he's a friend of Leon Taggart."

Eli and she exchanged surprised glances. She definitely hadn't expected Oscar to come to them, though she was certain Eli would have gotten around to getting in touch with the man.

"Check Oscar for weapons," Eli instructed, causing her heart rate to spike. She hadn't considered that he'd come here to attack them, but she should have. She should be thinking worst-case scenario right now so she could make sure Cora stayed safe.

"Move over here," Eli told her after Gunnar had left, and he motioned for her to come behind the desk. Once she'd done that, he positioned himself in front of her, and he put his hand on the gun in his holster.

Maybe it was Eli's stance, but it caused the wiry, gray-haired man to come to a stop in the doorway. She'd never met Oscar, but as Ashlyn studied him, she realized she'd seen him in court when Leon had entered his plea before the judge. Oscar was about the same age as Leon, late forties, but he was a good foot shorter than Leon. She'd always thought Leon looked like a criminal. Oscar certainly didn't, and his pale complexion and the cough that rattled in his chest made her think that he might not be in the best of health.

"Sergeant Slater. Miss Darrow," he greeted, and it wasn't a question. Obviously, he recognized them, too. "I heard about the trouble y'all had last night and figured you'd want to talk to me."

Eli just stared at him, and even though Ashlyn couldn't see Eli's face, she was betting one of his eyebrows was raised. "Why, did you have something to do with that?"

Oscar gave a dry smile, shook his head. "Dominick called me early this morning and said he intended to mention me in an interview. I thought I'd save you the trouble by coming here and letting you know I didn't try to kill either one of you."

Normally, Ashlyn would have liked his direct approach, but she wasn't about to trust this man. "How do you know Dominick?" she asked.

"That's just it—I don't. He called me out of the blue,

claimed he was looking into your background, and he wanted to know if I could tell him anything."

"Anything?" Eli snapped. "What specifically?"

"Didn't say, and I didn't ask. That's because I told him I didn't know Miss Darrow. Or you," he added to Eli. "Because he asked about you, too."

Ashlyn wanted to groan. Dominick was digging for dirt, probably so he could find something to use against her in a custody fight, and he would have gone to Oscar because of his connection to Marta and Leon.

"I figure this Dominick might be trying to set me up for something," Oscar went on. He coughed again. "I mean, why else would he call me and say he was going to mention me in an interview with a cop and Texas Ranger?"

"Good question," Eli said. "Why do *you* think Dominick would do that?"

Oscar lifted his shoulder. "I'm an easy target. I'm dying," Oscar added without any change in his tone. "Lung cancer. I'm home alone a lot with no alibis. Maybe someone like Dominick wants to do something bad—like go after the two of you—and then blame me for it. Whatever he's up to, I'm thinking it's no good."

Ashlyn thought the same thing. However, she could see this from a different angle. Leon and Oscar were friends, and maybe with Oscar dying, he wouldn't mind doing his old friend a favor by getting back at the two people who helped put him behind bars.

"I heard the deputy say that Remy's lawyer was here," Oscar went on. "I guess it doesn't surprise me that Remy would be a suspect in this, too."

"You know Remy?" Eli asked.

"Of course. And Marta," he readily admitted. Then he paused. "I've been hearing things lately. Rumors. They've got to be rumors," Oscar added as if talking to himself.

Eli kept his attention nailed to the man. "What have you heard?"

Oscar opened his mouth. Closed it. And he seemed to reconsider what he'd been about to say. "Leon's no threat to anybody. The man doesn't have a nickel to his name. But there could be other folks out there, drug dealers, who might not be pleased that Marta was tattling on them to the cops."

Everything inside Ashlyn went still. "What are you talking about?"

"Marta." That's all Oscar said for several long moments. "The rumors I've heard are that she's alive, that she faked her death to hide out from some of those dealers who might want her dead for real. If that's true, give her some advice from me. She'd better stay dead."

Chapter Eight

There was a whole lot of information—and questions—going through Eli's head. He'd thought that being at Jack's house would help him process all of it since it was quieter here than it'd been at the sheriff's office. But the processing just kept circling back to one of the questions.

Was Marta actually alive?

If she was, did that have anything to do with the attack and the mortician's murder?

No matter how it circled and mentally played out, Eli just couldn't see Marta faking her death and letting everyone believe she'd been murdered. Nor could he see Marta killing anyone, but maybe someone had done it on her behalf. Someone like Remy, who wanted to protect her from drug dealers who might come after her if they found out she was alive. But Remy had looked shocked when Eli had brought up the possibility of Marta surviving the shooting.

Real shock.

It was hard to fake that. Then again, the surprise could have been simply because Remy hadn't expected Eli to know anything about it.

While standing by the kitchen table, Eli drank more coffee, studied his notes on his laptop and then glanced at his phone. He considered giving Marta's father another call, but before he could do that, Ashlyn came into the kitchen. She looked exhausted with her pale face, heavy-lidded eyes and rumpled hair. Those were the first things he noticed. The second thing that snagged his attention was that despite the fatigue, she looked good.

Hell.

He might as well hit his head against the wall a couple of times. He'd known that hug in the observation room was a mistake, but Eli hadn't counted on it lighting a couple more fires that shouldn't be lit.

She glanced at Gunnar, who was grabbing a catnap on the sofa. "Cora's finally asleep," she whispered to Eli. She went to the fridge and got a bottle of water. "Gloria's with her."

Not a surprise, since Gloria hadn't left the baby's side since they'd arrived. That was good, and Eli hoped the woman continued to be okay with that arrangement since she might be there for a while.

"I'll text Owen and tell him to come so he can stay here while Gunnar, you and I go out to your place," Eli offered, and he fired off the message. "Or if you're having second thoughts about going, I can get the things you need and bring them to you. You could make a list."

She shook her head. "I want to make sure the horses are okay." Then she paused. "I want to make sure I'm okay, too. I need to be able to go back there, to prove to myself that I can do it."

Eli understood that. It was akin to getting back on a

horse that'd just thrown you. But the horse wasn't going to hire gunmen to kill you.

"It's my home," Ashlyn added as if she needed to convince him, but it sounded as if she was actually trying to convince herself. "If I can't stay there, then… well, it changes everything."

Yeah. She'd have to sell the house and land that'd been in her family for a couple of generations. She would have to give up her livelihood, too, at least until she found another place big enough for the horses.

He hadn't thought it possible, but Ashlyn now looked even more exhausted than she had when she'd first come into the kitchen. Eli wished there was something he could do to help with that. Of course, his stupid body came up with a few bad suggestions, but he shoved them aside. Holding and kissing her wasn't going to help.

"You scowl whenever I'm around," she said, and Ashlyn reached up and touched her fingers to the muscles that were bunched up there.

Eli probably should have just blown that off and gotten the conversation back on the right track. He could do that easily by telling her the bits and pieces of info he'd learned about the investigation. But apparently, this was going to be the day his brain joined the other stupid parts of him.

"Naked thoughts," he admitted.

Her eyebrow rose. "Of us." Now she got some color when she blushed. "Of us in your truck," she continued without waiting for him to say anything. "It's firm in my memory because you were my first. That creates a strange intimacy. A connection. No matter what happens afterward, it stays with a woman."

"It stays with a man, too." Apparently, the stupidity was just going to keep on coming from him.

The corner of her mouth lifted for a quick smile. "I wasn't your first," she pointed out.

He nearly blurted out that some were more memorable than others. Ashlyn had definitely been memorable. But he'd filled his dumb things to say quota for the day.

"Losing you was hard," she went on. "Then, hating you for Marta…" She stopped, waved it off.

Eli just stared at her and waited her out. It took her several moments, and she kept her gaze on the floor, but Ashlyn finally continued. "This might be easier if I really did hate you. I don't." She looked up at him, and yeah, their eyes locked.

"It wouldn't be easier," he assured her. "I didn't like you hating me."

She gave him that half smile again and brushed her hand down his arm. It wasn't a flirty kind of gesture. More the signaling of some kind of truce.

Despite that, it went straight to his groin.

That wasn't a good direction for any kind of feeling to go, and before Eli could talk some sense into himself, he slipped his hand around the back of Ashlyn's neck, pulled her to him and kissed her.

Eli grimaced at her taste. Not because it was bad but because it was damn good. Like a really nice present that he'd just unwrapped. A hot one, and that heat did a number on him when it slid right through him.

Ashlyn moaned, her pleasure mixed with some hesitation. Which meant she was smarter than he was right now because he couldn't muster up any hesitation whatsoever. None. Eli just hauled her closer and deepened the kiss until it was more than a mere slide of heat. There was need. An urgency. The kind of rush that upped the stupidity and made him remember being naked with her in his truck.

Gunnar's noisy yawn caused them to jerk apart—which Eli was certain he should see as a good thing. Once his body softened and the steam cleared in his head, that is. Gunnar lifted his head, glancing at them from over the back of the sofa. In that glance Eli got a reminder that Gunnar was a good cop, because he saw the realization in the deputy's eyes. Gunnar knew what they'd been doing.

"I'll be back," Gunnar mumbled, tipping his head in the general direction of the hall bathroom. That was no doubt an invitation for Ashlyn and him to continue the mistake they'd just been making. They wouldn't. But Eli figured he'd be thinking way too much about doing it again.

"I know you're sorry that happened," Ashlyn whispered. "There's no need to apologize."

She didn't give him a chance to even consider if he wanted to do that. Ashlyn went back to the fridge and took out one of the sandwiches that they'd picked up earlier from the diner. Apparently, kissing him made her hungry. He was hungry, all right, but not for food.

"Were you able to find out any more about Dominick's bank account?" she asked.

He reminded himself that talking about the investigation was a good thing. Whether it felt like one or not. "Nothing. No suspicious withdrawals." Of course, Eli hadn't expected there to be, since Dominick had voluntarily given them access. "I called the prison, and the warden is setting up a phone call with Leon. I want to ask him about Oscar, about what he said."

She nodded. "It's true that Oscar visited Leon?"

"Yes. He's been there three times since Leon's conviction, but two of those visits have happened in the last month. The conversations were monitored, but the recordings of the visits have already been wiped."

Judging from her expression, she wasn't any more pleased with the timing than Eli was. He was about to add that maybe they would get Leon to tell them what Oscar and he had discussed during those visits, but there was still way too much fog and heat cluttering his mind.

"Look, I just want to get this off my chest," he grumbled. "I didn't kiss you so that you'd stop hating me. Or so you'd stop feeling as if I didn't do my job the night Marta and you were shot. The kiss just happened."

He wanted to groan because that sounded about as stupid as the kiss itself had been. The fact that it was true didn't make it better.

She took in a breath and stared at him as if considering that. "I didn't think that. It didn't seem like some kind of ploy or test. It felt like, well, like what it actually was—lust." She glanced in the direction of his zipper and actually managed a smile.

That didn't make it better, either, but Eli found himself wanting to smile, too. Thankfully, he was spared from doing that because his phone rang. Not the prison, but it was a call he'd been expecting.

"It's Marta's dad," Eli let her know, and he took the call on speaker so that Ashlyn would be able to hear.

"Sergeant Slater," Gus greeted. "I didn't expect to hear from you."

And he didn't sound especially happy about it. Eli couldn't blame the man. Just hearing Eli's voice likely brought back a slew of bad memories. Eli figured that would only get worse with this call.

"Some questions have come up," Eli started. There was no easy way to say this so he just put it out there as fast as he could. "The mortician who handled your daughter's remains has been murdered. Marta's file was stolen. Her hospital records are missing. All of that doesn't add up to a solid conclusion, but I have to ask the question. Do you believe Marta's still alive?"

Silence. For a long time. "Is this some kind of sick joke?" Gus finally snapped.

"No," Eli assured him. "Do you believe she's alive?" he repeated.

"Of course not. I buried her. You know that."

Yes, he thought he did. Eli had gone to the funeral, but it'd been a closed-casket service. "Did you actually see Marta's body?"

"No, but—" There was another stretch of silence. "Tell me straight what's going on," Gus demanded.

Because he figured he would need it, Eli first drew in a long breath. "Like I said, what I have isn't close to being conclusive. A mortician's dead, files are missing, and I had a person come forward who claims to have heard rumors that Marta might have faked her death to hide from some drug dealers. I just need to know if you think there's any chance that happened."

There was another long silence. "I didn't ask to see her body. I couldn't."

Eli got that, but he wished that Gus had taken a glimpse of his daughter when he'd said goodbye. "I've done the paperwork to exhume Marta's body." Eli paused long enough to give the man time to object.

Gus didn't.

"You really think she could be alive?" Gus asked, and Eli hated the hope that he heard in the man's voice.

"I have to rule it out," Eli settled for saying.

"Then get it done. In fact, if it'll speed things along, I'll pay for it. I want it done immediately."

Eli wasn't sure he could make *immediately* happen, but he could press. "I'll see what I can do," he assured Gus, and he ended the call so that he could message Kellan to get him involved.

When he finished the text, Eli saw that Gus wasn't the only one with some hope. Ashlyn had it, too. Hell, so did he. But if Marta was alive, then it was going to pose a whole new problem for them. Such as—had Marta had any involvement in the attack from the hired guns?

Before Eli could give that any thought, his phone rang again, and this time it was the prison. As he'd done with Gus, he put the call on speaker, and after several transfers, he finally heard the familiar voice.

"Sergeant Slater," Leon greeted. His voice was low and raspy. "Long time, no see. You're alive and kicking, I guess?"

"Any reason I wouldn't be?" Eli countered, and he tried to make the muscles in his chest relax. Hard to do since this was the man who'd orchestrated an ambush that had killed one person and wounded Ashlyn.

Well, wounded Ashlyn, anyway.

With what he was hearing about Marta, he might have to amend Leon's label. His lawyers would want an amendment, too, and if Marta was truly alive, they could use that to get Leon a much reduced sentence.

"I heard about the trouble you had out at your place," Leon answered. "Lots of gossip about it, and it was on the news. The details are a little sketchy, but it sounds like someone took some shots at you."

Eli didn't doubt the news or gossip part, but that might not have been the reason Leon knew about it. He might have firsthand knowledge. "You're sure you didn't hire someone to kill me?"

Leon laughed. "You have access to my bank accounts. Oh, wait. I don't have any bank accounts because I don't have any money. You also have access to any and all of my visits so unless you think my lawyer floated me a loan, then you know I didn't hire anyone."

Yes, Eli did have access to those things, but that didn't mean something couldn't slip by. "You hate me. That means you might have found a way to come after me."

No laugh this time, but there was a heavy sigh. "I don't want you dead. Didn't want you dead that night, either. Drake said he needed to have it out with Marta, that he was going to convince her to quit ratting on him. You and Marta's friend, Ashlyn, were just in the wrong place at the wrong time."

Ashlyn went a little pale again, and she was no doubt battling the flashbacks from that night.

"So you didn't want me dead, only Marta?" Eli said.

"Didn't want Marta dead, either," Leon insisted. "I actually liked her, but Drake was paying, and I needed cash. It wasn't personal, just business."

There was no chance of Eli's chest muscles relaxing

with that. He wanted to reach through the phone and beat Leon senseless. "It was personal to me," Eli said, his voice a low, dangerous warning.

Leon stayed quiet a moment. "What's this call all about? Because I doubt you're just wanting a trip down that particular memory lane."

"It's about Oscar. Tell me about his visits."

"Oscar," Leon repeated, and he didn't sound surprised. More like resigned that his old friend was going to come up in conversation. "You think he's the one who hired the gunmen."

"Did he?" Eli pressed.

Leon gave another sigh. "Maybe. I honestly don't know for sure," he quickly added before Eli could challenge his answer. "Unlike me, what happened with Drake is personal."

Everything inside Eli went still. "Explain that."

"Oscar and Drake were like brothers, and Oscar wasn't happy when you killed Drake."

"Well, I wasn't happy when Drake gunned down Marta, shot Ashlyn and then tried to kill me. I get testy when things like that happen. What the hell did Oscar say to you when he visited you in prison?" Eli demanded.

"That he wasn't happy about some honor that you got," Leon answered after a short hesitation. "He got all worked up when you got a commendation last month."

Eli had indeed gotten that, because he'd tracked down a killer and saved the hostage that the killer had taken. The commendation had embarrassed him some since he'd just been doing his job, and now it had had this effect. But Eli hadn't seen anything "worked up" about Oscar when he'd come into the sheriff's office.

"Oscar was angry about that?" Eli pressed.

"Yeah, he said he didn't like that you were getting on with your life when you'd cut Drake's life short. And there's no need for you to remind me that Drake was trying to kill you. Oscar doesn't believe that. Oh, and he's riled about Ashlyn, too."

Ashlyn's eyes widened. "Why?" she asked.

"Because Oscar heard you'd adopted a kid." Obviously, Leon wasn't surprised that Ashlyn had been listening to their conversation. "It's that whole getting on with your life thing." He paused again. "Look, I think Oscar would like it better if you two were wallowing in grief over what happened."

Maybe they weren't exactly wallowing, but it was still haunting them. Worse, it could be the reason for the attack.

"Why did Oscar come to visit you twice in the past month?" Eli went on.

Leon groaned but also made a sound of dismissal. "He just wanted to rant, that's all. He went on and on about Ashlyn's kid and your medal. I told him to cool off, but it didn't help much. He hates your guts."

"That's it?" Eli didn't roll his eyes, but that's what he wanted to do. "He drove all that way there just to vent?"

"That and he wanted to know if I'd kept in touch with any of my old friends."

Eli got that feeling down his spine, the one that told him that he was finally onto something. "What old friends?"

"Just some guys I used to hang out with." Leon's

tone was casual, but there was nothing casual about what Eli was feeling, and it wasn't a feeling he intended to push aside.

"Are you talking about criminal friends?" Eli pressed.

"They've got records, yeah, but Oscar said he might needs some help at his pawnshop. I took that to mean he might need a little muscle or something like that. Maybe some protection in case he'd made some deals that could cause him problems."

"Criminal friends," Eli flatly repeated. "Were two of those guys Charles Cardona and Abe Franklin?" Eli didn't explain that those were the names of the two dead gunmen who'd tried to kill Ashlyn and him. He just waited for Leon to respond, and it didn't take long.

Leon cursed. "I think it's time I called my lawyer."

And with that, Leon ended the call.

Chapter Nine

Ashlyn listened as Eli made the follow-up calls about Oscar and Leon. Calls that might hopefully link Oscar to the attack. Of course, Leon had already linked the man by what he'd told Eli and her, but they would need more than the hearsay of a convict to consider Oscar a real suspect.

Eli was just finishing up those calls when Owen and another deputy, Raylene McNeal, arrived. Ashlyn hadn't expected the second backup, but she was pleased about it. They had the ranch hands keeping an eye on the place, but she preferred having two trained law enforcement officers guarding her daughter while Eli and she were at her place.

"Oscar's not answering his phone. It went straight to voice mail," Eli told her, and he filled in his brother, Gunnar and Raylene while Ashlyn did a quick check on Cora to make sure she was still asleep.

She was.

Maybe they could make it back from her house before the baby woke up. Then she could spend some time with her while she helped Eli unravel this thread that Leon had given them.

When she went back into the living room, Gunnar and Eli were already at the door. Owen, too, and she heard him lock the door as soon as Gunnar, Eli and she were out and heading to the cruiser.

"Is there any reason for Leon to lie about this?" Gunnar asked once they were inside. It was a good question and something that Ashlyn was already considering.

"Maybe Leon's just ticked off at Oscar about something and thought this was the way to get back at him." Then Eli shook his head. "But if that were true, Leon would have already figured out a way to get in touch with me so he could blab. What he told us felt more spur-of-the-moment."

Ashlyn made a sound of agreement. "And Leon's worried that he could be considered an accessory after the fact for the attack."

That got nods from both Gunnar and Eli, and while she knew they'd heard every word she'd said, they both had their attention on their surroundings. It was all rural property between her place and the Slater ranch, which meant there were plenty of places for a hired gun to lie in wait.

"When SAPD and the Rangers were investigating Marta's murder, nothing came up about a connection between Drake and Oscar?" Gunnar asked. He was behind the wheel, and he made brief eye contact with Eli in the rearview mirror.

"Oscar was interviewed, but so were nearly a hundred others." Eli cursed under his breath. "It was a connection I should have made."

Ashlyn huffed to let him know that there was no way he should put this on his shoulders, and then she realized the huff was a sympathetic show of support. Something Eli wouldn't want. Something that was a by-product of the kiss in the kitchen.

A kiss that had changed everything.

Actually, the change had started before that, around about the time she'd realized they were in this together and that they needed to trust each other. But the kiss had sealed the deal, and no matter how Ashlyn spun it in her head, it had reminded her of a man—or rather a boy—that she'd once loved enough for him to be her first.

Now she wanted him all over again.

She huffed again at that, causing Eli to look at her. Gunnar gave her a glance in the mirror, but thankfully she didn't have to explain herself because Gunnar took the final turn to her place.

Ashlyn automatically moved closer to the window when her house came into view. Before the attack, there'd been only good memories here, but now she could hear the sounds of those gunmen. Feel the hit from the stun gun. And the terror. Most of all, she remembered the absolute terror of them taking Cora.

She jolted when Eli slipped his hand over hers. Obviously, she was past being just on edge. Ashlyn had never had a panic attack before, but she was worried that it might happen now.

"We don't have to do this," Eli said, his voice a soothing whisper. She wanted to latch onto it. Onto him. So she gripped his hand harder and steeled herself.

"I hate them," she murmured. "The gunmen. Even though they're dead, I hate them for bringing this to my home." She shook her head to try to clear it. "I won't let them take this away from me."

"Good." Eli's voice wasn't so soothing now. "Don't let the SOBs take away anything from you. You're tough. Hell, you survived getting shot. And you can get through this."

She looked at him to see if it was lip service. But it wasn't. She could tell that from his fierce expression and his eyes. Ashlyn was about to say he was wrong, that she wasn't tough, but she rethought that. She would do anything—anything—to keep her daughter safe, so that meant she could get through this.

Gunnar pulled to a stop in front of her house and looked back at Eli and her. "Why don't I check on the horses? I can make sure they're fed and have water. Ashlyn, you can pack the things you need."

Considering that Eli agreed so quickly, it meant Gunnar and he had likely already worked this out so that she'd be in the house and not out in the open. Ashlyn didn't argue, but she hoped she got at least glimpses of the horses so she could see for herself that they were okay.

Just as they'd done the other times at Jack's house, Eli moved her fast from the cruiser to her front door—after Gunnar had already opened it. She was outside for only a couple of seconds while both Eli and Gunnar protected her. Ashlyn hated that they had to put their lives on the line for her like that, but maybe they'd get answers soon so that Eli could make an arrest.

Gunnar did a quick check of the house, something that sent her heart pounding because it was a reminder that someone could have broken in. Someone who might be still be there and was lying in wait for them.

But nothing, thank goodness.

Once he'd finished his search, Gunnar went straight out the back door, hurrying, no doubt so he could finish the chores and get them out of there fast. Ashlyn headed to her bedroom and tried not to focus on the signs of what had been a struggle between her and the gunmen. A broken lamp and toppled furniture.

Eli stayed right next to her as she walked down the hall, but he stopped in the doorway of her bedroom when his phone dinged with a message.

"We got the approval we needed to exhume Marta's body," Eli relayed to her. "They'll start digging soon."

Which meant that it wouldn't be long before they had answers. If Marta was truly alive, then that would start a whole new investigation.

She grabbed a suitcase from her closet and stuffed in some clothes and then went into the adjoining bathroom to do the same with her toiletries and meds. When she came back out, she saw Eli glancing at the books on her nightstand while he kept watch at the window.

"Parenting books," she explained, though Eli could easily tell that from the titles. "I wanted to do everything right. I didn't want to take a chance of messing it up. It's the most important thing I've ever done."

Eli didn't seem surprised by that. Probably because even in high school she'd mentioned that someday she wanted kids.

"I've seen how you are with Cora, and you're a great mom," he said, his glance going to her this time.

Ashlyn wasn't sure why that felt like such high praise coming from him. And then she remembered something else. "You wanted kids, too." But the moment the words left her mouth, she winced. After that kiss, he might think she was trying to thrust both a relationship and fatherhood on him. "Sorry. That didn't sound right."

He lifted his shoulder and seemed more, well, amused than manipulated. The expression didn't last long, though. His forehead bunched up, and he hurried out of the room.

"Stay away from the windows," Eli warned her as he ran.

The chill rippled over her skin, and just like that, her heart began to pound. With her suitcase gripped in her hand, Ashlyn followed Eli and saw him in the kitchen. She didn't go closer because there was a wall of windows above the sink and counter, and from those windows, she had a clear view of the barn.

"What's wrong?" she asked once she had gathered enough breath to speak.

Eli didn't jump to answer, and he continued to fire his gaze around the yard and barn. "Maybe nothing. I thought I saw someone, but I could be wrong."

She wanted to believe that. Ashlyn wanted to latch onto it so she could try to tamp down the nerves that were now raw and hot.

"I'm texting Gunnar to have him come back inside," Eli added a moment later. "We're leaving."

Good. She didn't want to be there if there was some kind of danger, and she set down her suitcase, waiting to find out what was going on.

Eli took out his phone, but he didn't manage to send the text before the bullet came crashing through the window.

ELI DIDN'T SEE the shot coming, but he sure as hell heard it. And he felt it.

The glass exploded, sending sharp pieces right at him, and he felt one of those pieces slice across his sleeve and arm. There was a quick jolt of pain, which he ignored, because he lunged at Ashlyn, pulling her to the floor with him.

They fell hard, causing Eli to see stars when he crashed onto the floor. Not a second too soon. Because another bullet bashed through the window and into the kitchen.

"Gunnar," Ashlyn said on a rise of breath.

Yeah, Eli hadn't forgotten about the deputy and hoped like the devil that he'd also taken cover. Better yet, Eli wanted Gunnar to be able to take out whoever was firing those shots. There was no chance this was just some random attack, and that meant either there was another hired gun or the boss was there to make sure the job was done right.

That sent a slam of rage through him. Here Ashlyn was in danger again, and they still didn't know why this was happening or who was behind it. That would change, though. As soon as he could get her safely out of here, Eli would make certain that he caught this SOB. First, however, he had to get Ashlyn out of here.

Eli's phone dinged with a text. Gunnar. Anyone hit? Do you have eyes on the shooter?

No to both, Eli texted back. He nearly added for Gunnar to make sure he stayed out of Eli's line of fire, but it wasn't necessary. Gunnar was a good cop and knew that Eli would be looking for this snake.

"Stay down," Eli told Ashlyn.

"You stay down, too," she insisted, her voice shaking.

No way could he do that. He couldn't give the shooter a chance to move closer to the house so he or she would have a kill shot.

Eli got up, took his backup weapon from his ankle holster and slid it her way. It would probably make her even more terrified than she already was, but the security system wasn't on, and that meant someone could sneak in. If that happened, he at least wanted her to have something to protect herself.

"Keep watch on the front door," he added. Again, that wasn't going to steady it, but Ashlyn was smart so she'd not only keep an eye out, she'd also listen for any sounds of footsteps.

"I have my phone now," Ashlyn said. "I'll text Kellan and tell him what's going on."

His brother would send backup, and it wouldn't take long for someone to get there. But Eli hoped he had this situation under control before a cruiser could respond. This time, though, maybe he'd be able to only injure the person so he could take them alive. And question them.

Two more shots came, but these didn't go crashing into the window. They hit the back door, a sign that the shooter was indeed moving. But Eli wouldn't stand still, either. He had to at least know the person's position to be able to stop them.

Staying down, he went to the window and peered out. He saw Gunnar by the barn—on the opposite side from where those shots had been fired. Good. That meant the deputy had some cover.

And could possibly be in a position to be ambushed.

Gunnar had his back against the barn wall, and with

his gun gripped and ready, he was keeping watch. Still, that didn't mean someone couldn't take him out with a long-range shot.

Eli fired glances all around, but he didn't see their attacker. So he waited. Hard to do since this clown could send a deadly shot straight into the house. Still, he forced himself not to move and risk having the shooter see him.

Where the hell was he or she?

There was a fence, but Eli would be able to at least partially see him if he was there. That left some trees and shrubs just beyond the fence and a water trough just inside it, but Eli caught no glint of metal from a firearm, no movement.

Another shot came. It also hit the back door, but this one had a different angle, meaning the shooter had moved again. Since Eli still hadn't seen him or her that meant he or she was likely on the ground. A belly-down prone position wasn't the best if a gunman wanted to get off a series of rapid shots, but it was damn good for accuracy.

Eli tested that. He took off his hat and flung it at the window. Sure enough the shot came, and the bullet tore through it. Eli didn't need another reason to hate this piece of dirt, but that did it because it was his favorite hat. Still, it was worth the sacrifice because he now had this idiot's location.

The shooter was on the ground by a water trough.

Eli made a quick check on Ashlyn to make sure she was still down on the floor. She was. She had her phone in her left hand, the gun in her right, and her attention was fixed exactly where Eli needed it to be. On the front door.

With his back covered, Eli leaned out and sent a shot to the side of the trough where he'd pinpointed the gunman. His bullet only kicked up some dirt, but it was enough to get the guy scurrying to the side.

"He's by the trough," Eli called out to Gunnar. It was possible that Gunnar would have a better angle on the shot than he would.

From the corner of his eye, Eli watched the deputy lean out from cover. Eli did the same, and he waited for Gunnar to fire. Gunnar's shot slammed into the fence, sending a spray of splinters. Not a hit, but it got the gunman scrambling back toward the trees.

That's when Eli took his shot.

He sent a bullet right into the guy's shoulder, and Eli knew he'd hit pay dirt when the guy dropped to his knees. But he wasn't down. The idiot twisted his body, taking aim at Gunnar. And that's when Eli knew he had no choice.

He fired.

This time, it wasn't a shot to disable him but rather one that would likely kill. The shooter took two bullets to the side of his chest before he collapsed face-first onto the ground.

Chapter Ten

Ashlyn tried to make sure she looked a lot steadier than she felt. That's because Eli was watching her, no doubt to make sure she didn't fall apart.

She wouldn't.

No way did she want to add more to his shoulders than was already there.

Eli was blaming himself for the attack. She could sense that in his stiff posture and tight jaw as he paced across the living room and continued the string of calls that'd started as soon as he'd killed the gunman. Eli was angry and frustrated—two things that she completely understood. She had gone through that as well, but then it'd been eased some when she'd gotten back to Jack's and had seen for herself that Cora was okay. There hadn't been a second attack at the ranch.

She looked down at Cora, who was now in Ashlyn's lap, and the baby smiled around the bottle she was sucking. Ashlyn automatically smiled back and felt some more of the tension ease away. Things weren't perfect, not by a long shot, but it was impossible not to be at least somewhat happy with her baby cuddled like this in her arms.

Owen glanced over at her when Cora cooed, the sound obviously getting his attention. He wasn't pacing. He was in the kitchen with her, sipping coffee and standing guard. She didn't miss the quick checks he was making in the backyard. In the front room, Eli was doing the same in between his pacing.

Owen reached down, brushed his fingers over Cora's bare toes, causing the baby to smile again. "If you go back out with Eli when he questions the suspects, you'll leave her here with Raylene and me," Owen said.

It wasn't a question, but Ashlyn nodded anyway. She wouldn't take Cora out of the house, but the rest of what Owen said puzzled her.

"Is that what Eli's doing—setting up another round of interrogation?" she asked Owen.

He nodded, sipped his coffee and studied his brother. "I don't think his temper is going to help in the interviews."

No, it wouldn't. Eli had been forced to shoot two men who'd tried to kill them. Dealing with that alone was enough, but he had the added pressure of not knowing which of their suspects was behind this.

Remy, Dominick or Oscar.

All of them had means, motive and opportunity, which meant Eli and she weren't any closer to learning the truth than they had been before this latest attack. She knew that Eli hadn't had a choice about killing the gunman, but part of his anger and frustration had to be because now the man couldn't tell them who'd hired him.

"You might want to try to calm him down a little," Owen continued, tipping his head to Eli.

Ashlyn lifted her eyebrow. "Why would you think I could do that?"

"You always could," Owen assured her. "I remember at the end of a football game when someone on the opposing team gave him a sucker punch as they were heading to the locker rooms. Eli punched back, and likely would have kept on punching if you hadn't stopped it."

She had no trouble recalling that. Or the fact that it'd happened a decade and a half ago. "High school," she reminded him. "I don't have that kind of…influence over him now."

"Sure you do." Owen gave her a wink.

Ashlyn would have disagreed with that, but Owen didn't give her a chance. He scooped Cora up from her arms, kissing the baby on her cheek. Cora must have liked the move because she gave him a big smile.

"I'm good at burping detail," Owen insisted, and he headed out of the kitchen just as Eli was coming in. Obviously, this was Owen's ploy to give her some privacy so she could try to do the soothing that he'd just suggested. She wouldn't.

Or rather she *couldn't*.

But it certainly seemed as if Eli needed something. As he got closer, she could practically feel the anger radiating off him.

"What the heck is he smiling about?" Eli growled when he looked in Owen's direction.

"Burping duty," Ashlyn mumbled, causing Eli to snap toward her. "He says he's good at it," she added when he just stared at her.

Skepticism replaced some of Eli's anger, and then his scowl deepened. "He told you to calm me down."

"Yes," she admitted. "I'd try if I thought it'd do any good." She took hold of his hand. "This wasn't your fault."

"The hell it wasn't. I knew it was a bad idea for you to go back to your place."

Ashlyn sighed. "All right, then it's my fault because I'm the one who insisted I go."

That didn't improve his glare. Not at first anyway. Then he groaned and squeezed his eyes shut a moment. When he opened them again, she'd hoped to see less anger there. Nope. So she leaned in and brushed her mouth over his. Eli stiffened, but when his gaze met hers, his eyes weren't nearly as narrowed as they had been.

Only then did she remember that she'd done that very thing the night of that football fight.

"You're trying to distract me," he grumbled. "But it'll take a hell of a lot more than just a kiss to do that."

Even though his tone was still rough, she relaxed a little because she could feel him doing the same. She wanted to push it even more. To say something light. But she still wasn't feeling steady enough to do that.

And Eli saw that in her eyes.

He cursed softly, pulled her to him and brushed a kiss on the top of her head. "You're going to have some bad dreams tonight," he whispered. "Not much I can do about that, so I'm sorry for that, too."

She pulled back, looked up at him. "I know there's plenty you will do to help with those dreams…and the threat of another attack." Things that involved more than hugs and kisses. "I heard one of your phone calls. You're bringing out some Ranger friends to search the grounds and keep watch. You're adding some security cameras with motion detectors. And I suspect you'll sleep on the hall floor outside the bedroom again."

He frowned. "How'd you know I slept in the hall?"

"Because I know you." Ashlyn ran a hand down his arm and felt the muscles respond beneath her touch. "You'll do whatever it takes. So will I."

His frown had lightened up a little, but it deepened again when she added that last sentence. "What do you mean by that?"

Since this would require a deep breath, she took it. "Owen said you were bringing in all the suspects. When?"

"ASAP. I told them if they didn't get into the sheriff's office that I'd arrest them and charge them with obstruction of justice."

Ashlyn bet none of them cared much for that threat, but it might get them there sooner than later. "I think that's a good idea, but I also believe I should be there when you talk to them."

Now his eyes narrowed, too.

"We won't take Cora with us," she went on. "She'll stay here with an army of law enforcement officers to protect her. She'll be safe." Ashlyn had to believe that because the alternative was unthinkable. "But I should be there to talk to Dominick. I know him. I've dealt with him. And if he's lying, I believe I'd be able to tell."

Eli didn't jump to respond to that. Not verbally, anyway. However, he did grind out some profanity under his breath. "It might not even be Dominick. It could be

Remy. Hell, or Oscar. I'm trying to get an ID on this latest shooter so I can see if he's linked to Oscar like the others."

She nodded. Ashlyn had heard bits of that conversation as well. "And if he is, maybe you'll have enough to make an arrest."

"Yeah." Eli didn't sound very hopeful about that, though. "I also asked the Rangers to do a deeper financial dig on Dominick and Remy."

Good. She hadn't heard that part of the call, but Dominick was definitely capable of hiding funds. She suspected Remy was, too, especially if he'd hired someone to murder the mortician and steal those files.

"It just seems stupid that Oscar would hire gunmen that we could so easily connect back to him," Eli continued. He paused, groaned softly. "But then that might have been exactly why Oscar would do that."

A sort of reverse psychology, she supposed, but it might not be as complicated as that. It could be that Oscar was reacting out of anger and hired the first people he could think of. Even as the owner of a seedy pawnshop, there probably wasn't a slew of potential candidates for hit men so he might not have had a lot of options in that area.

"The timeline bothers me," Eli went on. "I mean, Oscar waiting so long to come after us. It makes me wonder if he's working with one of the other suspects."

Interesting. Ashlyn hadn't considered that, but it was possible either with Remy or Dominick. One of them could have stirred up Oscar's old anger enough to cause the man to snap.

"If that's true, maybe both of them paid the gunmen," she threw out there. "If so, there would be smaller amounts withdrawn from their individual accounts." Which wouldn't be good because it would make those payments harder to find.

Eli nodded and absently ran his hand down her back. "Remy must have known that he'd be a suspect right from the get-go, so I'm betting he would have made sure a suspicious withdrawal didn't show up in his account."

Ashlyn made a sound of agreement. "It's the same for Dominick."

He nodded again, paused. "But if we go with the theory of two of them working together, Remy or Oscar could have given Dominick the names of the gunmen. Those men might have connections to Remy, too."

Eli's phone rang, the sound jangling her nerves more than it should have. Any unexpected noise was having that effect on her, which meant Eli was right, too, about this latest attack giving her another round of bad dreams.

"It's Gus," Eli said when he looked at his phone screen, and as he'd done with some of the other calls, he put it on speaker.

Ashlyn checked the clock on the stove. There'd been enough time for the exhumation, so Gus was likely calling about that. She stepped back a little and tried to tamp down the nerves that were already firing beneath the surface of her skin. She also tried to brace herself for whatever Gus was about to tell them.

Gus made a hoarse sob, and with just that sound alone, Ashlyn heard the heavy emotion. "She's not there," Gus blurted out, his voice choppy. "Marta's not there in the grave. The coffin is empty."

ELI FELT AS if someone had slugged him in the gut. Hell. What was going on?

"This means my girl is alive," Gus continued a moment later. "Alive," he repeated, crying now. "I have to find her."

Eli agreed with that, but it didn't answer a really big question. How had Marta managed to pull this off? Eli could figure out the why. Well, if he was to believe Oscar. Marta had faked her death to hide from some drug lords with ties to Drake.

But that didn't feel right.

"I'm going to make some calls," Gus went on. "The first will be to Remy—"

"Hold off on doing that. Remy should be arriving at the sheriff's office here in Longview Ridge at any moment," Eli explained. "I want to see how he reacts when I tell him Marta's body wasn't in the coffin."

"Remy will know where she is," Gus argued. "I need to talk to him."

"If you tip him off, Remy might go rabbit on us. He's got the money to do that now, and if he disappears, we might lose our best chance at finding out where Marta is. Just hold off talking to him for a couple of hours—that's all I'm asking."

"My daughter's alive." The man's voice broke. Then he paused. "I'll give you those two hours, but I'm coming to talk to Remy in person."

Eli knew he stood no chance of talking Gus out of doing that. If their positions had been reversed, no one could have convinced Eli to stay back while the law got involved. That's why he just thanked Gus and ended the call.

"Let me make a quick check on Cora, and I'll go with you to Kellan's office," Ashlyn insisted.

He wasn't surprised she was sticking to her guns on this. Especially now. Marta had been her best friend, and if the woman was truly alive, then Remy would almost certainly know where she was.

"Am I staying here or going with you?" Gunnar asked Eli after Ashlyn hurried into the bedroom.

"You're coming with us. I can't guarantee you, though, that you won't get shot at again."

Gunnar lifted his shoulder. "I'm hoping we've met our bullet quota for the day. Plus, Owen and Raylene are better with baby-guarding duty than I am."

Eli could agree with all of that. Or rather he wanted to agree on the bullet quota, but there could be another hired gun. While he waited at the front door, he wondered if it would do any good to remind Ashlyn of that. It wouldn't, he decided. She was seeing the big picture here, and that meant they had to cut off the head of this snake to stop any other attacks.

He made a quick call to Kellan to update him about Marta and asked his brother to pass along the info to SAPD. Since the cops there were primary on the mortician's murder, they'd want to know. And they would almost certainly want their own interview with Remy.

"Be careful," Owen warned Gunnar and Eli as he came out of the bedroom with Ashlyn. "Don't worry. We'll keep watch," he added to Ashlyn. "And there are two Rangers on the grounds along with the hands. We'll make sure no one gets to Cora."

She thanked him, and as if it were the most natural thing in the world, she gave Owen a quick hug. It was amazing how an intense life-threatening situation could change things. It was as if they'd stepped back in time to when she'd cared for Owen like a brother.

And Eli as a lover.

It riled him that his mind kept going back to that. He had plenty of things to do, and none of them involved taking Ashlyn to bed.

Even before they hurried out to the cruiser, Eli glanced out the window, looking for any kind of threat. Both Gunnar and Ashlyn did the same, but Eli didn't see anything other than some armed ranch hands who were clearly standing guard.

"Remy might have murdered the mortician," Ashlyn said as she, too, kept watch.

Eli made a sound of agreement. That was one of the first things that had occurred to him, and he'd need to press Remy on not only his alibi but that deeper search into his financials. Motive was easy to figure out. Remy wanted to keep it secret that Marta was alive. But that only worked if Remy was aware of that. He might not be.

"Thanks for not giving me an argument about this," Ashlyn murmured a moment later, drawing his attention back to her.

Eli hoped he didn't regret giving in on this, but he had to consider that whoever had hired those gunmen would be getting desperate. Three hired killers—all dead. That was a lot of money down the drain, and that had to be beyond frustrating for the person who'd hired them.

His phone dinged with a text, and Eli read the info that Kellan had just sent him. And he cursed. "They got an ID on the latest dead gunman. Jay Hamby. I know him. He was a criminal informant."

Ashlyn shifted in the seat toward him. "I never heard Marta mention him." But then she shook her head. "She didn't talk about that side of her life very often, though. Is Hamby connected to Oscar, too?"

"Don't know yet, but that's something I intend to find out." However, Eli was guessing that would be a yes, that there was indeed a connection. Now he'd need to figure out if Hamby had been hired to frame Oscar or if Oscar had just tapped someone that he already knew to do the job.

"How soon do you have Oscar and Dominick coming into the sheriff's office?" she asked.

"They might already be there. I didn't exactly treat them with kid gloves when I ordered them to come in."

That, of course, meant they'd be showing up with their lawyers. Eli didn't mind that. He just wanted them in the box so he could grill them about both of the attacks.

The moment that Gunnar pulled to a stop in front of the sheriff's office, Eli spotted Remy, who appeared to be pacing across the reception area. He looked about as riled as Eli was. Ditto for the suit—the lawyer, no doubt. He was a wiry man with white hair and a steely expression. Eli gave him steel right back, and he knew for a fact that he was better at it.

"What the hell is this about now?" Remy snapped the moment they were all inside.

Eli didn't answer but instead turned to Kellan, who was sipping coffee while standing in the bullpen. "I frisked Remy. He's not armed. And I read him his rights."

That was exactly how Eli wanted to start this meeting. "This way," he told Remy.

Eli started toward the interview room. That would not only get this started, it would also take Ashlyn away from the windows. Eli was about to tell her that she'd have to wait in observation for this leg of the chat, but Remy started up before they even reached the room.

"I asked you a question," Remy went on, his voice as sharp as a bullwhip. "Why did you say you'd arrest me if I didn't come in? I've cooperated with you, and I've done nothing wrong." Remy opened his mouth again, no doubt to continue his verbal fire, but Eli stopped him cold.

"Marta's coffin is empty," Eli said, turning in the hall so he could study every bit of Remy's reaction. By telling him this way, Ashlyn would be able to do the same. "There's no body."

Remy pulled back his shoulders, his gaze firing to Ashlyn as if he expected her to confirm or deny that. She didn't say a word. Neither did Eli. They both just stood there, waiting.

"No body," Remy repeated. Groaning, he spun around, pressing his head to the wall. Eli was skeptical enough to believe the man had done that to hide his expression rather than his attempt to deal with the shock.

"What's this about?" the lawyer asked. "What's going on?"

But Remy waved him off. With his breath coming out in short bursts, Remy finally turned back around to face him. "How'd you find this out?"

"Marta's father had the body exhumed," Eli answered,

still watching Remy. There wasn't so much shock or surprise now, but something else. Urgency, maybe?

"Where's Marta?" Remy demanded. "Did Gus say?"

The tone seemed right for a man who'd just been given a big shock like this, but Eli wasn't ready to buy it just yet. "Gus doesn't know. Do you? Do you know where she is?"

"Of course not." The anger flared through Remy's eyes again. "I had no idea. I went to her funeral. I watched them put her coffin in the ground."

Eli didn't point out that a burial could be faked as well as a death. Instead, he went with another facet of this. "Did you steal Marta's hospital and funeral home records?" he came out and asked.

"No," Remy howled while the lawyer barked out a protest about Eli badgering his client. The noise must have alerted Kellan because he stepped into the hall with them.

"A problem?" Kellan calmly said.

"Yes!" Remy snapped. "Your brother just accused me of murder."

Eli lifted his shoulder. "I hadn't gotten around to doing that, not specifically, but the question would have come up soon enough. A missing body and files. A dead mortician. And you with a recent inheritance. That could all equal a whole lot of felonies."

That set the lawyer off howling again, and Kellan merely tipped his head to the interview room. "Why don't I start this interrogation with Remy? There's something on my desk that I think you need to see."

Part of Eli wanted to stay put and yank the information from Remy, but judging from Kellan's expression, whatever was on his desk was important.

Eli put his hand on Ashlyn's back to get her moving out of the hall. They didn't get far, though. That's because Oscar came in.

"I don't appreciate being ordered in here like this," Oscar grumbled.

"Welcome to the club." Eli tipped his head to Remy. "Others feel the same as you."

Oscar looked at Remy just as Remy turned in his direction. Their gazes practically collided. "I know you," Remy spat out.

Oscar's eyes narrowed. "So? A lot of people know me."

"You were friends with Drake." Remy's eyes had narrowed, too. "You're the one who helped Leon set up the attack in that alley."

Eli hadn't counted on being the one who was surprised today, but that did it. "How'd you know Oscar and Drake were friends?" Eli asked Remy.

Remy's shoulders snapped back again, just as they'd done when Eli had told him about Marta's empty coffin. But this time it wasn't shock, pretend or otherwise. Eli was pretty sure this was raw anger.

"How did you know Oscar and Drake were friends?" Eli repeated when Remy didn't answer.

"I need to talk with my client," the lawyer insisted, taking Remy by the arm. Remy didn't put up a protest when the attorney led him into the interview room.

Since this delay might give Remy plenty of time to doctor his answer, Eli turned to Oscar. "You know Remy?"

Oscar didn't dodge the question. "I know of him. He was Marta's hotheaded boyfriend. I'm guessing he's got some kind of grudge against me. Like you," he added to Eli.

"No grudge," Eli assured him. "Just looking for the truth."

Kellan took things from there. "Come this way to interview room two, and we can get started. No lawyer?"

"He's on the way," Oscar said, but his attention wasn't on them. It was on the room where Remy's attorney had taken him.

Later, Eli would want to know if Oscar was the one who was holding grudges and if the man knew anything about Marta's whereabouts. For now, though, Eli sent off a text to one of his Ranger friends to request a favor, and then he went with Ashlyn to Kellan's office. It didn't take him long to see the report that his brother had left for him on the center of his desk.

"It's the detailed financials on Dominick that the Rangers ran," Eli relayed to her as he scanned through it. It didn't take him long to see what had caught Kellan's eye.

A second bank account that had been hidden under several layers of security.

Ashlyn made a strangled sound of surprise because she'd seen it, too. And the info just below that.

Dominick obviously had some explaining to do.

Chapter Eleven

Twenty-five thousand dollars.

That was a lot of money, and Ashlyn immediately thought of how Dominick could have used it—to hire those three gunmen.

"Yeah," Eli grumbled, letting her know they were having the same train of thought. "He's got means, motive and opportunity."

Dominick did, but it sickened her to even consider that he'd want her dead so he would stand a better chance of getting custody of Cora. And that sent a new wave of alarm through her.

"Olive Landry. Cora's biological mother," she managed to say. "She could be in danger."

Eli nodded so quickly that it meant he'd already considered it. "I alerted Austin PD to the possibility of that. They've been checking on her. I'll have them talk to her to see if she wants police protection."

Ashlyn didn't exactly breathe easier about that, but she was glad Eli was already on top of it. Maybe it would be enough. While she was hoping, she added that maybe Oscar and Remy would give them some information that would help put an end to the danger.

"Dominick should be here soon," Eli reminded her. "But I'd like to hear what Remy's saying to Kellan."

Ashlyn did as well, and she followed Eli to observation, which was located between the two interview rooms. Oscar sat alone in one of them, but Kellan appeared to already be deep into questioning Remy. Remy looked just as flustered and upset as he had been earlier when he'd confronted Oscar.

"You believe Remy didn't know about Marta's empty grave?" Ashlyn came out and asked.

"I'm not sure. He's lying about something. What, exactly, I don't know. But if Marta's truly alive, I can't see Remy not knowing about it."

She agreed, so maybe what Remy was lying about was his part in the attacks. After all, he had money, too, and while there had been a cash withdrawal from his account, it wasn't as large as the one Dominick had made. However, it didn't mean Remy hadn't gotten his hands on the cash to do the job.

"If Oscar knew the gunmen, Remy could have, too," Eli pointed out. Then he paused. "But without the money trail, we don't have probable cause to hold Remy. Besides, letting him go might give us more answers."

Ashlyn looked at him and thought about that for a moment. "You're going to put a tail on him?"

Eli nodded. "If he knows anything about Marta, we'll soon find out."

Good. Even if Remy wasn't up to something illegal, they might be able to exclude him as a suspect. And if he was guilty, then Eli could arrest him. However, this could go well beyond that.

If Marta was alive, Remy might lead them to her.

Just considering that possibility sent Ashlyn's heart into a tailspin. All this time she'd grieved for her friend. No, more than that. She'd felt guilty for not being able to save Marta. Ashlyn would be relieved if Marta was actually alive, but it was going to cause an avalanche of emotions that her friend had let her believe that she was dead. And more. Maybe Marta had been the one to hire the gunmen.

Ashlyn continued to watch as Kellan pressed Remy on the subject of those hired guns. And as expected, Remy denied everything. No way would he just confess to hiring hit men when there was no solid evidence against him. Kellan pressed on Marta, too, but again nothing. After that, Kellan was forced to let him go.

Remy stormed out, and as he went past the observation room, he shot Eli and her a glare. Kellan came out as well. No glare from him. Just the same signs of frustration that Ashlyn was sure were on her face.

"I need some coffee," Kellan said to Eli. "If you've got anything to ask Oscar, you'd better do it now before I start the official interview."

Ashlyn knew that was the advantage of having a brother who was a sheriff. If Kellan had gone by the book on this, Eli and she wouldn't have been a part of this.

Eli thanked Kellan and didn't waste any time going into the interview room with Oscar. Ashlyn stayed right by Eli's side in the doorway.

"You're here to have another go at me," Oscar immediately snarled.

"Jay Hamby," Eli said, not responding to the man's comment.

As Ashlyn had done with Remy, she watched Oscar

to see how he reacted to that name. But Oscar merely shrugged. "I know him. He's a bouncer at a bar just up the street from my shop."

Eli didn't say anything else. He just stared at Oscar and waited for the man to continue.

Oscar finally cursed, and his mouth twisted as if he'd gotten a bad taste of something. "Let me guess—he's the guy you shot and killed at Ashlyn's place."

"How'd you know about that?" Eli fired back.

"Word gets around." Oscar cursed again, shook his head. "And now I get why I'm here. You think because I know...*knew* Jay Hamby that I hired him to take shots at you. I didn't."

"Any reason I should believe you?" Eli asked.

Oscar's eyes narrowed to slits. "Yeah. Because it's the truth." He looked away from Eli and repeated some of that profanity he'd been spewing. "Someone's trying to set me up. That's the only explanation as to why all three hired guns could be connected back to me."

"Not the only explanation," Eli assured him. "You could be guilty. Are you?"

Oscar's gaze came back to Eli. "No. And I'm not saying another word until my lawyer gets here."

Eli made a suit-yourself sound and walked away, leading Ashlyn back in the direction of Kellan's office. Kellan was on the phone, and he held up his finger for them to wait a second while he finished. Ashlyn tuned in to the conversation when she heard Kellan say, "Ashlyn's horses."

She certainly hadn't forgotten about her horses or her small ranch, but it was a reminder that one of the animals could have been hurt. After Eli had shot the gunman, he'd gotten her out of there so fast that she hadn't had time to check for herself.

"Everything's okay," Kellan assured her as soon as he finished the call. "The CSIs are out at your place again, and I sent two of my ranch hands out to tend your livestock and get your things."

"Thank you." She hadn't realized just how thin her breath had gotten until she tried to speak. "I'd already packed a suitcase, but I left it on the floor in the kitchen."

He nodded and sent a text. No doubt to let his hands know where it was. "I've also arranged for Cora's crib to be taken to Jack's." Kellan scrubbed his hand over his face. "I considered moving all of you back to Eli's since it's bigger, but I think it's safer if she stays put."

Ashlyn felt the same way, but there was something in Kellan's weary eyes that made her realize there was more.

"The CSIs found Hamby's car," Kellan added several moments later. "It was parked on a side road just up from Ashlyn's. There are signs that two people were in the vehicle. Two fast-food bags and drinks. Hamby also had a burner cell phone in it, and he got a call right after he was shot. It came from another burner."

Ashlyn followed the thread of that. "There's a fourth gunman?"

"Probably," Kellan admitted. "Either that or the person who hired him could have been in the vehicle. If so, that rules out Remy, because he has an alibi. He said he was at a doctor's appointment, and I just confirmed that."

"Any prints or trace in Hamby's car?" Eli asked.

"Plenty. Along with the receipt for the fast food. It'll take them a while to sort through all of it, but we might get lucky."

Maybe, but she wondered if whoever had hired Hamby would be careless enough to leave evidence behind.

Kellan tipped his head to the man in the suit who came in the front door. "Oscar's lawyer. I'll get started with the interview, and when I'm done, I'll press the CSIs to get us anything they can from that car." He started out but then stopped, his gaze connecting with Eli's. "Dominick should be in soon. You want to interview him?"

"Absolutely. I want to ask him about his secret bank account and that big withdrawal."

Ashlyn knew it would take more luck to pin Dominick down on that. Especially if he had indeed hired those gunmen.

As soon as Kellan walked out, Eli took hold of her hand and moved her out of the doorway. Out of view from the windows, too. She hadn't needed a reminder of the danger, but that gave her one anyway.

"There are too many puzzle pieces," she said. "In the meantime, you and I—maybe Cora, too—are in the crosshairs of a killer."

He didn't argue with her. Couldn't. Because it was true, a frustration that they both felt. That frustration was in every muscle of his body when he pulled her into his arms. As he'd done in the kitchen, he brushed a kiss on the top of her head. A kiss of comfort.

And it worked.

Ashlyn could practically feel some of the tension

slide right out of her. Of course, the heat came in its place. No surprise there. She'd been dealing with it for much too long.

He pulled back just a little and looked down at her with those smoky gray eyes. They weren't stormy now but had some of the same fire that she was certain was in her own.

"Yeah," he said as if he'd known exactly what she was thinking—and feeling. "If we were still in high school, I would just coax you into taking a trip out to my truck. That won't work this time, though."

"No." Since he could be dangerous. And also since sex should be the last thing on their minds. But Ashlyn wanted to make this moment a little lighter than spelling out those reminders. "Because we're sensible adults now."

The corner of his mouth lifted, causing a dimple to flash in his cheek. Yes, a dimple. It was another weapon in the arsenal of Eli Slater, hot cowboy. But the smile didn't last long.

"Soon, we're going to have a brief talk about this," Eli drawled, his voice all smoke and heat. "And then we'll deal with it. I've got some ideas as to how we can do that."

Now she smiled, and even though she figured it was a mistake, Ashlyn brushed her mouth over his. Again, not a full-fledged kiss, but it could have qualified as foreplay. *Short* foreplay. They moved away from each other when they heard a familiar voice in the squad room.

Dominick.

Ashlyn whirled around, and the first thing she noticed was that Dominick had seen her in Eli's arms. She silently groaned. She didn't especially want to keep her feelings for Eli secret, but she figured it wasn't going to please Dominick. Of course, nothing would likely please him at this point.

"I see you've found a way to keep yourself busy," Dominick snapped. "And where's Cora while you're here with Slater?"

"Cora's safe," Ashlyn settled for saying.

With his lawyer right on his heels, Dominick came closer. "I want to see her, to make sure you're not lying to me."

"Uh, you're here for an official interrogation," Eli interrupted. "Not to visit a baby. So you can just cut the demands. The only rights you have are to remain silent and have your attorney present. That's it."

Dominick's icy gaze cut to Eli. "I'm here because Ashlyn has talked you into harassing me. What the hell do you want this time?"

Eli stepped out and used his fingers to motion for Dominick to follow him, but Eli made sure that he was between Dominick and her. On the way to the interview, he recited Dominick his rights. That only added more steel and ice to Dominick's expression.

"You'll have to wait in the observation room," Eli whispered to her. "I need to keep this official."

She nodded, though she would have preferred to confront Dominick face-to-face. Still, she'd be able to see him and gauge his reaction. It was obvious he was more upset now than he had been during his other visit.

So was she, Ashlyn realized.

Dominick's demand to see Cora had cut her to the

bone. And also riled her. If he truly was so interested in the baby's safety, then why would he insist on seeing her at a time like this? She'd already known Dominick was pigheaded and used to getting his way, but he had also claimed to love Cora. If that was true, he sure wasn't putting his granddaughter first.

Ashlyn flipped the switch to get the audio, and she listened while Eli worked his way through some preliminary questions. Dominick didn't hesitate when questioned about his alibi during the time of the latest attack. He said he was in a meeting with four other people. She didn't doubt it, either. If he was behind this, then he would have made sure of a strong alibi.

"Tell me about your secret bank account," Eli threw out there the moment Dominick had answered the previous question.

Dominick visibly stiffened, opened his mouth. Probably to claim there was no such account. But then he stopped and had a short whispered conversation with his lawyer.

"It's not a secret," Dominick said when he faced Eli again. "It's an account I'd set up so I'd have funds to buy my wife gifts and such. That way, whatever I bought her would be a surprise. After she died, I didn't close it. Sentimental reasons," he added with a smirk.

"Sentimental reasons," Eli repeated. No smirk, but he sounded plenty skeptical. "The account had a lot of layers of security on it for something that's supposed to be legal and aboveboard."

Dominick calmly lifted his shoulder. "My late wife was very good at snooping."

"Yeah." Eli's skepticism went up a notch, but Ashlyn knew that with the woman dead it wasn't something they could prove. "Do you use the account for things other than surprise gifts?"

Now a faint smile crossed Dominick's lips. "Yes. Recently, I withdrew funds to do some remodeling at my house."

"Really?" Eli challenged. "You used cash for that?"

"Yes. I thought it'd make things easier for the contractor. And before you ask, there was nothing illegal about it."

"You've got receipts?" Eli pressed.

"I can get them." Dominick no longer smiled or looked smug. The anger was creeping back into his expression and tone.

While Eli continued to press him on that, Ashlyn took out her phone and called Sue Malloy, the nanny Dominick had hired for his visits with Cora. Even though Ashlyn had never left Cora with the woman, Sue had given Ashlyn her number.

"Ashlyn," Sue said the moment she answered. "I was surprised when I saw your name on my phone screen. I heard about the attack. Are Cora and you okay?"

"Yes. We're fine. But that's not why I'm calling." She paused, tried to figure out how to say this. She didn't want to put the woman on defensive. "Have you recently been at Dominick's house?"

"I have," she readily admitted. "He converted one of the bedrooms to a nursery. You know, in case he got the overnight visits approved for Cora. He wanted her to have her own room, and he asked me to make sure it had everything she might need."

Considering that Dominick was a suspect in attempted murders, that tightened Ashlyn's stomach, but she reminded herself that he could be innocent. He hadn't lied about the bank account, and while it still didn't seem aboveboard, he had told the truth about the renovation.

"Is there a problem?" Sue asked.

"No. I was just checking. Thanks." And she ended the call before Sue could press her for more info.

This time when Ashlyn looked at Dominick through the glass, she did so with less anger and nerves. Maybe he was innocent about everything other than wanting more time with his granddaughter. If so, she'd owe him an apology, but she wasn't about to do that until the person who'd hired those gunmen had been caught.

She heard the footsteps in the hall and automatically tensed again. But it wasn't a threat that her body was preparing for. It was Gunnar. He glanced through both observation windows. Kellan was still in interview with Oscar. Eli with Dominick.

"Any idea how close they are to wrapping things up?" Gunnar asked.

"It shouldn't be long on Dominick. I'm not sure about Oscar." She hadn't been listening to that interrogation.

"Good. Because Eli's going to want to hear this." Gunnar went to the interview room door and knocked. "The tail we had on Remy just called, and he says something suspicious is going on and that Eli should get out there right away."

Chapter Twelve

Eli took one look at Ashlyn and Gunnar, and he knew something was wrong. Something that was going to delay finishing his interview with Dominick. He stepped out into the hall with them, shutting the door in case this was news about that hidden bank account.

"The reserve deputy, Manuel Garcia, we had on Remy followed him to a small farmhouse about ten miles from here," Gunnar explained. He glanced down and read from a note he was holding. "The place belonged to Remy's grandmother. It's in his name now, but it's been empty for a couple of years since the grandmother got moved into a nursing home."

Eli took a moment to process that but figured there had to be more or Gunnar wouldn't have pulled him out of the interview. "What happened?"

"Garcia parked on a trail so he could keep watch, and he saw Remy go to the backyard. He says that Remy then dropped down and started crying in front of what Garcia thinks is maybe a headstone. You know, a grave."

Beside him, Ashlyn made a sharp sound of surprise. "Are any of his relatives buried there?" she asked.

Gunnar shook his head. "There's no burial record for anyone at that location, and Garcia figured the way that Remy was carrying on that it probably wasn't a pet." Gunnar paused. "I thought you'd want us to go there and check things out."

"I do." Eli had to give the logistics of that some thought. "Get the cruiser ready, and I'll let Kellan know what's going on."

Eli was about to tell Ashlyn that she'd be staying there at the sheriff's office, but then he considered that she would be there with two of their prime suspects. Of course, Kellan would protect her, but his brother already had his hands full with the interviews.

"You want to come with Gunnar and me?" Eli asked her.

She gave each of the interview doors a glimpse and then nodded.

Eli hoped like the devil that it wasn't another mistake, but this could be a "damned if he did, damned if he didn't" situation. Rather than stand there and lose time, he went in and had a quick chat with Kellan. Once he got the green light from his brother to leave, Eli headed toward the front.

Gunnar and Ashlyn were already there, waiting for him, and they rushed out and into the cruiser. Gunnar took off as they all kept watch around them. However, keeping watch wouldn't be easy with this trip because it was already starting to get dark.

Great.

Just what he didn't want—more obstacles to keeping Ashlyn safe.

"A grave," Ashlyn said. She still sounded shocked about that. "Maybe it's some kind of memorial for Marta?"

Yeah, that had been his first thought, shortly followed by the possibility that it could be a ploy to throw them off the scent that Marta might be alive. If Remy showed them a memorial like that, he might believe it would convince them to stop looking for the woman.

It wouldn't.

But maybe Remy was desperate.

Eli heard Gunnar's phone ding with a text, and the deputy passed it back to Eli so he could read it. What he saw on the screen had Eli cursing.

"Garcia says that Remy's walking away from the headstone," Eli relayed to Gunnar and Ashlyn before he handed it back to Gunnar. "It looks as if Remy is about to leave."

Eli wanted Remy on scene, and there was little chance they would make it there in time before he left, so Eli took out his own phone. He didn't have Remy's number in his cell so he went through dispatch to have them call the man. Eli wasn't sure Remy would even answer, but he did on the fourth ring.

"Who the hell is this?" Remy snapped.

"Eli Slater. Just checking to see how you are." Eli didn't bother to sound sincere since Remy wouldn't have believed him anyway.

"How the hell do you think I am?" Remy countered, and Eli had no trouble hearing the man's sob.

"Did something happen?" Eli pressed. "Are you okay?"

Remy didn't jump to answer that time, and then he cursed much as Eli had done just seconds earlier. "I see a car. You had someone follow me." It wasn't a question. "You SOB. You put a tail on me."

"Yeah, I did," Eli readily admitted. "Now, you want to explain to me who's buried in that grave you were just crying over?"

That only brought on more cursing, and Eli waited him out while he mouthed for Ashlyn to use Gunnar's phone to keep track of Remy through Garcia. If Remy tried to leave, he wanted Garcia to stop him.

"You had no right to follow me," Remy finally said.

"I beg to differ. The badge gives me that right. Now tell me who's in the grave, or I'll get a bulldozer out there tonight, and I'll have it dug up."

"You can't!" Remy shouted. He repeated that a couple more times and broke down into another sob.

Ashlyn nudged Eli to show him Garcia's text message. Remy's pacing in the backyard. He's not heading back toward his car.

Good. He wanted Garcia to have backup before he tried to restrain Remy. The man could be armed. Heck, and he could be dangerous.

"I won't let you dig it up," Remy insisted.

"Then tell me who's buried there." Of course, Eli would have it dug up anyway, no matter what Remy told him.

Remy sobbed several more seconds, which Eli considered a good thing. Each second brought them closer to the place.

"She's here," Remy finally said on a choked breath. "Marta's here."

Eli felt the stillness slide through him. "Marta's buried in that grave?"

Again, Remy paused, cried. "Yes. She's here. I couldn't have her buried so far away. I needed to be able to come and talk to her. I needed her to be close to me."

The stillness didn't last inside Eli. A new wave of grief came, and it was just as raw and fresh as it had been the night Marta had been gunned down. For a few hours, he'd allowed some part of himself to believe that she might be alive. But she wasn't.

"How'd you get Marta's body?" Eli pressed.

"The mortician," Remy answered after a long pause. "I bribed him, but I didn't kill him. I swear, I didn't."

Eli wasn't going to take the man's word for that. "And what about Marta's hospital records?"

"I didn't take those. There would have been no use in me doing that because she was dead. I only wanted her body so she could be close to me."

Eli tried to think of a reason why Remy wouldn't admit to stealing records when he'd just confessed to much worse, but he couldn't come up with anything. Well, unless Remy was just so upset that he had no idea what he was saying.

Ashlyn nudged Eli's arm again and showed him Garcia's latest text. Remy's walking toward a small barn that's off the backyard. You think he's in danger from himself?

Eli had to shrug. He had no idea what was going on in Remy's mind right now. "Tell Garcia to keep watching," he mouthed. "When I get there, we'll go inside the barn and arrest Remy."

And that would be just the start.

He'd need to do a tough interrogation with Remy and put in a call to Gus to let him know what was going on.

Oh, and arrange for the body to be exhumed. Judging from Remy's extreme reaction and his confession, Eli figured this time they would indeed find Marta.

"Remy?" Eli asked.

No answer. And a moment later, Remy ended the call.

"We're almost there," Gunnar whispered as he took a turn off the main road. "We're only a couple of minutes out."

Good, because if Remy truly was suicidal, they needed to stop him. Maybe they would get there in time.

Gunnar's phone rang. Not a text this time, but a call from Garcia. Eli took the cell from Ashlyn and put the call on speaker.

"We've got a problem," Garcia immediately said. "Some guy just came out from the trees that aren't too far from the barn. He's got a gun."

Hell.

Eli had no trouble hearing what Garcia had said, and he felt the immediate slash of fresh adrenaline. Not again. Not another attack.

"Gunnar, turn off your headlights," Eli instructed. "When you reach Garcia's car, pull in behind him."

Eli looked ahead and spotted the unmarked sedan, and Gunnar came to a stop behind it. He saw the deputy crouched behind his door, and he had night goggles pressed to his eyes. The house and barn were in the distance, not far at all, but there were no signs of Remy or a gunman.

"I'm sorry," Eli said to Ashlyn, causing her to look at him. "We have to stay. We have to give Garcia backup."

"Of course you do." She kept her shoulders straight,

trying to show him that she was a lot stronger than she likely felt. "I know the drill. I'll stay in the cruiser and will keep down."

It wasn't enough. Nowhere near it. But maybe this "damned if you do, damned if you don't" situation would end without Ashlyn getting hurt.

"Stay here with Ashlyn and call for backup," Eli told Gunnar, and Eli brushed a quick kiss on her mouth before he reached for the door.

"Be careful." Her voice was shaky now, and even in the dim light he saw the fear in her eyes.

"I will be," he promised her as he hurried out.

He eased the door shut so that it wouldn't make any noise, and he heard the clicks of Gunnar locking it. Eli trusted the deputy and knew he'd do whatever it took to keep Ashlyn safe, but Eli hated that he couldn't be in two places at once.

"The guy with the gun is on the left side of the barn," Garcia told him when Eli reached him, and he passed his goggles to Eli.

Eli didn't have any trouble spotting the man. Tall, lanky, dressed all in black. And he did indeed have a gun.

"Remy's still in the barn," Garcia added.

He hoped Remy wasn't doing something dangerous in there, but for now Eli had to go with the immediate threat—the gunman. The guy wasn't moving, but that didn't mean he soon wouldn't be. But who was his target?

Remy?

Or had the gunman known that Remy would lead them here?

"I'm going to cut around on foot and try to come up behind the thug," Eli instructed Garcia. "You move closer to the barn—also on foot—but try to keep an eye on the cruiser. I don't want them getting ambushed."

Garcia made a sound of agreement, and keeping low, the deputy started moving—fast. Eli did the same, after he put his phone on vibrate, and he tried to push aside any thoughts of all the things that could go wrong. So far, all the breaks had gone against them, and something had to go their way.

Despite it being past sunset, it was still hot, and it didn't take long for the sweat to start trickling down Eli's back. He swiped his forehead with the back of his hand and kept going. Kept listening. And watching. There was still no sign of Remy, but once Eli reached the house, he got a better look at the gunman. His attention was fastened to the barn.

And that's where he had his weapon aimed.

So, he was after Remy. Well, maybe. Since the guy hadn't fired a shot, it could be that this was a setup to make them believe that Remy was a target.

As Eli got closer, he tamped down the thud of his heart so that it wouldn't interfere with his hearing, and took extra care to make sure his footsteps stayed light. He definitely didn't want to do anything to alert this clown.

He threaded his way through the trees, cursing when the underbrush crunched beneath his boots. The gunman immediately whipped in the direction of the sound—just as Eli managed to duck out of sight.

Eli stayed still, but thankfully he didn't hear the gunman coming his way. When he peeked out, he saw that the guy's focus was back on the barn.

Blowing out a quick breath of relief, Eli started moving again, and he made sure he maneuvered himself behind the man. That's when he realized the guy didn't have his weapon actually pointed at the barn. He was just watching.

Why?

Had someone sent him here to keep an eye on Remy, or was this going to be another attempted murder? Eli hoped he got the chance to find out.

He stopped just long enough to glance across the yard to see if he could spot Garcia. No sign of him, which was a good thing. It meant the deputy was managing to stay hidden enough while he made his way to the barn.

Soon, very soon, backup would be arriving, and they would make a silent approach. Maybe it wouldn't catch the attention of the gunman, because Eli didn't want the guy even looking in Ashlyn's direction. He wanted her safe, and the best way to do that was to stop this potential threat.

Eli crept closer, thankful for a gust of wind that muffled his move. Thankful, too, when the gunman's next glance was in the wrong direction. Eli was on his blind side, and he took full advantage of that.

"I'm Sergeant Eli Slater, Texas Ranger. Drop that gun or you're a dead man," Eli warned him.

The gunman spun around, getting ready to take aim, but Eli already had him beat. His weapon was ready to blast the snake to smithereens. Plus, Eli was still partly behind cover of one of the trees.

The man froze. Cursed. And Eli saw the exact moment the guy realized he was outgunned and outsmarted. Still cursing, he dropped the gun and without prompting, he lifted his hands in the air.

"Get facedown on the ground," Eli instructed. "Hands tucked behind your head—though I'm pretty sure you know how this all works. I'm guessing this isn't your first rodeo."

Eli kicked the guy's weapon away so that he wouldn't be able to reach it, took out a pair of plastic cuffs from his back pocket, and he restrained him while he read him his rights.

"I'm remaining silent," the man snarled.

Eli would do everything possible to change his mind during interrogation. For now, he texted Gunnar to let him know he had the gunman. Something that Gunnar had likely figured out since he had no doubt been watching. Gunnar would send the backup to help haul the man back to the sheriff's office.

Any word from Garcia? Eli added in his text.

Eli didn't have to wait long for a response. His phone vibrated with an incoming call, and he saw Garcia's name on the screen. Maybe this meant Garcia had Remy in custody.

Or not…

When Eli answered the call, he heard Garcia's single word of raw profanity, followed by, "Remy's not here. He got away."

Chapter Thirteen

From the doorway of Kellan's office, Ashlyn just stood back and watched the chaos in the squad room. Gunnar was booking the gunman while Eli was on the phone, barking out orders to the team of Rangers and deputies that he had out looking for Remy.

So far, there'd been so sign of the man.

Since no one had heard the sounds of a vehicle after Remy disappeared into the barn, it meant he'd fled on foot. Ashlyn doubted he'd done that solely because he was so upset over being at Marta's grave. No. Remy had run because there would be charges brought against him.

Maybe murder charges.

After all, someone had murdered the mortician, and right now Remy had the strongest motive for that. With the mortician dead and those files missing, there'd be no proof that Remy had indeed stolen Marta's body. Well, no proof other than the body itself. But what if it wasn't there?

She immediately shook her head, rethinking that. Remy had been very upset as he stood by that headstone. She'd practically been able to feel his grief, and Ashlyn didn't think he'd be able to fake that.

Ashlyn continued to watch as Gunnar stood with the still-cuffed gunman, and Gunnar motioned for Garcia to follow him. The two deputies led the man not toward lockup but in the direction of the interview room. Maybe that meant the guy was willing to talk. A few minutes later, Gunnar returned with Kellan. Eli quickly ended his call and joined them in Kellan's office.

"The guy's name is Al Waite," Gunnar said. "And you were right about him having a record," he added to Eli. "B&E, assault, drug possession. He's only thirty-one, and he's already spent nearly seven years behind bars."

"Did he say who hired him?" Eli immediately asked.

"No, but you'll be able to press him on that. I put him in interview room one since Dominick and his lawyer are still in the other."

Shortly after she'd arrived back at the sheriff's office, Ashlyn had heard that Kellan was still in interview, but she hadn't known if he was with Oscar or Dominick. She hoped that Dominick would just leave quietly because she wasn't up to another confrontation—with anyone. She just wanted to get all of this resolved so she could get back to the ranch with the baby.

"Waite had a tranquilizer gun on him," Gunnar went on, snagging Ashlyn's attention again.

Eli's head jerked back, and Ashlyn knew the reason for his surprise. Maybe he hadn't gone there to kill Remy after all.

"You think Waite was waiting for Remy to come out of the barn so he could kidnap him?" Ashlyn asked.

"It's looking that way. In addition to the tranquilizer gun, he had some tape and restraints on him."

"But he didn't go closer to the barn when Remy went inside it," Eli said as if thinking out loud. "Unless he didn't see Remy go in."

True. Garcia didn't spot Waite until after he'd told them about Remy leaving the backyard and going to the barn.

"Waite could have been waiting for Remy to come back out, too," Kellan suggested.

That was a possibility as well, but she figured they had all considered something else, and it was Eli who voiced it.

"Remy could have used Waite to distract us so he could get away. And so it would make him look like a potential victim rather than the person who hired Waite."

Both Gunnar and Kellan made sounds of agreement.

"When I moved up behind Waite to take him," Eli went on, "his attention was on the barn. I believe he knew Remy was in there."

And that meant Remy had maybe played them all. Including Waite. The gunman might not have known that the evening would end with his arrest.

"What can you charge Waite with?" she asked.

Gunnar scrubbed his hand over his face. "Parole violation for carrying a weapon. That would send him back to jail to finish out his five-year sentence."

So, not too much time. If Remy had paid him well, that might be enough to set up this ruse. But why?

"If Remy wanted to escape, why didn't he just try to drive off?" she pressed.

"That's what I'll ask Remy when we find him," Eli assured her. He checked his watch. "Let me question Waite, and then I can drive you back to the ranch. Is Cora okay?"

"She's fine. Gloria said she's already tucked in for the night."

Eli nodded. "I'll try to hurry so you can get back to see her."

She wanted to jump at that offer, but more than that, she wanted answers. "Take your time. I want to know who hired him." She looked at Kellan. "I'm guessing Oscar or Dominick didn't make any confessions?"

"Nothing," Kellan answered on a weary sigh. "But then they both know there's only circumstantial evidence against them. Neither of them is running scared like Remy."

Yes, but that didn't mean one of them wasn't guilty.

Eli started out, heading for the interview room, but his phone rang after he'd only made it a few steps. He hesitated for just a couple of seconds when he looked at the screen, and Ashlyn didn't think it was her imagination that he was steeling himself.

"It's the CSIs," Eli relayed to them. He took the call, but this time he didn't put it on speaker.

The moments crawled by, and while she could hear the chatter on the other end of the line, Ashlyn couldn't make out what the caller was saying. Gunnar and Kellan stayed put, too, obviously waiting to hear.

"You're sure?" Eli asked the caller, and he gave a resigned nod before he ended the call. "The Rangers sent in imaging equipment. Ground-penetrating radar."

He paused, his gaze locking with Ashlyn's. "There's a body buried beneath the headstone at Remy's place."

A body.

Marta.

Ashlyn hadn't expected the news to hit her as hard as it did. After all, Remy had told them he'd had her buried there. Still, she'd held on to a thin thread of hope that he'd lied, that Marta was out there somewhere and alive.

"They'll exhume the body," Eli went on, "so that we'll have confirmation."

Yes, that was a legal necessity, but all four of them knew the truth. They hadn't been mistaken about Marta being gunned down in that alley.

"I can take the interview with Waite," Kellan offered.

But Eli shook his head. "You're about to drop on your feet. Get some rest, and I'll have a go at him."

Kellan didn't refuse. "I'll catch a nap in the break room." He looked at Gunnar. "Come and get me if anything breaks."

Gunnar assured him that he would, and Kellan walked out. Eli stayed put, and he caught on to her hand. "Are you okay?"

"I was about to ask you the same thing," she admitted.

He gave a dry smile that didn't make it to his eyes, and he pulled her into his arms. "Having hope can make you end up feeling like you took a punch to the gut, huh?"

Yes, it could.

"I replay that night all the time," he went on, not waiting for her to answer. "I go over all the things I should have done. If I'd just seen how things were going to play out, I could have stopped it. Marta would be alive, and you wouldn't have been shot. In my mind, I undo the mistakes and make it all right."

Ashlyn tightened her grip on him, eased him closer. "I do the same thing. Not just with what went on that night but how I dealt with the aftermath." She looked up at him. "I was wrong to blame you, but you were alive and an easy target."

Eli shrugged, but she knew there was nothing casual or dismissive about it. Her blame had hurt him. Maybe even crushed him. She could see that now, and while it wouldn't go back and undo those scars, she hoped the kiss she brushed on his mouth would help with the healing.

"I'm in love with you, Eli," she said. "I have been for years." Then she winced at his stunned expression. "Yes, I know. The timing sucks." Ashlyn huffed, kissed him again and then eased him back away from her. "Go ahead and talk to Waite. I'll be in the observation room, and when we're done, we can finish this conversation."

Because he didn't budge, she thought he might refuse, but then he cursed, caught on to her hand and headed toward the hall. They were nearly at observation when Dominick and his lawyer came out of the interview room.

Ashlyn groaned before she could stop herself. She was emotionally wrung out, and she was positive that showed on her face. It certainly showed on Dominick's. Over the past couple of months, she'd seen him angry and combative, but she'd never seen him look exhausted.

"Ashlyn." The weariness was in his voice, too. "My

lawyer and I were just going over my statement. I just signed it," he added to Eli.

Eli made a sound that could have meant anything, and he would have moved Ashlyn past them if Dominick hadn't stepped in front of her.

"It's not a good time to annoy me," Eli warned him, and every part of him was dark and dangerous.

Dominick nodded, and if he was bothered by Eli's show of temper, he didn't react. "I only wanted to tell Ashlyn that I was sorry. I can't imagine how stressful the attacks have been for her."

The apology seemed sincere, and she thought that Dominick wanted her to respond with some kind of olive branch of her own. But he didn't wait for that. Motioning for his lawyer to follow him, Dominick walked out.

Just seeing the man leave helped Ashlyn settle some of her nerves. So did the hand that Eli ran down her back. It stilled her. And surprised her. After she'd just dropped the *L*-word bombshell, she'd figured he would try to put some distance between them. At least until after this interview. He didn't. In fact, Eli dropped a quick kiss on her mouth before he left her in observation and went into interview.

"I'm Scott Sanders," the lawyer said, standing. "My client and I want a bail hearing ASAP."

"You and I both know your client won't get bail." Eli sat across from Waite. "He was carrying a gun, which is a violation of his parole. His parole officer has already been contacted."

The lawyer didn't even react to that and instead looked at his phone screen—and frowned.

"I found that gun," Waite insisted. He was a wiry man with beady eyes that darted around as if he expected someone to jump out at him. Maybe he just needed a fix, but Ashlyn couldn't see why anyone would have hired him to go after Remy or anyone else, for that matter.

"You found it," Eli repeated. He couldn't have possibly sounded more skeptical.

"Yeah. In the woods, there," Waite added. Beneath the table, Ashlyn could see his legs fidgeting as much as the rest of him." My car wouldn't start so I started walking, looking for help. That's when I found the gun."

Eli calmly leaned forward, and even though Ashlyn couldn't see his face, she'd bet he was giving Waite a hard glare. "Why didn't you just use your phone to call someone? You had a cell in your pocket."

Waite went stiff, and he looked up at the ceiling as if to find the answer there. Since he obviously didn't, he didn't say anything.

"You had a tranq gun and duct tape on you," Eli went on. "And before you give me some lame excuse to explain those things, I should probably tell you that a deputy sheriff had you under observation from the time you stepped onto the property. He saw enough that you'll be headed back to a cage."

Eli leaned back and waited.

It didn't take long.

"I want a deal," Waite said, and he shook off the grip that his lawyer put on his arm.

Eli didn't jump on that, either. He just took his time. "What kind of deal?"

"I tell you what I know, and I don't go back to jail. I can't go back there, man. You gotta give me a break."

"I don't have to give you anything," Eli assured him. "But if you tell me what you know, I'll consider it. I'll even put in a good word for you with the DA."

She hadn't thought it possible, but Waite's fidgeting got even worse. "Okay," Waite said after giving that some thought. He shook off his lawyer again. "Someone paid me to go out there. I don't know who," Waite quickly added.

"And what exactly were you supposed to do?" Eli pressed.

"Just grab the guy and drop him off at that old abandoned gas station up the road. I wasn't supposed to hurt him or nothing. It wasn't even like a serious crime or anything."

"You were supposed to kidnap a man, tranq him, tie him up and put duct tape on his mouth. Sounds plenty serious to me." Eli sat back again and waited. "I'll bet it sounds even worse to the man you were supposed to kidnap."

Waite's eyes darted around. "Well, I didn't do it, and I'd changed my mind before you even got there and arrested me. I wasn't going through with it."

"Right," Eli grumbled. "Who's the *someone* who hired you to do this? Give me a name, and I'll push to get you a deal."

"No," the lawyer blurted out. "Don't tell him anything...not until he puts it in writing. You can't trust him. He'll lie to get the information he wants."

"I'll put you back in a cage to get the information I want," Eli calmly answered. "But I just offered you a deal, and I meant it. Give me a name, and if it pans out, you won't be charged with a parole violation."

Waite kept his gaze nailed to Eli's, and when he opened his mouth, Ashlyn automatically moved closer to the glass. Her heart was pounding now. Her breath, held. Maybe they would finally know the truth.

However, before Waite could say anything, the lawyer's phone dinged with a text message. Since she could clearly see Sanders, she thought maybe there was relief, as if this was something he'd been waiting for.

Yes, definitely relief.

Ashlyn saw even more of it when he silently read whatever was on his phone screen. Sanders showed the text to Waite, his eyes darting across the message, and he swallowed hard. Every drop of color seemed to drain from his face.

"No deal," Waite said. His voice was suddenly as shaky as he was. "I'm not saying another word to you."

Chapter Fourteen

Eli had already used every curse word he knew. Multiple times. And he would have used them all over again if he'd thought it would help. It wouldn't. No matter how hard he'd pressed Waite, the man had just clammed up.

Or rather he'd been threatened if he continued to speak.

Eli knew that in his gut.

Waite had been ready to spill. Eli was absolutely certain of that. But the confession had been nixed because of whatever was in the text that Waite's lawyer had shown him. Now, even after all that cursing and the phone calls, Eli still didn't have proof of who'd sent that text.

Eli reined in any urges to belt out more profanity, and he stopped pacing when Ashlyn came into the kitchen. The moment they'd gotten back to Jack's house, she'd gone into the bedroom to check on Cora, and judging from her expression and the fact that it was a short check, everything seemed to be okay there. He figured her raised eyebrow was for him and not anything going on with the baby. Ashlyn wanted an update on the case, especially since the danger was breathing down their necks.

"Nothing," he volunteered, keeping his voice at a whisper since Gunnar was already asleep on the sofa. "It was a no-go on getting the lawyer to reveal any info about that text."

Of course, Eli hadn't expected anything different. After all, the lawyer could claim it was client-attorney privilege, but it still riled him to the core. Waite and the lawyer were on the same payroll, and Eli wanted the murdering SOB who was paying them behind bars.

"What about the tails you had on Oscar and Dominick?" Ashlyn asked. "Did they see anything?"

"Oh, yeah." And that was the second source of Eli's extreme frustration. "According to the deputy on Oscar, she saw him use his phone right about the time of the text which means he could have been the one to tell Waite to shut up. Of course, Oscar isn't willing to just hand over his phone, so I'm having to work on a court order to get that, too."

He'd get the court order, but if Oscar was truly behind this, then he'd likely used a burner, something that couldn't be traced. Something that Oscar would have already ditched.

"What about Dominick?" Ashlyn walked closer, and she slid her hands into the back pockets of her jeans. "Did he come up with the receipts for the renovations?"

"More or less. There are receipts, all right, for the nursery redo, but we'll have to check and make sure they're legit. I still think that's way too much cash for a single room."

Proving that, though, wouldn't be easy, and like the

text, it could be impossible to get to the truth. Someone like Dominick could have easily paid a contractor to falsify receipts.

Since Eli didn't want to dump that bad news on Ashlyn, he changed the subject. "Is Cora okay?"

She nodded. "Whoever brought in the crib put it in the spare room where Gloria's asleep."

"Good. It's best if Cora's not alone in the bedroom."

The moment Eli said the words, he wanted to wince. On the surface, it was an innocent thing to say, but Ashlyn and he weren't anywhere near the "surface." There was the blasted attraction. And more. It was what she'd said to him earlier.

I'm in love with you, Eli.

That was definitely deep stuff, and Eli knew he couldn't continue to step around it. However, before he even had the chance to bring it up, his phone buzzed to indicate he had a call. He scowled when he saw the name on the screen and immediately showed it to Ashlyn.

Remy.

Since Eli definitely wanted to talk to him, he motioned for Ashlyn to follow him to the bedroom he'd been using. That way, the conversation wouldn't wake up Gloria, the baby or Gunnar. Eli shut the door and put the call on speaker.

"Hold on a second, Remy," Eli told the man, and he texted dispatch so they could try to trace the call. "Where are you?" Eli demanded once he'd done that.

Remy didn't jump to answer, though. It took him several long moments. "I'm in hiding. Someone wants to kill me. That's why I sneaked out of the barn and went on the run."

Eli huffed. "You're sure you didn't run because you're guilty of the attacks?"

"No." Remy didn't hesitate that time. "I didn't have anything to do with them, I swear."

"Don't hold your breath waiting for me to believe you about that. You stole Marta's body, then hid it, and you're on the run from the law. That's three strikes in my book, and it doesn't add up to someone I intend to trust. Now, where the hell are you?"

"I don't want to tell you because I don't trust you, either. You haven't done your job and fixed this. Someone was following me, and after everything that's happened, that person might want me dead, too. Who's doing this, Eli? Who wants to murder us?"

Eli wasn't buying into Remy's denial, but the man certainly sounded afraid. Of course, fear could be faked, and Remy had a strong motive for wanting to kill him. Maybe Remy had stretched that motive to include Ashlyn as well, but if so, Remy was also coming after the baby, since she was in the middle of this mess.

"You need to arrest whoever's trying to kill us. Until you do that, I'm protecting myself, and it starts by not telling you where I am. Find him, Eli, or I will," Remy warned him, and he ended the call.

Eli groaned, and even though he knew Remy hadn't been on the line long enough, he called dispatch anyway. "Nothing," Eli had to relay to Ashlyn once he had his answer. "They weren't able to trace it."

Frustrated, he put his phone back in his pocket and mentally replayed everything Remy had just told him.

Which wasn't much. However, if Remy did indeed try to play cop and find their attacker, then he could put himself right in the path of a killer. If Remy wasn't the killer, that is. If he was, then his call had merely been an attempt to make himself look innocent.

It hadn't worked.

He intended to keep the man on his suspect list.

Eli looked up when he felt Ashlyn touch his arm, and he immediately saw the fresh concern in her eyes. He knew that she just wanted this to be over. So did he. But Remy was right about one thing. Eli did need to arrest the snake who kept putting them in danger. So far, they'd gotten lucky by getting away from the gunfire, but their luck might not hold out much longer.

Ashlyn kept her gaze on him, and after a few seconds, Eli didn't think her expression was only one of concern. Well, it wasn't solely about the attacks anyway. That worry was there all right, but there was also something else.

That *I'm in love with you.*

"I know what you're going to say," Ashlyn blurted out before Eli could broach that subject. "You don't want me to be in love with you, and I get that. Believe me, I get it," she added in a frustrated mumble. "If I could change how I feel about you, I would."

Okay, that spelled it out for him. She wasn't any happier about this than he was. But then she shook her head. "That's not exactly true," she amended. "I probably wouldn't change things in the feelings department."

"You should," he insisted right off. "I'm bad news, Ashlyn. I can't make the past go away."

Her gaze came back to him, and she gave him a

blank stare. "There were some good things in that past. And yes, I know it's hard to see the good what with all the bad. I hung on to that bad for a very long time, blaming you for something that wasn't your fault." She stepped closer, laying her palm on his chest. "It wasn't your fault."

He wanted to believe that. Better yet, Eli wanted her to believe it, but the hurt would always be there.

And apparently so would the attraction.

Certain parts of his body took her touch as some sort of signal that more should happen to tap into that attraction. Eli was almost certain he could have resisted, almost, if Ashlyn hadn't come up on her toes and put her mouth close to his. She didn't actually kiss him.

So Eli kissed her.

Even though he knew there was a high chance of regretting this, Eli dragged her to him and finished what Ashlyn had started. And there it was. That kick of heat so strong that he wondered how the heck he'd ever resisted her in the first place.

Ashlyn melted right into the kiss. She melted right against him, too. With her hand trapped between them, she pressed her body to his, a reminder of just how well they fit together.

Eli deepened the kiss, letting it fan the fire even more until the kiss and the body contact weren't enough. He needed more, and judging from the way Ashlyn was struggling to touch more of him, she felt the same way.

Her free hand slid down his back, urging him closer and closer, and the sound that she made in her throat was one of pure desire. Eli hadn't needed anything else to rev him up, but that did it.

He shoved up her top, lowered his head and kissed the tops of her breasts. All in all, that was a good way to take things to next level, but soon it wasn't enough, either, and Eli found himself backing Ashlyn across the room. First, he locked the door, and then he led her in the direction of the bed—while he kissed her again.

They fell back, sinking into the feather mattress while the sides of it swelled around them. Everything around them was soft. Except for Eli. And he could feel his body going steely hard.

Ashlyn went after his neck, kissing him there, while she fought with his shirt to get the buttons undone. It wasn't easy since Eli was waging his own battle against her clothes. He finally managed to peel off her top, then he pushed down her bra so he could kiss her breasts.

She stopped with his buttons, arched her back to move her breasts even closer to his mouth, and she made another of those sounds of pleasure. Since it was something she obviously liked, Eli lingered there a few more seconds until the urgency kicked in again, and Ashlyn went after his zipper. As soon as she got it down, she slid her hand down into his boxers.

He could have sworn his eyes crossed. It certainly robbed him of what little breath he had. Eli ground his teeth and let her touch spear the pleasure through him.

Man, he wanted Ashlyn, and he wanted her now.

Eli had to push her hand away so he could get his jeans unzipped. Ashlyn finally gave up her touching quest and helped him with that. Together, they shimmied off her jeans. Her panties, too.

"Now," she insisted.

He definitely wanted to give her "now," but Eli kissed her again and skimmed his hand from her breasts down to the inside of her thighs. That was pleasure for both of them, because Ashlyn ground herself against him, seeking the cure for the pressure cooker of heat that they'd built together.

She repeated her "now" while she groped the waist of his jeans to get them down. As much as Eli was enjoying the kissing, he knew it was time to cut the foreplay and finish this. He got off his boots and jeans and remembered to take the condom from his wallet before he tossed his clothes and boxers onto the floor.

He kept it gentle as he slipped inside her and even stilled to give Ashlyn a moment to adjust to the pressure of him filling her. But Eli quickly learned that it wasn't gentleness she wanted. Ashlyn hooked her leg around his lower back and gave him a push while she lifted her hips to meet his thrust.

Eli took things from there. It was obvious she didn't want him to treat her like someone fragile or broken, so he didn't hold back. He gave her, and himself, exactly what they needed. The movement came harder. Faster. And with each plunge inside her, it took them closer and closer to the edge.

Ashlyn went over first, the climax rippling through her and gripping on to him like a fist. After that, Eli couldn't have hung on even if he'd wanted to. His body needed release.

And *he* needed Ashlyn.

Those ripples of her body coaxed and pushed him until Eli buried his face against her neck and let himself go.

ASHLYN HADN'T REMEMBERED to keep her scars hidden away. That was a first for her, but then sex with Eli apparently could rid her of any self-consciousness, including what she had about those scars from her gunshot wounds.

Of course, he'd already seen them because she'd shown them to him. However, that'd been a quick glimpse, and it would likely be a whole lot more than that now what with her naked.

The moment that Eli moved off her and dropped on his back next to her on the bed, Ashlyn reached for the cover to drape it over her body. Eli stopped her, though, by catching on to her hand. First, he frowned, and then he kissed her.

Before he looked at those scars.

His frown deepened for a moment before he leaned down, kissed them, too, and he got up, gathering up his jeans and boxers before he headed into the adjoining bathroom. Only then did Ashlyn release the breath she'd been holding.

Thank goodness, the scars hadn't brought back the memories of that awful night, and there'd been enough heat left in his eyes to tell her that they hadn't been a turnoff, either. What could be a turnoff, though, was when he had time to think about this, because he would almost certainly see it as a mistake.

And maybe the timing exactly was.

After all, they had plenty they should be doing to get to the bottom of who was trying to kill them. But it was hard for Ashlyn to regret her finally making love to Eli. In fact, she doubted anything would make her regret that. Including a broken heart.

Eli wasn't in love with her. Ashlyn was pretty sure if he had been that he would have said something about it by now, and it was probably bothering him that he didn't feel the same way about her that she did him. That would cause him plenty of regrets, too, but she doubted he'd be able to deal with his feelings or anything else personal until the danger was over.

Remembering that danger, Ashlyn got up so she could get dressed and check on the baby. She hadn't heard any sounds coming from across the hall, and if Cora had indeed woken up, Gloria would have certainly let her know. Still, she wanted to see her daughter, and maybe that would help settle the nerves that were starting to jangle inside her.

And speaking of jangled nerves, Ashlyn got more of them when Eli came out of the bathroom. He'd put on his jeans, but since he was shirtless, she got a nice view of his toned and perfect chest. Too bad she hadn't taken the time to savor that, but then making love with him had seemed too urgent for foreplay.

He stopped in the doorway of the bathroom and combed his gaze over her. It wasn't exactly regret that she saw on his face, but there was some concern.

"Please don't tell me you're sorry this happened," Ashlyn told him before he could say anything.

His eyes stayed on her. "Well, I am sorry you're dressed." And he flashed her a smile that warmed her all over again. If a mere smile could do that, she figured another kiss would land them back in bed. However, there wasn't time for that, because Eli's phone buzzed.

"Kellan," he relayed to her after he glanced at the

screen. Eli put the call on speaker and laid his phone on the bed so he could get dressed.

"Everything okay there?" Kellan said the moment he was on the line.

"So far. Please tell me you've got good news."

"Some. The CSIs found Waite's prints in Hamby's car. That's enough for me to threaten him with accessory to attempted murder. His lawyer will come back in first thing in the morning so I'll have a chat with Waite then."

Good. And attempted murder just might be enough to get the man talking. If so, that could lead to Waite giving them the name of the person who'd hired him.

"I want to be there when you question Waite," Eli insisted.

Kellan didn't argue with that. "I'll let you know where it's all set up, but considering the other attacks, I think you should leave Ashlyn there. I can send out a pair of the reserve deputies to stay with her."

Ashlyn didn't like the idea of Eli going out there and opening himself up to another attack. Nor did she especially care for being with the reserve deputies. Still, she doubted Eli would agree to letting her go back to the sheriff's office with him.

Eli had just finished putting on his shirt when his phone dinged with an incoming call. "Gotta go," he told Kellan. "One of the hands is trying to ring in."

Hearing that automatically kicked up Ashlyn's pulse, but she reminded herself that this could be just an update since the hands were keeping watch of the grounds.

"Eli, this is Jeremy," the hand said after Eli had answered.

Jeremy Cranston, one of the top hands. Ashlyn knew

him, and the last time she'd seen him, he'd been in the front pasture.

"There's a car that's stopped just up from the ranch road," Jeremy went on. "The headlights are on high so I can't see through the glare to get a glimpse of who's inside."

"Can you read the license plate?" Eli asked.

"Sure." And Jeremy rattled that off to Eli.

"Thanks," Eli told him. "Hold on just a minute while I have dispatch run the plates—"

"The car's moving," Jeremy blurted out, his voice louder now and edged with even more alarm. "Fast… hell! Eli, the car just broke through the fence and is headed right for us."

Chapter Fifteen

Eli knew in his gut that this wasn't just some driver who'd gotten turned around. No. This was probably the start of another attack. A stupid one. Because in addition to Gunnar and him, all the hands were armed and ready for something like this.

"Make sure the baby is okay," Eli told Ashlyn, though he knew that Cora was fine. Still, he wanted Ashlyn to stay put. Best to not have her anywhere near the front of the house until he made sure that she wasn't in danger. "If you hear anything, go in the room with Cora and Gloria and make sure all of you stay down."

She gave a shaky nod and didn't question him as to what he meant about hearing "anything." Ashlyn knew they'd all be listening for the sound of gunshots.

Because he thought they could both use it, Eli brushed a quick kiss on Ashlyn's mouth and headed for the front door. "Wake up," he told Gunnar as he hurried past him.

The deputy did, and he automatically drew his gun. "What's wrong?"

Eli looked out the small window on the side of the door, and he cursed. There was indeed a car coming across the pasture. A dark sedan. It tore through the section of wood fence and came right toward the house.

"Want me to try to shoot the driver?" Gunnar asked.

Eli considered it. Heck, he wanted to do it himself. But he didn't know what they were up against.

"Hold off just a second," Eli told him, and he took aim. Gunnar did the same at the other side window.

The car jolted to a stop about ten yards from the house, but Eli didn't have any better luck than Jeremy had at seeing inside the vehicle. The high beams were cutting through the darkness, though, and it meant if someone got out, Eli and Gunnar would have no trouble spotting them. However, someone could possibly sneak out of the trunk, so Eli took out his phone to warn Jeremy about that, but before he could do that his phone buzzed again with a call.

Remy.

Eli wanted to let it go to voice mail because he didn't want the distraction of another round of conversation with the man. But something in his gut told him to answer. The moment he did and put the call on speaker, he heard Remy's frantic voice pour through the room.

"Don't shoot me," Remy said. "I have a hostage."

Eli hadn't thought his muscles could go any tighter, but he'd been wrong. "What hostage?" Eli demanded.

There were some muffled sounds. Maybe a struggle going on. "I'll kill you if you move again," Remy growled, and Eli was pretty sure the man wasn't talking to him.

"Who's your hostage?" Eli ordered Remy, and he tried not to think the worst. That maybe Remy had taken one of the hands or an innocent bystander.

"I've got Dominick," Remy spat out. "And if he keeps trying to get his hands untied or kick me again, he'll die."

"Dominick?" Eli heard Ashlyn repeat. He glanced over his shoulder to make sure she had stayed put. She had. Ashlyn was in the hall just outside the door where Cora was sleeping. She looked shaky but confused, too. Eli was on the same page with her. What the hell was going on here?

"Why do you have Dominick?" Eli pressed, and that was just the first of many questions he had for Remy.

Eli turned his attention back to Remy's vehicle. Or rather to the vehicle that had crashed through the fence. The odds were that Remy was indeed inside. Maybe Dominick, too. But Eli also knew this could be a trap and that Remy's call could be just a distraction.

There could be gunmen inside that car, and they could be waiting to come out shooting. The fact that they'd gotten this close to the house riled Eli all the way to his bones. This wasn't like the other attack on the road. It was worse. Because this time Cora could be caught in the crosshairs of a killer.

"Text Jeremy and tell him to keep an eye on the trunk," Eli mouthed to Gunnar, and the deputy immediately took out his phone to do that. "And then let Kellan know what happened."

"You're gonna listen to me," Remy carried on, "or Dominick will die. So help me, I'll put a bullet in him."

Remy certainly sounded desperate enough to do something that stupid, but it still didn't make sense to Eli. "I'm listening," Eli assured him. "Now, tell me what you want and why you have Dominick."

"I don't want Marta's body moved," Remy insisted. "I don't want anyone touching her."

Eli listened for any hint that the demand didn't ring true, but it did. Well, it did if Remy had gone off the deep end. Since the man had been acting more erratic than usual, that was possible.

"You need to stop this idiot!" Dominick shouted, and the sound of his voice didn't just come over the phone line. Eli heard it from within the car. Of course, it could be some kind of recording, something meant to be a decoy or distraction, but Eli was starting to believe this was what it appeared to be. Remy losing all control and taking a hostage.

Except there was a problem with that.

"How the hell did you manage to take Dominick?" Eli asked Remy. "Better yet, *why* did you take him?"

"I needed leverage," Remy answered almost immediately. "I knew you'd listen to me if I had a hostage, so when I saw Dominick coming out of the sheriff's office, I followed him."

"The idiot used a stun gun on me," Dominick snarled. The man's anger certainly seemed genuine. "He tied my hands when he got me in the car and then drove around crying," Dominick added with some disgust.

"I can't lose Marta," Remy snarled back, but then it sounded as if a hoarse sob tore from his mouth. "I lost her once, and that can't happen again."

Eli doubted the best response to that would be to remind Remy that Marta was already dead. Obviously, the man was well past the point of reasoning.

"Whose car do you have?" Eli pressed. "Because the

one in the yard isn't yours." And he needed to make sure it wasn't some kind of decoy.

"It belongs to a friend. I had him come and get me after I ran from the barn."

"Is that friend in the car with you now?" Eli added.

"No, it's just Dominick and me. Now, here's what you're going to do," Remy went on without waiting for Eli to respond. "You're gonna call Marta's dad and get it *in writing* that he won't try to move her. I've been trying to reason with him, but he blocked my calls."

Eli didn't blame Gus for doing that. After all, Remy had stolen Gus's daughter's body.

"When you get Gus on the line, I want to talk to him," Remy went on. "I want to hear him say that he agrees to it, that he'll let her stay near me. Then he can put it in writing. I want that done right now."

As demands went, it wasn't an especially hard one. Or rather it wouldn't be if he could get in touch with Gus right away. Still, even if Remy got that guarantee, he had a hostage. And he'd committed a serious crime. Eli was going to have to defuse the situation and arrest the man.

"Okay," Eli said. "We'll try to call Gus right now." Since Eli didn't want to take his focus off the car, he motioned for Gunnar to do that.

Even though Eli's pulse was drumming in his ears, he could still hear the ringing sound when Gunnar tried the call. Eli dragged in his breath, waiting, but Gus didn't answer.

Hell.

This just got a whole lot harder.

"Gus didn't pick up," Eli relayed to Remy, "but I know he'll agree to this. He wouldn't want to see a man hurt."

"It has to be in writing!" Remy yelled. "That's the only way I let Dominick go. Try to call Gus again, and keep calling until you speak to him."

Eli nodded for Gunnar to keep trying. The deputy would, but while they waited, Eli was going to have to do something to defuse this. Thankfully, he had some backup. In the distance he could see a vehicle approaching on the ranch road. Kellan. At least he hoped it was. But if not, maybe this vehicle wouldn't break through the fence, too.

"You don't need Dominick as a hostage," Eli told Remy. "You've got a gun, and I can't risk you firing shots this close to the house. That's enough to keep you safe so you can let Dominick go."

"He's staying put," Remy snapped. "I don't trust you."

The feeling was mutual. Of course, Eli wasn't certain he could trust Dominick, either, but that was something he'd have to work out later.

Gunnar tried Gus's number again, and Eli finally released the breath he'd been holding when he heard the man answer.

"Tell him what's going on," Eli instructed Gunnar, and he turned back to Remy to let him know they'd reached Marta's father.

Before Eli could do that, though, he heard something he definitely didn't want to hear.

A gunshot.

ASHLYN HAD NO trouble realizing someone had just fired a gun, and it sent a jolt of fear and terror through her. After the attacks, she'd become too familiar with that horrible sound. And she knew what it meant.

They were in danger again.

Turning to go to Cora, she was about to shout for Eli to get down. He was right at the little window by the door, and a bullet could easily go through the glass and kill him. But Eli mumbled something to Gunnar, something she didn't catch, and the deputy turned and ran toward her. Gunnar shoved his phone into his jeans pocket, took her by the arm and moved her into the open doorway of the bedroom that Eli had been using.

"Go into the bathroom," Gunnar told her.

She frantically shook her head. "I need to make sure Cora's okay," Ashlyn insisted, fighting to get out of his grip.

"I'll do that. You go into the bathroom."

Ashlyn didn't do as he'd ordered. She stood there, watching, and she had to fight against all her maternal instincts to go with the deputy. She was the one who should be checking on her child. She should be there to protect Cora if she needed it. However, Ashlyn could see into the room when Gunnar eased open the door. Gloria was already out of bed, and she had a sleeping Cora clutched to her.

"Go in there," Gunnar instructed, tipping his head to the attached bath. "Lock the door behind you. Then, get in the tub with her and stay down until I tell you it's okay to come out."

It was a small claw-foot tub, only large enough for one person, but Ashlyn thought it was deep enough that it would protect Cora and Gloria if someone fired another bullet.

She prayed it was enough.

Gloria hurried into the bathroom and disappeared out of sight. Ashlyn's fear spiked even higher, and the jolt of adrenaline she got made it nearly impossible to stay put. She wanted to take her baby and run to safety, but she had to remind herself that right now staying put could be the right thing to do.

Ashlyn glanced back at the bathroom that Eli had used earlier. It was just as small as the other one, and instead of a tub, it had a shower. She hadn't gone inside it, but she was certain it wouldn't have the space for Gloria, Cora and her.

"Remy?" Eli shouted, and she realized he was talking into his phone. "Are you there?" If Remy answered, she couldn't hear what the man said.

"What's happening?" Ashlyn asked Gunnar when he came back to her. "Did Remy fire that shot?"

"We're not sure yet. It looks as if Remy's taken Dominick hostage, and it sounded as if some kind of struggle was going on in the car."

Oh, mercy. Dominick a hostage? One that Remy had brought here to the ranch. That was more than enough for her to process, but Ashlyn hadn't missed Gunnar's "looks as if Remy's taken Dominick hostage."

"You think Remy could be lying?" she asked.

Gunnar lifted his shoulder. "Remy's definitely not thinking straight, and he said he wants to use Dominick to get Gus to agree not to move Marta." Gunnar didn't look at her though when he spoke. He kept his attention nailed to Eli.

So if Remy had told them the truth, this was about Marta and maybe didn't have anything to do with the other attacks. That didn't mean, though, that one of them couldn't be hurt.

"I need a gun," Ashlyn told him. "Just in case Remy or someone else gets inside the house." Because she had a really bad feeling about this.

She could see the debate going on in Gunnar's eyes over her request, but he finally reached down, took out a small weapon from his boot holster, and he handed it to her.

"Giving you this doesn't mean I want you out in the open. If you don't stay down, you'll have to answer to Eli. So will I," he added under his ragged breath.

Ashlyn knew that was true, but if they did have to answer to Eli, that would mean this had all been a false alarm. That the only danger was to Dominick and not any of them.

When Ashlyn started across the hall toward Gloria and Cora, he stopped her again. "Eli wants you to hunker down in the shower," Gunnar reminded her.

"And I need to prevent anyone from getting to Cora," she snapped.

Ashlyn made sure her tone and expression let him know that she wasn't going to budge on this. She moved into the doorway of Cora's and Gloria's room. That way, she could easily hear them in the bathroom, and she could keep an eye on the window opposite the bed.

Eli had told her that all the doors and windows were wired into the security system, but she wanted to be there if someone tried to break in. If that did indeed happen, Ashlyn consoled herself with the reminder that Gloria had locked the bathroom. That meant an intruder would not only have to get past her but also break down the door.

Gunnar huffed, cursed and then glanced back at Eli, who was still by the front door. Eli hadn't moved, and there hadn't been any other shots, but he was clearly still standing guard.

"Remy?" Eli shouted again. Like before, he got no response that Ashlyn could hear.

"Maybe Remy shot Dominick," Ashlyn said.

"Maybe," Gunnar agreed. "Or else Dominick got the gun from Remy and turned it on him."

That was possible, but if so, then why hadn't Dominick just come out of the vehicle? She was certain he hadn't, or Eli would have already told Gunnar.

"I'll see what I can find out," Gunnar told her, and he gave her a warning glance to stay put before he hurried back to the front door next to Eli.

Ashlyn wanted to hear their conversation, but she didn't want to move any farther away from Cora and the bedroom window. So she stood there, the gun gripped in her hand, and she waited. She could tell from Gunnar's expression that he didn't have good news when he came back to her.

"Neither Dominick nor Remy is responding," he said. "Either Remy turned off his phone or it's not working."

Ashlyn had no idea which of those could be true, but it was possible the shot she'd heard had damaged the phone. "What happens now?" she asked.

"Kellan's here in the cruiser, and he's about to drive closer so he can try to see in Remy's car. If Remy killed

Dominick, accidentally or otherwise, he might be too scared to come out."

True. Or Remy could be lying in wait to gun down Kellan or anyone else who approached him. If the man truly wasn't thinking straight, then there was no telling what he would do.

"Is there any way of knowing where the shot went?" she pressed. Ashlyn hadn't heard it hit the house, but there were plenty of ranch hands patrolling the grounds. She hoped it hadn't hit one of them.

Gunnar shook his head. "The windshield on the car is intact, but it's possible the shot went out the back. Kellan's not going to let this drag on," he added. "He's already called for more cruisers, and when they get here, they can box Remy in."

Since the cruisers were bullet-resistant, that would hopefully mean Remy wouldn't be able to fire a shot into the house. Also, if he lowered his window to try to do that, Kellan or one of the hands would almost certainly take him out.

Ashlyn hated the thought of someone being killed, especially just yards away from her baby, but Remy might not give them a choice. If he'd truly lost his mind, then there might not be any turning back from this for him.

Gunnar went back to the front, taking up position on the other side of the door from Eli. Ashlyn kept her attention on them, and that's why she didn't miss when Eli glanced back at her. Their eyes connected, and she could almost feel his worry and regret. He would blame himself for not being able to stop this, blame himself for not realizing just how close to the edge that Remy had been.

Eli's gaze slashed back to the window when there was another sound. Not a gunshot, thank goodness. This was a screech of tires, and for a moment she thought it was Kellan moving in with one of the cruisers.

But no.

Ashlyn's heart jumped to her throat as she saw Eli's and Gunnar's reactions. The two bolted away from the door, both of them running in her direction.

And the car crashed through the front of the house.

ELI WAS CURSING and praying at the same time. There'd been only seconds to react. Seconds between the time Remy had gunned the engine and used his car as a battering ram to tear into the house.

The front of the car did plenty of damage, breaking down the front door and shattering windows. And setting off the security alarm, which immediately started to blare. If the crash hadn't woken up the baby, that would certainly do it, and despite everything else going on, Eli added a prayer that the little girl wouldn't be scared.

Ashlyn and Gunnar took aim at the car, and while Eli appreciated their quick backup, he wanted Ashlyn away from this. Well, as far away as she could get, which would mean going in with Cora and Gloria. For now, though, Eli used his phone to turn off the security alarms so he could hear.

He heard all right. The sounds of the car engine crackling from the impact. Wood and glass falling. But beneath all of that, he also heard the moans. Someone was hurt. Hopefully, Remy. Eli didn't have any sympathy whatsoever for the man since he'd endangered not only his hostage but everyone in the house.

The moaning picked up a notch, and then the front passenger's door of the car creaked open. Dominick stuck out his head, and since the lights were still on in what was left of the house, Eli had no trouble seeing the blood on the man's head. It looked as if he'd hit it during the collisions.

"Remy set a fire inside the car," Dominick said, and his voice was a mix of pain, fear and anger.

Eli had already noticed the smoke, but he'd thought that had come from the crash. Apparently, though, Remy was determined to do even more damage than he already had.

"Let Kellan know about the fire," Eli told Gunnar. Kellan would almost certainly be approaching the vehicle, and he'd need to be aware what he was up against.

"Is Remy alive?" Eli asked Dominick. He didn't go to the man to help him out of the car and wouldn't until he was positive that Dominick hadn't had some part in this.

Dominick opened his mouth to answer, and then he cursed and groaned. A moment later, Eli saw why Dominick had had that reaction. He got out of the car, and Remy was right behind him.

Remy had a gun pointed at Dominick's head.

Hell. They still had a hostage situation on their hands, and the smoke from the car was getting worse, which meant if there was indeed a fire, it could soon spread into the house. Worse, Kellan wouldn't be able to do anything about that fire as long as Remy had Dominick. Of course, his brother might be able to get a clean shot to take out Remy, and if so, that would put an end to this.

Remy staggered out of the car, and Eli could see that he, too, had a head injury. There was a line of blood snaking down his temple all the way to his jaw, but Remy didn't even seem to notice it. His face was tight with rage and determination. Not a good mix when it came to an out-of-control armed man who seemed hell-bent on doing as much damage as possible.

"Get in the room with Cora," Eli told Ashlyn. Thankfully, she did move but only into the doorway of the bedroom. He would have preferred her to be in the bathroom, but at least she wasn't in the direct line of fire.

Gunnar and Eli took cover, too, both of them scrambling behind the sofa. It wouldn't give them much protection if Remy started shooting, but Eli hadn't given up on reasoning with the man. Maybe that wasn't even possible, but he had to try especially since Kellan was going to be tied up trying to deal with the car.

Behind him, he could hear Cora crying. Could also hear Gloria trying to soothe her.

"Remy, you need to put down your gun," Eli warned him. "We have a baby here, and you could hurt her."

"That baby is my granddaughter," Dominick spat out. He angled his narrowed eyes back at Remy, who now had him in a choke hold. "So help me, if you put one scratch on her, I will kill you."

Remy didn't have a reaction to that, either. He seemed to be in shock as he forced Dominick through the debris from the crash and into the living room. However, Eli rethought that "shock" diagnosis when Remy positioned himself so that his own back was to the wall.

It would make it much harder for Kellan to get off that shot. Ditto for Gunnar and Eli. Right now, neither of them could fire because they would almost certainly hit Dominick.

"You need to stop this, Sergeant Slater," Dominick spat out, saying "Sergeant Slater" as if it were the profanity he added after his demand. "You need to kill this lunatic before he does any more damage."

"And you need to stay quiet," Eli told him. It definitely wouldn't help if Dominick agitated Remy even more than he already was.

Dominick glared at Eli and gave him a look that could have frozen hell. Apparently, the man wasn't going to make this easy, so Eli needed to try to defuse this as fast as he could.

Through the gaping hole in the front of the house, Eli saw Kellan and one of the hands inching toward the car. Since the smoke was still spewing from it, maybe they'd be able to deal with that. If Remy let them, that is. If Remy saw them, he might try to shoot them. And that's why Eli had to keep Remy occupied.

"Before you crashed your car into the house, I had Gus on the phone," Eli told him. Not a lie but what he would say next would be. "He agreed not to move Marta's body, and yes, he'll put that in writing."

Gus would probably agree to it only to appease Remy enough to have him put an end to this, but Eli was betting there was no way Gus was going to let Marta's body stay where it was.

Remy didn't say anything, but his gaze continued to fire around the room and toward the car. His eyes were wild, and his hand was shaking. Clearly, he wasn't in control, which made this situation even more dangerous.

Kellan leaned into the smoking car, and using his hat, he batted at the flames. Eli couldn't tell if he'd managed to put out the fire because there was still plenty of smoke. Smoke that was seeping into the house.

"I need a car or truck so I can get out of here," Remy finally said.

Eli huffed. Well, at least it was a demand he could work with. A demand that didn't make sense, though. "Why'd you crash your own car if that's what you wanted?"

Remy shook his head, and yeah, he was dazed. "I didn't intend on doing that. It just happened."

"I was trying to get away from him," Dominick volunteered, "and the idiot jammed his foot on the accelerator."

So that hadn't been part of the plan. Of course, neither had Remy holding Dominick at gunpoint in the living room.

"Obviously, we're not dealing with a bright bulb here," Dominick added in an enraged grumble.

Remy might have been dazed, but he didn't care much for Dominick's insult, and he ground the gun even harder against Dominick's head. "I want a car or truck," Remy repeated, and his words were suddenly as fierce as his expression. "Get it now. I know Kellan's out there, and I can use his cruiser."

Eli nodded. "That can be arranged. I'll have Kellan bring in the keys."

"No," Remy snapped. He glanced out at his car again, and even though Kellan and the hands were no longer in sight, Eli knew they were nearby and waiting to respond.

Dominick huffed. “Like I said, he’s not very bright. You’ll need the keys, moron,” he added, tossing Remy another look from over his shoulder.

Eli wished the man would just shut up, because that put a new layer of rage on Remy’s face. “Tell Kellan to leave the keys in the ignition of the cruiser,” Remy ordered. “I want the engine running and ready to go. And I want her.”

Remy looked past the sofa, past Eli, his attention going into the hall. And Eli’s stomach went to his knees, because he knew that Remy was talking about Ashlyn.

“I’ll take her instead of Dominick,” Remy went on. “She’s not as likely to put up a fight, and I’m betting Kellan or you won’t fire any shots at me if I’ve got Ashlyn with me.”

“You’re not taking Ashlyn,” Eli snapped, though he wasn’t sure how he managed to speak with everything churning even harder inside him.

Remy’s gaze slashed straight to Eli’s. “Then I start shooting. You don’t want that to happen because like you said, the kid could get hurt. I’m betting Ashlyn will come with me to stop that from happening.”

“I will,” Ashlyn said.

Eli didn’t look back at her. He didn’t want to take his attention off Remy, but he wanted to give her a back-off warning. No way was Eli going to let her leave with Remy. In the man’s state of mind, he could kill her.

“Take me hostage,” Eli insisted. “Kellan and Gunnar won’t fire if I’m with you.”

Eli could see Remy considering that. And he also

saw him dismiss it. "I want Ashlyn. She's likely to give me less trouble than you would."

Yes, she was less likely because she wouldn't be able to defend herself against Remy, who was much larger than she was. Which was another reason why she wasn't leaving with him.

"I won't be armed," Eli said, trying again to reason with Remy. "I'd leave my gun here."

Again, Remy considered that, and this time there wasn't an immediate dismissal. Not from Remy anyway, but Eli heard Ashlyn mutter a soft "no." There was plenty of emotion in that single word. Especially plenty of fear, because she had to know just how dangerous Remy was right now.

"All right, Eli, we'll deal," Remy finally answered. "Put down your gun and have Gunnar cuff you. I want your hands behind your back. Then you and I will walk out of here and go to the cruiser."

The cuffing wasn't ideal because Eli wouldn't be able to fight back, but he trusted Kellan to stop Remy before they could make it to the cruiser.

Remy's eyes narrowed even more than they already were when he looked at Eli. "If you try to pull anything stupid, I start shooting. The kid could get hurt."

Eli hoped like the devil that Gloria had stayed in the tub with Cora. While he was hoping, he added that they were all right. He could no longer hear the baby crying, so maybe that meant she'd gone back to sleep.

"Here's my gun," Eli said, sliding it across the floor toward Remy. He had a backup, but Remy didn't ask for that.

Remy nodded. "Okay, Gunnar. Get the cuffs on him. And I want to watch you when you do that."

Eli motioned for Gunnar and him to stand, and he went ahead and shot that warning glance at Ashlyn. She was still there in the doorway. Still had a grip on a gun that she had aimed in Remy's direction.

When Eli stood, he eased his hands behind him, and Gunnar moved closer so he could start putting on the plastic cuffs.

"Remember, no tricks," Remy warned them. "If you pull anything, I shoot, and it wouldn't be my fault. It'd be yours if the kid gets hurt."

Dominick made a deep throaty growl of outrage, and while Eli could understand why the man was furious with Remy's threat, it wasn't a good time for Dominick to be anything but cooperative. Dominick, though, obviously had something different in mind.

Something that could get them all killed.

"This ends now," Dominick spat out, and before the last word had even left his mouth, he whirled around. In the same motion, he took hold of Remy and slung the man across the room.

Remy slammed against Eli, sending them both to the floor.

And Remy pulled the trigger.

Chapter Sixteen

The sound of the shot was deafening, and it was like a blast roaring through Ashlyn's head. She could have sworn she felt the vibration of it all the way to her bones.

She also felt the slam of fear that quickly followed.

Oh God. Had Remy managed to shoot Eli? Or had the bullet gone into the bathroom where Cora was?

She fired glances all around her but didn't see the signs of where any gunshot had landed. However, she did hear Gloria and Cora. Cora was crying, causing Ashlyn's fear to spike even more.

"Cora!" Ashlyn shouted.

"We're okay," Gloria called out. "We're not hurt."

The relief came flooding through her. Her baby hadn't been harmed. The relief was short-lived, though, because Ashlyn knew there could be other shots. Plus, she still wasn't sure if Eli was okay. He certainly wasn't calling out to her to let her know he was all right.

Ashlyn blinked back the tears that automatically started to burn her eyes, and with her gun ready, she hurried out of the doorway of the bedroom and into the hall so she could see what was going on.

And what was going on was chaos.

Eli was alive, thank goodness, but she saw that there was blood on his hands. That tightened the muscles in her chest so that it was hard for her to breathe. The slam of adrenaline didn't help, either. Everything inside her was screaming for her to get to Eli to save him.

But Eli was trying to save himself. He had his hands clamped around Remy's, and the grip no doubt stopped Remy from firing again.

Dominick reached down, scooping up Eli's gun from the floor, and he took aim at Remy.

"No," Gunnar told Dominick, taking the word right out of Ashlyn's mouth. "Don't shoot. You could hit Eli."

Thankfully, Dominick held back, but she could tell from the way he was moving around that he was trying to find a clean shot. Gunnar was doing the same, but Remy wasn't making that easy for them. He and Eli were locked in a fierce battle, rolling around on the floor while Remy kicked and punched at Eli. Somehow, despite all of the blows he was getting, Eli managed to hang on to Remy's shooting hand.

"The fire's out," Kellan said when he hurried in through what was left of the front door. He also had his gun drawn, and he cursed when he saw the struggle that was going on between his brother and Remy.

"Was Remy alone when he brought you here?" Kellan snapped at Dominick.

Dominick nodded and kept moving. Kept looking for that shot. It was obvious he was furious with Remy, and Ashlyn didn't think it was solely because of the kidnapping. She'd heard the rage in Dominick's voice when Remy threatened to fire shots into the house.

Kellan moved to the side of the room, looming near

Remy and Eli, and he tipped his head to Dominick. "Move. Go back toward the door and stay down. This clown could get off a shot."

Yes, a shot that could go anywhere, including into Eli or Cora.

"Did you see any other gunmen?" Gunnar asked Kellan.

The question gave her another hit of adrenaline along with another jolt of fear. Eli was in a battle for his life, but she needed to make sure no one tried to climb through the window to get to Cora. Now that Eli had turned off the security system, they wouldn't even know if a hired gun broke in.

Ashlyn hurried back to the doorway, and she volleyed her attention between Eli and the window. Cora had stopped crying again, but it still wasn't easy to hear if someone was approaching the house because of the shouts and curses from the living room.

Even though Ashlyn had tried to steel herself for it, the next shot still stunned her. And put her heart right in her throat. From her position she could partially see Eli, but Kellan was in her way so she couldn't tell if Eli had been hit. Kellan's next round of ripe profanity didn't help that, and he moved in, kicking at something.

Remy's arm, she realized.

Remy howled in pain, and Ashlyn moved out a few inches so she could get a glimpse of Eli. He was still down, and he had Remy's hand pinned to the floor. That didn't stop Remy from pulling the trigger again.

This time, Ashlyn didn't have to guess where the bullet had gone because she saw it blow out a hole in the wall just above Eli's head. Another couple of inches, and he would have been killed.

"Enough of this," Eli snarled.

Ashlyn held her breath and watched as Eli gave Remy's hand another bash on the floor, and then he rammed his elbow into Remy's chest. The man sputtered out a cough, and that split-second lapse was enough for Kellan to move in. He latched onto the back of Remy's shirt collar and dragged him off Eli.

But Remy somehow managed to keep hold of his gun.

A gun that he aimed at Eli.

Ashlyn heard herself yell for Eli to watch out, but he was already scrambling to the side while he reached to draw his backup from his boot holster. He was still reaching for it when the next blast roared through the room.

She froze, her feet seemingly frozen in place, but that didn't stop the horrible thoughts from racing through her head. "Eli," she managed to say. Ashlyn would have gone to him, but Kellan stepped in front of her again.

"You don't need to see this," Kellan said, spiking her fear even more.

Until she realized Eli was fine. Well, he hadn't been shot, anyway. He was on his feet, his backup weapon now in his hand, and he had it pointed at Remy.

Remy wasn't *fine.*

The man was no longer holding his gun. That was good. He was on the floor, his hands pressed to his chest, and Ashlyn had no trouble seeing the blood. It was seeping through his fingers and spilling down the side of his shirt.

"I had to shoot him," Kellan muttered, and it sounded as if he was talking to himself. He went closer and kicked Remy's gun to the other side of the room. "Remy didn't give me a choice about that."

No, he hadn't. Remy's choices had started when he'd taken Dominick hostage and then had come here to the house. Despite Eli trying to reason with him, he'd fired three shots, any of which could have hurt or killed. He had to be stopped, and thankfully Kellan had done it.

"I want to be with Marta," Remy said, his words choppy with his rough breaths. "I want to be buried next to her."

Eli certainly didn't give him any assurances that would happen, and she wondered if Gus would even allow it. Not after everything that Remy had done.

"I'll call for an ambulance." Eli holstered his backup, picked up his gun and then took out his phone to do that, but he also glanced over at Ashlyn. "Is Cora okay?" he asked.

She managed a nod, not trusting her voice. Ashlyn wasn't certain she could speak yet. Not sure she could move to Eli, either, even though that's what she wanted to do. She wanted to hold him, to feel for herself that he was safe. But Eli still had to wrap this up.

"Check on the car and make sure that fire didn't kick back up," Kellan instructed Gunnar.

While Eli continued to hold his gun on Remy, Kellan went to the man, stooped down and pressed his hands over Remy's. Probably to try to slow down the flow of blood. Ashlyn figured that wouldn't help, not with the amount of blood that Remy had already lost.

"Did you hire those guns who tried to kill Ashlyn and Eli?" Kellan asked him.

Remy opened his mouth, maybe to answer, but that's when she heard the rattling sound that came from Remy's throat.

And she watched as Remy died.

Kellan cursed again, probably because a confession would have tied up everything into a neat little bow, but they still might be able to get confirmation from Waite—who was still in custody. Eli had said they could hang charges of accessory to attempted murder over him to get him to talk.

Ashlyn turned to go into the bedroom so she could check on Gloria and Cora, but she'd only made it a step when she felt someone take hold of her shoulder. At first she thought it was Eli, but the grip was too hard. Hard enough to leave bruises. And the person spun her around, knocking her weapon from her hand and dragging her back against his chest.

Dominick put a gun to her head.

ELI'S HEART SLAMMED so hard against his chest that it felt as if he'd cracked a rib. Hell. This couldn't be happening. Not now, after everything they'd just been through.

He dropped down behind the side of the sofa and automatically brought up his gun, taking aim at Dominick. So did Kellan after he took cover behind the end table. But both he and his brother knew that neither of them had a clean shot. Just as they hadn't with Remy when he'd dragged Dominick from the car and into the house. That's because Dominick was now using Ashlyn as a human shield.

Eli couldn't help but see Ashlyn's face and the shock and terror that was on it. He hated that once again she was in danger. As bad as the other attacks had been—and they had been bad—at least the gunmen hadn't managed to get their hands on her. Now Dominick had managed that.

And he'd done it right in front of two armed lawmen.

Eli wanted to kick himself for not seeing what was about to happen. Kick himself, too, for not putting a stop to it. But that led Eli to a couple of questions. Had Dominick ever actually been a hostage, or had this been some kind of sick setup with Remy? Of course, the biggest question on Eli's mind was why Dominick was now holding a gun on Ashlyn.

"Throw down your weapons," Dominick told Eli and Kellan. "Then, listen carefully to what you need to do to keep Ashlyn alive."

Eli forced the muscles in his jaw to ease up so he could speak. "Trust me, I'm listening. Now, what the hell do you want?"

Dominick shook his head and made a sound of frustration. "I wanted things to go a heck of a lot better than this. Since that didn't happen, I'm now on to plan C."

Which meant two other plans had failed. Eli didn't have any trouble filling in the blanks on what Dominick had tried to do.

"You had your own granddaughter kidnapped," Eli started, "and you set me up for that by trying to make Ashlyn believe I was responsible for it. You wanted her to murder me, and once she'd been convicted and was in jail, then you would have had a clear path to get permanent custody of Cora."

Dominick didn't deny anything Eli said, not with words, nor with his expression. This was all about getting his hands on Cora.

Ashlyn's eyes narrowed, and Eli could see her fear and shock replaced for another emotion. Fury. He totally got that. This idiot had put Cora in danger not just by having those thugs kidnap her but also with the attacks.

Of course, Dominick likely thought the baby had never been in danger, but she easily could have been. The hired guns could have turned on Dominick and tried to hold the child for ransom. Cora could have been hurt or worse. And all because Dominick hadn't wanted to "share" her with Ashlyn.

"When Ashlyn didn't take the bait and kill me," Eli went on, "you set your goons on us. Goons who shot us when Cora could have been in the car."

"She wasn't." Dominick's voice took on even a harder edge. "They had orders to make sure she wasn't part of that."

"Orders that you trusted with hired killers," Eli pointed out. "I don't know if that makes you stupid or just plain careless with a child's life."

That sure didn't cool down the fire in Dominick's eyes, and he gave Eli a look that could have frozen hell. "Cora's my granddaughter. My blood kin," he emphasized through clenched teeth. "I will be the one to raise her."

Which meant Dominick was going to have to get Ashlyn out of the way. Along with Kellan and him, too, and any other witnesses.

From the corner of Eli's eye, he saw Kellan move. His brother was shifting his position, trying to get into a better angle to put a stop to this. But Dominick saw it, too, because he immediately turned, keeping Ashlyn in a chokehold in front of him.

"Did you not hear that part about keeping Ashlyn alive?" Dominick snapped. "Trying to shoot me is a surefire way of getting her killed."

Kellan froze. But Eli knew they couldn't just stand there and let Dominick do whatever he was planning on doing.

Eli listened for any sign that Gunnar was still nearby. He didn't glance outside because he didn't want Dominick to be reminded that the deputy had gone out there. Not that Dominick had forgotten that, but Dominick wasn't a hired killer, and he might not be thinking straight right now. All they needed was some break, a distraction, just enough for Ashlyn to bolt out of Dominick's grip so that Eli could shoot him.

Eli very much wanted to shoot him. And that was a reminder for him to tamp down his anger. That wasn't going to help Ashlyn right now. He needed to keep a clear head.

"Here's how this is going to work," Dominick said. "Ashlyn and I are going to get Cora, and we'll walk out of here. I don't want to use the cruiser that Remy wanted because I suspect there's a tracker on it. Idiot," he grumbled when he glanced at Remy's body.

So that meant Dominick likely hadn't been working with Remy after all. Not that it mattered now, but when they got out of this—and they would—then Eli would want to build a solid case against Dominick. He wanted him in a cage for the rest of his miserable life.

"I'm guessing the reason for this desperation is because you got wind that Waite was about to spill his guts," Eli went on. He wanted to keep Dominick's attention on him so that he didn't notice Gunnar or Kellan. "Waite will confess that you're the one who hired him and his buddy. He must have told you that when you were at the sheriff's office visiting him—right before Remy kidnapped you."

Again, Dominick didn't deny it, but his silence put a cold hard knot in Eli's gut. All along Dominick had been a suspect, but Eli hated that he hadn't gotten the proof sooner. He definitely hadn't wanted things to play out like this what with Ashlyn, Cora, Gloria, Kellan and Gunnar in danger. Plus, some of the hands could get hurt, too, if Dominick tried to escape.

"Your son, Danny, didn't want you to raise Cora," Ashlyn said. "In fact, before he died, he made it clear that he didn't want you anywhere near her."

Dominick tightened his grip on Ashlyn's neck, and Eli could feel the man's anger go up a notch. Obviously, this was a sensitive subject, and while Eli wouldn't have minded pushing some of Dominick's buttons, he didn't want to do that while he was holding a gun on Ashlyn.

"My son was on drugs and confused," Dominick spat out. "If he'd been thinking straight, he would have made sure that she wasn't put up for adoption where anyone could have ended up getting her. She's my granddaughter, and with Danny dead, she belongs to me."

In his own way, Dominick was just as crazy and obsessed as Remy had been. That only made him more dangerous, because there was no way to reason with someone this bent on getting his way.

"Cora belongs to me," Ashlyn snapped, and she was

just as angry as Dominick. Definitely not good. Eli didn't want her to do anything that would goad the man into pulling the trigger.

"Until you can prove to me that she has your DNA, then she's mine." This time Dominick dug the gun even harder into her head just as Remy had done to him minutes earlier.

"Both of you want what's best for Cora," Eli interjected, trying to get Dominick to turn back to him. "Just make sure you don't fire any shots that can go through the walls."

That did get Dominick's attention, and he finally turned his glare back on Eli. "If I shoot, I won't be aiming at a wall."

No. He'd be shooting at Ashlyn, and she'd be a very easy target. But for now, Dominick almost certainly wanted to keep her alive because he thought she was his ticket out of there. With his money and resources, he no doubt planned to take the baby, murder Ashlyn, and then he'd disappear with Cora.

Eli didn't intend for any of that to happen.

"I need a vehicle," Dominick reminded them. "I'll take the keys to your truck." He meant that for Eli. "First, put your gun on the floor. You, too, Sheriff Slater. And before the two of you think of delaying that some more, just know that I will shoot. Nowhere near where Cora is, but that end table isn't giving the sheriff much protection. I'm thinking a bullet could go through that without a problem."

It could, and Eli wasn't immune to the threat of having his brother shot. Or of having any gunfire. There'd already been enough bloodshed. But Eli also had no intention of facing Dominick while he was unarmed.

Eli slid his gun across the floor toward Dominick, and in the same motion, he drew his backup from his boot holster. He kept that out of sight. From behind the table, Kellan did the same, drawing his backup as well.

"Good," Dominick continued. "Now, go ahead and take your keys from your pocket and slide them over here. Remember not to do anything that'll get your lover killed. That includes giving me the wrong key and trying to charge at me when I reach down for them."

Eli doubted that Dominick had any proof that Ashlyn and he were indeed lovers, but it was possible they were giving off some kind of vibe. Eli knew he wasn't reining in all his emotions when he looked at her, but he didn't want Dominick using that in some way.

He took out his keys and as instructed, Eli slid them toward Dominick. They stopped just a few inches from his feet. Dominick tightened his hold on Ashlyn even more, causing her to make a gasping sound. A sound that made Eli want to do that charging that Dominick had already warned him about.

Eli moved back behind the sofa and waited for any chance he had to put a stop to this.

Dominick stooped down, dragging Ashlyn with him. "Pick up the keys," he told her.

She did, closing her fingers around them, and when her gaze met Eli's, he wanted to curse. Because he could tell that Ashlyn was about to make a move. A move that he prayed wouldn't get her killed.

Before Dominick had fully stood back up, Ashlyn turned, ramming the keys into his face. The metal gouged his cheek, causing him to shout out in pain, and he cursed her, calling her a vile name. However, the injury wasn't enough for him to break the hold he had on Ashlyn. He yanked her, hard, against him, and this time she did more than gasp.

Dominick was choking her.

"Gloria?" Dominick called out. "I know you're back there, and you have Cora with you. Bring her out to me now, or Ashlyn dies."

Chapter Seventeen

Ashlyn prayed that Gloria would stay put in the bathroom. She started to shout to the sitter to do just that, but the chokehold Dominick had on her was so tight now that she couldn't speak.

Couldn't breathe.

Plus, Dominick had threatened to shoot Kellan. And she was certain the man would do just that. In fact, he'd be looking for any excuse right now to eliminate the lawmen in the room, because that would give him a clearer path to killing Gloria and her. That had to be his end goal, to get them all out of the way so he could walk out with Cora.

It sickened Ashlyn to think that his plan could possibly work. No way was anyone going to risk firing shots at Dominick if he had the baby in his arms. Then, once he had Cora in Eli's truck, he could simply disappear.

Even if she managed to stay alive, Ashlyn might not ever find her baby. That's why she had to stop Dominick now. It didn't matter if Cora and he had DNA in common. She was Cora's mother, and Dominick was a monster and had no right to take her.

She clawed at Dominick's hands until he finally

eased up on his grip. By the time he did that, Ashlyn's lungs were aching, and she gulped in several quick breaths, causing herself to cough. However, she did manage to hold on to the keys, and she hoped she got a chance to use them again. She poked the largest key through her fingers, turning it into a weapon, but she also kept it down by her side so that Dominick hopefully wouldn't see what she'd done.

"Gloria?" Dominick yelled again. "I start shooting if you don't come out here now with Cora."

Again, Gloria didn't answer, but Ashlyn was positive the sitter had heard the threat and was no doubt debating what to do. Ashlyn was doing the same, and maybe Gloria would just stay put until Eli, Kellan or she could stop Dominick.

Or maybe Gunnar could.

Ashlyn had been glancing outside but hadn't spotted the deputy in the last five minutes or so. Certainly, Gunnar had heard what was going on and had hopefully called for backup. Or else he was waiting and trying to work out a way to get inside and sneak up on him.

She didn't think Dominick had brought any hired guns with him. If he had, he would have already used them. So that meant Gunnar wasn't likely to be ambushed. That was something, at least. But she had to wonder if Dominick was working alone in this.

"Did you team up with Oscar or Remy?" she managed to ask, though it was still hard to talk with his tight grip on her neck.

Dominick made a quick sound of surprise. Or maybe disgust. "No. Both are idiots."

So Remy's kidnapping had been just that. A kidnapping that'd stemmed from desperation.

"Oscar might be useful, though, if I can set him up for this," Dominick added in a mumble.

Ashlyn hoped it didn't come down to that. Because if it did, it would mean she, Kellan, Eli and Gunnar would be dead. So would any of the hands who'd witnessed any of this.

"Tell Gloria to come out," Dominick snapped to Ashlyn. "Tell her Eli will die if she doesn't. I can put a bullet through that couch and straight into him. He'll die because of you. Do you really want to see someone you love die right in front you again?"

No. She didn't. In fact, just mentioning that triggered some flashbacks that she had to force away. She couldn't let that play into this now. She had to keep her focus. Ashlyn shook her head, not sure of what she should do, but Eli spoke before she could figure it out.

"Let Dominick shoot me," Eli said, his voice calm and hard at the same time. "That means he'll have to take the gun off you, and when he does, Gunnar will kill him with a shot to the head."

Ashlyn felt the muscles tense in Dominick's arm and chest, and even though she couldn't see his face, she thought maybe his gaze was firing all around.

"Yeah," Eli added. "Gunnar's got sniper skills, and he's got a gun aimed at you right now. All he's doing is waiting for you to move. An inch is all he needs to end your worthless life."

"You're lying," Dominick spat out, but he didn't sound as if he was so certain of that.

Neither was Ashlyn. She knew it could be a bluff,

but Gunnar was indeed out there somewhere, so it was highly likely that he had Dominick in his sights.

"You really think I'm lying?" Eli taunted. He kept his gaze nailed to Dominick. "If you honestly believe that, then you should be checking out the window to see for yourself who's watching you."

Ashlyn saw Eli shift a little, leaning out from the sofa as if daring Dominick to take aim at him. That caused her heart to jump to her throat. She didn't want Eli putting himself in the line of fire like this. She definitely didn't want him hurt or dead because he was protecting Cora and her.

Again, she felt Dominick tense, and maybe he did glance outside. If so, it wasn't for long, and he didn't shift his position enough because Eli stayed put. He didn't get that shot that he was no doubt hoping for.

"Ashlyn and I will go and get Cora," Dominick finally growled. "Tell your deputy friend that he'd better back off."

Neither Eli nor Kellan did that, and she saw both of them move again when Dominick started down the hall with her. He kept her in a chokehold and took slow, cautious steps backward. He was almost certainly glancing behind him as well as keeping an eye on Kellan and Eli.

It didn't take long, only a few steps, before Ashlyn lost sight of Eli. Kellan was still there, though, but that was because he inched to the side of the table. That's when Ashlyn noticed the gun he was holding. His backup weapon, no doubt. Good. He had a way to fight back if it came down to that.

Even with the porch light still on, it was hard for her to see in the yard, but she searched through the darkness to try to spot Gunnar. Still no sign of him, but she heard movement. Apparently, so did Dominick, because he stopped.

"Just remember that at any time, I can put a bullet in Ashlyn," Dominick called out as a warning. "It won't kill her, but she'll be in a lot of pain, and it'll all be your fault."

No, it wouldn't be. The blame for this was solely on Dominick, but Ashlyn doubted anyone would convince him of that.

Dominick stayed still several more seconds. Clearly, he was listening, but Ashlyn was thankful what he wasn't hearing were any sounds coming from the bathroom. Cora wasn't crying, and Gloria was keeping quiet. Of course, that might change once they made it to the door, and she figured that wouldn't take much time. There wasn't much space between the hall and that bathroom.

"Don't do anything stupid," Dominick warned her again, and he started moving. Walking backward until they made it to the doorway of the bedroom.

Ashlyn glanced inside and didn't see anyone, but there was light spilling from beneath the bathroom door. She also noticed that the room seemed warmer than the rest of the house. For one terrifying moment she thought maybe the fire from the car had spread back here, but the fire wasn't spreading. Plus, it wasn't that kind of heat. It was just the humid hot air from the night.

And that's when she noticed the bedroom window.

It was open, causing the curtains to flutter in the breeze. Since it had been closed before this whole ordeal had started, it meant Gunnar had likely opened it.

Maybe so he could get inside, or he could have done it to give himself a better shot.

Dominick stopped, and he cursed when he saw the window. That sent him snapping in all directions, dragging her along with each move he made. He shifted his gun, taking aim at each corner of the room, but if someone was there, they were staying out of sight.

"I'll kill her if you make it necessary," Dominick spat out, speaking to no one in particular.

His breathing was a lot faster now, practically gusting, and Ashlyn could feel his heart thudding against her back. She didn't mind if he was scared, but she didn't want him to panic and do something dangerous that could get Cora hurt.

She heard someone moving around in the living room. Kellan and Eli no doubt. The only way they could access the bedroom from inside the house was to come down the hall. A hall that Dominick was still clearly watching. But if either Eli or Kellan went outside, they could come in through the open window.

Dominick kept moving, inching his way to the bathroom door, and when he reached it, he used his foot to knock. "Open up, Gloria!" he shouted.

No answer.

Ashlyn tried to tamp down her own pulse so she could hear any sounds of her baby, but nothing. That didn't help with the fear that was already skyrocketing. Mercy, had something happened?

"Gloria?" Dominick banged his foot even harder against the door, but he stopped abruptly and pivoted her in the direction of the hall. Adjusting her so that she was squarely in front of him. And Ashlyn soon saw why.

Eli.

He was no longer by the sofa but was peering out from the wall that led into the hall. He was close, but he still wouldn't have a clean shot. Not with Dominick's position. If Eli missed, the bullet could go through the door and into the bathroom.

"Gloria!" Dominick shouted, and she could feel the rage bubbling inside him. He was quickly losing control.

She adjusted the grip on the keys, getting ready to make her move. Ashlyn figured she wouldn't be able to go for his face this time, but she would jam the keys like a knife in his thigh. If that was enough to break the hold he had on her, then she could drop to the floor and hopefully drag him down with her.

Dominick's next shout for Gloria was even louder, and without warning he turned and bashed his body against the door. Again and again. Harder and harder.

Until the door flew open.

Dominick pivoted to the side, no doubt looking around the small room, just as Ashlyn was doing. And what she saw caused her heartbeat to go into overdrive.

The bathtub was empty.

Neither Gloria nor Cora was there, and there wasn't any place in the room for them to hide. They were simply gone, and not knowing where they were or what happened to them nearly sent Ashlyn into a panic.

Dominick cursed, his words vile and raw, and his profanity only got worse when his attention landed on the open bathroom window. But Ashlyn wasn't cursing. The relief came because she knew that Gloria had managed to escape. Maybe with help from Gunnar. If so, she prayed that Gunnar had them tucked somewhere safe. Away from Dominick and any shots he might fire.

"Call out for Gloria," Dominick demanded, strangling her again. "Tell her to bring Cora in here right now!"

Even if Ashlyn could have spoken at that moment, she wouldn't have done that. Not even if Dominick threatened to kill her again. No way would she do anything to bring her baby back into the middle of this.

Since the strangling was blurring her vision, Ashlyn figured she didn't have long before she passed out. That meant she had to do something now, especially since Dominick was already dragging her toward the window—maybe so he could take her outside to look for Cora.

Ashlyn pinpointed all her strength into her hand, and she rammed the keys into the side of his leg. Dominick howled in pain, cursing her again, but he also staggered back. It was just enough for him to move the gun away from her head. Also enough for him to ease up on the chokehold. Ashlyn took advantage of that and dropped to the floor.

Even though she was gasping for air and her throat was throbbing, she swung out at him again with the keys, digging them into his other leg. As he roared with pain, their eyes met, and in that instant she saw that rage had tightened all the muscles in his face. There was pure hatred in his eyes. And she also saw something else.

That he was about to shoot her.

Dominick shifted, taking aim with his gun to do just that, and she knew at that range, he wouldn't miss.

The blast came, thick and loud. It echoed through the room. Through her head. And it was followed by a second shot, one just as loud as the first.

Ashlyn braced herself for the pain. But it didn't come. It took her a moment to realize that she hadn't been shot.

But Eli had been.

Eli was in the doorway of the bathroom, and there was blood on his shirt. God. *Blood.* But despite that, he still had his gun aimed at Dominick. He was bleeding, too, and it was spreading across the front of his shirt. Eli and he had exchanged shots, and both had been hit.

Groaning, Dominick turned and jumped out the window.

Escaping.

Eli took aim again, but it was too late. Dominick was gone.

Chapter Eighteen

Eli felt the burning and the pain in his arm and knew he'd been shot. Despite that, plenty of things had just gone right. Ashlyn hadn't been hurt, and Dominick hadn't managed to get to the baby.

Now Eli had to make sure things stayed that way, along with catching Dominick and making sure he paid for all the things he'd done. Things that could have left all of them dead and Cora in the hands of a killer.

"Cora!" Ashlyn practically shouted.

Despite the alarm on her face when she looked at his bloody shirtsleeve, she scrambled away from him to get to the window. No doubt because she thought that Cora and Gloria were out there where Dominick could still get to them.

Eli hurried to her, took hold of her and pulled her from the window. He also slapped off the lights so that Dominick wouldn't be able to see them.

And shoot them.

Because while Cora and Gloria weren't out in the yard, Dominick was.

"Gunnar has Cora and Gloria," Eli told Ashlyn, and even though she was still struggling to get away from him, he maneuvered her out of the bathroom and back into the hall where they wouldn't be in Dominick's line of sight.

It obviously took several seconds for his words to sink in, but Ashlyn finally stopped trying to fight him off, and blinking, she stared up at him. "Cora's all right?"

Eli nodded. "Gunnar texted me about five minutes ago. He went in through the bathroom window, got Gloria and the baby out, and took them to the cruiser. It's bullet-resistant," he reminded her. "Gloria has the baby on the floor of the car so Dominick can't see them. The hands are guarding them to make sure Dominick doesn't get close."

Her breath swooshed out, and she practically sagged against him. "Cora's all right," she said. "My baby's all right."

But her relief was very short-lived. Almost immediately, the alarm returned to her eyes, and Ashlyn's gaze slashed to his shirtsleeve.

"Oh God. You've been shot," she blurted out. "Dominick shot you."

"It's okay. *I'm* okay." Though Eli thought it was more than just a scratch, he had no intention of telling Ashlyn that. Not when she was so close to panicking.

Ashlyn volleyed her attention between his face and the wound, and she shook her head. "How soon can an ambulance get here?" So, she wasn't buying his *I'm okay*, and she eased up his sleeve to take a look.

"Soon. Kellan called for one, but it won't be able to get on the grounds until we're sure it's safe."

"Safe," Ashlyn repeated. "You mean not until Dominick is caught." She paused, her bottom lip trembling a little. Considering everything she'd just been through, that was a fairly mild reaction. However, he was betting that every nerve in her body was rattled right now. "You shot him."

Eli nodded. Then he silently cursed himself. "I should have gotten off a second shot so he couldn't get away. I should have killed him."

Apparently, Ashlyn wasn't the only one with rattled nerves, but it had cut him to the bone to see Dominick holding that gun to her head and hearing the man threaten to take Cora. It had also cleared Eli's mind in a very unexpected way. The fear had cut through the old wounds, their pasts, and it had made him realize just how much Ashlyn and Cora meant to him.

They meant everything to him.

Everything.

"You need an ambulance, and I need to see Cora," Ashlyn said, shifting his attention back to her. Not that it had strayed too far away, but Eli was keeping watch to make sure Dominick didn't try to get back in the house.

"Soon," Eli assured her.

Because he thought they could both use it, he brushed a kiss on her cheek. That's when he noticed the bruises already forming on her temple and throat. Both were reminders of what Dominick had done to her. That caused a whole new round of anger to slam through him.

"How soon will the ambulance be here?" she pressed, and Ashlyn ripped off part of his sleeve to form a makeshift tourniquet on his arm.

"After Kellan and the hands find Dominick and arrest him."

She looked up at him, and he saw her blink back tears. "They have to find him, Eli."

Yeah, they did. And while Eli was certain that would happen, he also knew that Ashlyn and he wouldn't be breathing easier until the man was in custody. As long as Dominick was out there, he could manage to escape and get away from the ranch. Maybe even get help and recover from his gunshot wound, and that meant he could try to come after Ashlyn and Cora again.

That sent a new round of anger through Eli. Ashlyn and Cora had been through enough, and he didn't want them having to live out their lives while keeping watch for a snake like Dominick.

"The danger has to end," Ashlyn said, her voice more breath than sound, and she put her arms around him, pulling him close to her.

He didn't have any trouble making the contact even tighter. He looped his good arm around her, and this time when he kissed her, it wasn't on her cheek. He really kissed her, pouring all his anger and relief into it. It helped. Well, it helped him, but it caused his wound to throb. That didn't make him let go. Just holding her like this gave him another of those realizations like the one he'd gotten when Dominick had her hostage.

Eli wanted Ashlyn and Cora in his life.

He was about to tell her that when his phone dinged with a text. "It's from Kellan," he told Ashlyn, and he read through the message. "No sign of Dominick yet, but Gunnar's going to pull the cruiser right up to the door. Kellan wants you and me to get in it. Then Gunnar can get us out of here."

Eli didn't add that his brother was concerned about

Dominick trying to double back and sneak into the house. Best not to put that idea in Ashlyn's head, especially when she already had enough bad memories and nightmare images there.

"I can see Cora," Ashlyn muttered. "And if there's a first aid kit in the cruiser, I can take care of your arm until you can see an EMT."

There was that, and Eli wanted to be closer to Cora so he could make sure she was safe. But Eli also knew this meant having Ashlyn go out into the open. Even if it would only be for a few seconds, it was still a risk. A risk that Kellan must have thought was worth taking. Maybe because Dominick was still close to the house?

Hell.

Eli hoped not, but if so, he would have to stay on guard and be ready. He watched as the cruiser drove up, moving as close to the house as the driver could get. The ranch hands hurried to flank the car, one on all four sides, and each of them was armed.

"Move fast," Eli told her.

Though the reminder wasn't necessary. The moment the front passenger's door opened, she took hold of Eli and started running. Ashlyn scrambled in first, moving to the middle of the seat next to Gunnar, who was behind the wheel. Eli got in right after Ashlyn.

The first thing Eli heard was Cora. The baby was making cooing sounds, and when he looked in the back seat, he saw the baby smiling as Gloria talked to her. Thank goodness Cora wasn't scared—though Eli could see plenty of fear on Gloria's face. However, there was relief on Ashlyn's.

Ashlyn, too, was smiling when she leaned over the

seat to kiss the baby, and Eli found himself smiling right along with them. Yeah, he definitely wanted them in his life and would figure out a way to make that happen as soon as they were all safe.

"The ambulance is just up the road," Gunnar explained. He glanced at the blood on Eli's arm and frowned. "Sorry that happened."

Eli shook his head. "It's nothing. Thanks for getting Gloria and Cora out of the house."

"Yes, thank you," Ashlyn echoed.

She was still leaning over the seat when Eli heard something else. Something he didn't want to hear.

"Watch out!" someone shouted. Kellan. "He's coming your way!"

Eli pivoted to the sound of his brother's voice, but instead of seeing Kellan, he spotted Dominick. The man was coming out of the house and running straight toward them. Kellan was on the side of the house. Also running. But he might not be able to intercept Dominick in time.

"Get down now," Eli ordered, and he hoped that Ashlyn and Gloria would listen.

Dominick was a mess with blood all over the front of his shirt, and he was staggering, but he still had a gun. A gun that he had pointed at the cruiser. Even though there was little chance a bullet would be able to get through, Eli didn't take any chances. Barreling out of the cruiser, he took aim.

And fired.

This time, he didn't hold back. He sent three shots straight into Dominick's chest. There was a startled look on Dominick's face as if he couldn't believe what'd just happened, but the look was gone in a flash. His expression went blank, and Dominick collapsed onto the ground.

Dead.

Eli was sure of that, but he kept his gun on the man as he hurried to him. He kicked away Dominick's gun, leaned down and touched his fingers to his neck. He was definitely gone.

"Sorry," Kellan said, running in behind Eli. "I spotted Dominick, but he got away from me. I didn't want to shoot because I wasn't sure if Ashlyn and you were still in the house."

Kellan stopped and cursed when he saw the blood on Eli. "Let me get the EMTs up here for you."

Eli didn't stop him from doing that, but right now his injury wasn't his main concern. Ashlyn was. She had no doubt watched as he'd gunned down Dominick, and Eli had to confirm she was okay.

He made sure he didn't wince in pain when he made his way back to her. Ashlyn must have sensed it, though, because she got out of the cruiser, and she forced him to sit on the seat.

"It's over," she said, not sounding as shaky as he'd thought she would. She stepped closer, standing between his legs and looking down at him. "Thank you."

He didn't want her thanks. Didn't deserve it. Because he hadn't stopped the danger that'd led them to this.

"I should have seen how unhinged Dominick was," he told her.

The look she gave him turned a little flat. "I think Dominick hid it well. Until tonight, that is. But he'll never be able to come after us again."

True, and neither would Waite. Not that Eli thought Waite was a threat now. Not with Dominick's money fueling him. Still, Eli wanted him to pay, too.

In the distance, he heard the sirens from the ambulance. It wouldn't be long before it arrived, and he couldn't see how he was going to talk Ashlyn and Kellan out of making him go to the hospital. Besides, he was pretty sure he needed stitches, and he'd need to be examined if only to stop Ashlyn from worrying about him.

"When you told me you were in love with me," he started, "I dismissed it."

She gave a heavy sigh. "It's okay. I understand."

That made him frown. "Well, you shouldn't understand, because I had no right to dismiss it. Not when I feel the same way about you."

He'd said those last words fast, just to make sure he got them all out before the ambulance got there. And even though he was certain that Ashlyn heard him, she didn't have the response he wanted.

She gave him another flat look. One that went on for several too-long moments. And then Ashlyn smiled.

"You're in love with me?" she asked.

Gunnar cleared his throat, obviously trying to remind him he was there, listening. Eli didn't care. He had a sudden, unexplainable urge to shout it from the rooftops, and he might just do that after he got stitched up. And after he kissed Ashlyn.

"I do love you," Eli told her, and he got busy with the kiss.

Eli pulled her down to him, easing her into his lap so he could do it the right way. He kissed her long and deep, and he didn't stop, not even when the ambulance pulled into the yard. He just kept kissing her until what he felt for her washed away some of the ugliness of the night. Heck, it was the cure for a lot of things, because he felt a whole lot better.

Ashlyn gave "better" a notch up. "Good. Because I'm still very much in love with you."

Their gazes connected, and they shared another smile. Another kiss. Eli hadn't thought there could be any more notching up, but he was wrong. Ashlyn took Cora when Gloria handed her to Ashlyn, and suddenly Eli had a beautiful, smiling baby in both their arms.

"Cora and I are a package deal," Ashlyn reminded him.

Eli didn't have to think how he felt about that. He knew. He gathered both Ashlyn and Cora close and kissed them both. Because this was one package deal that made everything perfect.

* * * * *

deep, and he didn't stop, not even when the ambulance pulled into the yard. He just kept kissing her until what he felt for her washed away some of the ugliness of the night. Heck, it was the cure for a lot of things, because he felt a whole lot better.

Ashlyn gave [illegible] "Good. Because [illegible] very much in love with you."

Their gazes connected, too, and they shared another smile. And a kiss. Eli hadn't thought there could be any more [illegible], but he was wrong. Ashlyn took a step [illegible] Cora [illegible] to Ashlyn, and suddenly Eli had a beautiful, smiling baby in both their arms.

"Cora and I are a package deal," Ashlyn reminded him.

Eli didn't have to think how he felt about that. He knew. He gathered both Ashlyn and Cora close and kissed them both. Because, yes, it was one package deal and it made everything perfect.

* * * * *

UNRAVELING JANE DOE

CAROL ERICSON

Chapter One

The smell of burning rubber assailed her nose and woke her with a jolt. Her head snapped up. Pain seared through her skull.

Her eyelids flew open. She blinked at the upside-down tree.

She clenched her teeth at the sound of a wheel spinning around and around, squealing with every turn. Her jaw throbbed.

The seat belt dug into her neck, and she reached down to tug on it. Her fingers crawled to the side of her head to probe the area that screamed with pain. The tips slid through strands of sticky hair.

She pulled her hand away and held it in front of her face. She tried to focus on the red streaks running down her arm. Blood. Her blood.

She swallowed and gagged. Swallowing and hanging upside down had its difficulties. She snorted out a laugh. People stuck on an amusement park ride must feel something like this—only this was no amusement park.

Her hand followed her seat belt to the latch. If she released too quickly, her head would bang against the roof of the car. It already hurt like hell. She didn't need any more injuries.

She braced one hand on the roof of the vehicle and

unsnapped the seat belt with her other hand. Her body slumped and curled in on itself in a fetal position as she rolled to her side.

She felt for the car door handle, but when she reached it, the handle wouldn't release. Her fingers scrabbled to find the button for the door locks, and she clicked them open. She tried the handle again. This time, the door opened but not all the way. Repositioning herself, she shoved at the door with her feet, the edge of it scraping through dirt and sand.

When just enough of a space opened, she started to slither through it. Voices above her caused her to freeze with her feet just outside the car.

A man's voice carried through the air, over the sound of the spinning wheel. "Should we go down?"

Another man answered him in accented English. "What do you think? I haven't seen a thing move since it crashed."

Terror seized her. Their words, their tone, their *something* pumped adrenaline through her system, revving up her sluggish, aching body.

She wriggled the rest of the way through the car door and crouched in the dirt beside the mangled, upended car. It lay at the bottom of a gully on the desert floor.

She peered over the top of the wreck at the ridge above and at two pairs of boots standing at the edge. The owners of those boots couldn't see her, and for some reason, she wanted to make sure they never did.

One pair of boots, black with silver tips that glinted in the sun, made a move, and several pebbles tumbled down the embankment.

The owner of the boots said, "We have to be certain."

"You go, man. I'm not going down there. What if the car explodes?"

"I'd rather be in a car explosion than face El Gringo Viejo and tell him we're not sure she's dead."

"I have an idea. You see that gasoline leaking?"

The smell of gasoline now permeated her nose. Why hadn't she noticed it before? The car could've gone up in flames at any time.

"Give me the cigarette, *cabron.* You're too chicken to get close enough."

If she ran now, they'd see her. Better to let them think she'd gone up in flames with the car. She coiled her body, her muscles quivering.

A few more pebbles rolled down as the man with the silver-tipped black boots ventured down the embankment sideways. He stopped, and she held her breath.

The other man laughed from above. "You missed."

Two seconds later, a fire whipped up on the other side of the car. Fueled by the gasoline, it roared to life.

Using the flames and smoke as cover, she crawled through the sand toward that upside-down tree she'd spied through the cracked windshield, now right-side up. Leaning against its rough bark, she drew her knees to her chest, willing herself to shrink into the bark. Willing the two men to stay away.

When the car exploded, a door sailed past her and black smoke billowed into the blue cloudless sky. She stayed put, folding her arms across her body, fingers digging into her biceps.

A hot breeze carried the two male voices toward her, but she couldn't make out their words this time over the crackling blaze. She squeezed her eyes shut and mumbled to herself, "Go away. Go away."

A car started—maybe not. A small explosion sent another flurry of debris skyward, and she covered her nose and mouth with her hands to block out the acrid smoke and ash.

Her head hurt. Her lungs hurt. Her ribs hurt. And still she sat. She sat as the car burned out behind her. She sat as a lizard skittered across her toes. She sat as the sun dipped behind the hills. She sat as feral eyes glowed at her through the darkness.

Finally, her muscles stiff and her throat parched, she peeled herself away from the tree and cranked her head around. Wisps of smoke still rose from the torched husk of the car. It crouched in the desert like some watchful creature.

She patted the pockets of her pants and pulled out a few pesos from the front and a knife with a fancy handle from the back. She hit the button on the side of the knife, and a shiny blade materialized. She just might need that. She retracted the blade and shoved it back into her pocket, stepping away from the tree and scanning the ground.

The light from the half-moon provided scant illumination, but she spotted some debris in the sand. She squatted and picked through some scraps of paper, empty cigarette packages, receipts and bits of paper and plastic bags.

She snatched up one piece of paper stirring in the faint breeze and flattened it out on her knee. Someone had sketched the face of a man with longish hair and glasses—just more trash. She swept it from her leg and scanned the ground for something useful.

The desert floor stared back at her with hooded eyes, giving up nothing.

She glanced up at the ridge where the two men had stood and discussed her demise. They'd probably left hours ago, but fear had kept her attached to that tree. She needed a way out of here, water, food.

But most of all, she needed to find out who she was.

ROB CLIMBED INTO his Border Patrol truck and slumped behind the wheel, leaving his door open. He massaged his temples and whispered, "What a day."

The hushed voice came from a place of reverence for the desert and its undercover creatures. He could shout at the top of his lungs and no human soul would hear him.

He sat for a moment, his hands resting on the steering wheel, soaking in the peacefulness. As a Border Patrol agent, he knew this stretch of the desert didn't always host serenity. He'd experienced firsthand the headless bodies, the shoot-outs and the drugs—always the drugs.

His fingers curled around the steering wheel. Drugs had ravaged his life. They didn't represent some inanimate object to him. He viewed drugs as some great evil that had become his personal enemy.

He'd never expressed it quite like that when he'd applied for a job with the Border Patrol. The agency probably would've dismissed him based on his psych eval if he had.

He loosened his death grip on the steering wheel and ran a hand through his hair. He didn't want to pollute the evening with thoughts of home.

Easing the door of his truck closed, he started the engine. The sound would scatter all the shy creatures and maybe even a drug dealer or two, although his survey of the border today probably already did that.

He buzzed down his window and wheeled the truck around. The truck bumped along the dirt of the access road until it hit the asphalt, which didn't provide a much smoother ride. He flicked on his brights. He didn't want to mow down anything out here, and it wouldn't be likely that he'd be blinding another driver at this time of night.

The warm breeze from the window caressed his face, and he inhaled the scents from the desert, subtle but distinct. His nostrils flared at an alien odor.

Despite the hot and dry conditions of the Sonoran Desert, fires didn't commonly occur due to the lack of combustible vegetation, but he'd definitely caught a whiff of burning rubber and gasoline. He pulled over and adjusted his rearview mirror, studying the landscape behind him.

The road had crested and the desert floor had fallen away, down a steep embankment. Scanning the space to the side of the road, Rob detected a stream of gray smoke curling toward the sky.

He threw the truck into Reverse and backed onto the shoulder, giving himself plenty of space between his tires and the edge of the ridge that fell away about fifteen feet.

He left his headlights on and grabbed the flashlight from his truck. He exited his vehicle, planting his boots on the shifting gravel. Peering over the side of the road, he aimed his flashlight in the area where he'd seen the smoke.

The beam of light picked out the skeleton of a car, burned down to bare bones. "Damn."

Torched cars did occasionally appear in this part of the desert. Sometimes car thieves dumped the fruits of their labor here after stripping them of usable parts. Sometimes coyotes got rid of their vehicles after transporting their human cargo across the border. And sometimes people had accidents.

Rob edged sideways down the embankment, wedging his boots in the dirt and rock with each step. He called out for the hell of it. "Anyone here?"

If anyone had been in that car, he or she would've perished in the fire. The car hadn't crashed that recently, so even if someone had survived the impact and the inferno, that person probably wouldn't have survived exposure to these harsh elements.

When he reached the car, he kicked at the frame with the toe of his boot. It collapsed with a squeal. Walking around the vehicle, he searched for the VIN, license plate and any other type of identifying information. He couldn't even tell what kind of car it had been.

As he turned toward the embankment leading back up to the road, a rustling sound stopped him in his tracks. He glanced over his shoulder. It could be anything.

He eyed the paloverde tree and a few scrubby bushes to the right of the car. He'd probably startled an animal holing up there. Running his flashlight over the vegetation, he squinted at the outlines of the tree's low branches. Something bigger than a longhorn sheep could be hiding out there, something as big as a person.

"Hello?" He started walking toward the tree. "Anyone there?"

Something decidedly human coughed, and a shape emerged from behind the tree.

"Are you all right? Is that your car?" He swept the beam of his flashlight over the figure.

A woman stepped forward, blinking in the light. She raised her arm, her hand gripping a knife, and said, "Take one more step and I'll gut you."

Chapter Two

Rob stumbled back, the light from the flashlight crisscrossing over the woman's body. His hand hovered over his gun holstered in his belt. He couldn't shoot an accident victim. She'd probably lost her senses out here alone.

His gaze darted past her. She *was* alone, wasn't she? Maybe he'd walked into some sort of ambush.

He flexed his fingers near the butt of his .45. "I'm not going to hurt you. Are you injured? Is that your car?"

"I'm fine. You can keep moving." She flashed the knife, and it glinted in his beam of light.

She'd clearly lost it. "Keep moving? No way. You're not fine. You're a bloody mess."

She touched her hair, clumped with blood, and then drew back her shoulders. "It's nothing."

"Look, ma'am, you don't have to be afraid. I'm a Border Patrol agent. My truck's on the road above." He jerked his thumb over his shoulder in case she'd forgotten the direction of the road.

"Border Patrol? What border?" Her eyes gleamed in the dark like some feral creature's.

He pulled his badge and ID from his pocket and extended his hand toward her. "Mexican border."

He couldn't tell in this light if she were Latina. Could that car have belonged to a coyote transporting people across the border? That would explain her skittishness. She didn't have an accent, but that didn't mean anything.

She darted forward and snatched the ID from his hand. Cupping it in her palm, she squinted at it.

He aimed his flashlight at her hand so she could see his ID.

She read aloud, "'Roberto Valdez.'"

He raised his right hand. "That's me. I can take you to the hospital right now, or if you don't want to ride with me, I can call the police, an ambulance."

"No cops." She threw the billfold containing his badge and ID back at him. It landed at his feet. "No cops. No ambulance. No hospital. I'm fine."

"Ma'am, I can't leave you out here. You'll die. It's miles from the nearest town. There's a hodgepodge collection of campers and RVs closer than town, but it's not safe there."

"I'm not going with you to the cops or hospital." She dropped the knife and put a hand to her throat. "Please. I—I don't think I'd be safe there."

He tilted his head. "Why not? Did you come across the border illegally? Did a coyote bring you?"

"What? No." She shook her head, and the tangled strands of her hair whipped back and forth. "Nothing like that. Please. I-it's my husband, my ex-husband. He's after me, and I'm afraid."

Rob swallowed. If she just lied to him, she'd picked the best lie to tug at his heartstrings.

He waved his arm toward the burned-out car. "Did he do this?"

"I think so. I think he caused the accident and then made sure the car went up in flames."

"Why didn't you go up in flames with it?"

"After the accident, I saw him coming for me, so I hid

behind the tree and clump of bushes. He set the car on fire and took off. He never saw me. He thinks I'm dead, and I want to keep it that way."

"If we call the police…"

"No cops!" She dipped down and scooped up the knife. "I swear, you'll have to shoot me with that gun you keep touching, or I'll run off into the desert and you can forget you ever saw me."

"I'm not going to shoot you, but I'm not going to let you run away, either. What's your name?"

"J-Jane."

He narrowed his eyes. Blatant lie. "Last name?"

"Doesn't matter."

"Okay… Jane." He held out his hand. "I'm Rob Valdez, and I'm gonna help you out."

She folded her arms. "Not by taking me to the hospital and calling the police. That's not going to help me."

"We'll figure something out. Let's get you out of this desert. I have water in the truck." Locking his gaze with hers, he ducked to pick up his badge and ID.

"Water?" Her body swayed to the side and she braced a hand against a branch of the paloverde tree.

"That's right. You must be parched." He inched closer to her, shuffling his boots in the sand.

"Water?" As the word left her lips, she crumpled to the ground.

Rob lunged forward. He placed one foot on top of the knife, driving it into the dirt just in case this was some kind of scam.

He crouched next to her and whistled as he touched the wound on the side of her head. No scam.

He swept his light across the ground to see if she had anything besides the knife and the clothes on her back. She didn't.

He pocketed the knife, placed the flashlight between his teeth and slid his arms beneath Jane's lithe frame. He pushed up, clasping her to his chest, and picked his way over the ground.

Trooping up the incline carrying dead weight, even though that dead weight was as light as a feather, was proving to be a challenge. He pumped his legs, digging his feet into the sand with each step. When he reached the top, he placed Jane on the ground and scrambled over the ridge. He scooped her up again and placed her in the passenger seat of the truck, snapping the seat belt across her body. He reclined the seat and checked her vitals.

He wouldn't call her pulse strong, but it beat steadily beneath his fingers. Her parched lips parted, and she released a soft sigh. Her dark lashes fluttered.

He held his breath, willing her to come to. He'd rather have her conscious and threatening him with that knife than out like this.

Reaching into the back seat, he grabbed the first-aid kit every Border Patrol vehicle carried. He flipped it open and snagged some gauze and antiseptic from two compartments. He lifted the top tray and pinched a clean cloth between two fingers. He soaked it with water from his bottle and dabbed the cut on Jane's head. Head wounds always bled all out of proportion to their seriousness, but this nasty gash had him worried.

He should just drive her straight to the hospital and let a professional take care of her. Even if her ex found her out, the cops could protect her.

His hands froze and he snorted. He knew better than anyone the fallacy of that misplaced belief. He finished cleaning the dried blood from her cut and applied some antiseptic.

Her breath quickened and her eyelids squeezed tighter.

"Jane?" he whispered in her ear, but it probably wouldn't do much good. If her name was Jane, his was Tarzan.

He wrapped some gauze around her head like a hippie headband to cover the injury in case her movement caused it to bleed again. Then he dumped some water on another clean cloth and pressed it against her lips.

She moaned and shifted in her seat.

"I've got you. You're safe. Wake up and drink some water."

She mumbled something and moved her arm.

"That's it. Come out of it."

Her eyes flew open, and she stared at him. Panic flooded her face. She jerked forward against the seat belt and lurched back against the restraint.

"You're all right. You're all right. Remember? I'm Border Patrol agent Rob Valdez. You passed out down there, and now you're in my truck."

Her hands flailed for a few seconds. "No police."

"I didn't call the police. I didn't call anyone." He held out the bottle of water. "I cleaned your wound. I did the best I could, but..."

"No hospital." She shook her head, gasped and then cradled one side of her face with her palm.

"Okay, no hospital, either, but you need to take it easy." He held the water to her lips. "Drink. You're dehydrated."

Closing her eyes, she gulped back the water, finishing almost half of the liquid. She shoved the bottle between her knees and wrapped both hands around it, denting the plastic.

Rob cleared his throat. "Is there someplace I can drop you? A friend? Relative? Bus station? I can drive you up to Tucson, if you like."

She opened one eye. "Tucson?"

"Isn't that where you were headed when you had the crash?" He'd just assumed that. *Jane* hadn't told him a whole helluva lot outside of the story of her abusive ex. He tilted his head. "Where were you headed? How'd you wreck that car?"

He should've been asking these questions before he got her in his truck.

"I wasn't running toward anything or anyone." She put a hand to her throat, and her voice hitched. "I was just running away."

"You don't have any friends or relatives in this area? No bags? No money? No car?"

"Everything burned up in that inferno." She swept her hair, clumped with blood, from her cheek where a single tear sparkled. "I'm so tired, so weak."

Rob patted her knee and pushed up to his feet. What kind of brute was he, interrogating her on this desert road when she needed food and meds and rest?

"I can take you back to my place for now, so you can get your bearings. Is that all right?"

"How's your family going to feel about it? I don't want to put anyone out."

"I don't have a family—at least not one I live with. If you'd rather stay with a family, I can probably drop you off with my buddy and his wife." He scratched his chin. "I *think* that would be okay."

Whom was he kidding? Clay Archer played by the rules, even if his wife, April, didn't. Clay would call the cops for sure.

"Your buddy? Is he a Border Patrol agent, like you?"

"He is."

She held out a hand. "That's okay. I trust you. I mean, you rescued me. I just need a day to regroup."

"Of course, yeah, regroup. I have more water at my

place and some leftover food, and even some ibuprofen, which seems to be missing from my first-aid kit."

He closed the door of the truck and went around to the driver's side. Sliding behind the wheel, he glanced at the petite woman in the seat next to him, her dark lashes creating two perfect crescents on her cheeks.

Maybe it would be better if he didn't call his coworkers on this one. They were always telling him how impulsive he was, and this would give them more ammunition.

He studied Jane's profile, convinced she was faking sleep, and started the truck.

The woman had to be about a 110 soaking wet. He'd feed her, let her get some rest and get her bearings.

How much trouble could she be?

THE BORDER PATROL AGENT... Rob...prodded her shoulder. "Are you awake? Conscious?"

She stretched her arms and rubbed her eyes. She'd been awake the whole way but didn't want to face any more of his questions. How could she? She didn't have any answers.

She'd learned she was somewhere between the Mexican border and Tucson, but how she got here, she hadn't a clue. Scratch that. She'd been driving that car when it crashed. She hadn't even thought to grab anything from the car before she scrambled out of it.

Now she had nothing...except that knife, which he'd taken. She slid a gaze at the earnest young man beside her. Well, nothing except this hot Latino with his soulful dark eyes and ready sympathy.

"Feeling any better?"

"Not much." She clapped a hand on the back of her neck and twisted her head from side to side. "I'm feeling stiff."

"This is my place." He pointed out the windshield as they pulled into the driveway of a small house with lights burning in the front windows. "I'll get you some ice, ibuprofen, food and water—in whatever order you want—and then you can make your plans in the morning."

"Water, pain meds and ice first." She finished off the bottle of water still clutched in her hands. Her plans for the morning swam in her head in a misty fog with all the other confusing thoughts—including her identity.

Jane—what an idiot. Why didn't she just call herself Jane Doe? Rob didn't believe her for a second. What else hadn't he believed?

At least he hadn't run to the cops. She'd felt sure a Border Patrol agent would be duty-bound to call the police and report the accident and its strange victim.

His face had softened when she'd told him the story about the violent ex-husband. She cringed a little inside when she saw how her lie had affected him… But it could be the truth.

Maybe one of those men who'd planned to kill her by setting fire to the car was an ex. She couldn't remember their words right now, but they'd come to her later—unless she had some sort of weird short-term memory loss where she couldn't remember even recent events.

She remembered Rob Valdez, though, and his kindness. Her gaze flicked over him. And the way that shirt from his green uniform hugged his shoulders and tightened across his chest when he moved. She couldn't be too messed up if she could still appreciate a handsome man in uniform.

She jumped when he put his hand on her arm. His touch sent some sort of electric current through her system, or it made her nervous.

He snatched his hand back. "I'm sorry. Did I hurt you?"

"No. I'm still on edge."

"If you're nervous about coming into my house, I can check with my coworker and his wife. You might feel more comfortable there."

She doubted she'd feel more comfortable with another Border Patrol agent. She couldn't possibly get lucky a second time with a law enforcement official who wouldn't run straight to the cops.

"It's not that. I'm still nervous about my ex…and what he did to me." As she threw that last bit in there, Rob's eyes turned into liquid velvet. His pumped-up frame housed a soft heart—and she had to take advantage of that soft heart right now, no matter how wretched it made her feel.

He snatched his keys from the ignition, and all that softness morphed into hard lines and a clenched jaw. "I can imagine, but you'll be safe here."

And she believed him—not only that she'd be safe with him but that he *could* imagine. Of course, what did she know? How could she read people when she couldn't remember any people in her own life?

"I'll help you out." He clambered from the truck with his equipment belt squeaking and a backpack slung over one shoulder.

By the time he came around to her side of the truck, she'd unlatched her seat belt and grabbed on to the water bottle—her single possession at this point besides her dirty and tattered clothing.

He opened the door and held out his hand. "Hang on."

She did hold on to his hand while he guided her out of the truck and walked her up to his house. The blue door with the light above it stood out against the beige stucco of the house. The door fitted into an arched entryway that led to a courtyard with potted cactus and chairs gathered around a wood-burning potbellied stove. He wouldn't have need of that during what must be summer.

She placed a hand over her heart. She didn't even know the season, but the intense heat marked it for summer.

"Are you all right?"

"You're a kind person."

A flush edged into his face just beneath his mocha skin, and he snorted. "Kind? Okay."

They crossed the courtyard, and he unlocked the front door. The tile floors and adobe walls created a cool cocoon, and she released a long breath.

Rob dropped his stuff on a bench in the foyer and brushed past her as he strode into the living room. He gathered some throw pillows on the couch and bunched them up on one side. As he patted the cushion, he said, "Sit right here. I'll get you some cold water and ice for your head."

She sank to the couch, propping her arm on top of the pillows. "Can I use your restroom?"

"Of course." He smacked his forehead with the heel of his hand. "What am I thinking? Second door on your right down the hall. Do you need help?"

"I think I can make it." She rose to her feet and headed for the hallway. She pushed open the door of the bathroom and held her breath as she squared herself in front of the mirror.

She sucked in a breath at the reflection that stared back at her. She flicked a strand of light brown hair as her brown eyes surveyed the unfamiliar face. No, not unfamiliar. Had there been a spark of recognition at the unexceptional features? Brown hair, brown eyes, slightly upturned nose. Nothing that would make her stand out in a crowd—she liked that.

She patted the clumped hair on the side of her head and gritted her teeth as she traced the bandage Rob had wrapped around her head.

He tapped on the door. “Everything okay?”

Oh, yeah. Just getting acquainted with my face.

Inserting a finger beneath the gauze, she said, “Should we take off this bandage?”

“I can replace that with something better. I have a whole first-aid station out here when you’re ready.”

She flung open the door and he jerked back. “I’m ready.”

“Worse than you expected?” He cocked his head.

“Better, a lot better.” She followed him into the living room and took her place in the little nest he’d fashioned for her on one side of the couch.

He’d arrayed bottles, bandages, water and an ice pack on the coffee table in front of her.

“Let’s replace that bandage. I can do a better job now.” He sat beside her and unwound the gauze from her head. He dabbed the edge of a wet towel on her wound, cleaning more blood from her scalp.

As he applied more antiseptic, she flinched.

“Sorry.”

When he finished with the bandage, he offered her two ibuprofen cupped in his palm. She downed them with the water.

“Now you need some food.”

Her gaze shifted from his face to the small kitchen behind him. “Don’t go to any trouble.”

“You won’t let me take you to the hospital. I can’t let you starve.” He jumped up and swept up several items from the table. “No trouble, either. I have some leftover albondigas soup and half a turkey sandwich I swear I didn’t touch.”

"That sounds good, but what are you eating?" She would've killed for a sandwich this afternoon, but she'd gotten used to the hunger clawing at her stomach.

As he walked into the kitchen, he glanced over his shoulder. "I ate dinner hours ago. You do realize it's almost midnight?"

She didn't know much, but she'd noticed the time when she got into his truck. It had been light outside when the car crashed.

"Just want to make sure I'm not stealing your leftovers."

"Not at all." He ducked into the fridge and pulled out a bag with one hand and a plastic container with the other. He tipped the container of the soup back and forth. "I'll heat this up."

She toed off her canvas shoes, dirty and filled with sand, and curled one leg beneath her. Releasing a long breath, she relaxed her shoulders for probably the first time since she'd awakened in that car. She didn't want to think about tomorrow. Didn't want to think about who she was and why two men were trying to kill her.

The beep of the microwave penetrated her thoughts, and she sat forward, her mouth watering at the spicy aroma of the soup.

After clinking around in the kitchen for a few minutes, Rob emerged carrying a tray. He set it on the coffee table in front of her and even shook out the cloth napkin and placed it on her lap.

"What service, but I feel guilty." She waved a spoon at him.

"Don't worry about me." He backtracked to the kitchen and grabbed a bottle of beer from the fridge and twisted off the cap. "This is all I need right now. It had been a rough day even before I spied your car off the road."

She paused in the middle of stirring the soup, the little whirlpool in the liquid mimicking her mind. "You saw the crash from the road?"

"I saw the smoke. I know that piece of desert like the back of my hand." He took a swig of beer. "I'd offer you one, but I don't think alcohol is a good idea in your condition."

He had no idea. "Don't think so, either. Water's fine."

"Can I ask you what happened out there? Was someone chasing you? You lost control?" He'd sat down in the chair across from her, rolling the bottle between his hands.

"Yes." She blew on a spoonful of soup. Better to stay as close to the truth as possible.

"Did your ex see the car go over?"

"I think so." She pressed two fingers against her throbbing temple. "I don't remember that much about the crash and the aftermath."

"And he just left you there?" Rob dragged a fingernail through the damp label on his bottle. "Damn."

"He must have." She lifted one shoulder and slurped up some soup.

"Where were you coming from? Where do you live?"

She squeezed her eyes closed. "I'd rather not talk about it. Is that okay?"

"Sure, sure." He tipped his head. "How's the soup?"

"Delicious." She scooped up another spoonful of veggies and tasty broth. "Did you make this?"

"No. A woman who owns a restaurant in town always makes up a batch for me because I told her it was just like my *abuela*'s."

"Are you from… Tucson?"

"LA, originally." His hand tightened on the beer bottle

for a second. “I moved to Paradiso when I got hired on with the Border Patrol.”

“Paradiso?”

“That’s the town we’re in now. You must’ve seen the signs for it on the road up from…wherever.”

She nodded so hard, a shaft of pain skewered her skull. She pushed the soup aside and dug into the sandwich. Maybe if she kept her mouth full, Rob wouldn’t ask her any more questions.

He let her eat in peace as he finished his beer, and when she popped the last of the sandwich into her mouth, he made a move for the tray.

Putting a hand on his arm, she said, “I’ll do it. I need to move from this spot.”

“If you say so.” He carried his empty bottle into the kitchen.

She pushed up from the couch and dropped her napkin onto the plate. Then she reached up to stretch and bent over the coffee table to pick up the tray.

Rob called from the kitchen. “Who’s Rosalinda?”

She almost sent the dishes crashing down. “What?”

He reached behind him and rubbed his back. “That tattoo on your back. Who’s Rosalinda?”

Chapter Three

She froze, gripping the tray with both hands, wanting to drop it and tug down her shirt. Instead she composed her expression, popped up and spun around. "Sh-she was a friend of mine who died. All of us, her particular friends, got her name tattooed on our backs."

"That's quite a tribute."

"She was murdered." She snapped her mouth shut. Why was she throwing out all these details? It might make her story more believable but easier to debunk—not that Rob Valdez would be debunking anything about her. She'd be out of his wavy, dark hair tomorrow.

"I'm sorry." He parked himself in front of the sink and rinsed out the plastic soup container.

The air crackled between them. She knew he had questions on his lips, but he knew by now she'd shut him down.

Was her name Rosalinda? Did people tattoo their own names on their bodies?

She delivered the tray to the kitchen, and he snatched the dishes from it and ran them under the water.

"I have three bedrooms in this place. One of the extra rooms is an office and the other is a spare bedroom. You're welcome to sleep there. The door has a lock on it."

Leaning her back against the counter, she folded her hands behind her. "I trust you."

His eyebrows quirked over his nose for a split second. "You shouldn't be so trusting."

"Of you?" She pressed a hand against her stomach. Had she totally misread Rob Valdez? Being in law enforcement didn't automatically make him a good guy. Maybe he'd been so accommodating about not calling the police because he wanted to…take advantage of her in some way. Who knew he had her here? Nobody.

"Sorry." He grabbed a dish towel and waved it in the air like a white flag. "I didn't mean to freak you out. You have nothing to worry about from me. I'm just saying, in general, you've been very trusting tonight—except for the part where you pulled a knife on me."

"Not putting my faith in anyone all day almost got me killed out there in the desert. I figured if I were going to trust anyone, it would be a Border Patrol agent."

"That makes sense. I'm glad it was me."

"Me, too." And she wasn't even talking about the way his shirt stretched across the muscles of his back as he washed the dishes, or even the fact that he was washing dishes. Rob Valdez possessed a calmness that inspired the same in her. She didn't know who she was or who was after her, she'd survived a car crash and a day in the desert without food or water, and yet she'd managed to chow down some food and felt ready for bed…sleep.

"Can I—" she plucked the blood-and-dirt-stained T-shirt from her body "—shower?"

"I'll get you a towel and one of my T-shirts. If you want to give me your stuff, I can stick it in the washing machine." He reached out and tugged on the hem of her ripped shirt. "Can't do much about that."

That rip had exposed the tattoo on her back, but at

least it had given her a clue to her identity. Maybe she'd wake up tomorrow morning and remember everything. Maybe she had a frantic husband or boyfriend somewhere.

Her gaze slid to Rob, still in possession of her T-shirt. Then she'd end this interlude and be on her merry way. Merry way with two guys out to kill her?

Tomorrow morning, she'd try to remember what they'd said, but now she just wanted sleep.

"I'll probably just toss it when I get…home, but yeah, putting on some clean clothes tomorrow would help a lot."

He released the shirt, a flush rising from his chest. "I'll get that towel. You can use the same bathroom you were in before."

"Thanks. I really appreciate everything you've done tonight. You didn't have to do anything, especially when I brandished that knife at you."

"I couldn't leave you there, and that knife?" He winked at her. "I could've disarmed you and taken you down at any time."

He pivoted and exited the kitchen. She watched his departure through narrowed eyes, his broad shoulders and pumped-up arms lending truth to his claim. Despite his caring nature and surface geniality, it would be a mistake to underestimate Rob.

She dried the dishes he'd left in the dish drainer and was putting away the last one when he returned.

"You didn't have to do that."

"I'm not as bad off as I look. I was wearing my seat belt."

"But the car was upside down, wasn't it? I could tell that even from its condition." He shook his head. "You're lucky to be alive."

She shivered and folded her arms. "I am."

He gestured behind him. “I put a towel and one of my T-shirts in that bathroom. There’s soap and shampoo, if you think you can wash around the bandage.”

“I’ll do that later.” She grabbed the plastic water bottle he’d given her in the car and slid open his trash receptacle.

He jerked forward. “You don’t need to do that. I recycle. I have a bin in the back.”

Could the guy be any more perfect?

“Admirable, but you forgot this one.” She plucked his beer bottle out of the trash and set it on the counter next to the water bottle.

“Oh, thanks. Everything’s locked up for the night, so I’ll be in my bedroom if you need anything else.”

She could think of quite a few things she’d want from Rob, but none was appropriate for a crash survivor who didn’t even know her own identity. She squeezed past him out of the kitchen. “Thanks.”

When she made it to the bathroom, she stripped off her clothes and dropped them to the floor. Facing the mirror naked, she studied her body for any more tattoos or identifying marks.

She discovered tan lines from a bikini, and a few more bumps and scratches from the crash. Her toes sported purplish polish, and although no such color tipped her fingernails, they looked neat. So, she probably wasn’t a homeless person. She skimmed her hands over her forearms and wrists—no needle tracks.

She twisted around to try to get a look at the Rosalinda tattoo. She caught the tail end of a flourish with a rose. She’d have to get ahold of a hand mirror to see it completely.

She cranked on the water and stepped into the warm spray, wincing as it hit her sore body. Did she want to reclaim the identity of a person who had people out to kill her?

Those guys believed she'd died in the crash, or at least the fire. She'd be safe as long as they maintained that belief.

She couldn't have Rob or anyone else plastering her picture anywhere or looking into any missing persons reports—not yet, anyway. She needed more information before she could step back into what was obviously a dangerous existence.

She might just hang out in Paradiso while she investigated. If Rob had friends here, she could get a job without ID. She had to support herself until her memory returned.

And if it never did?

She could forge a new identity. She could start life anew in Paradiso...with Rob Valdez as her first friend.

THE FOLLOWING MORNING, Rob plunged his hand into the pockets of Jane's pants. Empty. Why had she had a knife in her pocket? It must've been in her pocket, or she'd grabbed it when she escaped from the car. But why grab a knife and not a purse with your ID and money?

To protect herself against the violent ex?

He tossed the olive green pants into the washing machine and then shook out the torn T-shirt. He fingered the label that claimed its origin as Mexico. Lots of clothes were made in Mexico.

He dropped the shirt in the machine with the pants. That was all she had.

He added a few more clothes to the wash and strolled into the kitchen. He'd let Jane sleep and put on some coffee.

He had other reasons for letting her sleep in. He grabbed a plastic bag from a drawer and picked up the water bottle she'd drunk from last night, pinching the neck between two fingers. He dropped the bottle into the bag.

It might be a little late to check Jane's fingerprints, as she could've stabbed him in his sleep last night, but he deserved to know whom he had in his house. If she'd committed a crime anywhere, she'd be in the database. If not, he'd be back to square one—housing a woman who was lying about her identity.

If she had a violent ex-husband after her, he could understand her hesitance, but if she trusted him enough to stay here, she should be able to trust him with her real name.

He sealed the bag and stuffed it into his backpack. Pulling a chair up to his kitchen table, he dragged his laptop in front of him. When he launched a search engine, he entered *Rosalinda murder.*

He clicked on a few promising articles but, after fifteen minutes, gave up on finding a murder case involving a girl named Rosalinda. He'd need a last name, a city.

Jane would never give him that info. The only reason she'd told him about her friend was because he'd spotted that tattoo. He dragged a hand through his hair and hunched over the laptop.

Why did he care? She'd be gone this morning, and he'd chalk it up to a strange encounter—one of many in his life. He'd keep it to himself. He should've reported that crash and burned-out car, but he understood and sympathized with people who wanted to stay beneath the radar, especially women on the run from domestic violence.

As he heard the water run in the bathroom, he wiped out his search history and brought up his email. He pushed back from the table and stuck his head down the hallway.

He called out. "How are you doing this morning?"

She shouted over the running water. "I feel okay. I appreciate the water and ibuprofen you left on the nightstand. Are my clothes done?"

He edged closer to the bathroom door and placed a hand against it. "Not yet. Wash is almost done, and then I'll put them in the dryer. I'll get some breakfast together."

Without waiting for a reply, he returned to the kitchen and broke some eggs in a bowl. He mixed them with some milk, dashed some pepper in there and dumped them into a frying pan sizzling with butter.

"Smells good." Jane wedged her hip against the counter, tugging at the hem of his T-shirt, which—even though it hit her midthigh—had never looked so good.

"Just some scrambled eggs and coffee." He stirred the eggs. "Toast?"

"I can do the toast." She took two steps into the kitchen, and he immediately felt her presence engulf him.

For a petite woman, she had an overwhelming presence. At least for him.

Still prodding the eggs in the pan, he reached across the counter, flipped up the lid on the bread box and grabbed a loaf of wheat. "You can use this. Do you take cream or sugar with your coffee? I don't have cream, but you can dump some milk in there."

"Black."

He tapped the spatula on the edge of the pan. "You can help yourself to the coffee."

She reached around him and poured out two cups of steaming, fragrant java.

He scooped the eggs onto plates and carried them from the kitchen, relieved to escape the close quarters with Jane. As he put the plates on the table, the buzzer from the washing machine went off. "That's your laundry. You can start eating without me, if you want."

He strode into the laundry room and transferred the clothes from the wash to the dryer. When he returned to the kitchen, she'd placed silverware, napkins and their coffee on the table.

"The toast just popped up. Butter and jam or just butter?"

"Just butter for me. I don't even know if I have jam."

She brought the toast to the table, as he sipped his coffee.

"Why are you waiting on me? You're the accident victim." He took the plate of toast from her and pulled out a chair. "Sit."

She touched her bandaged head. "I feel fine, except that my head throbs when the ibuprofen wears off."

"You might need stitches." He held up a hand. "You should see your doctor when you get home."

"Maybe I don't want to go home." She crunched into her toast, and a shower of crumbs fell onto her plate.

"You can't hide from him forever."

"Really?" She speared a clump of eggs on her plate. "Do you think you could find me a job in Paradiso?"

"A job." He sputtered up his coffee. "Here?"

"Seems like a good place to lie low for a while. Maybe you know someone who could, you know, hire me off the books for a bit just so I could make a little money."

The thought of Jane staying in Paradiso sent a cascade of emotions tumbling through his system, but the ones that affected his body got the jump on the ones that affected his mind, and he blurted out, "Yeah, I do."

"You do?" She scooted up in her seat, wrapping her hand around her coffee cup. "Who? Where?"

"It's nothing fancy, but the woman who makes the

soup you had last night runs a small café in the middle of town and her niece is heading back to college and can't help her out anymore." Why was he dragging Rosie into this? "Do you have any experience in food service?"

"I do. I worked in fast food in high school and did some bartending in college." Her light brown eyes widened for a second, and then she rushed on. "I'd be happy to help your friend out with her business, and if she needs to get rid of me when her niece comes back, no problem."

"We'll go see her today." Rob shoved some toast in his mouth to keep himself from offering her anything else. At least if she stayed, he'd have some time to find out her real story.

As if to avoid questions, Jane kept the conversation through breakfast light and superficial.

After wolfing down most of her food, she waved a fork at him. "You're not in uniform. Do you have to work today?"

"Not until later." He eyed her hair tousled around the bandage and a small bruise high on her cheekbone. "Are you sure you don't need medical attention?"

"Why?" She clicked her coffee mug onto the table. "Do I look like I do?"

"You look..." He was going to say she looked even more appealing than she had last night, but his big mouth had already gotten him into enough trouble. "You look amazingly well after walking away from that accident and spending the day in the desert."

She patted her head. "I feel fine and so grateful to have gotten away from...my ex."

The buzzer from the dryer in the laundry room saved him from analyzing why she paused before mentioning her ex-husband—but he'd come back to that.

He jumped up from the table. “Your clothes are done. You can take a shower, and I’ll take you to Rosie’s.”

“She’s the woman with the café?”

“That’s right.”

“Thank you so much.” Jane rubbed her nose with the back of her hand. “I’m glad you stopped.”

“I don’t know what you thought you were going to do out there at night by yourself with just a knife.”

“I—I must’ve been stunned, disoriented.” She sipped her coffee and her eyes met his over the rim. “Where is that knife?”

His heart stuttered in his chest. He had no intention of arming his strange guest. Of course, she could’ve grabbed a kitchen knife at any time last night and stabbed him through the heart—if she’d wanted to.

He jerked his thumb over his shoulder. “I think I left it in my truck. Why’d you have it?”

“Excuse me?” She folded her hands on the table like an innocent schoolgirl.

She always answered a question with a question to buy time. He didn’t need the academy to teach him that—he’d lived it with his *familia*.

“The knife. Why did you grab a knife, of all things, when you escaped from the burning car? Why not grab your purse? Your phone?”

“I didn’t grab the knife. It was in my pocket.” She slurped the dregs of her coffee. “Protection.”

Man, she was good.

“You don’t need protection here.”

Her jaw hardened. “I appreciate that, but I’d still like my knife back… Sentimental value.”

“Sure.” He raised his hands as if in surrender. “I didn’t mean I was keeping it forever. You can get it when we go out to the truck.”

"I can wait. I don't need it now." She laughed, which snapped the wire of tension stretched between them. "Point me to the laundry room, and I'll get my clothes."

"Through the kitchen." He leveled a finger at the slatted door between the kitchen and the laundry room.

She gathered the plates on the table, including his, and placed them in the sink on her way to the laundry. "Thanks for the breakfast."

Several seconds later, she emerged, clutching her pants and T-shirt to her chest. "The sooner I shower and dress, the faster I can get out of your hair."

"Happy to help."

Nodding, she sidled out of the kitchen and turned the corner to the hallway.

When he heard the door snap close and the water start, Rob let out a long breath. He didn't know what to make of Jane. Should he be foisting her onto Rosie?

He'd let Rosie make the determination. He had faith in her ability to judge someone's character—at least more faith than in his at the moment. Being near Jane scrambled his senses for some reason.

Less than fifteen minutes later, Jane emerged from the bathroom. Her wet hair lay in tangled waves over her shoulders.

Rob jumped up from his laptop. "I'm sorry. I should've put out a comb and some hair products for you."

She shrugged. "You can be excused. You're a bachelor…aren't you?"

"Look at this place." He swept his arm to the side, taking in the neat room, every pillow and book in place, and his face warmed as Jane cocked her head.

"Doesn't look like any bachelor pad I've ever seen."

"I'm kind of a neat freak, but you won't find many feminine touches or niceties in here." He marched past her. "However, I do have sisters, and they usually need an army of products and a ton of time to make themselves presentable."

She tugged on the ends of her wet locks. "Not very presentable, huh?"

He glanced over his shoulder, his face heating up even more. "I didn't mean that. You look amazing for being in that car accident yesterday. How's your head?"

"I think it looks better without the bandage—less severe, and I can cover it with my hair. It feels fine."

She wouldn't tell him if it didn't. He swept into his bathroom and grabbed some hair products and other toiletries. He carried out an armful and dumped them on the vanity of the guest bathroom.

When he turned, he almost plowed into Jane standing in the doorway. "Help yourself."

"Thanks. I'll see if I can look more…presentable."

She came out the second time, bunching the ends of her hair into her fists. "I guess I'll leave it curly."

"Looks fine. Can't even see the wound on your head."

"That's crazy that such a small cut could cause so much…blood."

"Head wounds bleed." He closed up his laptop. "Are you ready?"

She tucked the ripped hem of her shirt into her pants. "I am now. I hope your friend Rosie isn't picky."

He hoped Rosie didn't think he was crazy. They walked out to the Border Patrol truck, his own truck parked on the street in front of his house. He opened the door for her and helped her in with a guiding hand on her back, which stiffened at his touch.

If her ex had abused her, he could understand her jitters, but that still remained an *if* in his mind. A lot of her story didn't add up.

He scooted behind the wheel and she said, "My knife?"

Yeah, a lot of things didn't add up.

Reaching beneath the seat, he said, "I think I stashed it here."

His fingers traced the edge of the knife's handle, and he pushed it farther under the seat. "It's not here. I'll have a more thorough look later. Is that okay?"

She snapped her seat belt and gripped the strap with two hands. "Yeah, sure."

On the ride to Rosita's, Jane peppered him with questions about the town. When she'd gotten her fill, she slumped in her seat. "You know a lot for being relatively new here."

"I made it my business to find out everything I could about Paradiso. I probably know more than some natives. You know how that goes."

She nodded. "I do."

He slid a gaze in her direction and then pointed out the windshield. "That's it."

"Cute."

He pulled in front of the café, and before he could get Jane's door, she'd hopped out and stood in front of the restaurant with her hands on her hips.

"Looks closed."

"She opens for lunch, but I know she's here." He raised an eyebrow. "Chickening out?"

"It's a restaurant, not a roller coaster." She charged past him and yanked open the front door.

He followed her into the cool confines of the tile-floored café with framed photos of Pancho Villa on the walls.

He called out, "Rosie? It's Rob Valdez. Are you here?"

The grandmotherly woman bustled from the back,

patting the long braid, streaked with gray, that wrapped around her head. "Rob, it's too early for *desayuna*."

"I'm not here to eat, Rosie." He nodded toward Jane, twisting her fingers in front of her. "I have a…friend, Jane, who's looking for a job—short term. She's in a little trouble, Rosie."

Rosie's warm brown eyes turned to Jane, assessing her from head to toe. Her face broke into a smile. "*Sí, sí. Puedo ayudar.* I can help. Have you had some experience, *mija*?"

Jane smiled back, the expression lighting up her face. Then she broke into fluent Spanish that put his to shame.

Chapter Four

Her lips were moving faster than her brain and her brain was freaking out, but when Rosie responded to her in Spanish, Jane kept the smile plastered to her face.

How did she know Spanish so well? The mirror had shown her paler skin than Rob's, but that didn't mean anything. She could be half-Latina. The Rosalinda tattooed on her back? Maybe that *was* her name, a family name.

She held up one hand and said in English, "I'm a little rusty. Do you mind continuing in English?"

Rosie chuckled and nudged Rob with her elbow. "She's being polite, Rob. Her Spanish is better than yours."

Rob's eyes narrowed as they assessed her. "It is, isn't it?"

Jane swallowed and turned to Rosie. "I do have another favor to ask of you. As I explained to you, I had to leave my situation quickly and I'm trying to keep a low profile. That means I don't have any of my credit cards or any cash. Would you be willing to pay me in advance so that I can get a motel room and maybe a few things to wear?"

Rosie's bright eyes flicked from her to Rob. "I thought you and Rob..."

Rob cut off Rosie with a sharp cough. "Jane *is* my

friend. Of course, you're staying with me, Jane. I thought I made myself clear."

"Rob is a very good man—the best." Rosie folded her hands and held them beneath her chin. "I know he will help you."

Rob smacked his hand on the countertop, probably wondering how he'd gotten in so deep. "I have a few things to do before I report to the station, so I'll leave you ladies to get ready for the lunch crowd. Thanks, Rosie. Good luck, Jane."

When the door closed behind Rob, Rosie asked, "Are you a friend of Rob's from LA?"

Los Angeles? That was big and sprawling enough to cover all situations.

"Yes, we're friends from LA."

Rosie shook her head. "Such a sad situation for him, but he's a strong man."

"He is." Jane bit her bottom lip. Had his wife left him? Was he in witness protection? Did his dog die?

"I'm glad you're here, Jane." Rosie brushed her hands together. "I'll explain what I need, and you can let me know if you have any questions."

For the next few hours, Jane wiped down tables and plastic menus, refilled the condiments at each station, prepped little plastic baskets for chips by dropping a sheet of paper in each one and stacking them, and even helped out Sal the cook in the kitchen.

Her head still throbbed a little and her memories were as elusive as ever, but this job had given her a purpose for now and that was what she needed—along with money, clothes, an ID. At least she had a place to stay.

She wouldn't hold Rob to that promise made for Rosie's benefit. Maybe the advance Rosie gave her would be enough to get into a motel.

She knew she couldn't stay in this town forever, pretending to be someone she wasn't, someone without an identity, someone without a home or family. But the thought of delving into her past frightened her. She'd be walking right into a murderous plot.

Paradiso could be her jumping-off point, a place from which to launch an investigation of her identity. And maybe Rob Valdez could help her.

"Two minutes until opening." Rosie stood in the middle of the floor, hands on her ample hips. *"Estás lista?"*

"I'm ready." Jane used the corner of a white towel to rub an imaginary spot on one of the tabletops. "Let 'em in."

Rosie unlocked the door and flipped the sign to Open. "It's a slow stream at first, but then we get the employees from the pecan processing plant and there's a rush."

"Bring 'em on, Rosie."

Jane handled her first few tables as if she'd been born to it. Maybe she was a waitress—with people out to kill her.

The lunch rush had her hopping, and she reconsidered the notion that she'd been a waitress in her previous life as she forgot items and spilled iced tea all over.

Rosita's did a brisk take-out business, and a line of customers had formed at the counter to pick up their orders.

Jane's gaze flicked over the line of people, and when a man yelled out that he wanted extra chips with his order, her blood ran cold in her veins. That voice.

With trembling hands, she delivered the salsa to her table and scurried back to the kitchen, keeping her head down. She pressed a hand against the butterflies in her belly as she leaned against the food prep counter.

The man who'd yelled out for food sounded like one

of the guys who'd set her car on fire. Why would he still be in this town? She wiped her sweaty palms on the pants covering her thighs. She'd imagined it. What had she really heard of that man's voice?

She ducked her head to peer through the window from the kitchen to the dining room. She hadn't seen the men at the scene of the accident and couldn't identify them, which put her at a distinct disadvantage. She remembered the black boots with the silver tips, but any number of people could be wearing those.

"Taking a break?" Anna, the other waitress, backed into the kitchen, her hands clutching two empty plates. "It can get hectic. If you need a breather from the dining room, you can package some of these to-go orders."

"I-if that's okay." Jane surveyed the containers of food crowding the countertop. Even if the voice didn't belong to one of the men from the highway, it had rattled her. She didn't want to serve food looking over her shoulder.

"More than okay." Anna picked up a slip of paper on top of one of the containers and waved it in the air. "Here are the orders. Just bag them and staple the slips to the handles of the plastic bags. Rosie will grab them and call them out by number."

"Got it."

For the remaining fifteen minutes of the lunch rush, Jane packaged the orders and kept her head down. She'd been mistaken. There would be no reason for those men to be in Paradiso. They thought she was dead, incinerated in that car. They'd be reporting back to whoever wanted her dead. Husband? Boyfriend?

She shivered and then jumped when someone patted her on the shoulder.

Rosie's pat turned into a squeeze. "I'm sorry I scared you, *mija*. I just wanted to let you know you did a good job today. I'm glad Rob brought you to me, and now he's here for lunch. Go see."

A lock of hair had escaped from Jane's ponytail, and she tucked it behind her ear as she sidled past Rosie out of the kitchen.

Seated at a table by the window, Rob raised his hand. Her heart skipped a beat when she saw him, which she put down to the fact that his was the only familiar face she had in her sparse memory bank.

On her way to his table, she touched Anna's arm. "Do you need help with the tables?"

"Jose will clean those. Go have lunch and leave. You did all the setup today, so I'll take care of closeout."

Lunch? Was that what Rob was doing here? He wanted lunch with her. This morning it seemed he couldn't wait to wash his hands of her. That was before Rosie corralled him into taking her in.

As she approached Rob's table, he jumped from his seat and held out her chair. She smiled her thanks.

Rob had already proved his trustworthiness. He hadn't run to the cops, even though he was part of law enforcement himself. She should tell him about her predicament. She needed an ally.

Anna had already delivered a basket of chips, a bowl of salsa and a couple of glasses of water to Rob's table. Jane looked at the chips and wrinkled her nose.

"Hazards of the job. You're sick of chips and salsa already." Rob grabbed a chip and dunked it into the salsa. "If you haven't tried Rosie's salsa yet, you're missing out. It's the best north of the border...and maybe even south."

Jane took his advice and scooped up a healthy dose of salsa with a sturdy chip and bit off the corner. The heat of the jalapeño made her eyes water, but just a little.

She sniffed and said, "It's good."

"How did your first day of work go?"

"Rosie is so sweet and Anna, Sal, Jose—all of them." She flicked at the corner of the plastic menu in front of her. Could she keep working here if her tormentors had stayed in the area? Where would she go if she didn't?

Rob briefly touched her hand and then snatched it back. "Is everything okay? How are you feeling? How's your head?"

She stroked the hair on the side of her head, covering the gash in her skull where her memories had leaked out. "It throbs now and then, but it's not giving me any trouble."

"I still think you need to see a doctor, sooner rather than later."

Jane nudged his foot with hers as Anna came up to the table. "Ready to order?"

"You know me, Anna. Same old, same old."

Anna tapped her head. "Burrito with carnitas, wet with green. How about you, Jane?"

"I've been eyeing those chicken tacos all day."

"Good choice. Drinks?"

They both ordered iced teas, and then Rob planted his elbows on the table. "Tell me what happened."

Jane blinked. "What happened? At work?"

He swept his hand across the surface of the table. "You had an abusive ex, you left him and he came after you. Did he cause the car accident? Are you going to report him?"

She licked her lips and took a sip of water. "It may be worse than that."

Folding his arms, Rob hunched forward across the table, his dark eyes burning into her. "You can tell me."

Could she? How did she even begin to tell him of her predicament? He'd probably want to take her straight to the hospital. Straight to the police. She couldn't allow that. For some reason, she couldn't allow that.

She rubbed her arms and opened her mouth to speak, but Anna interrupted with their iced tea. "Food will be up in a minute. More salsa?"

"Please." Rob tapped his glass. "And more water when you get the chance, Anna."

Anna spun around to get Rob's water, and he dumped a packet of sugar into his tea. "What were you going to say?"

"Before I get to that, can I ask you a question?"

"I'm an open book."

"I can second that." Anna returned with their food and topped off Rob's water. "This guy can't keep his mouth shut."

"Is it your job to eavesdrop now?" He picked up his fork and waved it at Anna's back. "You're setting a bad example for Jane."

Jane poked at her taco. If Rob were a talker, would he be able to keep her secrets?

He stabbed a piece of burrito and swept it through the salsa verde on his plate. "What's your question?"

"Why'd you agree to help me? I figured as a law enforcement officer, you'd feel bound to call the police."

He shrugged. "You were in a single-car crash. You didn't destroy any property or hurt anyone but yourself."

She stirred her tea with a straw, and the ice tinkled against the side of the glass. "It's more than that, isn't it?"

Rob sucked up half his tea through the straw before replying. "It was the abusive ex that got me. My mother had an abusive husband."

"Your father?"

"No." The line of Rob's jaw hardened, and he plunged

his fork into his burrito. "My stepfather. My dad died not too long after I was born."

"I'm sorry." She picked up her taco and tapped the edge of the hard shell against her plate. "And then your mother married a man who abused her."

"Yeah, and I was too young to do anything about it. I'm the youngest of five." He'd placed the tines of his fork on the edge of his plate, and his hand curled into a fist on the table.

"Is that why you went into law enforcement, to correct all the wrongs you couldn't set right as a kid?"

His head jerked up, and he took a gulp of water. "Maybe. Are you a psychoanalyst or something?"

Was she?

"N-no. And your other siblings? Did they go into the law, too?"

He snorted. "The other side of the law. I have two brothers and two sisters. One of my brothers is in prison. The other is an ex-con, an OG who still holds court in East LA."

"Wow. And your sisters? I'm afraid to ask." She took a bite of her food, her teeth crunching into the taco. She'd been trying to buy time, not realizing she'd get Rob's dramatic life story.

"My oldest sister is married to a criminal, repeating my mother's sad story, and my other sister is getting her doctorate at the University of Texas in Austin."

"How did you and your sister escape the family legacy?"

"Sheer willpower and a little luck."

She handed him his fork. "I didn't mean to ruin your appetite."

"Yeah, it's not exactly my favorite lunchtime topic." He attacked his food again.

Rob's attention to his lunch gave her some time to think of how she was going to frame her story. What was to frame? She lost her memory in the crash, and those two men gave her reason to believe she was in danger. Rob could help her.

She finished her food, took a sip of tea and patted her mouth with her napkin. As she took a deep breath, Rob's phone rang.

He glanced at it and held up one finger. "Excuse me. I gotta take this. It's work."

He tapped the phone. "Valdez."

He listened for a second, a crease forming between his eyebrows. "Yeah, yeah. You think it's El Gringo Viejo?"

Jane's heart slammed against her chest. El Gringo Viejo? Where had she heard that before? As she gripped the edge of the table with her hands, the voice of one of the men from the crash site came back to her and a piercing pain lanced the side of her head.

El Gringo Viejo was the person who wanted her dead.

Chapter Five

Rob half listened to his coworker as Jane's face turned white. He raised his eyebrows and pushed a glass of water toward her. Damn, she needed a doctor.

The voice on the phone repeated, "How many tunnels are left to check, Rob?"

"Maybe three. Hey, can we continue this when I get back to the station? I'm in the middle of something."

He ended the call with the other agent and grabbed Jane's hand. "Are you okay? You look like you're about to pass out or be sick or both."

"Just got a little woozy. I'm okay."

No matter how many times Jane said that to him, he didn't believe her. Who crawled from an accident like that with a head injury, on the run from some violent ex-husband, and refused to go to the police or the hospital? Refused to even call family or go home?

"Have some water."

Jane—whose last name must remain a mystery—had more secrets than a Vegas magician. But she was no criminal, at least not that he'd discovered, yet.

He'd run her prints and nothing had come back. That didn't mean a whole helluva lot. She could be a lucky criminal who'd never been caught. At least she hadn't tried to jack Rosita's.

Jane came up for air after chugging a glass of water, a little more color in her cheeks. "Do you mind if I take a nap at your place while you're at work? I think I just need some sleep."

A stranger in his house alone? A stranger swimming in secrets, steeped in lies? He'd offered. Did he think she'd be there only the same time as he would?

"Oh, oh." She covered her mouth with one hand. "You were just pretending before with Rosie, weren't you? I'm sorry. Of course you're not going to allow some random person to stay in your house while you're gone."

Heat suffused his chest and Rob took a deep breath, battling to keep it from washing into his face. He'd offered his home to her, and she'd taken him at his word. And he'd meant it…at the time. His fellow agents were always warning him that even though Paradiso was light-years from LA in danger, he shouldn't treat the place like a friendly little town.

They were too close to the border for that. Hadn't Las Moscas, the most active cartel in their area, left a couple of severed heads on a Border Patrol agent's doorstep?

Didn't stop him from feeling like a jerk.

"Look…" He held out his hand.

Shaking her head, she ignored the gesture. "No, really. I understand completely."

"Let me finish." He pushed away his plate. "I'll get you a room for the afternoon so you can sleep and rest up. Then you can come over for dinner, and we'll play it by ear. I'm not sure you should be alone anyway, whether at my place or at a motel."

This time, she put out her hand for a shake. "I accept your kind offer. I can pay you back for the room once I get some wages from Rosie."

He clasped her hand, feeling it tremble slightly in his. "Don't worry about paying me back."

"Sorry to interrupt." Rosie appeared next to their table, clutching a wad of bills. "This is for you, Jane, for your work today. I pay you in cash. You can come tomorrow, too, same time?"

"Absolutely." Jane jumped from her chair and hugged Rosie. "Thank you so much."

Rosie tapped her finger against the bruise beneath Jane's eye. "You take care of yourself, and I'll see you tomorrow. Do you need clothes?"

"I'll pick up a few things." Jane held up the money Rosie had just given her.

"I have that covered, Rosie."

Rosie winked. "You're a good boy, *mijo*."

As Rosie disappeared into the kitchen, Jane's smile faded from her face. "Was that offer for Rosie's benefit, too?"

Rob swallowed hard. "No. You look about the same size as my buddy's wife. I was going to ask her for a few things—I swear."

"I'm just kidding around." Jane pressed a hand against her heart. "I do understand why you wouldn't want a stranger in your house when you're not there. This all could be an elaborate ruse, and I might have an accomplice waiting outside town with a truck, ready to clean you out."

Rob tugged on his earlobe. "Wow. I didn't even think of that one."

"We'd better get going if I'm checking into a motel." Jane shoved away from the table and collected their dirty dishes. She carried them to the kitchen and said goodbye to the staff.

Rob waved on the way out of the restaurant. As he

helped Jane into his truck, he said, "We'll make a quick stop at the store for a few things."

The few things turned into a basket filled with ibuprofen, vitamins, bottled water, juice, a couple of T-shirts, snacks and other things to assuage his guilt.

He booked her into the Paradiso Motel and stashed her new belongings, her only belongings, in the room. He snapped the key cards on the credenza next to the TV.

"Should I take one of those, just in case?"

Her whiskey-colored eyes widened. "In case I pass out or die in the room?"

Fear tingled at the back of his neck, and he clapped his hand over it. "Don't say that. Just in case you need some help. Do you mind?

"I mean, I'm just as much a stranger to you as you are to me. You probably shouldn't give your motel key to a strange man."

"Strange man? I spent the night in your house last night, and you got me a job today." Her lush lips twisted. "I feel like I've known you all my life."

He grunted. "You're very funny."

"Take the key." She wedged a hand on her hip. "I'm going to ask for something in return, though."

"The knife."

"Read my mind. If I'm going to be alone in this room with an extra key floating around out there, I'd prefer to have a little protection." She widened her stance, as if digging her heels into the carpet. "I know it's in your truck, Rob."

"You're probably right." He grabbed a bottle of water from the minifridge. "Wait here and I'll get it for you."

The door to her room slammed behind him as he stepped outside. He'd get her the knife for kicking her out of his house. She must think her ex, or whoever, was headed this way.

He chewed on his bottom lip. She'd been about to open up to him over lunch, but they'd gotten off track. What had she said? The truth was probably worse than a violent, vindictive ex?

He ducked into his truck and felt under the driver's seat. His fingers wrapped around the knife and he pulled it out.

Cupping it in his hand, he examined the intricate metalwork in silver. The knife had been crafted in Mexico, like her clothing. Like her Spanish?

He'd get to the bottom of things tonight.

ROB SPENT MOST of the rest of the afternoon at the station doing follow-up work on the cartel's tunnels under the border. The Border Patrol had hit the mother lode when one of the agents, Clay Archer, had come into possession of a map detailing the tunnels Las Moscas had painstakingly created for their drug trade.

As Rob stretched at his desk and thought about Jane back at the motel, Clay plopped down behind his own desk and fired a pen at him. "Daydreaming, Valdez?"

"Yeah, daydreaming about getting out of here." Rob rolled the pen toward him with the toe of his boot and bent over to pick it up. Keeping his head beneath the desk, Rob asked, "Is April home right now? I have a favor to ask her."

"She's home. Do you want me to pass it along to her?"

Rob popped up from beneath the desk, holding the pen between two fingers. "I'll just drop by and see her. I know you're working late, and my request doesn't have anything to do with you."

"Mysterious." Clay held up a finger as the phone on his desk rang.

As Clay flipped through a file, Rob grabbed the opportunity to get out before Clay started asking probing questions. He shoved his laptop and some files into his shoulder bag and, on his way out the door, held up his hand at Clay still on the phone.

April would tell her husband everything, anyway. After the start those two had, they kept no secrets between them. But Rob didn't have to give Clay a head start on the ribbing.

He drove out to Clay and April's place and parked on the street in front. As promised, April was home. Her work as an accountant allowed her to work from the house.

Clay must've given her a heads-up because she came out to the porch to wait for him as he approached the front door.

She gave him a hug. "Clay told me you were on the way with a mysterious favor to ask."

"Clay's paranoid. It's not all that mysterious." He took off his hat as he stepped over the threshold, and their dog immediately bounded at him. He scratched Denali behind the ear. "Hey, boy."

"What do you need?" She picked up a glass of lemonade from the coffee table where she'd been working and raised it. "Can I get you something to drink? It's still hot as blazes and I heard we have a monsoon on the way."

"Yeah, the wettest winter I ever spent was a summer in Tucson, or something like that." He shook his head. "I don't need anything but your clothes."

April grabbed the hem of her T-shirt and wiggled her hips. "Ooh, no wonder you didn't tell my husband."

Rob laughed. "Not those clothes. I have a friend who's

in kind of a…situation, and she needs some clothes—nothing fancy, just a few pairs of shorts, a couple of T-shirts, maybe some jeans. She's about your size, maybe shorter, so I thought you might have something she could borrow."

April tilted her head and wrapped a lock of blond hair around one finger. "I have some stuff. Is this a *particular* friend?"

He kind of knew he wasn't going to escape April's matchmaking efforts. The woman had a caretaking streak a mile long and figured everyone needed to be as happy as she and Clay were.

"No, just a friend in need."

"Well, you know those are my favorite kind." She crooked a finger at him. "This way, Agent Valdez. I'll throw a few things together for your…friend."

Thirty minutes later, Rob staggered from the house, bags hanging from his fingertips that included enough clothes to outfit a sorority. With a wave out the window of his truck, he pulled away from the curb and made his way back to town.

He might as well pick up some dinner before he collected Jane from the motel. She could go through April's clothes at his place.

As he rolled up to the stop sign to turn onto the main street, his foot hit the brake hard and his truck lurched. He squinted through his sunglasses and watched as Jane tripped down the steps of the library.

What happened to her nap? Had she decided to get a Pima County library card while she hid out from her ex?

A car rattled past her, and she jumped, craning her head over her shoulder. She continued to glance behind her as she made her way down the street, never noticing him.

A breath hitched in his throat, as a man wearing a baseball cap and walking toward her seemed to slow his gait and flash her some kind of sign with his hand. Jane's step never even faltered, and Rob eased out a sigh.

He waited until she turned the corner, most likely on her way back to the motel, but even that seemed doubtful now. He wheeled onto the library's side street and scrambled out of the truck. He poked his head around the edge of the building to make sure Jane wasn't making a repeat appearance, and then strode to the entrance.

He eyed the three computers available for public use. A senior citizen was parked at one, playing a game of solitaire. The other two monitors glared at him.

She had to have been here using the computers. What else? She didn't walk out with any books under her arm. Standing between the two machines, he tapped the keyboards—one with each hand.

Password screens popped up, and the old man seated at the other computer pointed to a slip of paper attached to the top of the monitor, his crooked finger waving in the air. "Passwords are right there."

"Thank you, sir." Rob pulled one keyboard toward him and entered the password. The monitor woke up and displayed a desktop with several available applications.

Rob ran the mouse across the application icons, hovering over a web browser. "Did you see a woman using one of these computers while you were here? She just left."

The man removed his glasses, and his faded blue eyes assessed Rob from head to toe. He leaned forward and cupped his mouth with his hand. "Official business?"

"Yes, yes, it is. Official business." Rob cleared his throat.

"She was here." The old man raised his eyes to the

ceiling. "Pretty little thing with hair the color of caramel candy."

Rob's hand jerked. He supposed Jane did have hair the color of caramel. "That's her. Which computer was she using and…uh, did you notice what she was doing?"

"She was using the one on the end, but I could still smell her." The man's prominent nose twitched with the memory.

Rob raised one eyebrow. "Her smell?"

"Lemons—fresh and tart—just like my Lois." The man closed his eyes, lost in the memory of his Lois.

Rob coughed as he sidled in front of the computer Jane had been using. "Did you notice what she was doing?"

The man opened one eye. "Surfing the internet. Why don't you ask Julie, if this is official business? She can log you in to the young woman's session."

"I was just going to do that." Rob squared his shoulders and marched to the reference desk. The old guy obviously knew more about how the public computers worked than he did.

Julie looked up at his approach. "Hi, Rob. Do you need something?"

"A woman was in here using one of the computers, and I'd like to find out what she looked up."

"I can do that." Julie came from behind the reference desk and patted his arm. "All work and no play."

Rob ducked his head. Julie had a daughter somewhere in Phoenix she wanted him to meet, but he hated setups and he hated blind dates. "We're always busy."

Julie dropped her voice to a whisper. "Is this woman a drug dealer? A mule?"

"Nothing that serious." He put his finger to his lips and jerked his thumb at the man still playing solitaire.

Julie laid a hand on the man's shoulder. "Beating your own records, Frank?"

"I'm workin' on it, Julie."

Julie perched on the chair in front of the computer Jane had vacated recently and tapped on the keyboard. She logged out and then logged back in. A few clicks later and she pushed back from the table.

"There you go. We're back in her session. You can look at her browsing history to see what she's been up to." Julie traced the tip of her finger across the seam of her closed mouth. "And I won't tell a soul."

"Thanks, Julie."

"Anytime you get a break, I'll give you my daughter's cell phone number."

"I'll remember that." Julie's poor daughter would probably be mortified to discover her mother was playing matchmaker for her.

Rob scooted closer to the monitor and brought up the history of Jane's browsing session.

As he scrolled through the searches on drugs and drug cartels, his heart began to pound in his chest. When he got to the bottom and read the first search she'd entered, the blood pounded in his temples.

Jane had been searching for information on El Gringo Viejo—one of the most notorious drug suppliers in Mexico.

Chapter Six

The knock on the motel door made her jump. Wiping her sweaty palms on her pants, she stalked toward the door and leaned forward to peek through the peephole.

Rob took a step back so she could see his whole body. Several bags hung at his sides.

She puffed a breath from her lips, closed the knife and shoved it into her front pocket. She'd had a scare on the street earlier when a stranger wearing a cap had stared at her, and then flashed her a peace sign. She'd been afraid he'd followed her here.

She swung the door open and took a step back. "I thought maybe you weren't coming back to get me."

His eyebrows collided over his nose as he lifted his shoulders. "Why would you think that?"

"I don't know." She stood to the side and gestured him into the room. "Out of sight, out of mind."

"You may have been out of sight but never out of my mind." He held up the bags, stuffed with clothing, swinging them from his fingers. "I even got you some stuff to wear."

She pressed a hand against her warm cheek. What did he mean she was never out of his mind? And the clothes? She shouldn't get too dependent on Rob, but what choice did she have? He was it—the extent of her relationships.

She could probably add Rosie, Anna and the cooks and busboys at Rosita's to her list. And El Gringo Viejo.

Why did a drug dealer want to see her dead?

"Th-that's so thoughtful of you. I hope you didn't go to any trouble on my behalf." She lifted up one foot encased in a new sandal. "I was able to buy a few things at the thrift shop, too."

"Oh, you went out?" He turned the bags upside down over the bed and dumped out the articles of clothing. They landed on the bedspread in a tangle of colors and textures.

"Just for a short time." She sat on the edge of the mattress and picked through the items. "Where'd you get all this stuff? Looks all the same size and hardly thrift store quality."

"I hit up my coworker's wife. I figured you two to be about the same size." He cocked his head, his gaze scanning her from head to toe. "Maybe she's a little taller. My other buddy's girlfriend is maybe more your size, but..."

"But what?"

"She's a cop. She's attending the police academy right now."

Jane curled her hands around the edge of a floral sundress, bunching the silky material in her fists. "Oh."

"Yeah, oh." He ran a hand through his thick dark hair. "She'd be suspicious...and you wouldn't want that, would you?"

"No. I mean, the fewer people who know about my particular situation, the better."

"Your situation." Rob dropped his chin to his chest. "Anyway, the woman who gave me the clothes, April, she's always trying to help someone—to a fault."

"Sounds like you."

"I told you. I'm a sucker for...ladies in distress."

The tension between them vibrated like a plucked string. She grabbed one of the T-shirts and held it up. "Nice. Thank you."

"What did you do today besides hit the thrift store?" He meandered to the window and flicked aside the drapes, peering outside.

"Slept mostly." She patted her stomach. "I hope some dinner is in our future. I'm starving. I—I can pay half from the money Rosie gave me."

He dropped the curtain fold and pivoted toward her. "That doesn't make any sense. You need that money to get back on your feet, get yourself home or wherever it is you want to go. I already ordered us some dinner, and if we don't get going, the dinner is going to get to the house before we do."

"I'll try some of these things on at your place, then." She began to shovel the clothes back into the bags. "Tell your friend thanks for me."

"Will do." He waited for her with his back to the door, his arms folded.

Had April questioned him about her? Was he having second thoughts?

Maybe she should get out of Paradiso before El Gringo Viejo came looking for her. Hopefully the two men who'd set fire to her car had done a good job convincing their boss that they'd killed the prey.

She needed help—real help from a professional to get her memory back. She hadn't wanted to face her past, but now it seemed as if it were more dangerous not to remember.

She grabbed the bags full of clothes, patted the knife in her pocket and spun around with a smile pasted on her face. "I'm ready."

He opened the door and stood aside for her, saying, "I

kept the room for you, so if you want to get settled here, you have a place."

She nodded, blinking her eyes. Something had changed. Rob didn't want her in his house, didn't want to help her anymore. He'd be even more reluctant to help her if he knew she had some connection to El Gringo Viejo.

When they got to his house, he pointed to the room she'd used the night before. "You're welcome to try on some of those clothes. I'm sure you're sick of what you're wearing now, although that T-shirt from Rosita's looks good on you."

She pulled the T-shirt away from her body, glancing down at the logo for the café. "Rosie saved my life today…and you. Thank you. Have I said thank you?"

"You pulled a knife on me, instead."

She clutched a bag of clothing to her chest. "I'm sorry for that. You can understand why I did it."

"Sure." His lips stretched into a fake smile.

"I'll try some of these on." She dragged her feet down the hallway to Rob's guest room. He was definitely having second thoughts. Maybe April, the owner of the clothes, told him he was crazy. Maybe he'd told the other friend, the cop, and she was on her way right now.

She slammed the door behind her and dropped the bag of clothes on the floor. She'd stay away from Rob and his friends. Work at Rosita's for some cash, keep the motel room and make her way to Tucson and find herself a psychiatrist. If she were mixed up with this El Gringo Viejo and the cartels, she could disappear. Get a new identity. What would it matter? She had no identity now.

She pulled on and yanked off jeans, capris, shorts, blouses, T-shirts, sweaters. April had covered all the bases.

She left on a pair of olive capris and a red T-shirt and

surveyed the rainbow pile of clothes on the bed. She'd use the money Rosie gave her today to get settled, and she'd get out of Rob's way.

She swallowed the lump in her throat. Leaving Rob would be like losing her only friend.

Squaring her shoulders, she followed the smell of garlic into the kitchen. She tipped her nose in the air. "Italian?"

Rob glanced up from dumping some spaghetti onto a plate. "Is that okay?"

"Smells good." She popped a lid from a plastic container. "I'll do the salad."

Stepping back from his task, Rob waved a fork up and down her body. "The clothes fit?"

The look in his eyes sent a little tingle up her thighs. He may have changed his mind about being friends with her, but the attraction he had for her hadn't died out.

Her fingers fidgeted with the hem of the T-shirt. "Most of them. She *is* taller than I am, but it's close enough. Beggars can't be choosers."

"Don't think of yourself as a beggar." He nabbed a drop of marinara sauce from the counter with his thumb and sucked it into his mouth. "You're someone in need, and April likes nothing more than helping someone in need."

"Did you tell her about me?" She pinched the edges of the salad bowls between her fingers.

"Just a few basics. She's not the one you have to worry about." He turned his back to her, and she nearly dropped the bowls.

"Worry about?" She set the dishes on the table harder than she'd intended and they sent a clacking sound through the air that made her grit her teeth.

"I mean about being nosy. April just has to hear someone needs her help and she's the first to offer a hand. Emily's the cop—or at least she's going through the police academy right now. She's the one who'd want your life story."

Jane scooped her hair back from her face and said, "It's a good thing she's busy with the academy, then."

She hovered over the salads, her face turned away from him, waiting for a reply. All she got was the crinkling of foil.

"Do you like garlic bread?"

She supposed she did, as the smell of that bread had been making her mouth water ever since she'd left the bedroom. She took a deep breath. "I do."

He emerged from the kitchen, a plate of spaghetti and meatballs in each hand, a wedge of garlic bread balanced on the edge of the plates.

Rob tipped his head back. "Do you want to get some silverware? It's in the drawer by the toaster."

She ducked around him into the kitchen and pulled open the drawer. She grabbed two place settings and spun around, almost bumping into Rob, who'd already delivered the food to the table.

His eyes widened for a split second as his gaze dropped to the utensils clutched in her hands. "Knives for spaghetti?"

"Those meatballs looked pretty big. I'd prefer to cut mine with a knife civilly instead of trying to saw it with the edge of the fork and have it shoot across the table." Her lips turned up at the corners, but her grip on the silverware tightened. He didn't trust her with a knife in her hand.

Would he ever forget their meeting in the desert? What had he expected her to do when confronted with a stranger at night in the desert after someone had just tried to kill her?

Of course, Rob didn't know her whole story, and just as she'd been about to tell him, El Gringo Viejo had come between them. She couldn't tell him now. He'd never believe her.

"Good point." He scooted past her, his body tense. "I'll get some water. I'd offer you some wine, but I'm not sure your head needs alcohol right now—unless you want some."

"Water is fine." All she needed was to get drunk and babble her troubles into his sympathetic ears—ears that didn't seem so sympathetic now. Although maybe if she got loaded, her inhibitions would fall away and she might remember something of her life before the crash. She'd have to ask her psychiatrist if that would work—when she got one.

She positioned the silverware on either side of the plates in perfect order. How did she remember inconsequential stuff like place settings but not her own name? Another question for her future shrink.

She sat in front of one plate and waited until Rob returned with the glasses of water before plunging her fork into the steaming pasta. She twirled the spaghetti around the tines and sucked it off her fork. The red sauce dribbled on her chin and she dabbed it with a paper towel.

He pulled the salad bowl toward him and stabbed at a piece of lettuce. "How long do you plan to stay in Paradiso?"

"Until I feel safe." That was no lie. How could she go out into the world with people trying to kill her? They thought she was dead. They wouldn't be looking for her. Would they be watching the TV for news about a car wreck with a dead body burned to a crisp? And when they didn't see it, would they go back?

"You don't like the spaghetti?" Rob jabbed his fork in the air toward her plate.

"It's good." She picked up the knife and cut one of the huge meatballs in half and then quarters. "You see how neat that is?"

"I guess I'd better not stuff the whole thing in my mouth like I usually do."

Prodding the other meatball on her plate with her fork, she shook her head. "You're lying. I can't imagine you doing that."

"What would make you feel safe?"

She dropped her fork. Was he trying to catch her off guard?

"Oh, just to know my ex isn't looking for me." She toyed with the pasta. "Do you feel safe?"

Two could play this game.

His dark brows shot up. "From you?"

She picked up the knife and plunged it into a meatball. "Are you afraid I'm going to stab you in the night?"

"*Are* you?"

"I already slept under your roof one night—uneventfully. Besides, I didn't mean feel safe from me. Do you feel safe from your past?"

The Adam's apple in his neck bobbed as he swallowed—and he didn't even have any food in his mouth.

"My past? I feel safe. I escaped it, remember?"

She tilted her head. "Did you?"

"What does that mean?" He gulped some water. "Are you sure you're not a shrink? You talk like one."

"How do you know what a shrink talks like?"

"Got me." He formed his fingers into a gun and pointed at her. "Are you kidding? With my upbringing, the school was always sending me to the school psychologist. 'Are you okay, Roberto?' 'How does that make you feel, Roberto?'"

He'd changed his voice with the questions to mimic a woman.

"How did it all make you feel? The violence? The instability?"

He pushed away his salad and attacked his spaghetti. "Made me feel like taking control of everything and never letting go. Made me feel like hunting down every drug dealer and giving him some rough justice."

His words caused goose bumps to ripple across her skin, but she resisted rubbing her arms. She took a sip of water. "So, you became a Border Patrol agent."

He nodded, sucking the last of his pasta into his mouth. The action resulted in a drop of marinara landing on his chin.

She crumpled the paper towel in her lap and raised it to dab his chin.

He flinched, but she swiped it off anyway.

"Can't take me anywhere." He scrubbed his own paper towel across his mouth until his chin was redder than the original drop of sauce.

"Do you feel like you make a difference in the drug war?"

"I wouldn't stay in this job if I didn't think that." He dragged the tines of his fork through the sauce on his plate. "And what about you? Where do you live? What do you do for a living? Do you have any children?"

She pinned her hands between her knees. She shouldn't have gotten personal with him. He demanded reciprocity. He'd shown her his, and now he expected her to show him hers.

"I—I'm a teacher—an art teacher." She pressed a hand

against her heart. Something felt so real about that statement. Could it be the truth? Were her memories brimming at the edge of her consciousness, ready to overflow and make her whole?

He nodded, stuffing a meatball—just a piece of one—into his mouth. When he finished chewing and swallowing, he said, "That would explain what you're doing out here in the middle of the summer."

It *would* explain that. She obviously hadn't been going to or coming from a job. Had she been in Mexico? She hadn't noticed the license plates on the car before it went up in flames. If she had memorized the license number, maybe she would've been able to discover her identity. Had she left a purse in the car? ID? Money? Why hadn't she thought of all that before scrambling from that car?

"Are you all right?" Rob planted his elbows on the table on either side of his plate.

The words expressed concern, but his face didn't match. His dark eyes drilled into her, probing her vacant mind. If he could read it, more power to him.

"I'm fine. I'd rather not discuss my life." She pushed back from the table so abruptly the chair tipped over, and she saved it from falling.

She stacked her bowl onto the plate. "Can I get your dishes? Are you finished?"

Rob curled his fingers around her wrist, his light touch feeling more like a vise due to the intensity in his dark eyes.

Her pulse fluttered, as she leaned toward him, the magnetic draw of his gaze reeling her into his realm. This attraction between them couldn't be stopped, even though she hadn't a clue who she was. She could be married with four children, and not even that possibility could dampen the fire that kindled in her belly for this man.

Her eyes drifted closed. Her lips parted. Her breath caught in her throat.

But when she felt the warmth of his mouth inches from her own, the imminent kiss turned into harsh words.

"How the hell do you know El Gringo Viejo?"

Chapter Seven

Jane blinked her whiskey-colored eyes, and Rob clenched his back teeth, trying hard not to imagine whether or not her lips would taste like the color of her eyes. He could've satisfied his curiosity by indulging in a small nip before dropping his bombshell, but that just didn't seem right.

Realizing she was still poised for the kiss that hung suspended between them, Jane jerked back. Her gaze darted around the room as if looking for an escape. Then she took a deep breath, her chest rising and falling in the red T-shirt borrowed from April.

When her eyes found their way back to his face, they narrowed. Her nostrils flared, and she pulled back her shoulders. Ready for conflict.

"Why do you think I know El Gringo Viejo?"

Squeezing his eyes shut, Rob pinched the bridge of his nose. Did he think this was going to be easy? He scooted his chair out from beneath the table and clasped his hands on his knees. "I saw your search history on the library computer."

Her left eye twitched. "You were spying on me all this time?"

He'd been around criminals long enough to know they went with a swift offense when backed into a corner. "Did you think I'd let a strange woman into my home for an overnight stay without doing a little checking?"

"You didn't do any checking that first night." She thrust out her chin.

"You were injured, confused. I wasn't going to turn you away, but I did keep that knife from you and I retained your water bottle for fingerprints."

Her head snapped up, and she gripped the seat of the chair. "You ran my fingerprints? You know who I am?"

"You probably already know I didn't find a match." He tilted his head to the side, studying her face. "So, I know you're not an art teacher. Teachers' prints are on file."

Her shoulders slumped in disappointment. "You didn't find out my identity from running my prints, so you followed me around this afternoon and snooped into my activities at the library?"

"Snooped?" He rolled his eyes, smacking his hands on his thighs.

She flinched.

"You're giving me too much credit. I happened to see you walk away from the library when I went to the main drag to pick up some food for dinner. You told me you were going to nap this afternoon, so I got curious. That's when I discovered your first search was for El Gringo Viejo." He crossed his arms over his chest and leaned back in his chair, as if to give her plenty of room to hang herself. "Why?"

She sucked in her cheek before answering, formulating her lie. "If I knew who he was, like you claimed, why would I be searching him?"

He snorted. "You randomly did a search on El Gringo Viejo the first opportunity you had? If you didn't know him or know who he was, why would you do that?"

"But I had heard his name before." She held up her

finger and then lowered it to point it at him. "You mentioned El Gringo Viejo on a phone call you took during lunch at the café."

"You heard that and immediately did a search for him?" His fingers bit into his biceps. "That makes no sense. Try again."

"It sounded fascinating." She hopped up from the chair and spun away from him. "I was curious."

Hugging herself, she walked away from him and stopped by the window to peer through the glass.

"Jane."

She hunched her shoulders and leaned her forehead against the windowpane.

"Do you know what I'm thinking right now?" He couldn't explain to her exactly the thoughts crossing his mind because along with irritation with her lies and his suspicions, he had a strong desire to take her in his arms. He couldn't explain it to himself, so he sure as hell wasn't going to admit it to her.

She shifted to display her profile. The defiance had gone out of her chin. Her long lashes and parted, pouting lips suggested a vulnerability all out of proportion to a woman who was a liar and possibly connected to the cartels.

She'd been playing him since the moment she flashed her knife at him. A place to stay, a job, clothing, meals, sex… That hadn't happened, but if he hadn't uncovered her search history at the library, they might be tangled up in his sheets right this minute.

He cleared his throat and repeated the dangerous question, the one he hoped she couldn't guess in a million years. "Do you know what I'm thinking?"

She turned to face him, tucking her hands behind her back like a chastened schoolgirl. "You probably think I'm connected to El Gringo Viejo, that I was on some kind of drug run that went bad, or that I double-crossed him and the drug cartels and they retaliated by running me off the road and torching my car. Or you think I'm still in their good graces and this—" she flapped her arms at her sides "—is some kind of setup, some sort of infiltration into the Border Patrol through my seduction of you."

He felt his eyes pop out of their sockets like some kind of cartoon character, so he closed them and rubbed them with his fists. She'd come up with more scenarios than he'd let creep into his brain. Had she been seducing him?

"Is that close?" A little smile played about her lips, but her eyes drooped in sadness and he felt that crazy urge to charge across the room and engulf her in a bear hug.

"Close enough." He shoved his hands in his pockets. "Which is it, or is it all of the above?"

She turned back toward the window and doodled on the glass with her fingertip. "I don't know."

Rob blew out the breath he'd been holding, uttering a curse at the same time. "You're gonna have to tell me, or I'll have to...take action."

He crossed the room in a few long strides and touched her shoulder. "Just tell me, Jane. And why don't you start by telling me your real name?"

"I would...if I could." She pivoted and grabbed his arm. "Rob, I am connected somehow to El Gringo Viejo, but I don't know how. I—I think he's trying to kill me, but I don't know why. And my name? I don't have a clue."

His gaze dropped to her hand on his arm just to make sure she didn't have the knife. She wasn't right in the head...or maybe he wasn't. Either way, he couldn't make sense of her words.

"Wait." He held up a hand as much to stop her words as to stop the thoughts swirling in his clouded mind. "I don't understand what you're telling me. If it's more lies, I don't want to hear them."

"I wish I were lying, Rob. I wish I knew enough to lie." She rubbed the side of her scalp, digging her fingers into her hair. "It must've been the head injury. I don't remember anything before waking up in that wreck. I don't know my name. I don't know who I am, and worst of all, I don't know who's trying to kill me and why."

The words tumbled from her lips in a rush, too fast for his brain to sort and comprehend. "We need to sit down."

He collapsed on a cushion of his couch, and Jane sat beside him, folding one leg beneath her—almost too close to him for rational thought.

Now that the dam had broken, she couldn't stop talking.

"I heard those men talking about killing me, and that's when I first heard of El Gringo Viejo. I had the knife in my pocket, so when you came along, I thought you might be one of them."

Placing his hands on her shoulders, he pinched his fingers into her flesh beneath the light T-shirt. "Stop. Tell me everything from the beginning…and I'll decide if I believe you or not."

She took a deep, shuddering breath and folded her hands in her lap. "The first thing I remember is coming to in the car. It was upside down. I was disoriented right from the beginning."

He barely breathed as she told him about releasing herself from the car and then hearing another vehicle arrive and voices.

"Something made me hide from those men. Alarm bells were sounding in my head." She looked up, studying his ceiling as if searching for her memories there.

"I saw their shoes but not their faces. They couldn't see me at all. That's when I first heard of El Gringo Viejo."

He took his thumb out of his mouth, where he'd been gnawing on the cuticle, on the edge of his seat as she spun her story. "In what context?"

"Something about how El Gringo Viejo would be angry if they had to tell him they weren't sure whether or not I was dead."

"To be sure, they torched the car."

She nodded and drew her knees to her chest, wrapping her arms around her legs. "They thought I was still inside. Then they took off."

"Why did you hide in the desert? Why didn't you go up to the highway and wave down a car?"

"Why would I do that?" Her eyes widened. "All I knew was that someone was out to kill me, had probably forced me off the road. I didn't know who. I didn't know why. Those two men could've swung back around, and I wouldn't have even recognized them as my attackers."

"Okay, I get that you'd think that at the beginning of your...ordeal, but what about later? You had to figure they'd be long gone." He drilled his forefinger into his thigh. "And why not involve the police? Why didn't you want to go to a hospital? Get treatment? Report the accident? Tell the police about these two men?"

She hunched her shoulders. "I was afraid."

"Afraid of the police?"

"Afraid of not knowing." She tapped her head. "Do you know how it feels to have nothing up here? Of course you don't. The thought of people, strangers, coming at me and telling me who I am and where I should be...fills me with terror."

"You think your assailants would hear about the accident and the woman with amnesia and make a move?"

He scratched his chin. He could understand that, but it sounded more like a movie plot.

"Can you picture it? One of them could come to the police or the hospital and tell the authorities I was his wife. That we had an argument. That he didn't know where I'd gone." She splayed her arms to her sides. "What could I say?"

She made more sense than he'd expected—not that he would've handled the situation in the same way. He tugged on his earlobe. "What about your memory loss? Where'd you get the name *Jane*?"

"Where do you think?" She stretched out her legs and kicked them up on top of the coffee table. "All I could think of while I waited in the desert was that I was a Jane Doe—no identity, no possessions, no memories. So, when you asked me for a name, that's the first one that came to mind."

"Don't you want to discover who you are? Isn't it more dangerous not knowing?"

"I didn't think so at first, but I realize it now."

He jerked his thumb toward the window. "You're not going to find out working at Rosita's Café in a town where nobody knows you."

Her gaze dropped to her wiggling toes, and she glanced up at him through her lashes. "You know me. You're the only one who does."

"Jane, or whatever—" he clasped his hand on the back of his too-tense neck "—I don't know you. You must have family somewhere, a mother, a father, a husband…people who are worried about you."

"You think so?" She chewed on her bottom lip and examined the ring finger of her left hand, devoid of a ring or a tan line. "I don't feel married."

Rob snapped his fingers. "What about the tattoo on

your back? Rosalinda? You didn't know it was there, did you?"

"Of course not."

"Where did you come up with that story about the dead girlfriend?"

"My imagination." She scooped her tawny hair back from her face. "Where else?"

"I'm just wondering if any of those names and stories you came up with have some kernel of truth to them—something coming up from your subconscious."

"I can't tell you. The only thing that resonated with me was when I told you I was an art teacher, but you already blew that theory out of the water when you told me my fingerprints aren't on file. Teachers are printed, right?"

"What about the fluent Spanish?" He shook his head. "My mother would be mortified that some gringa speaks Spanish better than I do."

"Gringa." She pulled her knees to her chest again. "Why does that man, that drug dealer, want me dead? Maybe I'm a mule, a courier, a drug dealer myself."

Rob staggered up from the couch, not wanting to think about that possibility, even though it had been at the edges of his mind ever since he saw her search history at the library. "We need a pen and paper to start writing all this down—the car, the men, the knife, the tattoo, the name. All of it."

"Does that mean you believe me?" She twisted her hair into a ponytail with one hand. "I need you to believe me, Rob. I need help."

He ducked into the office and grabbed a legal pad from a desk drawer and a pen from the holder. Returning to the living room, he drummed the pen against the pad. "I suppose someone could make up a story this crazy to infiltrate the Border Patrol or to kill me, but there would be easier ways to do that—and I've seen that gash on your head. That head injury must've stolen your memories."

Rob perched on the arm of the couch, ankle crossed at his knee, pad of paper on his thigh. He wrote *Jane?* at the top of the page and started a bulleted list of everything she could remember.

He enlarged the dark circle next to the Rosalinda tattoo on the list. "This is the most distinct thing about you. We should take a stab at it."

"Not literally." Jane reached behind her and rubbed her lower back. "But that's what I thought when I looked in the mirror and saw myself for the first time—nondistinct. At the time, it pleased me, as I figured I could blend in, but a less bland appearance might help me figure out my identity faster."

Rob's mouth hung open. She couldn't possibly think she had a bland appearance. The color of her eyes, hair that couldn't decide between blond and brown and lush lips that turned up at the corners didn't equal mundane to him.

He muttered, "I think you lost your judgment along with your memory."

"What?" She prodded his leg.

"Never mind." He dropped the notepad on her lap and pushed up from the arm of the couch. "Now that we know Rosalinda is not the name of some murdered schoolmate, let's do another search."

He swept his laptop from the counter where it was charging and squeezed next to Jane on the couch. He launched a search engine and entered *Rosalinda* once more.

Jane ran her finger down the display. "A TV show, restaurants, people, a brand of tortillas. Do you think one of those Rosalindas could be me?"

"Only one way to find out." Rob clicked on the first Rosalinda, which turned out to be a politician in Texas, the smile on the middle-aged blonde's face promising more school funding and better infrastructure.

He went through all of the names, but not one of the Rosalindas matched Jane.

He slumped, tipping his head back and staring at the ceiling. "What else do people tattoo on their bodies?"

He could feel her gaze on him, assessing him in a way that heated his blood.

He rolled his head to the side. "What?"

"Do you have any tattoos, Rob?"

"No." The word came out in a burst and Jane reeled back.

"Not a fan of inking your body, I guess."

"Sorry, didn't mean to snap at you." Rob shoved a hand through his hair. "I was constantly pressured as a kid into getting the gang symbol tattooed on my arm. Both of my brothers had them. My refusal was kind of like a magical talisman in my head that assured me if I didn't get the tattoo, I'd never join the gang."

Jane squeezed his thigh. "And it worked."

"I've been tattoo-free ever since and probably always will be."

"But if you were a tattoo kinda guy, what would you get? What do your friends have? Your girlfriends?" She removed her hand from his leg and tapped her fingers on her knee.

"I don't have any girlfriends. Do you think I'd be running around with you, having you spend the night here, if I had a girlfriend?"

"You wouldn't be if *I* were your girlfriend." She brushed her hands together as if resolving that issue. "Tattoos."

If she were his girlfriend? He liked the sound of that and he didn't even know who she was.

"My buddies who were in the military have military tattoos, insignia, animals, stuff like that. The women, *not* my girlfriends, tend to have flowers, maybe little sayings, hearts." He shrugged. "Places?"

"Are there any towns called Rosalinda?" She flicked a hand at the keyboard. "We could go through each state. Rosalinda, Alabama. Rosalinda, Arkansas. Rosalinda, Arizona, of course."

"Rosalinda, Mexico." Rob clutched the sides of the laptop.

"Why Mexico?" She licked her lips and clasped her hands between her knees.

She knew.

He coughed. "Well, you speak Spanish fluently. Rosalinda is a Spanish-sounding name. We're close to the Mexican border."

"And I know El Gringo Viejo." She pressed her lips together in a straight line. "I'm not sure I want to know how well we're acquainted. Could he be my…husband? There weren't any pictures of him online."

Rob swallowed a lump in his throat. "There are no pictures of him. Nobody knows what he looks like."

"But with a name like that, *Viejo*, he has to be old… older." She interlaced her fidgety fingers. "People do have May-December relationships, though, don't they?"

He placed his hand over both of hers. He couldn't help it. "What made you think he might be your husband?"

"Because of the story I told you about escaping an abusive ex. Remember, we talked about kernels of truth."

"And remember you told me the only flicker of recognition you felt was when you said you were an art teacher." He stroked his thumb across the smooth skin on the back of her hand. "In all our years tracking El Gringo Viejo, nobody ever mentioned a spouse or partner for him."

She jabbed her finger at the monitor. "Enter it."

He typed *Rosalinda, Mexico* in the search engine and hit Return.

Jane leaned into his space, the ends of her hair tickling his hands still poised over the keyboard. "There's the TV show again. Maybe I'm just a big fan of that telenovela."

Rob eked out a breath. "Doesn't look like there's a town called Rosalinda, at least not one that rates top billing on this search engine."

"Rob." She grabbed his wrist. "There's an art gallery called Rosalinda. Right there."

He followed the direction of her trembling finger and clicked on an article from an online art blog that teased the name Rosalinda in the blurb.

He read it aloud, as Jane seemed to have been struck mute. "'For funky art pieces in a variety of media, some created by the gallery's owner, visit Rosalinda in Puerto Peñasco, better known to the gringos as Rocky Point. The proprietor and artist, Libby James, is knowledgeable about the…'"

Jane dug her nails into his flesh. "That's me. That's who I am—Libby James."

Chapter Eight

"Libby James." She said the name again, feeling it on her tongue, her lips, the roof of her mouth. "I'm Libby James."

Rob's arm went around her shoulders, and she leaned into him. "That's amazing. You remember. You can go to the police now, tell them about the accident and the men threatening you."

She stiffened. "I don't remember. I just know."

"You just know?" His arm sagged halfway down her back. "What does that mean? You don't remember your life as Libby James? Your association with El Gringo Viejo?"

She hated to disappoint Rob. He'd sounded so hopeful, so relieved that he didn't have to worry about her stabbing him in the gut while he slept.

Pounding a fist above her heart, she said, "I feel it here. I had that flash of recognition, that same flash I felt when I told you I was an art teacher. Don't you see? I *am* an artist, maybe I even teach others. The tattoo on my back is the name of my gallery."

"Maybe we can find out for sure." Rob placed his hands on the laptop's keyboard and typed in *Libby James.*

If Rob expected her face to pop up next to some biographical entry on her, he was hiding his defeat well.

Rob tapped his thumbs on the edge of the keyboard after his fruitless search. "I guess Libby James keeps a low profile."

"It makes sense, doesn't it, Rob? I'm fluent in Spanish because I live in Mexico. For the same reason, you weren't able to find my prints in your fingerprint database, or whatever it is you checked. I have the name of that gallery tattooed on my back. I *feel* artistic, and somehow I've run into, run across or run afoul of El Gringo Viejo in Rocky Point, which is a big tip for you."

"A big tip for me?" She followed his gaze as it scanned the screen, searching for her face, searching for some proof beyond her feelings.

"You all." She swiped her arm through the air. "Maybe El Gringo Viejo is in Rocky Point, too. You said law enforcement doesn't know where he is or what he looks like. Now you know he's in Rocky Point."

"I don't know, Jane." Rob rubbed his eyes and pushed the computer from his lap onto the coffee table. "We need some kind of proof."

"Libby." She pinned her shoulders against the back cushion of the couch, feeling stronger every time she said the name. "Start calling me Libby."

"You do look more like a Libby than a Jane."

"In what way?" She tilted her head, and her hair swung over her shoulder.

"Jane… I don't know. It reminds me of plain Jane and you're anything but plain."

A tingling warmth crept into her cheeks and she pressed her hand against one side as if to stop the color she was sure had accompanied the heat.

She snorted. "Yeah, plain doesn't cut it for a woman hiding out in the desert with ripped clothing and a gash on the side of her head."

Rob rolled his eyes.

Did he think she was fishing for more compliments? Was she?

"So." She laced her fingers and stretched her arms in front of her. "What's our next step? I don't think I should go running back to Rocky Point, do you?"

"Absolutely not. If you are Libby James from Rocky Point and in some kind of trouble with El Gringo Viejo, you don't want to return to the source of your misery—especially with no understanding of what that misery is."

Rob hadn't balked at her use of *our*. Whether or not he believed her about being Libby, he wasn't going to abandon her.

"You need to get your memory back. You need to find out why those men had instructions to kill you. You need to talk to someone." He held up a finger as she opened her mouth. "Not the cops."

"I know, a psychiatrist or psychologist—someone like that. I've already been thinking along those same lines. I suppose you don't have any mental health professionals here in Paradiso."

"We do. There's a therapist who works at the hospital, and I know she sees patients outside of her work there."

She raised her eyebrows at him.

He crossed one finger over the other. "Not me. I told you I had plenty of head shrinking when I was a kid in school. I don't need any more."

"Are you sure?"

"What does that mean?"

"You rescued a knife-wielding woman in the desert and took her into your home, didn't call the cops, didn't call the hospital, didn't report the accident—some people would say you're certifiable."

"Ah, don't remind me." He buried his hands in his hair.

"This cannot get out to my coworkers. They have this impression that I'm impulsive and careless."

"Do you think that's a reaction to being so very careful when you were growing up?"

His dark brown eyes narrowed. "I'll say it again. I think you're a therapist, not an artist. You have this tendency to analyze me when you're the one who needs analyzing."

"Maybe I'm just practicing for what's to come." She lifted and dropped her shoulders. "I don't need analysis so much as a swift knock on the head."

"I don't think you need that at all." He stroked his fingers over the hair covering her wound, and she melted just a little.

She sure hoped there wasn't a Mr. James out there looking for his wife.

He snatched his hand back from her head as if the same thought had just occurred to him. "If the psychiatrist at the hospital can't see you, she can recommend another therapist, although you might have to go to Tucson to see someone."

"I'd be willing to go a lot farther than Tucson to get help."

"I think your brain has done enough work for tonight. All signs point to Libby so far, but knowing your name isn't enough. You have to remember who you are to get this straightened out."

"I agree." She rose to her feet a little unsteadily, and Rob placed a hand on her hip. "Sh-should I go back to my motel tonight?"

"No, although I was ready to kick you out after confronting you about your library searches." He left his hand on her body as if she needed propping up. Maybe she did.

"After finding out, why did you bring me back here? Why did you feed me?"

"I wanted to trip you up. I wanted to discover your motive, and then I just wanted you to tell me the truth." He ran his thumb into the pocket of her pants. "Why didn't you tell me all this before?"

"I was afraid." She lodged her tongue in the corner of her mouth. "I was afraid of the unknown, of being taken to the police station and revealed as someone who had no memory, no ID, no life. You may have thought I needed to be in the hospital, but the thought terrified me. I didn't want to be captive somewhere for some stranger to come along and claim me like a stray puppy—tell me who I was and where I needed to be."

He nodded as he stood up beside her, removing his thumb from her pocket. "I get it. It must be strange not knowing who you are, like staring into an abyss."

"Take that and multiply it by a hundred, but then you came along and didn't push even though you didn't believe me." She turned from the magnetic hold his eyes exerted on her. "I appreciate that."

"My colleagues are not completely wrong about me. I can be impulsive. I can be naive about the crime committed out here in the desert, away from the big, bad city." He stepped over the coffee table to avoid squeezing past her on his way to the kitchen. "I'll even admit that some part of me did believe your story—a woman on the run from an angry ex. I've seen enough of that in my childhood. I could relate. I could sympathize."

"I had no idea I'd be pressing your buttons with that story. It just came to me as a possibility." She pointed past him. "We didn't finish cleaning up."

"That's where I was headed." He made a stop at the

table to collect the rest of their dinner. "I hate leaving a mess to clean up in the morning."

"I do, too." When Rob's head swiveled around, she held up her hand and said, "I think I do."

He tossed a dish towel over his shoulder. "I'm sorry. I'm going to make you anxious about recovering your memories if I jump every time you make a statement about yourself."

"I don't mind. Maybe it will all come back that way." She yanked the dish towel hanging down his back. "I'll dry."

He rinsed suds from a plate and handed it to her. "Memory's a weird thing, isn't it?"

"If I didn't think so before, it's taken on a whole new dimension of weirdness for me."

"I mean—" he handed her the second plate "—you don't remember your name or where you're from or who you are, but you clearly knew where Tucson was. And you remember how to speak Spanish."

She rubbed a circle on the plate until it glowed. "Maybe the psychiatrist can explain that. I imagine it has something to do with the parts of the brain injured."

"I suppose it doesn't matter, as long as someone can help you get on track. Then we can deal with those two men…and the rest of it."

She slid a glance at his profile as he worked at the sink, his jaw tight. Was he as worried as she was at what discoveries her true identity might bring?

As she dried the last of the dishes, he sprayed some green liquid on his granite countertops and ran a paper towel over the surface until it gleamed. Was he really this particular or just stalling for time?

He didn't think she'd fall into his arms or request they share a bed for the night, did he? Would she?

She said, "You can have your T-shirt back. April even threw in a couple of nightgowns with the tags still on them."

"Yeah, she really came through." He tossed the paper towel in the trash and rubbed his hands together. "I felt kind of crummy lying to her."

She touched her fingers to her lips. "I'm sorry. That's on me. She's not the cop, right? Maybe we can tell her the truth."

"April would help anyway. It doesn't matter to her. It's not like the woman hasn't told a few lies in her time—all for the greater good, of course."

"And that's what this is, Rob—the greater good. The fewer people who know my identity, or lack thereof, the better. It'll help me keep a low profile. Can you imagine the stir an amnesiac woman would cause in this town?"

"Everyone would be talking about you for sure. I agree, the greater good."

He held out his fist for a bump, and she tapped her knuckles against his awkwardly. Were they buds now?

"Tomorrow we'll visit Dr. Escalante at the hospital for some advice. Sound good?"

"Great—sounds great." She wiped her hands on the seat of her pants, even though she'd just hung up a perfectly good towel. She backed out of the kitchen and spun toward the hallway. "Same bedroom? I mean, the same bedroom I had last night?"

Rob coughed and made a job of intricately folding a dry dish towel over the handle of the oven door. "I just have the two bedrooms. The third I use as an office."

"Yeah, yeah, that's what I mean, the room I had last night." She waved like an idiot and snatched up the pad of paper from the living room. "Okay, good night. Thanks for your help, Rob."

She rounded the corner of the hallway and stubbed her toe on the edge. She bit her lip to suppress a cry and hopped on one foot to the bedroom.

She fell across the bed on top of April's generous donation, covering her face with one arm. She hoped Libby wasn't this lame in real life.

She pushed the pile of clothes onto the floor, knowing full well Rob would have a heart attack if he saw the tangled mess on the floor—but he wouldn't be in this room. Two rooms. He had two bedrooms and this was hers, for now.

With her ear to the door, she listened to the splashing water and electric toothbrush from the master bathroom buried deep in Rob's bedroom. In the midst of it all, she slipped into a coral-hued sheath with spaghetti straps and grabbed the little plastic bag containing the toiletries she'd purchased with her first salary.

Clutching the bag to her chest, she tiptoed into the bathroom next to her room and flossed and brushed her teeth. If Libby weren't a flosser, she'd start some new habits with her new life.

Rob's cell phone rang from his room and she heard his low voice rumble in answer. Maybe it was some woman wondering why he hadn't called her back, or maybe someone he'd met on one of those online dating apps setting up a first date.

She couldn't make out his words and didn't try. The man deserved some privacy in his own home.

As she spit into the sink, he rapped on the bathroom door.

"Ja… Libby?"

Frantic eyes flew to the mirror, her gaze dropping to the skimpy nightgown clinging to and outlining her braless breasts. What was April thinking?

"Yeah?"

"Can you open the door?"

He seemed to be forcing his words through clenched teeth. Obviously, an invitation to seduction didn't wait on the other side of that door.

She placed her toothbrush on the edge of the sink and contemplated the locked bathroom door between her and the tight-voiced stranger.

"Of course. It's your door." She took a few steps on the cold tile floor and threw open the door, the smile on her lips drooping. "Wh-what's wrong?"

"The Arizona Highway Patrol found your wreck."

She placed a hand on her stomach, against the slick material of the nightgown, all thoughts of covering her jiggling breasts lost in a flood of fear. "Why'd they call you?"

"They found something in the car."

Her heart pounded, causing the silky material covering her chest to quiver. "My ID? My purse? Why would they call you?"

"They didn't find that stuff." A muscle ticked in his jaw. "They found drugs. You were hauling drugs across the border... Libby."

Chapter Nine

Her fingers curled into the nightgown at her waist, bunching and twisting it.

Did she think that evidence would be burned beyond recognition, or did she really not remember? Either way, she had drugs in the car, whether or not she remembered.

She swayed on her feet and he had an urge to catch her, pull her into his arms, but he needed to stay objective—something he'd been failing at in a big way.

She shook her head slowly at first and then so vigorously, her hair whipped back and forth like a swirl of caramel. "Nothing survived that inferno. You don't think I checked it out when the fire burned down?"

"It would've still been too hot for you to do anything more than give it a cursory look." He set his jaw, but she'd planted a seed of doubt in his mind.

She must've seen the flicker and pounced. "You looked, too. Did you see any drugs or any packages that looked like drugs or were even intact? Pretty much everything was incinerated." She thrust out her chest and one strap of the flimsy nightgown slipped from her shoulder. "Where were they? What were they? Who found them?"

His gaze bounced from her bare shoulder to her scowling face. "Packages of meth, thrown from the vehicle.

They escaped the fire. The highway patrol spotted the burned-out vehicle and went down to inspect it."

"Meth? You mean like powder?"

"Crystals. Crystal meth in plastic bags, stuffed inside a paper bag." He scratched the stubble on his chin. "About ten feet from the crash site."

"How convenient. And you believe that?" Her nostrils quivered, and a red flush stained her cheeks. "You saw that area, and believe me, so did I. I searched around the car for anything that would tell me who I was and what I was doing there, and then I searched again for water, food, crumbs. There was nothing there but trash, debris from the highway."

Rob pinched the bridge of his nose. The scene of the crash swam before his eyes—desert, sand, dirt, cactus, a few bits of highway trash, a few trees. Had he done a thorough search of the area? It had been dark, and there was no blackness like nighttime in the desert without a full moon.

He huffed out a breath. "It was dark out there."

"I'm telling you there were no drugs." She slammed her hand against the porcelain of the sink, and her toothbrush bounced and fell to the floor.

"What are you saying… Libby?" He dug two fingers into his temple and massaged, as if that could get rid of the pounding in his head.

"Someone planted those drugs there, Rob." She wedged a fist against her hip, the curve of it just visible in the loose-fitting nightgown. "How did the highway patrol know about the accident? You said yourself you couldn't see it from the highway, but you smelled it and saw the smoke. That would've been long gone the next morning and certainly by today. So, how'd they know it was there? Helicopter? Drone?"

He still held the phone that had brought him the bad news in his hand and he tapped the edge against his chin. "Someone reported it."

"Aha!" She tossed her hair over her shoulder. "Don't you see? Somebody threw the drugs out there and then called the highway patrol about the accident so they'd see the drugs."

Libby would want to explain away the drugs so that he wouldn't connect them to her, but her claims held more logic than desperation. He hadn't seen anything out there on the desert floor. If the drugs had been secured in the car or hidden in the trunk, how'd they get thrown in the accident?

Her version might make more sense and clear her, but the implication didn't bode well for her safety and well-being.

"You know what you're suggesting?"

Her eye twitched. "I do. The men who caused my accident came back to check their handiwork. Maybe they wondered why there was no report of a dead body found with a crash and discovered it was because there *was* no body there."

"And that means not only do they know you survived the crash, they left those drugs there as insurance to implicate you if you went to the authorities."

"It almost worked, didn't it?" She stooped to pick up the toothbrush and ran it beneath the faucet. "You charged in here to accuse me of being a drug runner, or whatever."

"Do you blame me?" He reached back to shove the phone in his pocket and realized he'd rushed in here with just his boxers on. "We still don't know anything about you."

She placed her hands on either side of the sink and

leaned in to peer at herself in the mirror. "We know my name is Libby, I'm an artist and I own an art gallery in Mexico…and I'm in some kind of trouble with a drug dealer."

Feeling a sudden chill, Rob rubbed his arms. "I hope those two guys moved on after dropping those drugs… if that's what happened."

"Still doubting me? Why'd the highway patrol call you, anyway?"

"They didn't call me personally. They called the Border Patrol because of the drugs, and my supervisor called me to let me know. We have the drugs in our possession now, and you can bet I'm going to examine them for any identifying features."

"Drugs have identifying features?"

"Sure they do—consistency of product, purity of product, even packaging. That's why the highway patrol calls us." He took a step back. "I'm sorry I barged in here."

"I'm not."

He raised his eyebrows.

"I mean, I'm glad you came right to me and told me. I wish you'd done that when you discovered my search history at the library."

"You're one to talk about honesty and transparency. You didn't trust me enough to tell me you had amnesia."

"I didn't know you."

"My point, exactly." He wedged a shoulder against the doorjamb. "Libby, what are you going to do if you find out you are involved in the drug trade somehow?"

She lifted a shoulder. "Turn over a new leaf."

He retreated to let her finish getting ready for bed. He left his door ajar and stashed his gun in the drawer of his nightstand. He was no longer worried about the strange woman with the strange story he'd picked up in the desert… He was worried *for* her.

SHE SHOT UP in the bed, panic engulfing her, her heart rattling in her chest, her dreams breaking apart and skittering in all different directions.

She placed a hand to her heart, counting the beats, breathing deeply. She still didn't know who she was beyond a name and occupation, but she felt safe for the first time since coming to in that car crash.

She had someone in the other room who believed her. Maybe Rob believed her against all his instincts and better judgment, but she'd take it.

She'd come to the conclusion that Rob could afford to be trusting and a bit impulsive because he'd honed his instincts over the years. A person didn't grow up in the conditions Rob had faced as a boy without being able to tell good from evil, without sensing danger whether it stared you in the face or crept up on you around a dark street corner.

Most people didn't have that ability, so they approached every stranger, every situation with caution and fear. Rolling to her side, she pulled the pillow against her chest. Why did she understand Rob so much better than she knew herself?

She didn't even know what kind of person she was. Was she the kind of person who could smuggle drugs across the border? Drugs that hurt kids, ruined families and destroyed lives?

No. That wasn't her. Black boots and his cohort planted those drugs to get her in trouble. To keep her from reporting the accident. And that meant they knew she was still alive.

She pulled the covers to her chin. Had they seen her

in Paradiso? Had that voice she'd heard at Rosita's really been one of them?

Rob was right. She had to learn her identity sooner rather than later. And if she found out she had a husband and two children?

Her insane attraction to Rob could be based on the fact that he was the only man of her acquaintance and he'd rescued her from the desert, had even agreed not to call the cops even though he was one.

In fact, Rob Valdez was just about perfect without even taking into account his dreamy dark eyes, killer smile, hot bod and mocha skin… And he'd been beside her all night.

She hung over the side of the bed and picked up the notepad and pen she'd squirreled in her room. She couldn't sleep, so she'd stayed up sketching.

Rob's handsome face stared at her with a touch of sadness, or maybe distrust, from the top page. She flipped through the others to study the characters she'd drawn—a faceless, evil visage with silver-tipped black boots, Rosie's creased face wreathed in smiles and a fairy with curly hair and big eyes.

The knock on the door had her dropping the notepad and clutching the sheet to her chest like a virgin. For all she knew, she could be.

Rob called out in a singsong voice, "I made coffee."

"I'm awake." She kicked off the covers and dug through the clothes on the floor for a pair of sweats and a T-shirt. She didn't need to be shimmying around Rob's kitchen in the slinky nightie.

As she pulled on a pair of gray sweat shorts and a red U of A Wildcats T-shirt, she thanked the resourceful April. She'd pretty much thought of everything.

Her bare feet slapped the tile floor on her way to the

kitchen, the smell of bacon luring her in like a fish on a reel.

"I should be doing the cooking."

Rob looked up, a piece of bacon hanging from a pair of tongs over a sizzling frying pan. "You're still on the injured list."

She touched her bed-head hair. "This cut is nothing compared to the damage it did to my brain."

"While you were sleeping, I called Dr. Escalante at the hospital." He laid out the strip of bacon on a paper-towel-covered plate next to three other pieces, all running the same way, probably all equidistant, all done to the same level of crispness. He held up an egg. "Sunny-side up, over easy?"

She said without any hesitation, "Over hard with no runny yolk."

"I can do that." He cracked the egg on the edge of the skillet.

"I hope Dr. Escalante can see me and figure out why I can remember how I like my eggs but not my name or home." She grabbed the coffeepot and swirled the brown liquid in the pot. "You need a top-off?"

"I'm good." He carefully slid the crackling egg onto its other side. "Dr. Escalante referred me…you to a therapist up in Tucson. You up for a drive this afternoon after your shift at Rosita's?"

"Rosita's." She drove her heel against her forehead. "That just shows you how bad my memory is. I completely forgot about working today."

"I'm going in early to have a look at that packet of meth found near your wreck. I'll drop you off, and when you're done, we can take that ride up to Tucson. Dr. Escalante already called in your referral."

"Who's the doc?" She slurped at the black coffee,

convinced she'd never taken her coffee black before in her life.

"She's not a doctor. She's a licensed therapist and hypnotist."

Libby dropped the spoon she'd just grabbed from the drawer. "A hypnotist? She's going to hypnotize me?"

"Why not?" Rob crouched down to pick up the spoon and tossed it into the sink. "What do you have to lose?"

"Not more of my memory. That's not possible." She scooped another spoon from the utensil tray and poured some milk into her coffee. "Do you think you can find out who phoned in that tip about the accident?"

"Probably not if it was anonymous, and I gather it was, but I can do some digging." He slid a couple of eggs onto a plate, alongside two perfectly placed pieces of bacon. "I'm going to do some other digging, too. I want you to know that up front. I don't want to hide anything from you, Libby."

"You're going to dig around in Libby James's background, aren't you?" She watched the swirl of milk invade coffee. "Her—my criminal background."

"If there is one, but like I told you before, your prints didn't match any we had in the database. I'm also going to make sure nobody has reported you missing."

"Is there a database that you can check in Mexico?"

"Not that we can access." He carried the plates to the table and set them down on the woven place mats. "But there are a few other places I can look. Maybe I can arm you with a little more info before your appointment this afternoon."

"Or you can arrest me."

"I don't think that's gonna happen." He pulled out a chair at the table for her and sank into the other one.

He snapped a piece of bacon in two with one hand and watched it fall to his plate.

Her fork hovered over her eggs. "You're not so sure, are you?"

"It's not that, Libby." He popped one half of the bacon into his mouth. "I'm just wondering why someone felt it necessary to plant drugs at the scene of the crash."

"To shut me up."

"Then they know you're alive. How?"

"Maybe El Gringo sent them back to double-check. Maybe he sent them back to show proof of death—a picture of my charred body." She stuffed some food in her mouth so she wouldn't scream. After she swallowed and took a sip of coffee, she said, "They didn't find that proof, figured I walked away and left those drugs in case I got any ideas about ratting on them."

"Or maybe they're hanging around Paradiso and spotted you."

She leaned her fork against her plate, tines down, and folded her hands in her lap. "Thanks. You just ruined my appetite."

"I'm trying to look at all angles—no matter how ugly."

"Wouldn't you recognize a couple of strangers, thug types, wandering around Paradiso?"

Rob choked on his coffee and spit it into his napkin. "Thug types? How do you know they look like thugs? You didn't even see them."

"I thought you had superkeen instincts about these things."

"Did I say that?" He dabbed at the droplets of coffee he'd sputtered onto the table. "Sometimes thugs don't look like thugs, and sometimes people who look like thugs aren't thugs. There was a time in Paradiso, before my time, when strangers would stand out, but no longer.

Not since the pecan processing plant fired up, thanks to my coworker's family. The population boomed. We have more tourism. We have more tourists coming over from Tombstone and Bisbee. Now strangers aren't uncommon. Two guys, Latinos, are not going to make waves in Paradiso."

"They could be anywhere, watching me, and I wouldn't even know it." She stared at a picture of a café on a Mexican street, a green-and-red umbrella shading a couple hunched over a small table.

"What is it? Do you remember something?"

"Just a voice at Rosita's yesterday, someone in the to-go line. It struck a chord inside, and I panicked for a minute. And then there was a guy on the street in a baseball cap." She shrugged and picked up her fork. "I suppose those events jarred me because I already realized those men could be on the loose in Paradiso."

"If they are, they must know something's going on with you. Why else wouldn't you have reported the accident, reported them? They wouldn't be sticking around to drop off a stash of meth if they were worried about that."

"They must know there's some reason why I didn't call the cops after surviving that crash." She swallowed hard, all out of proportion to the soft eggs sliding down her throat. She didn't want to think she was involved in dealing drugs. She was sure she wasn't. Just as she knew she couldn't be so attracted to the man across from her if she were married, she knew her morals wouldn't allow her to engage in drug activity.

"The sooner you get through this morning and to that therapist appointment, the sooner we're going to figure out exactly what's going on. Once we do, I'll know how to keep you safe."

"That's important to you? Keeping me safe?" She

couldn't meet his eyes, so she drew crisscross patterns on her plate with the fork.

"It's become my top priority." Rob pushed back from the table so fast, his foot caught on the leg of his chair and he stumbled. A grin lit up his face. "If I could keep myself safe first."

Libby showered and dressed in record time. When she joined Rob in the living room, she tugged on the hem of the short-sleeved, dark green T-shirt. "At least my clothes aren't ripped today."

"That's a plus." He hitched his bag over one shoulder. "If something or someone makes you feel uncomfortable at work, just leave. Rosie will understand."

She sucked in her bottom lip as she walked out the front door. "I'll be in a public place. They're not going to come in and snatch me…are they?"

"Just be careful." He helped her hop into the truck. "These cartels are ruthless. Just a few months ago, two mules were executed at the border, beheaded. They were women—Tandy Richards and Elena Delgado. They don't care."

Rob's jaw formed a hard line as he slammed the door of the truck.

Rob *did* care.

By the time he dropped her off at Rosita's, her mouth was as dry as the desert floor. Rob hadn't meant to scare the stuffing out of her, but now she'd be looking over her shoulder all morning. Better to be on the lookout instead of getting ambushed in a surprise attack.

She sauntered into Rosita's with a swagger that masked her fear—or so she thought.

"I'm glad you're back, *mija*." Rosie patted her cheek. "You look better. Is Rob taking good care of you?"

"He is." As soon as he'd stopped believing she was a drug courier like those poor beheaded women.

She waved to the guys in the kitchen and got to work. She scrutinized every male customer, her glance taking in every pair of shoes, looking for the black boots. Nobody sparked any recognition in her, and nobody acted as if she should know him.

She soon got into a groove, and the morning passed quickly. By the time she wiped the last table, Rob poked his head inside the café wearing civilian clothes—a pair of faded jeans and a light blue tee.

"Are you almost ready?"

"Not fair." She waved her towel at him. "You had a chance to clean up and change."

"I can take you back to my place if you want to shower."

She reached around and untied the apron. "That's okay. Hopefully this woman likes the smell of chips."

Rosie scurried in from the kitchen, rubbing her hands together. "Do you want some lunch, Rob?"

"No, thanks, Rosie. We're in a hurry."

Rosie patted Libby on the back. "Don't hurry this one."

He saluted. *"Sí, jefe."*

Rosie shook her head and pressed a plastic bag into Libby's hands. "You take this anyway."

Libby thanked her, and then she and Rob got into his own truck.

As he clutched the steering wheel, he said, "That's another reason why I know you're a good person."

"Rosie?"

"You talk about my instincts. She can sniff out a phony like a bloodhound." He cranked on the engine. "She lost a son to drugs."

"Oh, no." Libby covered her mouth. "Overdose or some kind of drug violence?"

"OD. Happened before I moved here. Too bad." Rob's knuckles turned white as he squeezed the steering wheel. "Maybe I could've knocked some sense into him."

"You help enough people just by doing your job." She trailed her fingertips along his corded forearm. "You don't need to save the whole world."

"Maybe one person at a time." He threw the truck into Reverse and pulled out of the parking space. "Nothing unusual today?"

"No. You? Did you discover anything about Libby James?"

"Nothing criminal. That's quite a gallery she has down in Mexico, but she's camera shy. No pictures of her… you online."

"I guess that's not unusual. People want to see the art, not the artist." Libby gazed out the window. "I don't have much to offer the therapist."

"It's not your job to offer her anything. She's going to be helping you."

"Through hypnosis."

"You sound skeptical."

"Is she going to swing something in front of my face and tell me I'm getting sleepy?"

"That's what I mean." Rob slapped the dashboard. "You pulled that from your memory bank, and yet you can't access your personal memories."

"It's a weird condition to be in. It's like there's nothing personal there."

"There must be and this therapist—" he fished into the front pocket of his T-shirt and withdrew a slip of paper between his fingers "—Jennifer Montrose is going to help you bring it all to the surface."

About an hour later, they rolled into Tucson. They bypassed the downtown area and the university and aimed for the foothills.

Rob pointed out the window. "Looks like her office is in this business center."

Libby twisted her fingers in her lap. "What if I find out something I don't want to know about myself?"

"Whatever you find out is better than nothingness, isn't it?" He squeezed her knee. "What if you have a child somewhere?"

She flattened a hand against her belly, recalling the fairy she'd drawn last night who had borne a resemblance to her own face. "I can't. How could someone forget her own child?"

He parked the car and turned to face her. "You don't know what's going on in your head, what kind of injury you sustained. I don't think even an important memory has a chance to swim to the surface yet. That's why you're seeing Montrose."

"You're right." She released her seat belt and scooped in a deep breath. "I'm ready."

Rob checked his slip of paper for the therapist's suite number, and they walked up the stairs to the second level. When Rob tried the door with Jennifer Montrose's nameplate on the front, it swung open onto a small lobby with a few hanging plants and a blue love seat and matching chair facing each other.

Libby crept up to a closed door with a button like a doorbell on the side. Her forefinger hovered over it. "Should I?"

Rob checked his phone. "We're ten minutes early. Maybe wait until your appointment time in case someone's in there."

Libby meandered to the magazine rack and plucked up

a celebrity magazine, scanning the photos on the front. Why did she recognize these people but not her own face in the mirror?

The door behind her opened, and she jumped, dropping the magazine on the floor.

"I'm sorry I startled you." The smooth, low voice alone was enough to calm her down and put her under.

Libby turned and held out her hand to the petite, dark-haired woman in the patterned palazzo pants and long blouse. "I'm Libby."

The therapist's dark eyes didn't assess her or judge. She clasped Libby's hand in a firm grip that belied her size.

"Nice to meet you, Libby. I'm Jennifer Montrose. You can call me Jennifer."

Rob introduced himself, and Libby's heart stuttered when he sank into the lone chair in the room. He wasn't going in with her to hold her hand?

Libby's eyes flew to his face and back to Jennifer's. "C-can he come in with me?"

Jennifer said, "I don't think it's a good idea, but we can do this however you want."

What if she did remember being married to El Gringo Viejo or being a drug dealer or something even worse? Did she really want Rob there to hear it all?

"No, no. Of course not. I just had a minute of panic." She wiggled her fingers at Rob, who was half out of his seat. "I'm good. I'll be fine."

"I'll be right here waiting for you." Rob winked at her.

Swallowing, she followed Jennifer into the next room, the low lights already soothing.

Jennifer took a seat in a comfortable chair. "If you want to get right to the hypnosis today, you can take the seat across from me."

"I do. That's why I'm here. I lost my memory in a car accident, and what I heard from two men after that accident has led me to believe my life is in danger. I have to find out who I am."

"I got the summary from Dr. Escalante." Jennifer tilted her head to the side, the gentle smile never leaving her lips. "You told me your name is Libby."

"Rob and I discovered a few things. I—I have a tattoo on my back, and we think it might be the name of an art gallery in Mexico owned by a woman named Libby James. No pictures, but I have a feeling about it. I also speak fluent Spanish."

Jennifer nodded. "Thank you for the information. Hypnosis is a deep state of relaxation and has been useful in the past to help people access memories. I'm going to hold up this pen and I'd like you to follow it with your eyes and listen to my voice."

After several minutes of watching the pen and listening to Jennifer's soothing voice, Jennifer's words and the feelings they evoked washed over her. Images floated across her brain—pleasant scenes of the beach and the ocean and a small gallery tucked along a cobbled street, but Jennifer pushed her away from the serenity.

What had she forgotten? What did she want to forget? What made her fearful? Who made her fearful?

The rambling villa on the coast with views forever made her stomach twist. Her feet dragged over the rolling grass. "No!"

She wanted to stop, but Jennifer's voice prodded her onward.

She drew closer and closer to the object on the grass. Then she gripped the arms of the chair and struggled to resurface.

Jennifer led her back to awareness gently, but Libby's heart hammered in her chest as her eyes flew open.

"He's dead. I witnessed a murder."

Chapter Ten

Rob sat up straight in his chair, his nails digging into the fabric on the arms as he heard a cry—Libby's cry—from the other room.

She had to go through this alone. There had to be some trauma other than the car crash that had caused her to lose her memory. Was she reliving that trauma now?

Folding his arms, he jammed his fists against his sides. He couldn't do anything for her. Could he do anything for her if it turned out she was involved with the cartels or El Gringo Viejo?

People could reform. He'd seen it before. Even his brother in prison had repented and was trying to make amends.

The door eased open, and he jumped to his feet. The doorjamb framed Libby, a tissue clutched in her hand, her eyes wide and glassy.

Jennifer hugged her. "I'll see you next week. If you need to come in before that or give me a call, please do it."

Libby shuffled toward him and plowed straight into his chest.

He wrapped an arm around her, his mouth so dry he couldn't form any words.

She mumbled against his T-shirt. "I'll tell you outside."

When they walked out of Jennifer's office, Rob squinted in the sunlight and dropped his sunglasses over his eyes.

Libby blinked, her eyes watering, until he grabbed her cheap sunglasses from the side of her purse and handed them to her. "Put these on."

She obeyed but seemed out of it. He kept a hand on her arm, not trusting her to make it through the parking lot without getting hit by a car. When they got to his truck, he nudged her inside and she plopped on the seat.

He slid behind the wheel and started the engine to get the AC running. A crease had formed between her eyebrows and she seemed to be staring at something in the distance.

Rob cleared his throat. "Do you want to tell me what happened?"

She cranked her head toward him. "I witnessed a murder."

He caught his breath. "Do you know who it was? Do you know who killed him or her?"

As horrible as the memory was for Libby, a few knots unraveled in Rob's gut. For a minute he thought she was going to reveal that El Gringo Viejo was her vindictive spouse.

"I saw a man lying dead on the lawn. There was so much blood and I felt so much terror." She grabbed his arm, her nails digging into his flesh. "You don't think I did it, do you? Did I kill that man?"

Rob ran his hands along the steering wheel. "Was that your first feeling when you saw the body under hypnosis?"

She shook her head. "I knew he was dead, and I was afraid. Would I be so scared if I were the one who killed him? I felt a dark presence hanging over me, coming for me."

"Witnessing a murder would be enough to traumatize anyone." Rob rubbed his chin. "D-did you remember anything else? Do you know who you are?"

"I'm Libby." Her eyes widened for a second and she flipped down the visor. Scooting forward in her seat, she stared into the mirror. "I know I'm Libby James, Rob. I saw the gallery on a street in Mexico. That part was fine. It felt good…right."

"Did you remember anything else? The dead guy? His killer? Your…family?" He reached for the bottle of water in his cup holder and chugged it down so fast he coughed.

"Nothing like that." She traced a finger along her jawline as if drawing her face. "Just feelings, images, flashes of memory. Jennifer said that's completely normal and that it's a good sign I'll recover everything, eventually."

"Nothing about the car crash or the two men?" His staccato pulse returned to normal. She could handle witnessing a murder, and the fact that it shocked her was a good sign that she wasn't accustomed to the violence.

"We didn't go there. Jennifer wanted to lead me back to the events before the crash." Still watching her face in the mirror, she said, "Do you think that's why those two men were after me? Because I witnessed a murder?"

"Could be, or…" He pressed his lips together and shifted into Drive.

She jerked away from studying her reflection. "What?"

"We really don't know, do we? It's all guessing at this point. Let's wait for Jennifer." He pulled forward out of the parking space a little too fast and a car honked at him.

"You can't do that, Rob. I want all ideas on the table. Jennifer doesn't want me to wait for her. She wants me to dig whenever I can." She ran both of her hands across her face. "I'm okay. The whole hypnosis experience was strange. It rattled me, especially when I remembered that dead body on the lawn. But I'm okay."

"I'm just wondering what you were doing there with a murder victim. Were you also an intended victim? Did the killer hope to get both of you, and you escaped?" He held his breath. If she broke down, he'd have to pull over. If she returned to her semicatatonic state, he'd have to pull over. Hell, he shouldn't even be driving.

She grabbed her water bottle and shook what had to be lukewarm liquid inside. Then she screwed off the lid and took a sip. "Maybe."

His gaze slid from the road to her profile, which didn't look ready to crumble at all. "You keep talking about this lawn. Where was the man's body?"

She rubbed her bare arms. "It was on some beautiful, beachside estate—one of those lawns that runs down to the cliffs that drop off to the ocean."

"Yours?" Uneasiness stirred his belly again. Didn't much sound like the home of an artist.

"I hope not." She slammed the bottle back into the cup holder. "I don't know where it was or who owned it, but that place was pure evil. I felt that as if I were standing on the cliff's edge instead of sitting on a chair inside a therapist's office in Tucson."

"I wish this hadn't all taken place south of the border. It would be a lot easier to track Libby James if she lived in the US. There's only so much I can do to research you if you don't have many records here."

She clapped her hands together and rested her chin on the steeple of her fingers. "But I am Libby James. I'm sure of that now, and that feels good. Thank you."

"Me?" He drove a thumb into his chest. "You were more convinced of that than I was. It's a good thing you got that tattoo. That's what led us to Libby. We would've been lost without Rosalinda."

She closed her eyes and slumped in her seat. "I feel much better now. I really do. I have a name, a place and a reason why I was on the run."

"Maybe it's time to turn this over to the authorities."

"I don't have much to give them, Rob, and there are those drugs at the accident scene." She clasped her hands between her knees. "I don't want anyone else providing the narrative of my life before I have a chance to remember it."

With what she could give them now, the cops most likely wouldn't believe she had anything to do with the drugs in her car. He clenched his teeth. Yeah, they might. When he questioned a suspect, he came in with a healthy dose of skepticism, and Libby's story sounded outlandish on the surface.

He didn't know what had happened to that skepticism when he first came across Libby. Maybe it was the fear in her eyes. The story of abuse. Maybe it was the knife she was wielding.

She poked him in the ribs. "Why are you grinning? Are you thinking about my explanation to the cops about what happened?"

"Sort of."

"I hope you agree it's too early."

"I'm not going to force you to do anything you're not ready to do…except eat dinner." He patted his stomach. "I'm starving, but I can wait until we reach Paradiso."

"Maybe by then I'll have an appetite. Seeing that dead man—" she hunched her shoulders and a tremor shook her frame "—was almost like seeing him in person. In fact, it was all so real."

He stroked her arm with one knuckle. "I'm glad Jennifer helped you. Maybe that session unlocked the door, and the memories will keep flowing."

"I hope so." Closing her eyes, she scrunched down in the seat and leaned her head against the window.

Maybe she was trying to access more memories or maybe she was just sleeping. Either way, he left her alone for the rest of the drive back to Paradiso.

She didn't stir until he signaled to take the exit into town. She dragged her hand across her mouth and blinked. "Are we back yet?"

"Pretty much. Do you want to stop off and change?"

She yawned. "Are you still starving?"

"Ravenous." His eyes flicked over her body as she uncurled and stretched out.

"Then let's eat." She rubbed her chin. "Any drool?"

Just his own.

"No drool. You look refreshed." He reached over and tucked a strand of hair behind her ear. "Do you feel better about what you learned under hypnosis?"

"Anything, especially something that doesn't point to my involvement in the drug trade, is going to make me feel better at this point." She powered down her window a crack. "Of course, I don't know who that poor murdered man was."

"Do you remember what he looked like?" He hadn't wanted to upset her before by asking any details, but she'd calmed down and those details were important.

She screwed up one side of her face. "He was old. He had gray hair…matted with blood. I couldn't tell you his height because he was lying on the ground."

"Latino? White guy?"

"White—gringo." She clapped a hand over her mouth. "You don't think that was him, do you? El Gringo Viejo?"

"That wouldn't make sense if the two guys were afraid

to tell him they hadn't confirmed your death. If he were dead himself, he wouldn't care." He pulled onto Paradiso's main drag. "Burgers and fries or something more elegant?"

She pinched the material of her khaki-colored capris between her fingers. "Do I look elegant?"

"You look…fine."

"What if the man in my memory wasn't dead? What if he were just injured? He could still be El Gringo Viejo." Straightening in her seat, she pushed the hair from her face. "What if I injured him? That would be motive for him to come after me."

Rob rolled his eyes. "You're determined to make yourself the bad guy, aren't you? Your first impression of the man in your image was that he was dead—murdered."

"Maybe I thought I'd killed him but didn't. So, in my memory he'd be dead because I wouldn't have known any better."

He pulled the truck up to the curb of the Paradiso Café and cut the engine. "And why would the owner of an art gallery try to kill a drug supplier?"

"Argh, I don't know." She drilled her finger in the middle of her forehead. "This is what I come up with when I think about my past. You have to admit, my life has been pretty dramatic up to this point. Also, an American living in Mexico, running an art gallery with a drug dealer after her, has to be an adventurous person. Would you agree with that?"

"I would, but your association with El Gringo Viejo, if there is one, could be purely innocent, unintentional." He snatched his keys from the ignition. "Look, I know a lot of people in my old neighborhood who were not looking for trouble and got swept up in it anyway. Rocky Point may be a tourist area, but it's also on the edge of an area controlled by the Las Moscas and Sinaloa cartels. If you wander in the wrong neighborhood, you could be in a world of hurt."

She cocked her head. "I like that you're more optimistic about my background than I am. Rob Valdez, you're an optimist. Despite everything, you're still an optimist."

"I'd say I'm an optimist *because* of everything." He pushed open the door of his truck. "Let's eat."

As usual, she'd hopped out before he could get her door. He still went around to the passenger side of the truck and took her arm as they walked into the restaurant.

Being a little early for dinner, they had their choice of tables, and Rob led Libby to one by the window.

He snatched up two plastic menus from the side of the table as he sat down, sliding one over to her side. "They have more than burgers here, but the burgers are good."

She trailed her finger down the menu. "A burger sounds good."

"I'm going to have a beer, too."

"Me, too."

He raised his eyebrows at her. "Are you sure?"

"Who knows? Maybe if I get rip-roaring drunk, everything will come back to me. Jennifer explained that hypnosis puts you in a deeply relaxed state." She flicked her finger against the menu. "Maybe beer will do the same."

Sydney, the waitress, scurried over even though she had just two other tables. "You're early, Rob." Her gaze wandered to Libby, but he didn't feel the need to make introductions. Sydney could get her info like everyone else—from the town grapevine.

He pointed to Libby. "Are you going to order that beer?"

Libby picked out an IPA on draft and ordered a burger with avocado.

"Good choice." He ordered the same beer and a double-bacon burger.

Sydney returned minutes later with two frosty mugs of beer.

Libby planted her elbows on the table. "What am I keeping you from?"

He slurped his drink through the foamy head and asked, "What?"

"You've been babysitting me for two days now, got some clothes for me, took me to Tucson. What should you be doing instead and with whom?"

"I told you I didn't have a girlfriend." He licked his lips and gulped back more beer.

"You don't have any friends? Hobbies? Commitments?" She wrapped her hands around her own mug and took a delicate sip, which left foam on her upper lip.

Before he could make a fool of himself and wipe it off for her, she dabbed her mouth with a napkin.

"I've been with the Border Patrol just over a year. I just passed probation a few months ago. I didn't even live in Paradiso until a month ago. I was waiting to pass probation before making the move from Tucson."

"You commuted here all the way from Tucson?"

"Just in case I didn't make the department, I wanted to be in a place where I could look for other work."

"That's why your house is so neat. You haven't been there long."

"Yeah." He felt the warmth creep up to his hairline. He'd let her believe that instead of revealing his control-freak tendencies. Maybe that was why he'd jumped on her case. He'd wanted to control what happened to her. Better keep that to himself. The poor woman had enough problems.

"So—" she ran a fingertip along the rim of her mug

"—it's not because you like to control all aspects of your life because you had so little control as a child?"

Shaking his head, he said, "I'm telling you. You should hang your shingle right next to Jennifer's."

Sydney returned to their table with two baskets containing their food.

Rob pointed a French fry at Libby, attacking her burger. "Hypnosis must've made you hungry."

She circled her finger in the air while she chewed, and then said, "Once I got past the shock of seeing that dead man, I started to feel a lot better. Just confirming that I'm Libby James did me a world of good."

Rob kept his mouth full because he didn't want to rain on her parade by reminding her that the hypnotic state hadn't confirmed her identity. She'd made an assumption based on the art gallery and feeling at home there.

He hadn't seen her eat with such gusto since he'd picked her up in the desert, so he swallowed and stuffed another few fries in his mouth.

As they finished up their meal and Rob reached for his wallet, a dark-haired man stormed through the door of the café, his mouth agape and his eyes wide. Rob's muscles coiled, as the man made a beeline for their table.

"Mel!" The man tripped to a stop and made a grab for Libby's hand, which she jerked away from him.

"Mel, what's wrong? Thank God I found you. I've been searching the hospitals, everywhere."

Libby put her hands in her lap and hunched her shoulders. "Who are you? My name's not Mel."

The man's jaw dropped open, and his gaze flew from Libby's face to Rob's. "What do you mean, Mel? What's happened to you? Who's this man?"

Libby swept her tongue over her lips. "My name's not Mel. It's Libby, Libby James."

The man started to laugh and then choked. "What's going on here? Where have you been?"

"Hold on a minute." Rob stood up, towering over the shorter man with the ponytail. "Who are you? How do you think you know Libby?"

The man's dark eyes glittered, and a flush spread beneath his brown skin as he squared his shoulders.

"I don't *think* I know her. She's my wife, and that's—" he jabbed his finger in the air at a petite Latina holding a gurgling baby "—our baby."

Chapter Eleven

Libby swiveled in her seat to take in a young woman with an infant clinging to her side. The room spun, and she grabbed the edge of the table. "I—I'm not…"

She lost the words in a haze of confusion and despair, slumping against the vinyl banquette.

"Are you all right?" Rob shoved a glass of water toward her. "Drink this."

The man with the ponytail braced his hands on the table, leaning toward her, invading her space. "What kind of joke is this? What's going on?"

Rob held up his hand. "Back off a minute. Let's take this conversation outside."

Her so-called husband's hand formed into a fist, and he banged on the table. "Who are you to give me orders? Why are you with my wife? Where has she been the past two days?"

"I'll explain everything once we get outside." Rob tossed some bills on the table. He reached out a hand to Libby under the glare of the man with the ponytail, and then stuffed it in his front pocket. "Are you okay, Libby? Can you get up by yourself?"

The man snorted. "She's not Libby James, and what's wrong with you, Mel? Why can't you move on your own?"

Stepping closer to the man, Rob dipped his head.

"She's been in an accident. We'll talk outside. Get out of her space."

Libby grabbed her purse and hitched it over her shoulder, gripping the strap. Rob didn't believe this man, did he? Because she didn't…not for one minute.

Her gaze strayed to the sweet-faced young woman bouncing the baby. The girl gave her a shy smile and said, "*Hola*, Senora Bustamante."

Libby shook her head and covered her eyes with one hand. She wasn't married to this man. She didn't have that baby with him. He hadn't been in her recovered memories.

As she rose from the table, the stranger put his hand on her back, and she twitched.

He blinked his long lashes. *"Mi querida."*

She wasn't his dear or anyone else's. She longed to fall into Rob's arms right now, collapse against his broad chest. But she straightened her spine and walked away from both men, giving the baby a wide berth.

The eyes of the other customers tracked their progress out of the restaurant as Sydney called after them, waving the two twenties. "Thanks, Rob."

Out on the sidewalk, Rob took charge again. "There's a park across the street. Let's get the baby some shade."

"You took control of my wife, and now you want control of my baby, too?" The fake husband puffed up his chest.

"I'm not taking control of anyone." Rob dragged his wallet from his pocket and flipped it open. "If it makes you feel any better, I'm Border Patrol."

The man's eyebrows jumped to his hairline. "Is it the drugs? They're not ours."

Libby cleared her throat and found her voice. "Stop. Talking."

"It's not about any drugs." Rob curled his fingers into his hair. "There, on the bench under the tree."

When they got across the street, Rob placed his hand on the young woman's arm. *"Como se llama?"*

"Teresa."

"*Sientate, aquí con la bebe*, Teresa." Rob patted the back of the bench, and Teresa sank down, cuddling the baby in her lap.

"Your Spanish stinks." The man's lip curled, and Rob rolled his eyes.

"Yeah, I know." He turned to Libby and asked her if she wanted to sit down, with less solicitation in his voice than he'd had for Teresa.

Was he already starting to distance himself from a woman he thought was another man's wife? But she wasn't Senora Bustamante. He had to believe that.

She declined to sit and held on to the back of the bench for dear life instead. If Rob believed this man, she didn't want him framing her story, either. She had to grab hold of this narrative before it careened out of control.

She took a deep breath. "I was in a car accident. I had a head injury and lost my memory but I've already been under hypnosis to regain it, and I know I'm Libby James. I'm not married. I don't have any children."

"Thank you. That explains it." The man closed his eyes and placed his hands together. "I'm Pablo Bustamante, and you're my wife, Melissa Bustamante. This is our daughter, Luisa. We live in Rocky Point, as the American tourists call it, and you work at an art gallery—for Ms. Libby James."

Libby felt the world tilt again and dug her feet into the gravel beneath her. "I—I don't know you."

"Mi querida." Pablo put his hand over his heart. "That destroys me."

"Wait a minute." Rob's voice, rough around the edges, cut through Pablo's sadness…or feigned sadness. "What's your story? Why was your wife traveling in a car by herself up to the US?"

Pablo folded his arms. "We were taking a trip up north. Mel went in a different car to look at some art pieces. We were all going to meet up later in Tombstone, but Mel never showed up. Last I knew, she was heading up to the Paradiso area. When it seemed that her cell phone went dead and she wouldn't call me, of course I got worried. I came down here to look for her, checked the hospitals, called the police. I couldn't figure out what happened. Now that you tell me you lost your memory, Mel, it adds up, and I'm so relieved even if you don't remember me."

"I don't." Libby set her jaw, refusing to look at the sweet baby now tapping Teresa's face with her little fist. "Wait."

"Do you remember, *mi querida*?" Pablo stretched a hand out to her, adding a slight tremor for maximum effect.

"No, I don't remember, and neither does Luisa." She leveled her finger at the baby. "She seems much more interested in and engaged with Teresa than me. If I were truly her mother, wouldn't she be more excited to see me?"

Rob cranked his head back and forth, looking at the baby, a smile lighting up his face. "She has a point there, Pablo."

Pablo's eyes flashed for a second when he glanced at Teresa and Luisa. "Teresa is her nanny. This has been an issue between us before, Mel. Besides, this is stupid. Why would I come around and try to claim a stranger as my wife?"

"Good question." Rob's eyes narrowed.

"This is ridiculous. You're coming home with us, Mel, and we'll sort all this out when we get there. I'll introduce you to the real Libby James—your boss." He lunged forward and grabbed her arm.

Rob reacted with lightning speed, stepping between them and breaking Pablo's hold on her with a single, swift chop to the other man's arm.

Pablo gave a strangled cry and stumbled back while Teresa jumped up, clutching Luisa to her body.

As Pablo righted himself, his hands curled into fists at his sides.

"Don't try it." Rob flattened his hand across his body, revealing the outline of his weapon holstered on his hip. "I don't know what kind of game you're playing here, but if you think Libby is going to traipse off with someone she doesn't know to go God knows where, you don't know her at all and you sure as hell don't know me."

"You can't keep me from my wife." Pablo's lips curled into a snarl, the concerned husband and father disappearing.

"Even if she is your wife, which I doubt, she'll make her own choices about what she wants to do." Rob pulled out his phone. "If you want to give me your middle initial and birth date and any other identifying information, I'll run you and see if your story is true."

"Run me?" Pablo put his hand on the baby's back. "You're Border Patrol. I'm not giving you any information."

"Better yet, come down to the station with me and we'll fingerprint you. We should be able to confirm your identity, and then you and… Mel can work things out together, if she wants to. We can even call the gallery and speak to Libby James about her employee."

Rob shoved one hand in his pocket, as if his request

were the most natural thing ever, and wasn't it? Wouldn't a distraught husband be anxious to prove who he was?

Pablo said in a low voice, "I'm not doing that. Won't you just hold her, Mel?"

"Sure." Libby flipped her hair over her shoulder and held out her arms to Teresa.

The young woman slid a glance to Pablo, who gave her an almost imperceptible nod. She then peeled Luisa from her body and put her in Libby's arms.

Libby tucked one arm beneath the baby's bottom and patted her back, her baby-powder smell tickling her nose. "Hi, precious. What a sweet girl you are."

Luisa's dark eyes widened and her bottom lip quivered. She placed her little hands against Libby's chest and squirmed.

"It's okay." Libby stroked the baby's soft curls. "Are you looking for Teresa?"

Teresa started forward, but Pablo grabbed her upper arm, pinching her flesh.

Libby turned around so that Luisa could see Teresa and immediately the baby started to whimper and kick her legs against Libby's belly. "I know, sweetie. You want Teresa."

She poured the baby back into Teresa's willing arms and spun around on Pablo, her eye twitching. "That's not my baby. I don't know who you are or why you want me, but I'm not going with you…or anyone else."

"Mel! This is not over. I'll prove you belong with me."

Libby strode away from the little group under the tree on shaky legs. Rob caught up with her as she crossed the street and grabbed her hand.

"Are you all right?"

"Let's just keep walking to the truck. I'm going to collapse in the middle of the street if I stop moving."

When Rob handed her into the truck, she twisted her head over her shoulder. Pablo was waving his arms around and Teresa had sat back down with the baby, who looked as if she were crying. Libby shivered.

Rob slammed the door and gripped the steering wheel. "What the hell was that all about?"

"It's what I feared from the get-go." Libby folded her hands in her lap and dropped her gaze. "Someone coming forward claiming to know me. Some stranger taking me away."

"I'm not going to allow that to happen." He wedged a finger beneath her chin, tipping up her head. "Look at me."

She slid her gaze to the left, meeting his dark eyes burning with…some emotion she couldn't name.

"You're not going anywhere with anyone, unless and until you want to. You're not going to take some dude's word for it that you're married and have a child if you don't remember that marriage or that child."

"C-couldn't you have arrested him or something?"

"Nothing he did was a crime." Rob lifted his shoulders. "And while I wanted to punch him in the face when he grabbed you, I would've been the one arrested."

"What kind of a person would use an innocent child like that?" Libby shook her head. "I could tell Teresa, or whatever her name is, was scared out of her wits. Didn't you think?"

"I think—" Rob cranked the keys in the ignition "—Teresa is that baby's mother and Pablo was using both of them to lure you into his trap."

Libby pulled her bottom lip between her teeth. "He's not one of the men at the crash site, though. I'm sure of it—different voice. That means there are more than two.

Pablo must be working with the others, and they must know I have amnesia."

"He wouldn't have approached you otherwise with that story, but he didn't seem surprised when you mentioned Libby James and he knew Libby—you— Sorry, this is getting confusing. He knew you owned a gallery." Rob pulled away from the curb and headed in the opposite direction of his house.

Libby's heart skipped a beat. "We're not going back to your place?"

"I'm going to check out the Paradiso hotels first and find out where Pablo and Teresa are staying—and how they registered."

"Good idea." She twisted a lock of hair with her finger, let it go and wound it up again. "How did Pablo know I had amnesia? Only you, Jennifer and I know that. Not even Rosie knows it."

"Maybe they've been watching you. If you knew who you were and who they were, you'd report their actions or you'd continue to do what you were planning to do before they waylaid you."

"They planted those drugs at the accident scene to make sure I didn't report anything, or if I did, that I'd be arrested for those drugs."

"You drove up here to Paradiso for a reason—maybe it has to do with that dead body in your memory and maybe not. They stopped you but would've expected you to carry on with your mission…if you knew what it was." He tapped on his window as they rolled up to the Paradiso Motel. "They knew something was wrong when you stayed here and took a job at Rosita's. Now they know for sure because my guess is that you're no stranger to Pablo Bustamante."

She'd accept his explanation for now, but the notion

that people who meant to do her harm were watching her in Paradiso did nothing to calm her nerves.

The clerk at the Paradiso Motel didn't have anyone matching Pablo's and Teresa's descriptions staying there, and Libby and Rob didn't have any luck at the other two hotels, either.

After the visit to the last hotel, Libby climbed into Rob's truck and snapped her seat belt with a sigh. "At least we tried. I guess we can do a search on Pablo Bustamante, just like we did on Libby James, but I don't know how much we'll find."

"Well, I did get his fingerprints."

Libby jerked her head around. "You did?"

Rob pulled a pacifier from his pocket. "Like taking candy from a baby."

"You stole little Luisa's binky?" She punched his arm.

"Not exactly. It fell out of her mouth onto the ground. Pablo picked it up, left fingerprints and handed it back to Luisa, who promptly dropped it again. Pablo didn't notice this time, so I scooped it up with a tissue and pocketed it." He held up his hands. "Don't get too excited. We could have the same issue we had with your prints. If he's a Mexican national, his prints aren't going to be in our database. I have to go through other red tape to get that information, and nothing I'm doing is official at this point."

"It's a start. I never would've thought of that." She scooted down in the seat. "I'm exhausted. Just when I thought I unwound from my session with Jennifer, I get hit with Pablo. Did he really think I'd just waltz off with him?"

"He obviously thought the baby would be the clincher." He raised an eyebrow. "She *was* cute. How'd you resist?"

"Cute? She was adorable, but I knew she wasn't

mine. I had no feeling for her here." She pounded her fist against her heart. "I'd know. I'm sure I'd remember a baby…or a husband."

"You'd like to think you would, but who knows?" He slowed down to make the turn to his street. "I knew she wasn't yours by the way she clung to Teresa and barely looked at you. One of the other agents and his fiancée are adopting a baby, and that little guy is constantly zeroed in on his mama no matter who else is holding him. Luisa didn't have that for you."

"I agree." Libby shot up in her seat. "You have a visitor."

Rob rolled past the Jeep parked in front of his house and pulled into his driveway. "Friend, not foe."

Libby blew out a breath and threw open the passenger door before Rob even cut the engine. She could do with more friends and fewer foes.

A tall woman with a thick mane of blond hair and sun-kissed skin stepped out of the Jeep and waved. "Those pants actually look better on you than they ever did on me."

Libby stumbled and made a grab for the door of the truck. "I know you."

Rob came around to her side of the truck and hugged the blonde. "I should hope so. This is April Archer, your clothing fairy."

The adrenaline rushed through Libby's body, and she swayed on her feet. "No, I know this woman…from before."

Chapter Twelve

April glanced at Rob, a crease forming between her eyebrows. "Is she okay, Rob?"

Rob lunged back toward Libby, as she listed to one side. He caught her arm and steadied her. "Are you sure, Libby? This is April Archer, Border Patrol agent Clay Archer's wife. She's the one who loaned you the clothes."

April charged forward. "Rob, she needs to sit down. She needs water or a stiff drink. We can sort this out inside."

Rob knew better than to get into a struggle with April over taking care of someone. She was the pro.

Libby let April curl an arm around her shoulders and guide her to the house, so Rob sprang ahead of them to open his front door.

April walked Libby to the couch and patted a cushion. "Sit and tell me what's going on. Water? Tea? Whiskey?"

"Maybe some water." Libby rubbed the side of her head where her external wound was healing nicely. Soon there'd be no outer sign of her memory loss—just the vast emptiness inside her head.

"Rob." April snapped her fingers. "A glass of water."

Rob rushed into the kitchen and filled a glass with filtered water from the fridge. When he returned to the living room, April was seated next to Libby, whose face had returned to its normal shade.

April asked in a soft voice, "You think you know me from somewhere? Why does that worry you? Do you think I know your ex?"

Libby dropped her head back against the couch, staring at the ceiling. "Rob told you that story?"

"Story?" April glanced at Rob. "Is it a story? Whatever your story, you can tell me. No judgment."

Libby closed her eyes, and her chest rose and fell rapidly. "I don't have an abusive ex, or at least not that I know of. I was in a car accident the other day outside Paradiso, and I lost my memory. Rob's been helping me, and we've pieced together a few things."

"A car accident?" April tucked one long leg beneath her. "That burned-out wreck off the highway?"

"That's the one." Libby opened one eye.

"The accident found with the drugs?"

"Not hers." Rob perched on the edge of the chair across from them.

"Is that why you didn't report it? Get help?"

"Not at first, but those drugs haven't made it any easier." Libby launched into an explanation of the accident and the two men who set fire to the car.

"Oh, my God. You poor thing." April grabbed Libby's hand. "You still need to get checked out by a doctor. Rob, what were you thinking?"

"Don't blame Rob." Libby's gaze shifted to him, and his heart melted around the edges. "He was trying to protect me."

April asked, "So, where do I fit in? How do you know me, or how do you think you know me because I don't know you, Libby."

Rob hunched forward, his elbows digging into his knees.

Libby massaged her left temple. "I've never met you. I've never seen you in person, but I've seen a photograph of you."

Sitting back, Rob rolled his shoulders. "You probably saw a picture of her that I had somewhere. I told you. She's married to a fellow agent—my boss."

"That's not it, Rob. I didn't see a picture of April since I've been here in Paradiso. I saw it before…before I lost my memory."

"You saw a picture of her somewhere in Rocky Point, Mexico?"

"Rocky Point? That's where you're from?" April rubbed her chin. "That's cartel country. I wonder if my ex-fiancé…"

"Your ex-fiancé is a drug dealer?" Libby blinked her wide eyes.

"Was. He's dead." April waved her hand in the air. "Long story. Why did someone plant drugs at the scene of your accident? My husband told me those were packaged to sell."

"I hope I don't have an ex-fiancé who's a drug dealer, but I am mixed up somehow with those people." Libby pinned her hands between her knees and hunched her shoulders. "The two men who set fire to my wrecked car mentioned something about some guy called El Gringo Viejo. I've since discovered he's some sort of broker for the cartels."

April's lips formed an O, and she clutched her midsection. "El Gringo Viejo?"

Rob raised his eyebrows. Clay must share everything with his wife. He'd remember that the next time his boss got on his case. "Clay mentioned him to you before?"

"Not just Clay." April jumped up from the couch and did a circle around the room. "My brother, Adam, mentioned El Gringo Viejo to me long before I heard about him from Clay."

"Your brother." Rob cleared his throat. "He's the one who, yeah, had some problems with drugs?"

"He had a lot of problems, Rob, not just with drugs, but you know my history in this town, don't you?"

"I know your brother murdered your mother and let your father take the blame for it." Rob ignored Libby's sharp intake of breath. "I know your father disappeared after the murder and hasn't been seen since."

"Do you also know that Adam was convinced our father was El Gringo Viejo?"

"What?" Libby pushed up from the couch and grabbed April's arm. "Are you serious?"

"Wait, wait." Rob dragged a hand through his hair. "I never heard that your father, C. J. Hart, was suspected of being El Gringo Viejo. We don't know who he is. Nobody does."

"That's because I'm the only one, except Adam and he's dead, who suspects it. Clay dismissed Adam's rantings as wishful thinking, and, of course, he strongly advised me against going to Mexico to investigate the matter."

"What makes you think he's your father?" Libby dropped her hand from April's arm and stooped to grab her glass of water from the coffee table.

"Besides my brother telling me he was?" April flicked her hair over her shoulder. "The timing of my father's disappearance matches the emergence of EGV. Authorities are convinced my father slipped across the border after my mother's murder. My father had been dabbling in the drug trade before the murder, which is how my brother was able to convince him to go on the run. And, well, he's an old white guy."

"And now maybe I have further proof." Libby chugged down some water and offered the glass to April, who shook her head. "If I knew El Gringo Viejo in Rocky Point and he had your picture somewhere, it makes sense that I'd see it and recognize you from that picture."

"I'm glad you two have this all figured out." Rob rubbed his eyes. Was Libby imagining things? She still didn't remember her own name.

"I'm telling Clay about this. He's never believed this story about my father."

"Wait." Rob sliced his hand through the air. That was all he needed—his boss coming down on him because he'd gotten April involved in some wild-goose chase for El Gringo Viejo. "This is not proof. Did you miss the part where Libby told you she had amnesia? She could've seen you anywhere in town. She's working at Rosie's now."

April wedged a hand on her hip. "I haven't been to Rosie's this week, and I'm not going to drag you into it, Rob."

"I'm already dragged in. Libby's staying at my place. I rescued her from a burned-out wreck in the desert, and I didn't report that burned-out wreck to the authorities. How do you think that's gonna go over with Clay?"

"I'll handle Clay." April patted Libby's shoulder and smiled. "You guys have been speculating about EGV for years, and Libby and I may have just handed him to you."

Libby's eyes widened. "You don't mind that he's your father?"

"Might be." Rob pushed up from the chair. "Might be and probably isn't."

April gathered her hair in one hand, holding it back as she tilted her head to look him in the face. "I've lived with the idea of my father killing my mother and abandoning us for so long, this twist won't come as a shock."

"The only way we're going to know for sure is if someone goes down to Rocky Point to investigate, and that's not gonna be Libby—not for a while." He folded his arms and puffed out his chest in case there was any doubt he meant business.

April drummed her fingers on his forearm. "Ooh, I like a man who's large and in charge, especially when he's protecting his woman."

"Libby's not… I mean, of course I'm protecting her. She's vulnerable." He narrowed his eyes at April, the troublemaker. "Why exactly did you stop by, anyway?"

She winked at Libby. "Just to see how the clothes were working out and if *your friend* needed anything else. Do you, Libby?"

"You were more than generous, and I, for one, am glad you came by."

"Nobody handles Clay Archer, not even you, April."

"Don't worry about it." She floated to the front door and blew them a kiss before she left.

"That was strange." Libby dropped to the couch and covered her face with both hands. "When I saw her, it was like an immediate flash of recognition. It's happening, Rob. If I went back to Rocky Point and my gallery, I'm sure the memories would start rolling in."

He swallowed. He had no right to keep her here, but he'd do everything in his power, short of physical restraint, to persuade her not to return to Mexico. "I hope you realize going to Rocky Point would be the most dangerous move you could make right now. It's a catch-22, but regaining your memory is going to put you at risk."

"After that showdown with Pablo, they know for sure I don't have any memory of what I was doing in that car on that road. I'm safe…for now." She patted the cushion on the couch beside her. "Sit. Did I thank you for protecting me against Pablo?"

He lowered himself next to her. "I think you handled it."

"Only because you were there." She ran a hand down his thigh. "He wasn't about to try anything with you there. If you hadn't been…"

He cinched his fingers around her wrist, more to stop her hand traveling up his thigh than anything else. "I was there. I am here, and I'm going to see you through this."

Her bottom lip trembled. "I don't know how I got so lucky that you were the one who found me. If it had been anyone else, any other authority figure, my face would be plastered all over town or I'd be in jail for those drugs."

"I don't think so." He raised her hand to his lips and kissed the tips of her fingers, immediately regretting it. What kind of man took advantage of a woman with no identity? He didn't even know if she were free.

He loosened his clasp on her hand, but she curled her fingers around his thumb.

"Why stop?" Her whispered words echoed in his head, as if they'd come from his own brain.

"You know why. It's not a good idea for us to…hook up."

"It seems like a really good idea to me right now." She scooted in closer to him. "You're my anchor, Rob."

"I'm your only acquaintance. Of course you're going to feel this way about me."

She snorted lightly, her nostrils flaring with the effort. "Rosie is an acquaintance. April is an acquaintance now. I spent an intense hour with Jennifer today."

"They don't count. They're all women, and you're not living with them." He traced the curve of her neck with his fingertip. "You want comfort. I understand. It must be scary as hell to be where you are right now. I get it."

Turning her head, she pressed a kiss on his palm. "I don't think you get it at all, Rob. I'm attracted to you. I like you, and, yeah, it would feel great to be connected to someone, but not just anyone. I'm sure Pablo would've been more than willing to…connect with me. You're not just some port in a storm, my particular storm. You're Rob Valdez and I want *you*."

"Libby, what if you're married?" He clasped the back of his neck. "You saw that baby today. What if you had one of those, or two? A worried husband? A frantic boyfriend? I know I'd be in a panic if I lost you."

"You're not going to lose me." She cupped his face with her hand and toyed with his earlobe. "I'm not with anyone in my real life, Rob. I know that as much as I know I'm Libby James, as much as I know I saw a dead body, as much as I know I've seen April Archer's picture somewhere."

"Bad comparisons. As tenuous as your memories are of those things, you still have some proof or image that they're true. Just because you haven't had any flashes of memory about a husband and children, it doesn't mean they don't exist out there."

Sighing, she closed her eyes. "You don't want to make love with me because you're worried we're cheating on some nameless, faceless person who probably doesn't exist?"

Was he? He didn't like making mistakes in his life. He'd worked hard to avoid missteps. Falling for someone else's wife was not in his life plan.

But neither was picking up a strange woman and making all her problems his own.

He draped his arm around her shoulders and pulled

her close. He whispered in her ear, "There's no hurry, is there? When you get your memory back and know for sure you're single, we have time to explore if that's what you still want."

She nestled her head in the crook of his neck. "You don't have to be careful with me, Rob. In fact, I'm the last person you need to be careful with. I'm nobody. I'm a woman without a past and not much future."

"You're somebody to me." He rested his cheek against the top of her soft hair. "And you're worth protecting."

She curled her legs beneath her and slanted her body across his, wrapping one arm around his waist. Her hair fanned out across his chest and he took a strand between two fingers and ran them down to the ends.

Her body felt warm against his, and her breathing deepened. The bed was still made up for her, but he didn't want to move her. Didn't want to move himself. Didn't want to breathe.

He held her and looked down at her profile, studying every curve and her delicate bone structure. In sleep, her face lost its haunted look. Even when she smiled, it didn't light up her eyes. It was as if she had to know who she was, who she'd been, before she could allow herself to just be.

He knew her desire to have sex with him came from a need to get lost in her feelings, a chance to stop thinking.

When he made love to Libby James, he wanted to be with the real Libby, someone who could give him all of herself unreservedly because she knew exactly who she was and what she wanted.

Would he ever have that chance? Was Libby James a married woman? Engaged? In love? He could wait to find out. For now, he had this. He ran his hand down her back.

She arched like a cat, and then burrowed into his chest.

He could sleep with her next to him like this all night…and probably would. Closing his eyes, he tilted back his head.

A few minutes later, or maybe it was a few hours, someone pounded on his front door and a woman's cry pierced through the haze of sleep. He jerked forward, his arms going around Libby.

Thank God she was safe. Just as his heart rate returned to normal, he heard the cry again and the glass in his front door shook.

Libby sat up, blinking. "What was that?"

"Someone's at the door." He put his finger to his lips and scooted out from beneath Libby, still halfway draped across his lap.

He reached for his weapon on the end table next to the couch and staggered to his feet, shaking off the cobwebs of sleep.

Libby grabbed the back pocket of his jeans. "Be careful."

Rob crept to his door and stood to the side. With his gun raised, he flicked aside the curtain and swore. "It's Teresa…and she has the baby."

Libby stumbled against his back, her hand to her throat. "Is Pablo with her?"

"Not that I can tell."

"It's a trick, Rob. If you open that door, Pablo will come out of the shadows." She clutched his arm.

"I'm not so sure about that, Libby. Look at her face. She's been beaten." His finger twitched on the trigger of his gun as Teresa rapped on the window and uttered a garbled plea.

"What about the baby?" He couldn't take it anymore and turned the dead bolt. "If Pablo's out there and makes a move, he's a dead man. Stand back, Libby."

He yanked open the door and grabbed Teresa's arm through the narrow space. "Get inside."

Teresa tripped across the threshold, and Libby steadied her.

Then through swollen and bloodied lips, Teresa said in Spanish, "You have to get away. He was sent here to kill you."

Chapter Thirteen

Libby wrapped one arm around Teresa and held on to the baby with the other while Rob secured the front door.

He whipped around, still clutching his gun, and Teresa whimpered. "Is he out there? Does he know you're here?"

Teresa's eyes took up her entire face, which had blanched.

Scowling at Rob, Libby took Teresa's arm and led her to the couch. She could extend sympathy to someone in worse condition than she was. She spoke to Teresa in Spanish. "Rob's not going to hurt you. Where's Pablo?"

Teresa explained that Pablo had put her and the baby on a bus back to Mexico, but she'd gotten off two stops later and returned here.

"To warn Libby? What do you know about Libby? Who's Pablo? Who sent him to kill Libby?"

Libby held up a hand to Rob. "One question at a time, Rob. You're confusing her… And it doesn't help that your Spanish is atrocious and you're waving a gun around."

Rob shoved the gun in his waist in the back and crouched by the window.

Libby sat next to Teresa and stroked the baby's cheek. She spoke to her in Spanish. "Pablo didn't hurt the baby, did he?"

"No. He wouldn't hurt the baby. She's his daughter, and his name isn't Pablo Bustamante."

Libby nodded but pressed her lips together. He'd hurt his wife but not his daughter? How long would that last? "Why did he hurt you?"

"He said I didn't do enough to make you think Luisa was yours."

"I'm sorry, Teresa. If I thought he was going to harm you, I would've done a better job of playing along."

"No, no. He would've hurt you."

Rob perched on the arm of the chair across from them and asked, "Is she Libby James?"

"Yes." Teresa touched Libby's hand. "You don't remember? You're Libby James, the artist."

"I own a gallery in Rocky Point?"

"Yes."

"Why is Pablo, or whatever his name is, trying to kill me? Why did those other men try to kill me? Are they doing this for El Gringo Viejo?"

"No!" Teresa clutched the baby to her chest so hard, Luisa squeaked. "I don't know anything about El Gringo Viejo."

"But he's in Rocky Point." Rob hunched forward, his hands on his knees.

"I don't know. I don't know anything." Teresa whipped her head back and forth, and the baby whined.

"Your lip is bleeding." Libby touched her own lip. "Rob, can you please bring Teresa a towel and some ice? Water and ibuprofen would be good, too."

Rob stood up and cranked his head as he walked to the kitchen. "Ask her what she's doing here if she's not going to give up Pablo or El Gringo Viejo and can't tell you anything you don't already know."

Libby shook her head and drew a finger across her

throat. Seeing the gesture, Teresa started up from her seat on the couch.

"Don't worry. Nothing's going to happen to you here. Rob will protect you."

Teresa dropped back to the cushion and repositioned the baby in her arms. "I'm sorry. I can't tell you anything more about yourself. I know your name is Libby James and you're an artist who lives in Rocky Point. You crossed the cartels in some way, but I don't know how. You left Punto Peñasco in a big hurry, and they went after you. They tried to kill you but failed, so they sent…my husband after you. He brought me and the baby to make you think she was yours."

Rob came back with a wet paper towel, a glass of water and two ibuprofens cupped in his palm. "Why are you here? Why didn't you stay on the bus back to Mexico?"

Teresa's dark eyes glistened with tears. "I'm afraid he'll kill me one day. I—I have relatives in Texas. I want to go there, leave…him. You helped Libby. Maybe you'll help me, too."

"Here, let me have the baby. Take the pills and press that paper towel against your lip." Libby held out her arms for the sleepy baby and cuddled her on her lap.

Rob gave Teresa the makeshift first-aid supplies and jabbed his thumb into his chest. "What am I now, the savior of displaced women?"

Libby cocked her head at him and winked. "Maybe we just know a safe harbor when we see one."

"She does know I'm Border Patrol, doesn't she?"

"I don't think so, Rob, and you're not telling her. Let her go to her relatives. She's trying to help me, and we should help her."

"*Is* she trying to help you?"

"What does that mean?" Libby glanced at Teresa,

but she and Rob were speaking too fast for her to follow the conversation.

"Ask Teresa how she knew my house. How do we know Pablo isn't out there right now waiting for us?"

Libby asked Teresa and she admitted that Pablo already knew that Libby was staying with Rob and knew Rob's house. They'd driven past the house earlier. Pablo had asked her to write down the address and that was how she knew how to get back here.

"She's gonna have to give us more, Libby. If we're going to help her, keep quiet about her presence in the country and send her on her way, she has to give us more than your name and the fact that bad guys are after you. We know all that. We figured it out on our own."

Libby took a deep breath. How did you strong-arm a terrorized woman with a baby? "We want to help you, Teresa. We will help you and Luisa get to your relatives, but I have no memory and that puts me in grave danger. If there's anything else you can tell me—what the other men look like who are after me, why they're after me or even if there's someone I can call in Rocky Point for help, someone who knows me."

Libby slid a quick glance at Rob. Had he understood that last part? It's not that she thought she had a husband who could come to the rescue, but maybe she had someone who could fill her in on the details of her life.

Teresa stopped dabbing her lip, her gaze darting from Libby to Rob. She understood the implications of the questions. "I don't live in Punto Peñasco. I don't know you. I overheard my husband's conversations, and they want to stop you before you remember everything that happened. I don't know what that is. He never spoke of it in front of me. I do know when you left Punto Peñasco, you were coming here to Paradiso."

"Rob?" Libby crossed her hands over her chest. "Did you get that?"

Rob looked up from his phone. "Don't rub it in. You two are speaking too fast for me. What did she say?"

"She said she overheard a few of her husband's conversations, and from what she can gather, Paradiso was my destination when I left Mexico."

Rob shoved his phone in his back pocket. "That's weird. Why would you be headed here? It must be because of our Border Patrol office. We're the closest one to the border."

"How would I know that? Average, everyday people minding their own business do not generally know where their nearest Border Patrol office is—especially people living in Mexico."

"Ask her if she heard anything else, and let me have the baby." Rob crouched in front of her.

"Why?" Libby pushed a finger into Rob's chest. "You're not going to imply that you're going to take Luisa if her mother doesn't cooperate, are you?"

His dark eyebrows collided over his nose. "Never even occurred to me. It's great that you can't trust the only person you *can* trust."

"You are in law enforcement, Rob, and sometimes—" she shrugged "—you show that hard edge. I know you want to do your job, and I know you want to help me."

"Yes and yes, but not at the expense of a mother and her child. Ask her." He tilted his head toward Teresa on the couch. "She's beginning to think we're plotting against her."

Libby handed off Luisa, who'd begun fussing, to Rob, and she moved closer to Teresa. "That's helpful that you told me I was originally headed to Paradiso. Can you tell me anything else? Do you know why I was coming to Paradiso?"

"I don't know that—sorry." Teresa twisted the wet paper towel in her fingers. "I-is he going to help me?"

"Yes, we're going to help you." Libby put her hand over Teresa's. "You need money to get on a bus to Texas?"

"Yes, El Paso."

"Did you get that?" Libby twisted her head around to Rob, who was bouncing a giggling Luisa in his arms. "She wants to go to El Paso."

"Muy bueno." Libby winked at Teresa. "Can we do that?"

"She's gotta get a ride up to Tucson." Rob pinched the baby's chin. "Don't look at me like that, Libby."

She widened her eyes and fluttered her eyelashes. "Like what?"

"Like I'm the last hope for mankind."

"You are, or at least for displaced women. Can you take Teresa to Tucson tomorrow morning? Or—" she grimaced "—I guess that would be this morning."

"*We* can take her. I'm not leaving you here on your own, and this little one—" he held Luisa up in the air and jiggled her "—needs a car seat."

"Where are we going to get a car seat at this time of the morning?"

"I can borrow one from my buddy. He and his fiancée are adopting a baby, and even though the adoption isn't final yet, they do have a car seat for visits."

Libby turned and translated their conversation, or most of it, to Teresa, the crease finally disappearing between the other woman's eyes.

Rob handed the baby back to Teresa. "You two get ready to go. I'll get the car seat. Do not open that door. If you need it, there's a loaded pistol in my nightstand drawer."

While Rob went to his friend's place and made up some excuse about why he needed a car seat at five in the morning, Libby kept watch at the window with her hand curled around the handle of Rob's gun and watched Teresa feed and change the baby.

Nothing stirred outside until Rob pulled his truck into the driveway.

He used his key to get into the house, as he told her not to open the door for anyone—even him. He burst through the front door, rubbing his hands together. "All quiet here?"

"Everything's fine, and Teresa and Luisa are ready to go." Libby set the heavy weapon down on the table by the front door. "Did you have to do much explaining to get the car seat?"

"Luckily, my friend was home alone. His wife, who would be the one asking all the questions, had already left for the academy."

"Oh, she's the one who's going to be a cop." Libby wrinkled her nose.

"Yeah. My buddy's a lot more laid-back than she is, so when I told him I had a friend staying with me who needed to borrow a car seat for the morning, he handed it over with no more questions asked." Rob waved his hand behind him. "He's the one who owns all the pecan groves in town and has half ownership of the processing plant. The dude has no worries."

"Must be nice." Libby grabbed her purse and turned to Teresa. *"Estás lista?"*

Teresa nodded and answered in English, "Ready."

As they walked out to the truck, Rob led the way and called over his shoulder. "My friend Nash told me if the baby is under one year old, the car seat faces the back.

He helped me put it in. I never realized Nash knew so much about babies."

Libby said, "You're not so bad yourself in that department. I saw how you entertained Luisa. You did good."

"I have plenty of nieces and nephews—some with no fathers around. I learned by doing." He held the back door open for Teresa, who ducked in the truck to secure her daughter in the car seat.

Libby patted Teresa's shoulder. "You can sit in the back with Luisa. You'll be fine now. Does your husband know you have family in El Paso?"

Teresa shook her head.

Rob eyed his rearview mirror. "I'd stop for coffee, but I think it's best we get on the road."

Libby lowered her voice and touched Rob's thigh. "Do you think Pablo might be following us?"

"Don't know, but he's not going to follow us to Tucson, not if I can help it."

Both Teresa and Luisa fell asleep in the back seat, but Libby's nerves wouldn't allow her to doze off. She flicked her gaze to the side mirror almost as many times as Rob glanced at the rearview, her only conversation an occasional "See anything?"

As far as she knew, which wasn't much, she'd never heard of Paradiso before, had never been here, didn't know anyone here. Why would she be on her way to Paradiso?

If she had family here, wouldn't they have seen and recognized her by now? Maybe not. Paradiso was small, but as Rob had pointed out, it had grown with the pecan processing plant. She doubted she'd seen every person who lived in Paradiso.

The only person she wanted to see in Paradiso now was sitting right beside her. If Rob weren't so honorable, they could've made love last night. Maybe she just wanted him because she needed someone to feel close to, someone to fill all the emptiness inside her.

Maybe he was right. Even if she found out she didn't have a significant other in her real life, once she discovered that life she might feel completely different about him. Did that even matter? He didn't want to be hurt. She understood that. Despite his background, despite his buffed-up physique, Rob Valdez was a sensitive guy.

Once he fell for someone, he'd fall hard and never want to let go. Knowing that about him made her ache to be possessed by him, body and soul. You'd know who you were if you were loved by someone like Rob.

"We're just a few miles out. I'm going to take her directly to the bus depot downtown. She can get something to eat there." He flicked a finger at the rearview mirror. "We weren't followed. I know that for a fact."

"Good. He probably thinks she's on her way back to Mexico, still under his thumb. Even though she didn't give us that much info, I'm glad she came to us…you."

"She gave us another piece of the puzzle. We'd wondered where you were going when those two forced you off the road. Now we know you were close to your goal."

"But why?" She scooped her hair back from her face.

"We'll get that piece, too." He cranked his head around to the back seat. "Teresa, *estamos aquí*."

Libby turned around and patted a sleeping Teresa's knee. *"Estamos aquí."*

Ten minutes later, Rob pulled the truck into a parking space on the street and helped Teresa get Luisa out of the car seat.

Libby grabbed Teresa's small bag and joined them on the sidewalk in front of the bus terminal. Downtown was just waking up, but most businesses were still closed. Nobody on the street watched them or paid them any attention.

She and Rob escorted Teresa and her baby into the terminal. Rob checked the schedules and discovered a bus leaving for El Paso in thirty minutes. He handed Teresa enough cash to buy a ticket and get something to eat along the way.

When they saw the bus off, Rob expelled a long sigh. "At least that's taken care of. I don't know about you, but I need something to eat and I can't wait until we drive back to Paradiso this time."

"Breakfast sounds good. I feel like I haven't eaten in forever, so I'm up for anything."

Rob rolled his shoulders and flexed his fingers on the steering wheel. "I'm thinking we should publish your picture in town now. If someone there is waiting for you, they'll recognize your photo and come forward."

"Someone like Pablo Bustamante." She gripped the edges of the seat. "I don't know enough yet."

"You know you're Libby James, an artist from Rocky Point."

"What if another Pablo comes out of the woodwork?"

"I won't let you go…off with just anyone."

"I'll think about it." She snapped her seat belt. "Where to?"

"There's a place north of downtown called First Watch. Not sure where it is." He handed his phone to her. "Can you look it up?"

She looked up directions to the restaurant and let the GPS lady call them out to Rob. He navigated the streets of Tucson until he pulled into a shopping center.

"Yeah, I remember now, and it looks like it's open for business."

Several minutes later, they took a table by the window and ordered coffee. When it arrived, Libby dumped some cream into her cup.

Taking a sip, she closed her eyes. "Ah, I needed this. We didn't get much sleep last night, did we?"

"You seemed to sleep well." Rob slurped his own coffee and hid behind the menu the waiter had dropped off.

She tapped his menu. "Why didn't you go to your bedroom?"

"Like I said, you seemed to be sleeping soundly, and I didn't want to wake you up." He peered at her over the top of the menu. "I think I'm going to have one of these skillets."

"I don't think I would've woken up if you'd slipped out. You must've been uncomfortable sitting up all night."

"I kinda slumped over. It wasn't bad." He ran a finger down her menu. "They have some healthy stuff—oatmeal, yogurt and granola."

She raised her eyebrows. "Slumping over was comfortable?"

"All right." He snapped his menu down on the table. "I wanted to stay there and hold you all night long. Is that what you want to hear?"

"That's exactly what I wanted to hear." She smiled as she buried her chin in her hand and studied the menu. "Since you rejected me, flat out."

"Libby, you have no memory. Someone has to be thinking clearly for both of us."

The waiter's eyes popped open as he approached the table. "Y-you ready to order?"

Libby took Rob's advice and ordered the yogurt, granola, fruit bowl. When the waiter walked away, she hunched forward. "Wanting to be with you is the clearest thought I've had since climbing out of that wreck."

"What happens when you remember your husband?

You'd feel guilty. I'd feel…guilty." He gulped down some coffee, obviously burning his tongue, as he grabbed his water next.

"Rob—" she smoothed two fingers along the inside of his wrist, tracing the line of his veins "—Libby James doesn't have a husband. If she did, why wasn't he in the car with her…with me? Think about it. I witnessed something, probably a murder, and I fled. Wouldn't I go to my husband first?"

"Maybe your husband's in Paradiso." He swirled his coffee with one hand, leaving the other in her possession. "Did you ever think of that? You were running to him."

She sat back in her seat, pulling her purse over her head and setting it beside her. "That never occurred to me—and that's further proof he doesn't exist."

"Really." Rob folded his arms in that way he had that dared her to prove him wrong.

"The fact that it never crossed my mind proves that there is no husband. I think if I'm going to remember anything in a hypnotic state, it would be a husband, someone I loved and wanted to get to."

"Not necessarily. You remembered the incident that fueled your flight from Rocky Point first. That makes sense."

"Rob—" she curled her fingers around his wrist "—I can't ever imagine forgetting you, forgetting your face. Ever."

His dark eyes glittered, and she knew he felt the heat between them.

"California skillet." The waiter set Rob's plate on the table and slid her bowl of health in front of her. "Anything else?"

"My toast." Rob tapped her cup. "And more coffee when you get a chance."

Libby whistled and grabbed her spoon. "Saved by the waiter."

"I'm never going to forget you, either, Libby, but I don't want to make any mistakes."

Rob had obviously seen too many people make too many mistakes in his life.

"What if I never remember?"

"Jennifer believes you will. You've already started."

"I can't wait." She dug into her yogurt parfait.

"Once you remember everything, that'll go a long way to keeping you safe."

"Yeah. Can't wait for that, either."

While they ate, they tried to steer clear of her problems and his feelings. She pried into his family life a little more, and as that conversation was completely one-sided, she learned a lot about Rob Valdez—and liked him even more because of it.

After downing her second cup of coffee, she whipped the napkin from her lap. "I'm going to use the ladies' room before we hit the road back to Paradiso."

"I'll take care of the check."

Libby wove through the tables toward the restrooms near the entrance. She tried the door on one, which was locked, and shuffled to the other unisex bathroom as someone came up on her heels.

The handle turned, and as she pushed open the door, the man on her tail shoved her inside the bathroom, crowding inside behind her.

Her heart slammed against her rib cage. Spinning around, she placed her hands against his solid chest and opened her mouth to scream. It was then she felt the barrel of a gun jabbing her gut.

Chapter Fourteen

Rob glanced at the time on his cell phone. A flare of concern fluttered in his gut. Had Libby passed out or something?

He downed the rest of his water and Libby's and made his way to the front of the restaurant. He turned the corner that led to the small hallway where the restrooms were located and almost bumped into a woman coming through one of the two doors.

He caught the door before it closed and peeked inside, but these were single, unisex bathrooms and this one was empty. Sidestepping to the next one, he tried the handle. It resisted.

He knocked. "Libby? You still in there?"

A man's voice answered. "Still in here. Not Libby."

Rob's pulse jumped, and his head jerked to take in the exit door to the side parking lot. Had she gone out that way to wait by the truck?

He took one step toward the door and tripped to a stop. Pivoting back toward the occupied bathroom, he banged his fist against the door. "Libby? Libby, are you in there?"

The door burst open, hitting his foot, and a red-faced man with bunched-up fists charged into the hallway. "What's your problem, man?"

Rob pushed past the man's solid form and stumbled

into the empty bathroom. He tilted his head back to survey the sealed, frosted window. No way in, no way out of that.

He careened out of the bathroom and grabbed the jacket of the man, who by this time had dismissed him as a nut. "Who was in that bathroom before you?"

The man yanked out of his grasp. "I don't know what's wrong with you, dude, but you'd better back off."

"Sorry." Rob flipped out his badge. "Border Patrol. I need to know what happened to the woman who was in that bathroom before you."

"I don't know if it was the woman or the man who was in the john before me. They were both in the hallway and walking out the exit when I saw them." He shrugged. "I guess it could've been the girl in there before me."

"Was she wearing jeans and a green top? Long light brown hair?"

"I don't know what she was wearing. Yeah, probably jeans, but she had a rockin' body and it looked like her guy appreciated it, 'cause they were walking real close and he had his arm right around her."

Rob turned and ran for the door, every muscle in his body screaming. He shoved through the exit and rushed into the parking lot, his head cranking back and forth.

"Libby! Libby!"

"Rob! Ro..."

When Libby's cry reached his ears, adrenaline coursed through his body and he charged toward the sound. A shuffling, scraping noise got louder as he made his way to the edge of the parking lot.

Hot rage thumped through his veins when he saw Libby struggling against a man with a shaved head, trying to cram her into the driver's seat of a beat-up white sedan, a Wildcats sticker on the back.

Libby was hanging on to the door, her feet planted in the asphalt while the man had one arm hooked around her waist and a hand on her back—a hand holding a gun.

As the man started to raise the gun, Rob stormed at him, pointing his own weapon at his critical mass. "Stop or I'll take you down right now."

Rob held his breath while the man dropped his arm from Libby's waist. If he pulled Libby in front of him to use as a hostage, Rob would take the shot…a head shot.

Rob growled. "Don't even think about it."

The man released his gun and held up his hands. "Don't make a scene. There are some people coming this way, although they haven't noticed yet what's happening."

"Yeah, we wouldn't want to make a scene while you're abducting my…this woman." Rob's lip curled. What was he, some kind of gentleman kidnapper?

"I know it looks bad, but it's not." The man ran a hand over his shaved head.

Libby kicked the guy in the shin and ran to Rob. "He grabbed me in the bathroom and forced me out here at gunpoint, but when he tried to get me into the car, I resisted. I told him he'd have to shoot me first…and he didn't. Why didn't you shoot me?"

"My name is Troy. I don't want to hurt you, Libby."

"How do you know her name?" Rob's arm curled around Libby's waist, and her body practically vibrated against his.

Troy licked his lips. "I contacted her in Rocky Point. I'm the one she was on her way to meet in Paradiso. I swear to you. I have texts and everything."

Libby's frame had stiffened. "Are you going to tell me you're my husband, and I was coming to you for help? All you want to do now is take me back to Rocky Point and resume our happy life?"

Rob ground his teeth together, his muscles aching, his head throbbing.

Troy turned his head to the side and spit on the ground. "Oh, hell no. I've never met you before in my life, and I've already had two wives. I sure as hell don't want any more…especially ones who kick."

A flood of relief swept through Rob's body so fast, he had to lock his knees to keep upright.

Libby needed him to keep upright. Her body sagged against his. "Wh-what do you want? Who are you, and why did you abduct me at gunpoint?"

Tipping his head at the building behind them, Troy said, "Can we go back into the restaurant and discuss this? My weapon's on the ground, which you can take, and we're gonna start attracting attention. I don't want to explain myself to the police, and I'm guessing you don't, either."

Rob whispered in Libby's ear, "Stay here."

He crept toward Troy and the car, his gun still firmly clutched in his hand. "Kick your weapon toward me and don't try anything, or else one of those ex-wives is going to collect on your life insurance policy."

"That ain't gonna happen. My daughter gets it all." He nudged the weapon toward Rob with his toe. "Take it."

Without removing his eyes from Troy, Rob stooped to snatch up the gun. Then he approached the man, turned him around and shoved him against the car. A pat-down didn't reveal any more weapons.

"Start walking back to the restaurant, and remember…"

"Yeah, I know. My daughter's gonna collect that life insurance." He trudged past Rob, made a wide berth around Libby and plodded toward the restaurant.

If the hostess recognized any of them, she didn't let on,

waving them to a booth in the corner. Rob slid in first, letting Libby have the outside in case something went down and she had to make a quick getaway. He motioned Troy to the other side.

As Troy plopped down on the seat, Rob said, "I've got my gun pointed at you. One move and your daughter's going to be an only child."

Troy's eyes widened for a second and then he chuckled. "You're not so bad for a lawman, Valdez."

Rob's eye twitched. "How do you know me, and how'd you find us here? Nobody followed us from Paradiso. I'd bet my life on it."

"I didn't have to follow you." Troy laced his fingers together and cracked his knuckles. "I put a GPS tracker on your truck."

"Damn." Rob smacked the table with his open hand, and the silverware jumped.

A waitress scurried over. "What would you like?"

"Coffee all around." Rob swept his finger in a circle to encompass the table and then turned over his coffee cup.

Libby said, "Make mine a hot tea, herbal if you have it."

"Chamomile okay?" The waitress filled Rob's and Troy's cups to the brim.

"Perfect."

Rob pinned Troy with a stare. "When did you do that?"

"I'm not giving away all my tricks, lawman." Troy formed his fingers into a gun and pointed at Rob.

"Stop with the quips, Troy, and tell us what you want with Libby."

"Well, I wanted information." Troy rubbed the graying stubble on his chin with his knuckles. "Libby James was supposed to meet me in Paradiso to give me some information, but it doesn't look like that's gonna happen.

I figured out soon enough when I saw you in town that you had either changed your mind or had gotten a better deal. You didn't show up at our meeting place, and when I walked straight at you in the street wearing my San Francisco Giants baseball cap and flashing a peace sign, you didn't even blink. That's when I started thinking you didn't remember a thing."

"Oh, God." Libby squeezed her eyes closed and wrinkled her nose. "That was you. I remember now."

"Yeah, I wish you remembered more than that."

"Wait. This is all very clever, but why did you try to take Libby at gunpoint?" Rob drilled his finger into the table in front of Troy.

"You wouldn't have believed me if I'd come up to you and explained who I was." Troy snorted. "I saw what happened to the last guy who tried that."

"Pablo Bustamante." Libby crossed her arms on the table, rubbing at the gooseflesh on her skin. "What do you know about him?"

"Nada. Just that he works for the bad guys, and his name ain't Pablo Bustamante. I figured he was coming on like a husband and was using that baby as a prop. Am I right?" Troy dropped his chin to his chest and raised his brows to his bald head.

"You seem to be right about an awful lot." Libby drew back as the waitress placed her tea in front of her.

"Thanks." She smiled at the waitress and then turned her attention back to Troy. "Who are you, and what information did you hope to get from me?"

"You two haven't figured it out yet based on my slick moves?"

Rob grunted. "You're a PI."

"Bingo, lawman." Troy slurped up his coffee and then dumped some sugar into the cup.

"A private investigator?" Libby ripped open her tea bag and swung it around her finger, pointing at Troy. "Investigating what?"

"I'm investigating El Gringo Viejo. He's a..."

Rob sliced his hand through the air. "We know what he is."

"I figured you did, Valdez, but what about her? I mean, I know she knew about him before she lost her marbles, but does she know about him now?" He shook his head and folded his hands around his coffee cup. "Damn, this is getting confusing."

"I know what he is...now. The first time I heard his moniker was from the lips of two men sent here to kill me."

Troy's eyes bugged out. "That's it, then. He is in Rocky Point like I suspected, and you know who he is." Troy grimaced. "It's not surprising they want to kill you. You can't identify those guys?"

"That's why she's suspicious of everyone she meets—especially people who abduct her at gunpoint." Rob still had a grip on his own gun beneath the table. Could they trust this guy? If Troy *were* working for the cartels, Libby would be dead by now.

Libby fished her tea bag from her cup and watched the drops fall back into the steaming water. "What info was I supposed to give you about El Gringo Viejo? Did I know the man? Associate with him?"

"You and I weren't even sure this guy you knew *was* El Gringo Viejo, but if those two thugs sent here to murder you mentioned his name, it's a good bet he is."

"I know him?" Libby abandoned her soggy tea bag in the saucer and folded her hands in her lap. "How would I know someone like that?"

"You're an artist. You have some fancy art gallery in

town." Troy's eyes narrowed to slits. "The man with the big villa on the outskirts of town likes art. He'd contacted you before I did."

"The big villa on the cliffs overlooking the water." Libby's eyes grew glassy as she stared into her teacup as if hoping to read the tea leaves to her past there.

Troy scooted closer to the table. "You remember that?"

"I've seen a hypnotist."

Rob nudged her foot beneath the table. She must already trust this guy, but he'd rather do a little private investigating of his own first.

"Smart move." Troy snapped his fingers. "You didn't remember anything else?"

"I remembered the art gallery, but Rob and I had already done some sleuthing of our own and we deduced that I was Libby James, an artist and gallery owner in Rocky Point." Libby slid a glance at Rob, and he shook his head.

If Troy noticed the gesture, he didn't react. Rob didn't want Libby telling Troy about the dead body she remembered, or anything else, until he had a chance to check him out.

Rob blew out a breath. "Look, what's your name? Your last name. And why are you investigating El Gringo Viejo? How did you know he was in Rocky Point when the Border Patrol, DEA, FBI and the Federales don't know where he is?"

Troy plunged two fingers into the front pocket of his wrinkled shirt and pulled out two business cards. "One for you, and one for you."

Rob picked up the card Troy had placed in front of him on the table. "Troy Paulsen, private investigator. Oh, look here. You have a license and everything."

"That'll make it easier for you to run me, won't it,

lawman? I even have a license to carry that gun you're holding on me."

"You don't have a license to draw that gun on an innocent woman."

"I'm sorry, Libby." Troy spread his spatulate fingers on the Formica. "I needed to talk to you, and I knew you wouldn't remember me and our meeting. I was never going to hurt you. I was afraid to approach you in Paradiso with the cartel watching your every move."

"Don't remind me." Libby put her hand to her throat.

"Maybe you need to adopt some better business practices, Paulsen." Rob flicked the corner of the card. "You still didn't answer me. Why are you nosing around El Gringo Viejo, and how'd you get this far?"

"PIs aren't under the same rules and constraints as law enforcement. We can get information in ways you can't and from people who wouldn't give you the time of day. I know people in low places, lawman, unlike you."

"You have no idea." Rob twisted his lips. "Who hired you? Because I know you're not tracking down a cartel supplier out of the goodness of your heart. Is it one of the cartels? If it is, this stops here and now. Libby's not going to be involved with that business."

"No, no, nothing like that. I was working for Adam Hart."

Rob bared his teeth. "That's a lie. Adam Hart is dead, and I know the person who killed him."

"I said I *was* working for Adam Hart. I know he's dead, but it's not because he was looking for El Gringo Viejo."

"Not directly." Rob waved off the waitress hovering with the coffeepot. "Why are you still on the job if your client is dead? Hoping to cash in big if you bring EGV down?"

"Funny you should call him EGV. That's what she calls him."

Rob swallowed. "Who?"

"My new client, the person who hired me—Adam Hart's sister, April Hart, or I guess she's April Archer now. She hired me."

Chapter Fifteen

Libby gasped as Rob's stomach sank.

She dug her elbows into the table and propped her chin in one hand, as she leaned toward Troy. "April hired you to find EGV because she thinks he's her father."

"Wow. How do you know all that? Oh, yeah." Troy smacked his forehead. "She's married to a Border Patrol agent herself. You obviously know April, and you know what she believes."

"Does she know about this?" Rob wagged his finger back and forth between Libby and Troy. "Does she know you came to Paradiso to meet someone from Rocky Point who could ID EGV?"

"She doesn't know nothin'. I don't operate that way. Her brother didn't much like it, but I play it close to the vest. I don't give my clients nothin' until I can bring them results. April?" Troy dusted his hands together. "She doesn't even know what I look like. I contacted her after her brother died, told her what was going on and asked her if she wanted me to continue the investigation. She gave me the green light and transfers money to me when I send her my receipts and accounting every month."

"Sweet deal…for you."

"Hey, man. I get results." Troy drilled his knuckle

into the table with every word. "I got the heads-up that EGV was near Rocky Point. I went there for a vacation, put out some feelers and discovered this rich dude had a compound on the coast—electric fences, guards, dogs, the whole nine yards. I also found out he was an art lover. Then it got a little hot, and I had to leave, but not before I discovered the guy's interest in local art. So, I contacted Libby James."

Rob's hand curled into a fist. "And put her in danger."

"I didn't twist your arm, Libby. When I told you what I suspected, you were more than eager to help." Troy skimmed a hand over his head. "I don't know the details, but it seems like you had a particular reason to bring down this guy if he was involved with the cartels. You have no love for the cartels, Libby. You made that clear."

A crease formed between Libby's eyebrows. "Did you get the impression it was personal with me? Some hatred beyond what any decent person would feel for the cartels?"

"Oh, yeah." Troy drummed his fingers on the table. "Don't ask me, though, 'cause I don't know, and now I guess neither do you. What I don't get?"

"Yeah?" Libby met his gaze, and Rob placed a hand on her thigh beneath the table.

"How did EGV know you were on to him, and why did you have those goons on your tail on your way up here? This was supposed to be an informational meeting. You told me you had something to show me. Next thing I know, you blow off the meeting, don't acknowledge me in the street and Paradiso is thick with cartel members looking to kill you."

Libby's hand jerked and her tea sloshed over the edge of her cup.

"Sorry." Troy patted her arm with a clumsy hand. "I

suppose you don't have your phone, do you? I got the impression what you had to show me was on your phone, but you didn't want to send it to me."

"I'm assuming it burned up in the car along with my purse, my ID, my suitcase, my life."

Rob asked, "What about your phone? You said in the parking lot you had text messages between you and Libby for proof. I'd like to see those messages, see what she texted you before the accident."

"I have it..." Troy dug in his pocket and withdrew a phone with a pink sparkly case. "Damn, I don't have that particular phone on me. I have a lot of burner phones, and I swap them out just in case."

"Right." Rob snatched up Troy's phone from the table. "Passcode?"

Troy rattled it off, and Rob accessed his phone. He scrolled through enough text messages to see that Troy did have clients, and he had Libby's number saved. He called the number just for the heck of it. It rang and rang and rang.

"Libby's phone was probably destroyed in the car fire."

"I know that now. You don't think I've been trying it?" Troy slumped in his seat. "I guess it's back to the drawing board unless you get your memory back and can tell me what you had."

"Back to the drawing board for you. Libby's out of it."

"Lawman, she ain't gonna be out of it until she starts remembering. There are more Pablos out there, and they have orders to make sure Libby's gone before that happens."

LIBBY SAT IN Rob's truck, pressing her fingers to her temples on both sides of her throbbing head. "What do you think?"

"I think Troy Paulsen is a blowhard, and just listening to him tired me out."

"Do you believe him?" Rob must've believed some part of that story because he gave Troy's weapon back to him. "Because I believe him."

"I don't know why he'd lie about working for April Archer. That sounds like something her brother would get up to, and maybe she figured she'd go along with it to see if Paulsen could come up with something."

"Why do you think April didn't mention it to us when she came over? I realize she didn't know I had come across the border to meet with Paulsen, but El Gringo Viejo came up in the conversation and she even admitted that she suspected he was her father."

"I can give you one reason." Rob wiped his brow and started the engine. "Her husband. I'd bet my last dollar Clay doesn't know a damned thing about this investigation, and he wouldn't be happy about it if he did. April wasn't about to tell me."

He backed out of the parking space and pulled out of the lot.

"Why didn't you want me to tell him about the dead body from my memory?"

"You were spilling enough. No need to give him everything. I'm going to run him. If he checks out as legit, maybe we can schedule another meeting with him and you can tell him about the dead man. He might know who he is."

"Why would I have it in for the cartels?" Libby shoved her hands beneath her thighs to keep them from trembling.

"Why wouldn't you? They're a law unto themselves down there. They wreak havoc and pain up here. I've got it in for them. I would even if it weren't my job."

"Troy said I had a personal issue with the cartels." Libby gnawed at her bottom lip. "What if that dead body is someone I know? Someone I love?"

Rob's knuckles blanched as he seemed to tighten his hold on the steering wheel. "Troy made it sound like you had an issue with the cartels from before and that's why you didn't hesitate to help him. Don't you think you fled *because* of the dead body on the lawn?"

"I don't mean a husband or boyfriend." She trailed her fingertips along Rob's tensed forearm. "I think Troy made it clear I didn't have a significant other in the picture."

"Did he?" Rob dropped one hand from the steering wheel to his thigh. "He said you didn't have a husband."

"Okay, forget I said that." She kicked off her sandals and wedged her feet on the dashboard. "A loved one could be anyone, not just romantic love."

"Let me check out Troy, and if he's on the up-and-up, tell him about the dead body. Maybe he has some ideas. If his intel down there was any good, he should have an idea about who's in that complex with EGV."

"We should probably tell April we met her PI."

"Not a good idea. It doesn't sound like Troy was going to make himself known to her, so it's none of our business."

Libby's jaw fell open. "None of our business? We could put our heads together on this, and we could hand EGV to the FBI or the DEA. Isn't that important to you?"

"Keeping you safe is more important to me than catching EGV."

She stared at his profile, her mouth in danger of dropping open again. "You're kidding."

"Why would you think that? Haven't I upended my entire life since the day I picked you up?" He tapped the clock on the dashboard. "In fact, I'm going to be late for work."

"Um, you didn't seem that interested last night."

"That was sex. Wanting to protect you is something else, and turning you down, while it wasn't easy, is another way to protect you."

"That's nice to hear, Rob, but it's as much about protecting you."

"Me?" He jabbed a finger in his chest. "I know who I am. I know I'm not married or attached or even dating."

"Which means you're free and clear..." She whipped her head around. "You're not even dating?"

"Went on a few online dates in Tucson, but I've been busy. Then I bought my house. Next, I want to get a dog."

"Priorities." She raised her eyes to the roof of the truck. "What I was saying is that you're free and clear to fall for someone...fall for me. And if that happens and I turn out to have a husband and four children, where would you be? I know you're protecting yourself, protecting your heart, and I don't blame you, but, damn, we've got a thing here."

The corner of his mouth twitched. "Does having no memory give you free rein to say whatever comes into your head?"

"Pretty much." She punched his rock-solid bicep. "Do you deny we have some heat between us?"

Idling at the stop sign, Rob threw the truck into Park, leaned over the console and pressed his soft lips against hers. Her mouth opened, and he slid a hand into her hair and deepened the kiss.

Someone honked behind them, and they sprang apart.

Rob pulled away from the stop sign, the truck lurching as much as her heart, and touched his fingers to his mouth. "I do not deny any heat. In fact, my lips are on fire."

She traced her own tingling lips with the tip of her finger and sighed. "If we can generate that much passion with a quick kiss at a stop sign in a truck with our seat belts on, why the hell are we wasting time?"

Rob aimed his truck toward the on-ramp and punched the accelerator as he merged onto the freeway. "I've been through that before, Libby. I dated someone a few years ago who lied about her marital status. I'm just not doing that again. It was…messy."

She raised her eyebrows at him. "This wouldn't be like that, Rob. I wouldn't lie to you. I'd never lie to you."

"You're not in a position to know whether or not you'd be lying, and that's even…messier."

She puckered her lips, still feeling the stamp of his kiss on her mouth. How could something so messy feel so right?

They spent the rest of the ride to Tucson avoiding conversation about their feelings—and that kiss. They made good time, and Rob made a U-turn to drop her off in front of Rosita's.

As she reached for the door, he grabbed her arm. "Be careful. Don't go anywhere by yourself, including the restrooms. Use the ladies' room when it's crowded, during the lunch rush."

"I'll be fine. Are you going to look into Troy Paulsen's background?"

"I am, and there's something else he said that got me thinking."

"He said a lot that got me thinking. What did you pick up?"

"Your phone."

"Yeah, I'm pretty sure that burned up in the wreck. It wasn't on me and I didn't see anything in the husk of that car. That's why you didn't even get through to the voice mail when you called it."

"I didn't see anything, either, but Paulsen mentioned you'd been texting him. I'd like to get your phone records and take a look at your texts, if we can get them. Those could tell us a lot. I wish Paulsen would've had the phone he used with you. Those texts could've told us something."

Libby's heart skipped a beat. "Well, you have his card. You know, I never even thought about that. Just because the phone is destroyed doesn't mean the phone's records disappear."

"Exactly." Rob rubbed his chin. "I may not be able to get those records right away, but they'll definitely shed some light on your thoughts and actions before you hit the road to Paradiso."

"See? Troy was good for something." She kissed her fingers and pressed them against Rob's cheek. "Too messy?"

He slapped his hand against his face where she'd placed her fingers. "Just right."

Libby scrambled from the truck and got to work as soon as she entered the restaurant, her mind wandering to Troy's words during her busy shift. Why would a mild-mannered artist agree to infiltrate the compound of a suspected drug broker? Why would she put herself in danger like that unless she had a strong motivation?

Could that dead body be her motivation? Rob was right. If the dead body prompted her flight from Rocky Point, that person couldn't have been her impetus for getting involved with EGV in the first place.

It must've been something…or someone prior to that.

At the end of the lunch rush, Libby stood in the kitchen and ate a quick taco.

Rosie poked her head inside the window. "Rob is here to pick you up. He looks anxious to see you, practically hopping from one foot to the next."

"I didn't even know he was coming to get me." She called to Sal, "Sal, can you make a burrito for Rob Valdez? Carnitas, I think."

Sal grinned. "I know what Mr. Rob likes."

She wished she did.

Libby smoothed back her hair and traipsed into the dining room, walking in on a few patrons finishing up their lunches. She waved to Rob. "I ordered you a burrito. Did you find out anything about my phone?"

"I did." He pulled her into the nearest chair. "When I called Paulsen, he told me he fired up the phone he'd used with you and read some texts from you that are important."

"What is it?" Libby gripped the edge of the table she'd just cleaned.

"He wouldn't tell me over the phone. He's heading over here, but he doesn't want to be seen with us in case someone's watching you."

Libby glanced over her shoulder at the door, a chill claiming the back of her neck. "What's the plan?"

"He's going to come in here, place an order and leave his phone on a table, opened to the text he wants us to see. That's it. No other communication. All joking aside, the guy's spooked."

"I know how he feels."

Sal brought Rob's burrito to him personally in a paper bag. "Didn't know you were eating in, boss."

"How are the grandkids, Sal?"

"The oldest is up at U of A."

"Already? You need to retire, hombre."

"The wife and I have a little place on the Gulf. Going out there in a few weeks." Sal saluted and returned to the kitchen.

Rob pulled his burrito out of the bag. "I suppose I should pretend to eat this."

"Sal would be very disappointed if you didn't." She grabbed some napkins from the dispenser and shoved them at Rob, her gaze tracking over his shoulder. "Don't look now, but Troy just walked in."

"Keep an eye on him."

"He's ordering." Libby dabbed a napkin on the table. "He has his phone out. He's talking to Rosie."

Rob rolled his eyes. "I don't need a play-by-play."

"You asked." Libby scooted her chair back from the table. "He's walking this way."

Troy strode past their table on the way to the restrooms without a care in the world.

Libby kicked Rob under the table. "He left his phone at the counter."

"Go talk to Rosie and get his phone. Bring it back here." Rob's head swiveled back and forth. "I don't think we have to worry. Anyone left in here is a customer from before, right?"

"Yes, but how do I know one of them isn't spying on me?" She pushed back from the table and hung over the counter. "Hey, Sal, can we get some more salsa?"

She covered Troy's phone with her hand and slid it into her back pocket.

Rosie appeared from the back, carrying a dish of salsa. "The hot stuff."

"Thanks, Rosie." Libby carried the salsa back to the

table. Before she sat down, she pulled Troy's phone from her pocket and tapped it.

A set of text messages in alternating gray and blue popped up under the heading of *LJ*, which must be Libby James. She read them aloud to Rob in a low voice.

"'Where are you now?'"

"'Just crossed the border. I should turn off my phone and get rid of it.'"

"'Why?'"

"'I think I'm being followed. Maybe they're tracking my phone.'"

"'Info on the phone?'"

"'Yes, but I have something else to show you.'"

"'You're gonna toss your phone?'"

"'Have a place to drop it off. It's like a desert campsite for RVs. Unofficial. It's not far.'"

"'Go for it. Be careful.'"

The text messages between Troy and LJ ended, and Libby spun the phone on the table. "That's it. I left the phone at some campsite. How are we ever going to find that?"

Rob had stopped eating his burrito and held it midway between his mouth and the bag on the table. "I know exactly where it is."

"You do?"

Troy came barreling out of the bathroom, rubbing his hands together. "Is my order up?"

"Another few minutes, sir." Rosie greeted another couple coming through the door, and Libby swept the phone off the table. She cupped it between her hands.

"Done with this?" She grabbed the salsa and returned to the counter, making a wide berth around Troy.

She held up the salsa with one hand and slipped the

phone back onto the counter with the other. "Here you go, Rosie."

"You hardly touched it, Rob."

"I'm gonna wrap this up and take it home for later, Rosie."

As Libby sauntered back to the table, Rob folded the yellow wax paper around his food and stuffed it in the bag. He glanced up at her. "Ready?"

"Ready for anything."

When she got to the door, she waved to Rosie, who was handing Troy a bag of food. "Bye, Rosie. See you tomorrow."

"Day off tomorrow, Jane. We're closed on Sunday."

She and Rob slipped out the door and made a beeline for his truck. Troy wouldn't want to run into them outside.

Once inside the truck, Rob started the engine and took off down the street, back toward his house.

"Are you going to tell me where my phone is?"

"There's an RV campsite, and I use that term loosely, between Paradiso and the border. It's unofficial and unregulated. Lots of lowlifes there, so I'm not sure how you knew about it and why you'd leave your phone there."

"Are we just supposed to bust in there and ask for a phone?"

"If you left it there, you left it with someone. You must know someone there." He cranked up the AC and wiped his brow. "Believe me, strangers do not just waltz onto this property and ask nicely if they can stash their cell phones. A man was murdered there last month, a baby kidnapped."

Libby covered her mouth. "Is it safe?"

"Not really, but as much as I'd like to, I can't barge in

there myself. You have to come along and hope someone recognizes you and hands over your phone."

"Almost as important as the phone will be this person who knows me. Finally, someone who knows Libby James."

"But why there?" Rob chewed on the side of his thumb, and Libby slapped his hand.

"Stop that. I'll be okay—as long as I have you by my side. That's one thing Libby James does know."

Rob sped home and changed out of his uniform into a pair of jeans, a dark T-shirt and running shoes.

He pointed to her light-colored capris, filmy blouse and sandals. "You might want to change. It's a dirty, dusty place out there. Did you happen to buy a pair of sneakers when you went shopping the other day?"

"I did." She kicked off her sandals and hooked her fingers around the straps, dangling them at her side. "Why? Am I gonna have to make a run for it?"

"You never know out there."

She changed into clothes appropriate for a quick getaway, and Rob grabbed a backpack on their way out the door. He turned to her when they got to the truck and said, "We're going out past the site of the wreck. Can you handle it?"

"Do you mean am I going to freak out and have memory flashes that take me back to the crash?" She climbed into the truck. "I hope so."

Thirty minutes later, they passed the crash site without incident. Libby even tried to remember by squeezing her eyes closed and thinking the calming words Jennifer used to put her in a hypnotic state. Libby opened one eye and rolled it toward Rob. "Nothing."

He took her hand and threaded his fingers with hers. "It'll come, and this will all make sense."

"And maybe you and I…?"

"Maybe we will." He squeezed her hand.

She brought their clasped hands to her lips and kissed his knuckles. "It's the only hope I can hold on to right now, Rob."

When Rob turned off the main highway and the truck kicked up dust and dirt on an access road, Libby swallowed. "Where is this place?"

"Where nobody can find them. It's like a commune. People go there to drop out and live off the grid."

"I obviously know someone well enough there to drop off my phone." She ran her hands down the denim covering her thighs. "I hope that person is there today."

The desert undulated with one sandy hill resembling another, and the truck bounced and pitched as the road got rougher.

"Are you sure this is the right way?" Libby squinted out the windshield, and like a ragtag mirage, a collection of temporary and impromptu houses sprang up in the form of RVs, trailers and cars. "Those came up fast."

"There's a reason they chose this spot. Once someone comes over that rise like we just did, they can see 'em coming."

Libby licked her dry lips. "They're not going to charge us or anything, are they?"

"No." Rob hunched over the steering wheel. "But it looks like they're sending a welcoming committee."

Libby picked out two motorcycles heading their way, a cloud of sand following them. "Do you want your gun?"

"I've got it on me. Don't worry." Rob powered down his window and eased off the gas pedal.

One motorcycle veered right and one veered left, and then they both swung around to come up alongside the truck.

Rob slowed to a crawl and stopped, calling out the window at the rider on his side, “Can we help you boys?”

The biker, a tattoo snaking up his neck, shouted over the sound of his rumbling engine. “What do you want here?”

“We’ve come to pick up a phone.” Rob jerked his thumb to the side toward Libby.

The guy ducked his head and nodded. He circled his finger in the air and gunned the bike’s engine, sending a shower of sand and dust into the truck.

The biker on Libby’s side got the message and shot forward, both of them cruising back to the campsite.

Libby coughed and waved a hand in front of her face. “That was easy. I thought we were going to have to take them out for a minute.”

“They recognized you.” Rob rubbed the back of his hand across his nose. “They’ve seen you here before and you must be welcome, or they would’ve tried to stop us.”

“That’s a good sign, right?”

“Excellent sign. We’re in.” Rob followed the hazy air in the path of the bikes to the makeshift campsite.

When they arrived, the two watchdogs had already gotten off their motorcycles and were retreating to some dilapidated RV. Rob parked the truck just outside the official entrance to the compound and cut the engine.

“Just walk in there like you own the place, like a boss.”

“I’ve never felt less like a boss.” Libby hitched her purse over her shoulder, but this time she waited for Rob to come around and open her door. She had no intention of waltzing into that squalid encampment demanding her phone.

Rob took her arm, even though he couldn’t possibly know her knees were knocking together. He whispered in her ear, “It’s okay. We got this.”

As they scuffed into the center of the camp, a woman with cropped gray hair and an armful of tattoos floated out to greet them. She put her arms around Libby and said, "I'm glad you're safe, my sweet. I have your phone."

Libby reared back from the woman's embrace, tears stinging her eyes. "You know me?"

The woman's gray brows arched over her eyes. "What does that mean? Of course I know you, Libby. Your mother was one of my dearest friends. What's going on?"

"Ma'am." Rob held out his hand. "My name is Rob Valdez. Libby ran into some trouble north of the border. Some men forced her off the road. Her car crashed and she lost her memory. We've been able to piece together some things, but she has huge holes in her memory—and she's in danger."

The woman's light blue eyes grew larger and larger with every word from Rob's lips. Then she clasped Libby to her breast again and cried out, "I knew I shouldn't have let you go. Do you know you're Libby James?"

"I do." Libby inhaled the scent of this woman—herbs and earth and spice. Comfort. An overwhelming sense of calm seeped into Libby's bones. She knew this woman. "Luna."

Rob's head jerked to the side. "You remember her?"

"That's right, my sweet. I'm Luna." Luna patted Libby's back. "Do you remember me?"

"I—I remember your smell. Your name came to me from your scent."

"They do say smell is the most powerful sense and can evoke all kinds of memories." Luna smoothed her hand over Libby's face. "Were you physically injured?"

"Just a gash on my head. Otherwise, I'm fine."

Luna's gaze darted around the campsite. "Come to

my home. We're attracting attention out here, and I don't want anyone knowing our business."

With her arm curled around Libby's waist, Luna led them to her RV, one of the nicest in the collection, a colorful blue-and-white awning fanning out over some chairs and a small pit for a campfire.

Luna patted a canvas chair. "Sit here, Libby. I'm going to try to help you. I don't know why you were on the run from Rocky Point. You wouldn't tell me that, but I can help you with the rest. I can't imagine the fear of having a black hole for a memory."

Libby sank to the chair, crossed one leg over the other and promptly started kicking her leg. "It's been crazy, made worse because of the danger and made better because of… Rob."

"Call me old-fashioned, but I think everything's better with a partner by your side." Luna winked at Rob and waved him into a chair.

Libby blinked. "And you have a partner. He lives here with you."

"That's right." Luna nodded, a broad smile displaying her white teeth. "Zeke, who's scavenging in the desert right now. I'd say he's pretty unforgettable. See? You're remembering already. It must help to be with people you know. No offense, Rob."

"None taken."

"Luna—" Libby's blood bubbled in her veins "—you mentioned you were friends with my mother. Where is she? Is she in the States? Back in Rocky Point? Is she worried?"

The creases in Luna's lined face softened. "I'm sorry, Libby. Your mother is dead."

Luna's words punched her in the gut, and Libby pressed a fist to her belly. "H-how long ago? What happened?"

"It was just a few months ago." Luna clasped her hands around one knee. "Tandy was murdered, Libby."

Tandy? Rob sucked in a breath and choked out, "Oh, my God. Libby's mother was Tandy Richards?"

Chapter Sixteen

Libby stared at him, her eyes wide in her pale face. "Where have I heard that name before, Rob? I've heard the name."

"I guess I mentioned the name once, or you overheard me." Rob clenched his teeth. Libby didn't have to remember those details, and if she couldn't recall the conversation, he wasn't going to refresh her memory.

Then she wailed and doubled over, her forehead touching her knees. "She was beheaded. My mother was one of the mules who was murdered in the tunnel."

Luna stroked Libby's hair and glared at Rob over the top of Libby's head.

He'd gone from hero to zero with one stupid statement.

Luna murmured, "I'm sure that's just a rumor, Libby. There are all kinds of gruesome tales circulating around the border."

Libby straightened up, sweeping her hands across her wet cheeks. "No, you don't understand. Rob is a Border Patrol agent. He mentioned something about the two women, the two mules, who were decapitated at the border. He said their names, Tandy Richards and Elena something."

Luna pressed her lips into a straight, thin line. "You're Border Patrol?"

Rob lunged out of his chair and knelt before Libby, wrapping his arms around her waist and burying his face in her lap. "I'm sorry, Libby. I never in a million years would've connected you to Tandy Richards. I should've never mentioned that case to you."

Her fingers slipped into his hair. "My mother was a mule for the cartels?"

Luna said, "Your mother was a troubled woman, Libby, but she loved you and had the biggest heart."

"My father?"

Rob sat back on his heels and held her hands. He'd rather she have a husband in the wings than this.

Luna sighed. "Not in the picture. Your mother moved to Mexico with you when you were a child. She got mixed up with the wrong people."

Libby clenched her hands in her lap. "That's why I agreed to help Troy."

"Who's Troy?" Luna cocked her head, looking like a bird on alert.

"Never mind, Luna. Knowing my mother died at the hands of the cartels, as painful as it is, clears up a lot." Libby reached for Rob and touched his chin. "It's not your fault. This is the fear I have of remembering everything. I must have already grieved for my mother and it's hit me like a sledgehammer all over again."

Luna pressed a hand to her heart. "Please tell me you didn't decide to go after the cartels on your own to avenge Tandy's death."

"Not on my own, anyway. It's complicated, Luna."

Rob stayed crouched by Libby's side, his hand caressing her calf. "Do you have Libby's phone, Luna? We're hoping that's going to tell us even more."

"It's in the RV. I left it turned off, like you asked, Libby. It might need charging." Luna rose to her feet and climbed the two steps to the aluminum door to her home. She banged around inside and then called out through the window. "I'm charging it now. Give it some time."

Libby cupped his face with her hands. "I'm all right. I always felt there was something I didn't want to remember, and it didn't have to do with the dead body."

"If it makes you feel better, Tandy Richards did not come up on our radar as having any connections to the cartels or any drug dealers."

"She was a user, Libby." Luna picked her way down the steps, holding two cups of steaming liquid, the scent of peppermint wafting through the air. She handed one cup to Libby. "Do you want some tea, Rob? It's jade citrus peppermint. It'll relax Libby."

"I'll pass, thanks." He placed a kiss on the inside of Libby's wrist and backed up to his own chair. "What do you mean she was a user? Drugs or people?"

Luna shrugged as she sipped her tea. "A little of both. I think someone convinced her to carry for the cartels, or maybe she just went along with the other girl to give her some protection. That's something she'd do."

Libby inhaled the smell of her tea before taking a sip. "Were we in touch? Estranged? Did we live together?"

"Drink some more of your tea." Luna poked a stick at the firepit. "Gets a little chillier out here at night than in the city. A fire's nice. Rob, you wanna get one started? My man Zeke set it up before he left today."

Luna tossed a box of matches at him, and Rob caught them with one hand. As he shoved the kindling beneath the logs, Luna's low, soothing voice floated over him.

"Do you remember your mother, Libby? Pretty woman, like you, but she never had your strength. Always got by on her looks, Tandy did, and when those started to fade she panicked a little. Always enjoyed the company and flattery of men. Do you remember, Libby?"

Libby's eyes had drifted closed, as she drank more tea from her cup. "She was small, petite like a fairy, and she had a laugh that bubbled like champagne. I adored her, but as I grew up, I knew she couldn't protect me."

Rob glanced up from his Boy Scout activity, jerking his head toward Luna, who put a gnarled finger to her lips.

Luna's monotone voice continued. "She did secure the gallery for you, though, and a few wealthy investors. Do you remember?"

The smooth skin between Libby's eyebrows puckered. "We argued about it. She got money from her boyfriend, her rich, married boyfriend, and I told her that's the only way she ever got by in life—using men. I didn't want to accept the gallery, but she cried and said it was the only thing she had ever given me. I felt sad. I accepted the gallery."

"And made a success out of it."

"I wanted Mom to stay with me, but I told her she had to get off the drugs and booze. She wouldn't. We were estranged at the end. She wouldn't change, couldn't change." Libby's eyes flew open, and she pinned Rob with her gaze. "She knew that man in the palatial house. Somehow she knew him."

Rob struck a match and lit the kindling in several places with a slightly trembling hand. As the smoke curled up, he looked at Libby through the haze. "Do you remember now? Everything?"

Waving her hand in front of her face to dissipate the smoke, she shook her head. "Not everything. Not clearly. I can picture my mother. I know she talked to me about the man on the cliff and his interest in art. After she was murdered and Troy approached me, I knew I could get into the compound because my mother knew someone there. He sent her to her death, didn't he? El Gringo Viejo?"

"No, not directly, Libby. It was a small-time drug dealer working for the Las Moscas cartel who wanted to strike out on his own. He's the one responsible for your mother's death—and he paid with his own life." Rob stepped back from the crackling fire. "I wonder if EGV knew what happened to your mother. I wonder if you were in danger from the moment you stepped through the gates of his home."

"That's still a blank, Rob. I don't remember the man at the house. I don't remember the man who died."

"Someone else died?" Luna tossed the dregs of her tea into the fire, which snapped and danced. "You never told me any of this, Libby."

Libby held up her cup. "What's in this tea? I felt like I did when I was under hypnosis at the therapist's office."

"Hypnosis is just a state of deep relaxation. That's all I did." She pinged her fingernail against her cup. "I put you in a state of deep relaxation and gave you a few suggestions."

"It worked."

Luna asked, "Who's El Gringo Viejo?"

"You don't need to know." Rob circled around the fire and squeezed Libby's shoulders. "Are you all right?"

"I'm fine. I feel like the pieces are falling into place for me."

"Your phone is probably sufficiently charged to go through it." He held out his hand toward Luna. "Do you want me to take your cup? Is it okay if I go inside?"

"Take the cup, go inside, don't disturb the cat." She

handed him her cup. "The phone's by the sink, not that our place is all that big."

As he turned toward the steps, Libby grabbed his hand and said, "One more thing, Luna. I'm pretty sure I know the answer, but I'm not married, am I? Have any boyfriends lurking around?"

Luna chuckled. "You're one hundred percent single. Your mother was lamenting that fact the last time I saw her."

Rob swooped down and planted a kiss on Libby's mouth. "Thanks for asking."

He tromped up the two steps and yanked open the door to the RV. His nostrils flared at the smell of that tea in here. Luna must burn the stuff, too.

Spotting the charging phone on the small counter next to the stainless-steel sink, Rob took one step and reached for it. He could probably stand in the center of the RV and reach practically everything.

The gray tabby glared at him from his one good eye, and Rob yanked the charger out of the socket along with the phone before the cat got any ideas.

The battery meter in the corner of the display read half-full, so he held his thumb down on the power button. He stepped out of the RV as the phone came to life and tripped on the bottom step when he saw the familiar keypad for the log-in.

He held up the phone. "Good news and bad news. The phone is powered up and working, but you have a passcode."

"Let me have it." Libby snapped her fingers and opened her palm.

He placed the phone in her hand and hovered over her shoulder.

She hesitated for a split second, and then her thumb

darted over the keypad and the screen woke up. Cranking her head over her shoulder, she said, "I remembered, or my fingers remembered."

"Bring up your texts."

Luna half rose from her chair. "Should I leave you?"

"Stay, please, Luna." Libby flicked her fingers at the older woman. "I may need your help."

Rob poked at the screen. "There's your conversation with Troy."

"But I don't see anything that adds to that story." She tapped through the messages. "Wait."

Rob leaned forward, squinting at the lit display. "What do you see?"

"Text messages to and from a Charlie." She drummed her fingers against her chin. "Charlie."

Her phone dinged. "Hey, look. It's a text from Troy asking if I retrieved my phone."

Rob said, "You don't need to answer him now."

"Too late. I just responded Yes."

"Check your photos, Libby. You told Troy you'd have something to show him. You left your phone here to protect it when you knew someone was following you. It has to contain the info you were going to show Troy."

She tapped the photo icon. Gasping, she drew back from the phone. "I-it's Charlie. This is Charlie, Rob. The dead man. I took a picture of him before I left."

Rob's heart rate picked up as he made a grab for Libby's phone. Cupping it in his hand, he focused on the silver-haired man sprawled on the grass, blood soaking his shirt. "Charlie? This is the man you knew as Charlie?"

"Yes. He was my mother's friend or boyfriend. I went to see the man Troy suspected of being April's father about a purchase from the gallery and found Charlie dead on the lawn. That's when I ran."

"Libby, April's father isn't El Gringo Viejo."

"How do you know that? How can you be so sure?"

Rob tapped the photo on the phone. "Because your Charlie is C. J. Hart, and he's April's father."

Chapter Seventeen

"What?" Libby whipped her head around. "How do you know that?"

"I've seen pictures of C. J. Hart. He's still a wanted man. Even though his son may have confessed to murdering his mother, C.J. is still a fugitive. I know what C. J. Hart looks like, and this man is C.J."

"Oh, my God." Libby's hand dropped to her stomach, her fingers clutching the material of April's T-shirt. "I don't know what's worse, telling April her father is El Gringo Viejo and very much alive or telling her that he's Charlie Harper and very much dead."

"The latter—definitely the latter. So, he was living life as Charlie Harper."

Luna stretched her hands to the fire, wiggling her fingers. "Are you telling me Tandy was involved with a man, a wanted fugitive, who was involved with a drug dealer?"

"It seems so, Luna." Libby's lips trembled. "And he's probably the one who convinced her to go into that tunnel."

Rob slipped the phone back into Libby's hand. "Maybe not. He obviously helped you get onto the compound. He had to know what that would mean."

"It cost him his life. EGV must've found out what he'd done."

"Maybe he wanted his own revenge against him for Tandy's death." Rob placed a hand on top of Libby's head, her silky hair warm from the fire.

"But where's our proof?" She swept her fingertip from one picture on her phone to the next. "Was I just going to show Troy the picture of a dead Charlie? Was it to prove C.J. wasn't EGV? I don't think I ever heard of C. J. Hart."

"Why would EGV send his goons after you if that's all it was?" Rob sank to the RV steps. "Unless he knew the rumor about C. J. Hart being El Gringo Viejo. He may have even encouraged that rumor to keep the heat off of himself."

"There has to be something here, Rob. A picture of him. I must be able to ID him, and that's why he's so worried. That's why he's after me."

"Do you really think that man would allow you to take his picture? After all these years of staying under the radar? But you have seen him. You can identify him, and worse for him?" Rob extended his hands and flexed his fingers. "You're an artist. You don't need a photo of him. Once you remember everything about him, you can draw him."

"That notepad at the house—maybe I've already drawn him, just as I sketched my mother. I drew her as a beautiful fairy, how I wanted to remember her before disappointment and drugs stole her looks."

"I found that notebook." Rob shook his head. "You didn't draw any men, except for me and some faceless devil. Believe me, I looked...for other reasons. Our best move now is to somehow convince EGV that you've regained your memory—all of it. And you've ID'd him to the authorities. They'd have no reason to want to see you dead once you turn that information over to the cops."

"Except revenge." Luna spread her hands. "I'm sorry, but that's the way those guys are."

"The sketch must be somewhere. I probably had it with me in the car on my way to meeting Troy." Libby's heart flip-flopped in her chest. "Rob, I think I know where it is."

"A drawing of El Gringo Viejo?"

"Stupid, stupid me." She banged her fists against the arms of the chair. "It survived the car fire, and I just threw it away."

"What are you talking about? You had a drawing at the crash site?"

She balled up her fists against her eyes. "While I was sitting out there behind the tree waiting for…you, a piece of paper skittered past me. I snatched it up and smoothed it out. It was a drawing of a man—longish hair, glasses… I don't know. I thought it was trash. I never dreamed it came from the car… But it did. It must've been my drawing of EGV. I was bringing it to my meeting with Troy."

"What did you do with it?"

"I crumpled it up and tossed it." She hunched forward, gripping her knees. "It could still be there, Rob. It might be faster than waiting for my memory to return."

Luna coughed. "Not tonight you're not. Sun's already going down."

Rob rubbed his hands together. "Let's go back to Paradiso. We can head out to the crash site tomorrow morning. If we take some of Luna's magical tea with us, maybe we won't need to go out there. Maybe you'll get your memory back and you can draw it again. We can get it, and his name or alias, into the system and let him and his associates know we're on to him. It'll be too late for them then, Libby. They'll leave you alone."

"Except for that revenge thing." Luna pushed out of her camp chair. "Zeke's back. I hear his bike."

Tilting her head, Libby picked up the sound of a high whine in the distance of the still night. "If Rob was joking, I'm not. Can I take some of that tea with me?"

"Of course." Luna climbed the steps into the RV and returned with a plastic baggie of loose tea leaves just as a motorcycle pulled into the campsite.

The biker cut the engine and rolled his Harley to the RV. An old Native American climbed off the bike, throwing his long gray braid over his shoulder. "Libby's back."

Luna planted a kiss on the man's brown weathered cheek and turned to Libby. "Do you remember Zeke, Libby?"

Libby rose on unsteady legs, unsure what to do. Should she pretend she remembered him? Shake his hand? Hug him?

"Remember me? Have I aged that much in a week?"

"Zeke." Luna rested her hand on Zeke's shoulder. "Libby's had a rough time since she left us. She had an accident and lost her memory."

"That's crazy. How'd you make it back to Luna, Libby?"

"It's a long story, Zeke. I'll tell you about it later. These two have to get back to Paradiso." She thrust the bag of tea at Libby. "Take this. Relax, clear your mind, think."

Zeke stepped forward and wrapped an arm around Libby, squeezing her close. "Be careful out there, Libby. These desert roads at night… Just saw another car veer off the road, not far from here."

Luna's brow wrinkled. "Did you stop, Zeke?"

"There was another car behind him, and it pulled over. Didn't think an old guy like me without a phone would be much help."

"This is Rob Valdez." Luna waved her arm in Rob's direction. "He's Border Patrol… But he's helping Libby."

Zeke shook Rob's hand. "As long as you're helping our Libby, you're okay with me. She's had enough trouble rolling her way lately."

"She knows about Tandy." Luna stood on her tiptoes and kissed Libby's cheek. "Take care and let us know if we can do anything to help. You know, I don't like the direction this camp has been moving—too much riffraff, too many rough types. But those same rough types are not going to let anyone in here who's not on the guest list."

Rob jerked a thumb over his shoulder. "We noticed."

"We're going to hit the road, Luna." Libby rubbed her stinging nose. "Thanks for all your help. I'll be back—when I remember everything."

"When you do, and this man is caught—" her gaze flicked to Rob "—you can go back to your beautiful life. Because you do have a beautiful life waiting for you, Libby."

Zeke escorted them to the truck, and as he shook Rob's hand again, he said, "Watch yourself out there, but I suppose I don't have to warn a BP agent."

Zeke gave Libby another hug and stood at the entrance of the compound, watching them drive off.

Libby patted the baggie. "Maybe I should drink this at my next appointment with Jennifer. I can sort of see how this is going to work."

"How what's going to work?" Rob had started the truck and maneuvered back onto the access road with the truck shaking and rattling with every mile.

"This memory thing." Libby tapped the side of her head. "I thought everything would come back to me in a flash, but it's more like bits and pieces—conversations, scenes, faces, even feelings."

"As if we needed any more proof that the mind is strange and mysterious." He brushed her cheek with his knuckle. "I'm sorry about your mother. I don't care what she was doing—nobody deserves that. Maybe she was trying to protect Elena, the other woman."

"I'll hold on to that thought." She propped her elbow on the armrest and cupped her chin in her palm. "Now we have to tell April her father is dead."

"But we can also tell her he's not EGV." Rob accelerated when he hit the dark highway, his high beams creating a cone of light on the road.

"He was still involved with him in some way."

"She already knew C.J. was no angel. True, it turned out he didn't murder April's mother, but the reason his son was able to manipulate him into running was because of his association with the drug trade. When will people learn?"

"It must seem like easy money to them. Look at your own family. Is that what drove them? The money?"

"I'm sure that was part of it—power, control… There are a lot of moving pieces."

"But it never got you."

"It never got you, either."

They drove in silence for a while, maybe both of them pondering how they'd escaped the shared curses of their families.

Libby grabbed Rob's hand and kissed the back of it, savoring the feel of his flesh against her lips and the scent of the fire that lingered on his skin. "I'm so glad you found me that night."

"I am, too." His gaze flew back to the road and he jerked the steering wheel. "Whoa. That must be the wreck

Zeke mentioned, but it's still there. The car that pulled over didn't call 911?"

She jabbed him in the ribs. "Maybe someone else lost their memory and didn't want to notify authorities."

Rob's truck crawled up the road, and he swung into a gravel turnout. "I'm gonna check it out. Stay in the truck."

Rob dragged his weapon from beneath his seat and holstered it as he got out of the vehicle.

He'd pulled up behind the wrecked car at a crazy angle off the road, so Libby released her seat belt and scooted up in her seat to peer over the dashboard. A feather of fear whispered across the back of her neck as she watched him cautiously approach the damaged vehicle.

He'd left his headlights on to illuminate the scene, and Libby's gaze traveled from Rob to the car—an old white sedan, Wildcats sticker on the back window. Just like Troy's car.

Gasping, she braced her hands against the dashboard. It *was* Troy's car. She grabbed the door handle and scrambled out of the truck, her feet slipping on the gravel below.

She stalked toward Rob, now leaning forward, his face at the window—the shattered window. Her heart pounded, the blood ringing in her ears. "Rob!"

He spun around, his face white against the black backdrop of the desert night. "Stay back, Libby."

Her adrenaline spurred her forward, her feet barely able to keep pace with her intent. She rushed to the car and loomed over Rob's shoulder, gawking at the sight of Troy Paulsen—dead in the front seat, a bullet wound in his head.

Chapter Eighteen

Libby choked behind him, and Rob turned and grabbed her by the shoulders. "You don't need to see this, Libby. Go back to the truck. Hurry."

He looked around the scene, the desert floor cloaked in darkness. They could still be here. They could be anywhere.

He shook Libby's rigid frame. "Wait in the truck. I'm gonna check things out, and then I'm going to call it in. If the highway patrol can't get here fast enough, we're not going to wait. We're getting out of here."

Her head snapped up. "It was them, wasn't it? The same people who are after me, the people trying to protect EGV, killed Troy."

"Probably. That's why you have to get out of here. Duck down and lock the doors. The keys are still in the ignition. If anything happens out here, take off."

"And leave you? I'll mow them over with the truck first."

He landed a kiss on her forehead. "Not if they're shooting at you. Go."

She shuffled her feet and then turned and ran back to the truck.

Troy's door had been left ajar, so Rob nudged it open with his foot. They probably didn't want to make the same mistake they'd made with Libby. They wanted to make sure they killed their target this time.

He leaned into the car across Troy's body and studied the center console. A coffee cup occupied one of the cup holders and some loose change the other. Rob snatched up some receipts and scraps of paper. He didn't want to dismiss anything and possibly ignore any potential evidence.

He eased the door back into position and went around to the passenger side, shading his eyes and glancing back at the truck. No silhouette of Libby in the window, so she'd taken his advice and slumped in the seat.

Using his T-shirt to cover his hand, he opened the passenger door and ducked his head inside the car, his nose wrinkling at the smell of blood and death. He couldn't say he'd gotten accustomed to the smell, but at least he no longer puked like he had the first time he'd seen a headless body at the border. That body had been Libby's mother.

His gut knotted but he continued his search of the car. It wasn't here. They'd taken Troy's phone.

He dug his own phone from his pocket and called 911, the only call he could make out here. "I want to report a single-car accident about a mile and a half north of mile marker nine. The driver is dead."

After making the call, Rob stalked back to the truck and slid behind the wheel. He handed Libby the papers he'd retrieved from Troy's console. "Can you make any sense out of these?"

"Let me see." She hit the dome light button with her knuckle and dropped the slips of paper in her lap. "Did you find out anything?"

"I found out they took Troy's phone."

Libby's hands froze and one of Troy's receipts floated to the floor. "Then they know he texted me, and they saw my response that I picked up my phone. You were right. I should've never answered him."

"If Troy's even the one who texted you. It could've been one of them, testing the waters." He picked up her phone in the cup holder and handed it to her. "What time did you get that text from Troy's phone?"

She grabbed her phone and tapped the display. "At seven thirty."

He glanced at the time glowing on his dashboard. "It's almost nine o'clock now. We've been on the road for about forty-five minutes, which means we left the campsite around eight fifteen."

"It could've been Troy." Libby held out her hand and ticked off each finger. "Troy texts me at seven thirty, gets killed ten minutes later, and then Zeke sees the accident at seven forty and hits the campsite thirty minutes later?"

"He must've been driving awfully fast."

"He was on a motorcycle. He knows the lay of the land."

Rob placed a hand on Libby's bouncing knee. "Who are you trying to convince? It doesn't matter whether they sent the text or not. Even if Troy had sent it, they have his phone and they've seen the text exchange."

She held the phone in her lap. "Should I text him again? Play along like I haven't seen the accident, don't know Troy's dead?"

He didn't like the idea of Libby texting with a bunch of killers. "What would you text?"

"I would text him that the phone contains no information, no pictures, no names, no nothing. That it's useless and I remember nothing."

Rob expelled a ragged breath. "Do it."

Libby held the phone close to her face and tapped the

display, reading aloud as she typed. "'Got the phone. Nothing on it. Can't help you. Can't remember.'"

Rob held his breath as he watched the phone glowing in Libby's hands. When it dinged, he practically jumped out of his seat. "Response?"

"'Okay.'" She snorted. "Just 'okay.' Definitely not Troy Paulsen. I don't think the guy ever gave a one-word response in his life."

"At least your message is out there. They can believe it or not." He cocked his head. "Hear that?"

"Sirens. The first responders are here. What are we going to tell them?" She wedged her phone in the cup holder again.

"That we saw the wreck, determined the driver was dead and called 911." Rob shoved his weapon into its holster. "We don't know him, don't recognize him, didn't see anyone around."

"What about Zeke? Should we tell them Zeke is the one who spotted the wreck and another car in the vicinity?"

"Not without letting Zeke know first." Rob drummed his thumbs on the steering wheel. "In fact, I want to go back to Luna and Zeke's place and question him…and warn him."

"Warn him?" The lights from the emergency vehicles cast a red-and-blue halo around Libby's hair, making it look like fire.

"If the people who killed Troy saw Zeke's bike, noticed anything about him, he could be in trouble. He should at least know what he stumbled on. Luna mentioned she didn't much like the new residents of the camp. Maybe this is their opportunity to move on."

Libby clasped her hands. "I didn't even think about it. Luna and Zeke could be in danger."

"I suppose they don't have a phone, do they?"

"Nope."

"Then we'll have to drive out there when we're done with this." He squeezed her neck, his fingers pressing into her soft skin. "Are you up for that?"

"Of course. I don't want to see them get hurt. Those other bikers there might not provide any protection if they think the cartel will come after them, or if the cartel pays them off." She grabbed the handle of the truck when the first highway patrol pulled up. "The two dudes who came out to meet us didn't exactly look like Boy Scouts, did they?"

"Let me handle this." He caught a strand of her hair. "I'll tell them you didn't see anything, never left the truck. Okay?"

"Do you think they'll want to question me?"

Leaning forward in his seat, he pulled his ID and badge from his pocket. "Not when I show them this. As soon as I make it clear we don't know anything, they'll let us go. Then we can continue on to Zeke's place. The sooner we raise the alarm with him, the better."

She nodded and released the handle with a snap.

Shading his eyes, Rob marched up to the first patrolman and explained the situation. He ended by crossing his arms and saying, "Looks like the guy was shot, close range."

Another patrolman called from the wreck, holding up a bag. "Drugs."

Rob swore under his breath. EGV's people must keep a supply on hand to implicate unsuspecting and innocent people…and dead people.

The patrolman in front of him cracked a smile. "Looks like you boys might be getting this case anyway."

"Maybe so." Rob jerked his thumb over his shoulder.

"Can we be on our way now? You have my card if you need anything else, and like you said, we might be picking this up anyway."

"Yeah, sure." The patrolman stuck Rob's card in his front pocket and pivoted back to the scene.

Rob strode back to the truck and climbed into the cab. "That was easy."

"Professional courtesy?"

"Something like that." He cranked on the ignition. "Also, they found drugs in the trunk."

Libby covered her mouth. "Just like me. They want to make sure to blame the victim, don't they?"

"Blame the victim, muddy the waters, divert suspicion from the real motive. I hope Highway Patrol does throw the case to us. Then I can set things right for Troy. He deserves that."

"Rob?" Libby was turned around in her seat.

"What is it?" He shifted his gaze to his rearview mirror as they made a dip in the road.

"I saw some lights behind us. C-could that be the highway patrol following us?"

"No way." He squinted into the mirror and caught a flash of something coming over the rise. His foot came down hard on the gas pedal, and his V-8 roared.

Libby braced a hand against the door. "What is it? Is there someone behind us?"

"Someone who just cut their lights."

She whipped around in her seat again. "Why would someone drive without lights in the middle of the desert? I don't care how deserted it is, nobody would do that."

"Unless they didn't want to be detected."

"Rob, are you saying we're being followed? How? Why would they think we're out on this stretch of highway? They don't know anything about that campsite, or they would've paid it a visit by now to collect my phone."

Gripping the wheel, Rob tipped his head back and swore. "They have Troy's phone."

"So what? I didn't tell Troy where the phone was. They wouldn't be able to locate that site from the description I texted Troy. They may not even have the same phone with that text on it."

Rob turned off his own lights, and the darkness engulfed them. "Remember how Troy found us in Tucson after we dropped off Teresa?"

"He put a GPS tracker on your truck." Libby rubbed her arms. "What does that mean? How'd they get that GPS?"

"Libby, it's on his phone. They took Troy's phone after they killed him and found the tracking program." He pounded the steering wheel. "As soon as I learned Troy had a GPS on my truck, I should've demanded he remove it."

"C-can you find it now? Remove it now?"

"With that bearing down on us? I'm not going to take that chance with you in the truck."

She scooted forward in her seat. "We just left a gaggle of emergency vehicles back there. Can we turn around and get help?"

"We would have to drive straight back toward them. We'd have a shoot-out before we ever reached the scene of Troy's accident." Rob swallowed. "Do you know how much firepower these cartels have? I'm not bringing that to bear on those EMTs and patrolmen. There would be a slaughter."

"Your phone. I'll call the Border Patrol. You can let them know what to expect, and they can come prepared. Surely you guys can match them weapon for weapon?"

"You can try, but we usually can't get service out here, Libby. Texts, maybe. Phone calls? Not so much."

She pounced on his phone and tapped it. Held it to the window and tapped it. "But you used your phone back at the accident site."

"To call 911."

"Can I text?"

"Not the Border Patrol."

"How about the individual agents?"

"I don't want them walking into an ambush." He clenched his teeth. This was his mess. He wasn't going to put another agent's life at risk.

Libby stashed his useless phone in the cup holder and caught his arm. "Where are we going, Rob? We can't go back to Luna and Zeke. We're not bringing that to rain down on them, either."

"I agree. We need to get out of this on our own." His foot eased off the accelerator.

"What are you doing? It's time to speed up, not slow down."

"I can't take the next turn at this speed. We'll flip."

"Next turn?"

As he cranked the wheel to the left across the oncoming lane of traffic, the tires squealed and Libby's body fell against his arm. "Sorry. You okay?"

"I'm not okay, Rob. Where are we going? They're tracking us via Troy's GPS. We don't have a chance."

"We can do this, Libby. You just have to trust me. Can you do that?"

"I've done that from the minute you picked me up in the desert—or at least from the minute I dropped my knife."

"We're ditching the truck."

"Wait—did I just say I trusted you?" She pressed the

heel of her hand against her forehead. "Are you out of your mind? Once we ditch this truck, they won't be able to track us anymore but we'll be on foot. In the desert. In the middle of the night."

"C'mon. You've been there, done that." Rob leaned over the steering wheel. He wanted to ditch the truck but not crash it into a saguaro cactus. "Besides, as you pointed out, they can't track us without the truck."

"Why would they want to? They'll just find a couple of corpses."

"We still have a head start. They kept their distance because they had the GPS." He aimed the truck off the access road and toward a gully in the sand. "At the bottom of this dip, we abandon the truck and get out."

"Could we maybe search for the GPS on the truck first, remove it and get back in the vehicle…where it's safe?"

"This truck is not safe. It's a big target, although I'm glad it's black, and we don't have enough time to look for the GPS. Can't do it in the dark, and can't put the lights on." He halted the truck and cut the engine. "It's go time."

"It's go crazy time." She hung on to her seat belt strap as if daring him to pull her out of the truck. "I thought I was the one with holes in my mind."

Rob reached into the back seat and grabbed his backpack. "I didn't leave home without my bag of tricks because I didn't know what we'd find when we picked up your phone. Who knew we'd need it to…?"

"Survive, right? This is do or die?"

He hauled the backpack into the center console and kissed Libby's mouth. "It is. Let's get moving."

This time he was glad she didn't wait for him to get her door. She scrambled out of the truck and eased it closed.

Reaching into his backpack, he said, "I brought a

weapon for you. It's the one you had at my house when I left you alone with Teresa. Can you handle it?"

"Point and shoot. I'd rather have it than not." She patted the front pocket of her jeans. "I have my knife, too."

He grabbed her hand. "Follow in my steps. Even though I have a flashlight in my bag, I don't want to use it out here. We shouldn't use the lights from our phones, either."

"Won't they be able to follow our footsteps in the sand?" She glanced down at her own feet creating divots in the sand.

"Maybe they will, but it won't be easier than following a GPS… And I have a plan."

"That's good to hear. What is it? We must be close to the border."

"We are. That's why we're here. I know this terrain better than they do."

She huffed behind him. "There are snakes and tarantulas and other…things out here, aren't there? I got a look at a few of them after the accident."

"The most dangerous animal out here right now is the one coming for us, and you'd better believe nothing's going to stop him." Rob cranked his head over his shoulder. "If they've realized we've gone off-road, they know we're on to them."

"And they don't have to get out of their vehicle. They'll reach us faster now. Where are we headed? We can't hide out in the middle of the desert all night. I tried it."

"We're not going to be in the middle of the desert. We're going right there." He pointed to a ridge and some scrubby desert bushes.

"That doesn't look very promising to me." She leaned her head on his shoulder, her breath coming out in short spurts.

"You're not supposed to be able to see it, and neither

are they." He adjusted his backpack. "It's a tunnel, Libby, a tunnel that runs beneath the border."

"A tunnel? The tunnel where my mother was murdered?" Libby spun around in the sand, falling to her knees. "I can't do it, Rob. I can't go in there."

Chapter Nineteen

The sand and grit dug into her palms as she tried to push up to her feet. She couldn't—and she couldn't crawl into a tunnel, which had been the last thing her mother had done.

Rob dropped to the ground beside her. "It's not the same tunnel, Libby. We've closed all of those. We had three left to cut off, and this is one of them."

"I don't think I can, Rob."

"Your mother would want you to survive, wouldn't she? It sounds like she did everything she knew how to do to help you at the end. Don't waste that."

Libby sat back on her haunches and brushed her hands together. "Lead the way."

"First we're going to try to cover our tracks around here. Shuffle around in the sand from side to side."

They spent a few precious minutes scuffing through the sand to cover their footprints.

Rob braced his foot against a rock. "Now, follow me. We're going to hop from rock to rock to the entrance of the tunnel. We're gonna have to crawl on our bellies to get in, but if I recall, this particular tunnel is paved and we'll be able to stand to our full height—or you will be."

Rob jumped to the first rock and held out his hand to her. "As soon as I leave this rock for that clump of brush, take my place. Our stepping-stones don't have to be literal stones. There's scrubby brush we can use, too. Any hard object in the sand that's not going to show a footprint."

Like a couple of kids playing hopscotch, they jumped and careened and stepped from spot to spot toward that dark ridge that seemed to forecast her doom.

At the last anchor, she froze. "Rob, I hear an engine."

"I've been hearing it. They're on the way." He curled his hand. "C'mon. One more and then we hit the ground."

"Okay, I'm ready." She jumped toward Rob and he caught her, wrapping his arms around her. She wanted to stay here and forget about the men coming for them, forget about the tunnel at their feet.

"We're gonna crouch down here. The entrance is between those two rocks. It's big enough for a grown man to get through, so you won't have any problems." He placed his hands on her shoulders. "You can do this, Libby. I'll be right behind you."

"Behind me?" She gulped. "You mean I have to go through first?"

"I'm not crawling in there and leaving you out here by yourself. You'll be safe inside. Hurry."

Libby bent her knees, which felt stiff as boards. From above, Rob guided her. No wonder the cartels and coyotes got away with these tunnels. She was kneeling right in front of the opening and still needed Rob to tell her how to get inside.

As Libby crawled into the tunnel, she thought about her mother doing the same thing over a month ago. She whispered into the darkness, "Why, Mom?"

After several seconds of claustrophobia where she felt the dirt walls closing in on her, she took a breath that didn't result in grains of sand in her mouth. Her hands no longer scrabbled through dirt, but hit smooth cement.

Rob slithered through the entrance behind her, bumping her back with his head. "Is that you?"

"It had better be." Still on her knees, Libby stretched up. "There's a lot of room in here. I can't believe it."

"You'd be surprised at some of these tunnels." Rob crawled past her and sat up. "Can you stand?"

Holding her hands above her head, she rose to her feet. "Almost. Can we use the light from our phones in here, or will they see?"

"They won't see a thing from inside this tunnel."

Libby grabbed her phone from her purse and turned on the flashlight. She scanned Rob's face first, just to make sure he was beside her. "We made it. Now what?"

"They'll be coming after us. They might suspect we're in a tunnel, but they're going to have a hard time figuring out how to get in here." Rob tossed his backpack on the ground and plunged his hands inside.

"So, we're going to wait it out or what? They'll never give up, will they? We could cross to the other side of the border and get to a place where we can make a call from our phones."

Rob didn't answer her. He was busy pulling items from his backpack—scopes, wires, another gun, a rope.

Narrowing her eyes, she said, "We're going to use all that stuff?"

"If we hope to survive, we are." He picked up a pair of goggles. "These are night vision. We have to be able to see our enemies before we can take them out."

"T-take them out?" Libby ran a hand through her tangled hair. "We're not just going to hide? Wait for the cavalry? I didn't realize we were going to engage them."

"They will engage us. Make no mistake about it." He held a finger to his lips. "Shh."

Libby kept still, even though her insides quivered as she heard shouts from outside the tunnel.

She scooted next to Rob. "Can you hear them? Are they speaking Spanish or English?"

"They're speaking English—for my benefit. As far as I can tell, they're ordering us to come out from hiding."

"Or what?" She pulled the gun from her purse that she'd slipped in there earlier. "You tell me where to shoot, Rob, and I'll pull the trigger."

"I have no doubt about it, but don't get trigger-happy just yet."

A barrage of gunfire erupted outside, and Libby jerked back. "What are they doing?"

"Those are automatic weapons. They're shooting up the ridge. They must think they're gonna get lucky and hit us."

"Are we protected in here?"

"Stay away from the entrance and try to keep low to the ground when they're shooting."

She curled a finger around Rob's belt loop. "It doesn't sound like they'll ever stop."

And then silence descended and it was ten times worse than the bullets. "What's going on?"

Rob strapped on the night-vision goggles and did an army crawl toward the tunnel's opening, his gun clutched in his hand. He hoisted himself on top of the hunk of rock that blocked the rest of the entrance.

He aimed his thumb to the left and whispered, "They're that way. I can't make out what they're doing."

As his words ended, an explosion rocked the tunnel and threw her onto the ground. Her ears rang and she coughed up dirt.

The blast knocked Rob back, and he reached for her. "Are you all right?"

"I'm fine, but they're going to blast us out of here, aren't they? They have explosives, and they're just going to keep bombing away at us until we die or stagger out of here…and die."

"Nobody's gonna die—at least not us." He wiped dirt from his face and adjusted the goggles. "They're moving down the line. There's going to be another explosion, so brace yourself. Eventually, they'll stop in front of us—within my range."

Libby crouched on the floor of the tunnel, covering her ears. Preparing for the upcoming explosion didn't help much. This one rocked them even more than the first one. The next one would destroy the tunnel or them—or both.

When the dust settled, Rob got back into position. He murmured to himself, "C'mon, c'mon, you SOBs."

Rob's body tensed and Libby braced for the blast to end all blasts.

Instead, Rob fired off several shots. He cranked his head around, the goggles making him look like some alien desert creature. "I got 'em."

He scrambled from the tunnel, ordering her to stay behind. When he called her from outside, she wasted no time joining him.

Her jaw dropped as she picked her way over the rocks and debris outside the tunnel. Dust choked the air and filled her lungs. It looked like a war zone.

She averted her gaze from a man flung out on the ground, his silver-tipped black boots pointing toward the sky.

Rob growled, "He's dead, but this one is still breathing. I'm almost glad he is."

Libby came up behind Rob crouching beside the other man, blood pumping from a wound in his chest and bubbling from his lips, his fingers inches from a crude explosive device.

Rob shone his flashlight in the man's face and still Libby didn't recognize him. She'd never seen either of these men before that she could remember.

Rob leaned over the man, his lips close to his ear, and in a harsh whisper said, "We know El Gringo Viejo is in Rocky Point. Libby's going to be able to ID him, and it'll be all over. You should give thanks you're dying because you and your compadre there are the reason we're gonna get him. He's finished."

The man hacked, and his lips stretched into a gruesome smile through the blood. "El Gringo Viejo is gone. You'll never catch him."

Epilogue

Libby smoothed out the piece of paper that contained her drawing of El Gringo Viejo, a man she had known in Rocky Point as Ted Jessup.

The authorities didn't need her drawing now. She'd been able to tell them all about the man in the cliffside compound and his murder of Charlie Harper, or C. J. Hart, that she'd witnessed. She'd been able to direct them to the compound, and they'd conducted their raid.

But the man Rob had killed in the desert was right. El Gringo Viejo was long gone.

"You'd better watch that piece of paper, Libby, or Denali is going to snatch it." April grabbed the dog's collar and pulled him away. "Clay, teach your dog some manners."

Clay Archer whistled to Denali. "I get it. When he's doing something wrong, he's my dog, and when he's being all heroic, he's yours."

"Sounds about right." April winked at Libby.

"I'm sorry about your father, April." Libby took a sip of wine. "I think at the end, he really was trying to make amends for working with EGV all these years. He was ready to turn him in, give him up to Troy."

"Too little, too late." April dashed a tear from her cheek. "That's my dad."

"Rob, are you making arrangements for Libby? As long as EGV is on the loose, she's not safe." Clay walked up behind Libby and squeezed her shoulder. "I'm sorry, Libby. I mean, it helps that you're not the only one who knows his identity now. You can't tell us anything about him that we don't already know, but the man might want to take his revenge."

Rob rubbed a circle on Libby's back. "Now that I've passed probation and been on the job for over a year, I'm going to take a little vacation…with Libby. I'll keep her safe, and we'll figure it out from there."

"Hawaii's not a bad place to figure things out." April swirled her wine in her glass. "Do you remember everything now, Libby?"

"Almost everything." She patted Rob's thigh. "The important stuff. My therapist, Jennifer, said the rest will come gradually. I remember my mother. I remember learning about her death. I recall going to EGV's compound to show him some art and your father meeting me. Ted, EGV, meant to kill both of us, and your father saved me."

"I'm glad." April gave her a watery smile. Then she sniffled. "And I meant it. You can keep all those clothes."

"I didn't really invite you over here to return the clothes." Libby entwined her fingers with Rob's. "I just wanted to make sure you knew what your father had done for me."

Rob kissed the side of her head, and she snuggled in closer to him.

"I can take a hint." Clay jumped up and patted his leg. "Come, Denali."

April tossed back the rest of her wine. "Don't go anywhere without telling us first. You promise?"

Libby drew a cross over her heart. "I promise."

She and Rob stood on his porch and waved while Clay got Denali in the back seat of his truck and took off.

Rob draped an arm over her shoulders as they turned into the house. "Hawaii might be far enough away."

"Then what?" She stuffed a hand in his back pocket. "I stay in paradise while you go back to Paradiso by yourself? You can't expect me to stay away from you, Rob. Not when I've truly, truly found you."

He pulled her close, possessing her lips with his. The kiss he laid on her reached her toes, and she curled them into the floor.

When he came up for air, he placed a finger on her trembling bottom lip. "Can we stop talking? I've been waiting a long time to make hot, sweet love to Jane Doe."

"Jane Doe?" She broke away from his embrace and tugged at the hem of his T-shirt, yanking it halfway up his body to reveal a washboard belly that looked as if it had been kissed by the sun. She ran her hands across his mocha skin. "Should I be jealous of this Jane Doe?"

"Maybe you should be." He yanked his T-shirt over his head and threw it over his shoulder. "When I laid eyes on her, I lost all reason, even though she pulled a knife on me."

"Jane Doe doesn't sound very good for you." Libby placed a finger on her chin and raised her eyes to the ceiling. "I think you'd be much better off with Libby James."

"What does Libby have that Jane doesn't?" Rob hooked his fingers in the waistband of her skirt and pulled her toward him.

She cupped his face in her hands and kissed his mouth. "Libby's already half in love with you."

"Only half?" He swept her up in his arms and carried her off to his bedroom. Sitting on the edge of the bed, he cradled her in his lap. "I guess I have some work to do. I plan to give you a night you'll never forget."

She sighed against his lips. "As if I ever would."

* * * * *

Delores Fossen, a *USA TODAY* bestselling author, has written over one hundred novels, with millions of copies of her books in print worldwide. She's received a Booksellers' Best Award and an RT Reviewers' Choice Best Book Award. She was also a finalist for a prestigious RITA® Award. You can contact the author through her website at www.deloresfossen.com

Carol Ericson is a bestselling, award-winning author of more than forty books. She has an eerie fascination for true-crime stories, a love of film noir and a weakness for reality TV, all of which fuel her imagination to create her own tales of murder, mayhem and mystery. To find out more about Carol and her current projects, please visit her website at www.carolericson.com "where romance flirts with danger."

Also by Delores Fossen

Safety Breach
A Threat to His Family
Cowboy Above the Law
Finger on the Trigger
Lawman with a Cause
Under the Cowboy's Protection
Always a Lawman
Gunfire on the Ranch
Lawman from Her Past
Roughshod Justice

Also by Carol Ericson

Evasive Action
Chain of Custody
Enemy Infiltration
Undercover Accomplice
Code Conspiracy
Delta Force Defender
Delta Force Daddy
Delta Force Die Hard
Locked, Loaded and SEALed
Alpha Bravo SEAL

SETTLING AN OLD SCORE

DELORES FOSSEN

UNRAVELING JANE DOE

CAROL ERICSON

MILLS & BOON

First Published in Great Britain 2020
by Mills & Boon, an imprint of HarperCollins*Publishers*
1 London Bridge Street, London, SE1 9GF

ISBN: 978-0-263-28041-8

0820

MIX
Paper from responsible sources
FSC™ C007454

This book is produced from independently certified FSC™ paper to ensure responsible forest management.

For more information visit: www.harpercollins.co.uk/green

Printed and bound in Spain
by CPI, Barcelona